M000158924

SUSAN A. JENNINGS

The Blue Pendant

The Sackville Hotel Trilogy – Book One

SaRaKa InPrint

First published by SaRaKa InPrint 2021

Copyright © 2021 by Susan A. Jennings

All rights reserved. No part of this publication may be reproduced, stored or transmitted in any form or by any means, electronic, mechanical, photocopying, recording, scanning, or otherwise without written permission from the publisher. It is illegal to copy this book, post it to a website, or distribute it by any other means without permission.

This novel is entirely a work of fiction. The names, characters and incidents portrayed in it are the work of the author's imagination. Any resemblance to actual persons, living or dead, events or localities is entirely coincidental.

Susan A. Jennings asserts the moral right to be identified as the author of this work.

Susan A. Jennings has no responsibility for the persistence or accuracy of URLs for external or third-party Internet Websites referred to in this publication and does not guarantee that any content on such Websites is, or will remain, accurate or appropriate.

Designations used by companies to distinguish their products are often claimed as trademarks. All brand names and product names used in this book and on its cover are trade names, service marks, trademarks and registered trademarks of their respective owners. The publishers and the book are not associated with any product or vendor mentioned in this book. None of the companies referenced within the book have endorsed the book.

Cover Images:

Author photograph & Pendant- SAJ

Background - Pixabay.com

www.shutterstock.com/g/Irina+Alexandrovna www.shutterstock.com/g/photochecker

Second edition

ISBN: 978-1-989553-16-9

Editing by Meghan Negrijn

This book was professionally typeset on Reedsy.
Find out more at reedsy.com

For
My beloved Nana
Nancy Walker
1894 - 1965

Contents

II August 1919 - July 1935

I

June 1913 – July 1919

Bexhill-on-Sea, Sussex,
England

One

1913 – The Sackville Hotel

Nineteen-year-old Anna Neale stepped cautiously out of the Ladies Only carriage onto Platform 4 of the Bexhill-on-Sea train station. Scarcely able to take a breath, she seized her moment of freedom, anticipating the adventures that were sure to follow. Her fingers nervously twisted the black velvet ribbon at her neck and felt the coolness of its blue crystal pendant—Uncle Bertie's gift from India. His words echoed in her head, "Anna, follow your dreams and never let anyone destroy them." Bexhill-on-Sea may have been oceans away from India but this was Anna's first adventure.

Happiness percolated through her veins and a grin the Cheshire cat would be proud of spread from ear to ear as she walked distractedly along the platform. Startled by a blast of steam from the locomotive, she inhaled sharply, only to relax with the engine as it hissed its final breath, resting at the end of a long journey, and Anna, at the beginning of her own journey.

As the First Class passengers alighted, the platform buzzed with porters loading trunks and baggage onto carts, ladies huffing with displeasure, and their husbands stiff and strained, barely able to maintain their decorum. Nannies' frustrated voices could be heard trying to elicit good behaviour from children as excited as Anna. She gave a knowing smile to a little boy in a sailor suit and wished she could join him as he skipped up and down the platform. Intoxicated by the crowd, Anna watched families gather their belongings, fathers protecting and mothers fussing. A twinge of loneliness jabbed at her heart.

"Ouch!" she cried out as something sharp poked her arm.

"Sorry, Miss," said the boy in the sailor suit, clutching a shiny wooden boat, anxiety creasing his young face. Anna smiled to reassure him she wasn't going to chastise. A gentleman, the boy's father, doffed his hat to Anna, and pulled the boy away. Sadly, Anna thought, the boy *would* be chastised.

Loud squawks followed by several ear-piercing yaps made Anna turn her head looking for the offenders. A red-faced porter, his little round cap askew, was pushing an overloaded cart in her direction. Precariously balanced on top of a stack of trunks and bags was a birdcage, its gold satin cover having slipped to one side, revealing the source of the squawking—a loud, distressed parrot.

The yapping appeared to be coming from a grand, voluptuous lady who, in competition with the yapping, barked orders at the porter. Anna recoiled at the sight of such an imposing figure of a woman. Long black feathers sprang like tentacles seeking prey from an enormous black hat. Her black dress rustled with each determined step as she marched towards Anna. Two little jet eyes revealed the source of the yapping, a Pekingese snuggled protectively against an ample bosom. The yapping ceased. She averted her eyes, catching a steely look of disdain from under the hat. Anna felt decidedly Lilliputian.

A gruff voice called, "Miss Neale... Miss Anna Neale?"

"Yes, I'm Anna Neale."

A small man appeared from the crowd. "Name's Carter, Miss! Mr. Pickles sent me from The Sackville 'otel. This y'ur trunk?"

Anna nodded. Carter lifted the trunk onto his shoulder as though it was a sack of potatoes. His strength belied his short stature and greying hair.

"Follow me, Miss. I 'ope you don't mind a bit of a walk. I 'ad to park the buggy on the next street."

4

Anna nodded, but in truth she had trouble keeping pace and winced as her new boots pinched her little toe. Turning the corner onto the next street, the wind caught her hat. She grabbed it in mid-air, catching her fingers in the pale blue band, crushing the delicate blue and white flowers along the brim. She was annoyed that her long golden brown curls, wayward at the best of times, had loosened from their pins and would, she thought, resemble a bird's nest. But, better that than having her prized hat rolling down the dirty street. It had taken a great deal of whining and tears to persuade Papa that Mama could indeed take her to Mrs. Morton's Millinery Shop—an extravagance he could ill afford.

" 'ere we are," Carter said, dropping the trunk in the back of the buggy; the horse lifted its head and whinnied.

Carter skilfully manoeuvred the buggy between horses, landaus and automobiles as he pulled into the street. "Busy time," Carter said as he yanked the reins tight to avoid a carriage. "I think the 'ole of London comes 'ere for their summer 'olidays. It'll be like this all summer. Comings and goings, some stay 'ere all season. Bit early, June, it'll get frantic in late July and August. Mr. Pickles says it'll be a good summer, 'otel's already booked up."

The buggy leaned to the right rounding the corner onto the promenade, only inches from the shingle beach.

"Oh, the sea! And, how it sparkles like millions of dancing stars."

Carter slowed the buggy to a stop. "Y'ur first time at the seaside?"

Anna nodded, feeling the warm sun on her face and staring up at the bright blue sky. Carter lifted the reins and the horse moved forward and immediately in front of them stood The Sackville Hotel. "It's so big, and those towers... it looks like a castle!"

Overwhelmed by the size and grandeur of the hotel, Anna felt the euphoria slip away and the excited internal butterflies turn to anxiety. Her sister Lou's sarcastic words filled her head. "Maid's work, not good enough for... *our Anna*. What are you going to do when Papa isn't there to rescue you?" Lou had been right even if her remarks were made out of jealousy. How was she going to manage? The youngest of three siblings,

5

father's favourite and somewhat spoiled, Anna had learned to manipulate events and people to suit her fancy.

Carter looked sympathetic. "First time way from 'ome?"

Anna didn't answer, embarrassed to have shown her vulnerability. *Self-pity will get me nowhere*, she thought. *I must be strong.* She sat up straighter and lifted her chin a little higher, fluffing the flowers of her midnight blue hat before attaching it firmly to her head with a long hatpin.

"Whoa!" Carter pulled the horse to a stop.

"This is the *back* door," Anna said.

Carter looked puzzled. "Yes, we's staff, and staff goes in the service door. It's more than me job's worth if Mr. Pickles catches us at the front..."

"But I'm the front desk clerk, not a maid." Just the mention of the word *maid*, gripped her with fear; once was enough.

"Well aren't we hoity-toity!"

About to pout, Anna reminded herself that whether she liked it or not, she was an employee. Loosening her pursed lips, she smiled. "Sorry, Carter. I'm rather nervous."

"No matter, lass! 'Course you are, but nobody bites, they's a nice bunch on the 'ole. Mrs. Banks, she's 'ead 'ousekeeper, can be a bit strict, but that's her job. And Mr. Pickles, he's the 'otel manager, runs a tight ship—he used to be a ship's captain. They's fair, least Mrs. Banks is. Mr. Pickles has some strange ways about him." Carter lowered his voice and hesitated, "Mr. Pickles, well, he's... um... can be difficult," then he returned to his cheery self. "Mrs. Banks is always fair, and kind too."

"My uncle met Mr. Pickles on one of his trips to India," Anna said, feeling comfortable with Carter's friendliness. "That's how I knew about the position of front desk clerk."

"Anna, don't go braggin' about your uncle knowing Mr. Pickles to the others. They's a good bunch but they don't like favouritism, and they can be mean if you get above your station."

Carter's change in tone, kind but firm, perplexed her. She was proud of her Uncle Bertie's association with Mr. Pickles, and her position was superior. She mused. Was that bragging? She had the feeling Carter was giving her a warning.

Entering through the back door, Carter led her through a warren of passageways; Anna felt akin to Alice in *Alice's Adventures in Wonderland*. The hot, damp smell of wet linen mixed with soap and carbolic filled the hallway, followed by an unexpected hint of lavender and rose water wafting from an open door. Steam swirled around a young maid as she ironed. Anna gave a shudder—a memory better forgotten. The quietness and lack of people felt odd. As if Carter had anticipated her query, he said, "It's tea time. They's in the staff dining hall."

The laundry smell faded and the pleasant aromas of roasting meat, onions and some kind of baking filled Anna's nostrils, making her aware that she hadn't eaten since an early breakfast. Approaching a door opposite the kitchen, she heard a man's harsh voice and felt herself recoil as Carter opened the door. The voice stopped mid-sentence and all heads turned to look at Anna. Stricken by reality, she wanted to run but her feet were glued to the floor. It was impossible to move either way.

An enormous wooden table surrounded by dozens of chairs, most of them occupied, filled the room. A china cup being placed on its saucer broke the silence, and someone reached for a slice of cake.

Carter spoke first. "This is Miss Anna Neale, our new clerk."

The owner of the harsh voice, a tall, older gentleman with pointed features, shifty eyes and thin grey hair, immaculately dressed in black tails, striped waistcoat and white shirt, stood at the head of the table.

"Welcome to The Sackville Hotel, Miss Neale. I'm Mr. Pickles, General Manager. Once you are settled, you will be reporting to me in the front office."

The silence in the room drummed in her ears as she forced a reply, "Pleased to meet you, Mr. Pickles." She bobbed a curtsy. Hearing a maid giggle, she blushed, deducing the curtsy was inappropriate. Mr. Pickles' icy glare sent ripples down her back. Then he introduced Mrs. Banks, nodded dismissively to the staff and left the room.

Mrs. Banks had the look of a cross schoolteacher but the crossness softened in her brown eyes. Her grey-brown hair pulled into a too tight chignon gave her face a surprised look. She wore a neat brown dress trimmed with a white lace collar and a large ring of keys jangled at her waist.

"You must be tired after your long journey. Come sit." She pointed to the chair next to her. "Miss Romano, please pour Miss Neale a cup of tea while I introduce you all."

Anna declined to sit. Instead of feeling proud in her posh new travelling suit she felt self-conscious and quite aware of the inappropriateness of her attire in the staff dining hall. The brim of her hat, too-wide to fit between the chairs, would likely poke Mrs. Banks or Miss Romano in the face.

"Miss Sophie Romano is our senior housemaid and you will be sharing a room with her." Obviously Mrs. Banks considered sharing with Miss Romano, the senior maid, to be a privilege, but Miss Romano did not appear to agree. Her eyes bored into Anna with contempt. Anna, who had been expecting her own room, considered the contempt to be mutual.

Starting with the scullery maid, Mrs. Banks introduced the staff. Anna nodded at each introduction. The names and positions were becoming muddled and she was feeling lightheaded: chamber maids, scullery maids, laundresses, kitchen maids; as well as porters, cooks and kitchen staff, even a stable hand. Mrs. Banks' words merged together, her mouth moved in slow motion; muffled sounds surrounded Anna. She felt the blood ebbing from her head. Mrs. Banks' arms guided her into the chair, pushing her head towards her knees. "Miss Neale, keep your head down."

A sharp pain shot into Anna's head. Her hat caught on the table and pushed the hatpin into her scalp. Mortified, this was not the first impression she had intended.

"How long is it since you ate?" Mrs. Banks asked.

"I had breakfast before I left home." Anna kept her head down, unable to face the inquisitive stares.

"Silly child! No wonder you're faint." Mrs. Banks stirred two spoons of sugar into the tea. "Miss Neale, sit up slowly and sip some of this tea."

Anna raised her head trying to smile. "I must look a sight." Embarrassed, colour flooded into her pale face. She pulled the long pin from the hat and took the hat off handing it to Mrs. Banks, who gave it an admiring browse before placing it on the Welsh dresser.

A nice looking young gentleman, with blondish hair and haunting aqua-blue eyes, wearing a white chef's coat, handed her a piece of cake. "The best Victoria Sponge you'll ever taste this side of London," he said with a friendly smile. "I made it myself this morning."

"Thank you... um..." Anna looked up, frantically trying to recall his name.

"Name's Bill Blaine. I am the under chef, Chef Louis's assistant. Don't worry about names. You'll soon get to know everyone."

Tea cups clinked, the chatter and laughter resumed until the grandfather clock chimed the half hour. Everyone except Miss Romano and Mrs. Banks scurried back to their duties. Mrs. Banks finished her tea while anxiously studying Anna. Anna wondered whether her anxiety was due to her undignified fainting fit, or concern for her ability to fulfill her duties and get along with the staff. The latter caused an unpleasant memory flash of a spiteful maid at Lady Chartwell's, her previous employer.

"Are you feeling better, Miss Neale?" Mrs. Banks said with a stern expression, but unexpected kindness, in her voice.

"Yes, thank you, Mrs. Banks. The journey was perhaps more taxing than I thought."

"Miss Romano will take you to your room. You still look a little pale. I suggest you rest for a while. High tea, for those staff members who are free, is served at six, the rest eat when their duties allow. You will join me in my sitting room after tea and I will explain the rules. Tomorrow morning you will report to Mr. Pickles at eight o'clock for a list of your duties."

Miss Romano led the way down a short passageway, pointing to a sign that read *Head Housekeeper*. "That's Mrs. Banks' sitting room, and where she sometimes takes her meals, but she usually dines in the staff dining room. I think she likes to keep tabs on us. Her bedroom is upstairs in the staff quarters. Down there," Miss Romano pointed towards the end of the corridor, "is Mr. Pickles' suite—his study where he always dines alone and

9

his bedroom. He lives in during the week and goes home to his wife on Saturday and Sunday. The door next to it, the green baize door, is the staff entrance to the lobby, Mr. Pickles' office and the front desk. In case you are wondering, the baize door is soundproof, so the guests don't hear the staff."

"I know what a green baize door is," Anna retorted, sensing a pout on her lips and quickly reminding herself of her position.

"Oh you've worked in service, have you?"

Anna regretted her impulsive response. "The work didn't suit me and I left to go to secretarial school."

Miss Romano rolled her eyes. "You are lucky you had a choice. Don't be lording over me. I am the head maid and I work hard." Miss Romano ran up the four flights of stairs and stood on the landing watching Anna struggle, puffing heavily and limping from the pain of her toe.

"You'll get used to the climb. That's Mrs. Banks' bedroom." She indicated a door in the centre of the landing, which divided a long, grey, dreary hallway lined with doors all painted the same dull sage green.

Pointing to her left she said, "Those are the men's quarters and women are not allowed unless Mrs. Banks has given permission." Turning to the right, Miss Romano continued. "Here's the women's hall and no men allowed. If anyone is caught breaking the rules, dismissal without references is immediate." Miss Romano walked to the end of the hall and flung a door open. "This is *my* room. At least it was until you came here."

Ignoring the comment and struggling to hold her tongue, Anna followed her into a small attic room. Steeply sloping ceilings with barely enough room to stand except in the centre, made the room seem claustrophobic. A dormer window separated two beds, each with a chest of drawers at the foot. A wooden table and chair nestled under the window. Next to the door, on the only flat wall, a round mirror hung above a washstand with a basin and jug. Miss Romano opened a small door in the slanting wall, more roof than wall. "You can hang things in there. It's quite big inside. I use it as a wardrobe so make sure you push your stuff to the back."

Miss Romano pointed to the bed on the right. "That's my bed and chest of drawers. Don't touch my stuff." She wagged her finger at Anna. "I must go and make up some guest rooms before dinner." She spun on her heel and flounced out of the room, slamming the door behind her. Anna cringed, listening to Miss Romano's feet pound on the wooden floor.

Anna looked around the tiny room. The beds were old-fashioned iron bedsteads with brown horsehair blankets and clean, crisp, white sheets. The floorboards were bare except for a small rug by Miss Romano's bed. The bedsprings creaked and squeaked as she gingerly lay down. Stretching out on the lumpy mattress, she closed her eyes.

A rap on the door startled her. "It's Carter, Miss. I 'ave y'ur trunk." Carter placed her trunk just inside the door and left. His swift departure left her feeling abandoned. Feelings of loneliness and disappointment were foreign to Anna and she found the unknown alarming. Mrs. Banks had shown kindness when she had fainted, but the pursed lips and tight chignon gave the opposite impression. Anna chuckled; perhaps her stays were pulled too tight. She didn't trust or like Sophie Romano and the feeling seemed mutual. Just her luck, she thought, to be sharing a room with someone worse than her sister, Lou. And why didn't she have her own room? She deserved better. She would write to Papa and he would arrange for her to have her own room.

As much as she complained about Lou's annoying and bossy ways, she did love her. Anna and her soulmate brother, Charlie, daydreamed of sailing to far away countries like Uncle Bertie did. Father didn't approve of Uncle Bertie. He considered him an irresponsible wanderer, a womanizer and a generally bad influence. Mama adored her younger brother, so Papa tolerated him. Quite the opposite of Uncle Bertie, Papa was a precise man, an accountant by profession. Thinking of the family prompted tears, leaving wet spots on the ruffle of her white blouse. She was already having misgivings about her much-anticipated adventure.

It had not occurred to Anna, although when she thought about it, it should have been obvious, that a large hotel would require a large complement of staff. It had certainly never occurred to her that the hierarchy and duties of hotel staff were similar to that of servants in a large household. She swallowed the lump in her throat, afraid that The Sackville might open up some deep scars of injustice.

The memories of last year came flooding back. She had just turned eighteen when Mama announced that Thomas Tolford, a weedy looking farmer's son who would inherit his father's land, had asked Papa for Anna's hand in marriage. Anna overheard her mother say, "Taking a husband will cure our daughter's fanciful ideas of adventure." Anna was hurt and angry. She had always thought that her mother supported her yearnings to travel and her desire for independence. Not only did Anna have no affection for Mr. Tolford, she had no interest in marrying anyone. The thought of running a household and having babies made her feel quite ill. Anna had adamantly refused Thomas Tolford.

Mama and Papa were insistent that if she didn't marry, she must find something useful to do, always adding "until you do marry," which Anna had decided long ago was not going to happen. What could she do? Having never applied herself at school, becoming a teacher or governess was out of the question. Papa didn't approve of shop girls—he thought they were flighty. The obvious option open to her was service. To Anna, being a maid in service was almost as bad as marriage but no amount of pleading would change Papa's mind.

Anna was engaged by Lady Chartwell to assist her lady's maid, Dorothea. She thought this might be interesting. Lady Chartwell was a miserable, grouchy old lady who treated Dorothea unkindly, but for some inexplicable reason she treated Anna well, which did not endear her to Dorothea, or the rest of the servants.

Quite oblivious to the spiteful ways of servants, Anna's innocence led her down a dangerous path as imagination had taken her into an exciting dream world. A window to another life, she'd naively thought, of travel and adventure. Perhaps it was the constant praise that fuelled Anna's ego, and by her own admittance she enjoyed serving Lady Chartwell. However, she did not foresee how the praise would inspire hatred in Dorothea.

Fearing for her position, Dorothea plotted to get rid of Anna. While Anna was sponging and ironing one of Lady Chartwell's finest evening gowns, the kitchen maid conveniently called her away. Upon her return, to her horror, Anna found the hot iron burning a hole in the gown. As much as she claimed her innocence, she was dismissed in disgrace. Dorothea had burned the gown but denied it, and Anna couldn't prove she had even been in the laundry, let alone touched the gown.

Her confidence shattered, Anna had been miserable. It hurt to think that Lou and Mama were skeptical although they both had an awareness of the spiteful things that go on below stairs. Papa had considered it to be a domestic matter and no concern of his. Anna had moped around the house, afraid to do anything. It was Papa who'd come to the rescue and suggested that she try her hand at typewriting. Anna had then enrolled in Mrs. Wordsworth's Secretarial School for Young Ladies.

Anna relived the sense of pride and satisfaction she had felt when she soared to the top of her class, typing sixty-five words a minute. Pitman shorthand came to her easily. Her confidence returned and, once again, dreams of freedom filled her head. Her latest interest in reading books and newspapers had prompted her to question the role of women. She was intrigued by the success and notoriety of Florence Nightingale's nursing achievements during the Crimean War, and more recently by Emmeline Pankhurst, the leader of the British suffragette movement, and her fight for women. Although neither nursing, war, nor prison appealed to her (Emmeline was often arrested), the strength and independence of these women was a great motivator for Anna.

She affectionately remembered how she had persuaded dear Uncle Bertie to find her a secretarial position that would take her away from anything domestic. She grimaced, recalling the loud voices coming from Papa's study as Uncle Bertie had persuaded him that The Sackville was a prestigious hotel and Anna would be suitably chaperoned. Papa had finally given his permission, albeit reluctantly.

Mama had reprimanded her for unbecoming behaviour as she'd laughed and giggled and floated off into daydreams. She couldn't help herself. The prospect of leaving home and working in a big hotel had been an exciting adventure indeed. But now that she was there, standing in the tiny attic bedroom, the excitement had waned. Her palms were wet with perspiration, her throat constricted and tears rolled slowly on her face—her confidence slipping away with the receding tide of Bexhill-on-Sea.

Two

Papa's Little Girl Grows Up

Sophie Romano flung the bedroom door open and said, "Anna, it's six o'clock. Time for tea. Quick or we'll be late. Don't expect me to keep reminding you. Mrs. Banks only sent me because it's your first day."

"Thank you," Anna said, brushing her handkerchief across her wet cheeks. Noticing Sophie Romano had addressed her by her first name, Anna felt herself warming, just a little, towards her roommate.

The grandfather clock chimed the hour. Anna felt each stroke resonate inside her, validating her presence at The Sackville Hotel—there was no turning back. The deafening noise of wooden chairs scraping on the oak floor drowned out all possibility of hearing anyone speak. Not knowing where to sit, Anna looked to Sophie for guidance. She nodded towards an empty chair.

"Hey! That's my seat," a young bellboy yelled.

Anna jumped up. Sophie grinned and shrugged her shoulders. Mrs. Banks gave her a vexed look and pointing to the same chair Anna had sat in earlier she said, "This was Edith's place and now it is yours, Miss Neale." Anna detected a split second of tension at the mention of Edith's name.

The room erupted into clinking cutlery and clanging dishes, interspersed with chatting and laughter. Anna found the noise unsettling; meal times at home were quiet and formal. But, not having eaten a full meal since breakfast, she eagerly ate every morsel of the beef and mashed potatoes on her plate. The noise escalated as dishes were cleared away.

Mr. Blaine entered from the kitchen, balancing a large tray on his shoulder. The sweet smell of bread pudding and custard wafted towards Anna. Bill placed the tray next to her, giving her a smile and a wink.

When the meal was finished, Mrs. Banks invited Anna to her sitting room, where Amy placed a tea tray on a round table draped Victorian-style with a rich burgundy cloth topped with white lace. Anna remembered tiny, fair-haired Amy, ironing in the laundry room. Anna guessed she was no more than thirteen and wondered why she was not attending school.

An oversized broom cupboard with a fireplace would aptly describe Mrs. Banks' sitting room. A west-facing window filtered the rays of the setting sun, filling the room with a warm, orange glow and the soft scent of lavender hung in the air. The small wooden clock on the mantelpiece hummed a lyrical tick-tock.

Anna relaxed in spite of her nervousness; the cramped space contradicted the capacious sense of comfort and coziness. Mrs. Banks' demeanour mellowed as she lowered herself into a well-worn rocking chair. Sitting opposite, Anna glanced at a small dresser displaying three photos: a formal family gathering, a young man in uniform—perhaps a brother or beau—and another of a young girl, who could have been a young Mrs. Banks, holding a small dog. Several books lined the back of the dresser. Anna recognized titles by Mr. Rudyard Kipling and she immediately felt a kinship to Mrs. Banks—perhaps she shared her love of adventure. After all, Mr. Kipling did write about far off places. A thick, well-worn book overpowered the others: *Mrs. Beeton's Household Management*. It contained every detail about how to organize a household and she wondered how it would apply to a hotel. Mama called it her Bible and constantly quoted from it. Anna cringed, hoping she would not have to endure such recitations from Mrs. Banks.

"Miss Neale, as head housekeeper I am responsible for the discipline and care of all the female staff. In addition to etiquette, which I expect you to be familiar with, there are rules to be followed at all times. I am strict, but fair." As she spoke, her demeanour changed. Anna could have sworn her stays tightened, and the bun on her head pulled on its pins—she had Anna's attention.

"To break these rules may result in dismissal. Mr. Pickles looks after the male staff and he reports all staff activities directly to the owners, Kendrick Hotels Ltd., and is responsible for the overall management of the hotel. His word is final."

Mrs. Banks hesitated, cleared her throat, and took a sip of tea before continuing. "At times you will be working closely with Mr. Pickles in the office. Your predecessor, Edith was..." She hesitated again, taking another sip of tea. The cup rattled on the saucer. "Miss Neale, you will conduct your duties as instructed by Mr. Pickles." She cleared her throat. "But should you...," Mrs. Banks paused, "find his requests unusual or of a personal nature..."

The question was left hanging. Anna expected Mrs. Banks to finish the sentence but instead, she rambled on about more rules. Confused and bored, Anna began to fidget. She had a natural aversion to rules, but whether she liked them or not, she felt she had better comply.

"Have I made everything clear? Do you agree to abide by these rules?"

"Yes, Mrs. Banks."

"That is all. You will report to Mr. Pickles at eight o'clock in the morning in his office by the reception counter. Breakfast is served after six and no later than seven. Now off to bed with you and get some rest. We don't want any fainting spells tomorrow." Anna's cheeks flushed but Mrs. Banks smiled.

Reluctant to unpack her trunk, Anna stared mindlessly through the attic window. Her gaze fixed below on doll-sized ladies strolling along the Promenade under spinning parasols with gentlemen at their sides, all of them oblivious to Anna's loneliness. *Nothing more than ornaments beside the sparkling sea,* she thought. The pleasant scene below had no resemblance to what she considered to be the calamity of her first few hours at The Sackville Hotel.

Carter had called her hoity-toity. Her beautiful blue serge travelling suit and expensive hat had brought disdain, not the expected admiration from her peers. Tears of humiliation fell hot on her cheeks as she relived the fainting spell. Sophie Romano's anger reminded her of Dorothea and tightened her stomach. Only Mr. Blaine's caring smile gave her hope.

Her stare veered to the beach where the rhythmic waves felt hypnotic as they broke silently, receding invisibly into the horizon. Anna's spirits lifted as she imagined the promise of hidden quests and adventures waiting beyond those silent waves. "The tide always turns," she said, her breath escaping in a long sigh of yearning.

Stealing her gaze from the waves, she glanced around the sparse attic bedroom, comparing it to home. She hadn't expected to feel homesick; was that the cause of her ambivalence? Lou had selected the pretty pink-and-green floral wallpaper, Nottingham lace curtains, frilly counterpanes and a matching dressing-table skirt. The frills were not Anna's style, but sharing with Lou, meant sharing her taste. *What is my taste?* Anna wondered. The inside of the window in Rugby had looked pretty enough, but the view beyond those pretty lace curtains was of oppressive grey skies. Tall clay chimney pots billowing black coal smoke brought nothing more than the promise of soot-speckled laundry as it hung limply on the clothesline.

"What choices do I have?" she said, directing her question to the sea. "I can't go back to Rugby. Papa would not forgive me. Mama would have me married to Thomas the farmer." She shuddered at that thought. "And, Lou would say, 'I told you so.' Poor Charlie would be disappointed if I abandoned my quest for adventure. How I miss Charlie."

"My place is *here* for now," she said, pulling her trunk to the chest of drawers.

Anna finished her unpacking and laid out her clothes for the morning. She picked a simple high-collar white blouse with tight cuffs and just enough fullness in the sleeves to be fashionable, but appropriate for her desk duties. She decided on a dark brown skirt because it cinched her tiny waist; the hem fashionably above her ankles.

Perspiration trickled down Anna's back. The hot, stuffy attic room needed some fresh air. Inspecting the frayed sash cords of the window, she left it closed. She brushed her golden brown curls until they shone, twisting them into one long plait.

Gingerly, she extended her head into the hallway looking for the water closet. First she looked to her right—nothing but a blank wall with a small window. Turning to her left, the long hallway extended like a tunnel, with a speck of light at the end. She began to tiptoe towards the light, terrified of accidently stepping into the forbidden men's quarters. Then a terrible thought crossed her mind as she visualized the washstand in the bedroom. Maybe there was no water closet. Would she have to use a chamber pot? She let out an audible groan.

"Miss Neale, ar' y'u all right?"

Anna's hand flew up to her mouth to muffle her scream. She swung around to see Amy standing at the top of the stairs.

"Oh, Amy, you gave me such a fright." Anna let out a deep, raspy breath. "I was looking for the WC... we do have one, don't we?"

Amy giggled. "Course we do, it's a modern 'otel."

"Thank goodness. Could you show me where it is, please?" Amy pointed to the door behind her. Feeling foolish, Anna hustled inside, grateful for the privacy.

Back in her room she slipped on a thin nightdress, appreciating the cool cotton on her skin. She pulled the coarse brown blanket off her bed, thankful that she wouldn't need it tonight. *I'll send home for a softer blanket once I'm settled,* she thought, crawling into the creaky iron bed.

Anna awoke to unfamiliar noises. She rolled over, to see Miss Romano at the washstand, winding her thick, dark hair into a neat bun.

"Oh! *Her ladyship* is awake." Sophia's deep brown eyes catching Anna in the mirror.

"What time is it? It isn't hardly daylight," Anna said, choosing to ignore the sarcasm.

19

"Five o'clock. I have to help Amy get the maids up. The younger parlour maids can be lazy," she said, rolling her eyes. "There is much work to be accomplished in the salons. The dining room has to be spotless before the early rising guests come down for breakfast."

"What time did you finish last night? I didn't hear you come in."

"Usual, about eleven o'clock. Make the most of your first night. From now on you'll be working morning to night. That should take away some of those airs and graces."

In spite of her resolve not to pout, Anna's bottom lip trembled. "I don't have airs and graces. I have a different position from you, with different hours."

Pulling on her black dress, tying the white apron around her tiny waist and carefully pinning her lace cap on her head, Sophie giggled and turned at the door. "Pride always comes before a fall, your ladyship." She bobbed a pretend curtsy. "And don't get too settled, I intend to get *my* room back."

The razor sharp words rang in Anna's ears as she made her way to the staff dining hall for breakfast. The service stairs were teeming with activity: maids carrying trays of morning teas, parlour maids with carpet sweepers and feather dusters, porters and footmen with silver candelabras and brass coal scuttles, valets with jackets and trousers, and ladies' maids with gowns flung over their arms. Anna stepped to the side, pressing her back against the bannister, allowing a beautiful crimson gown to pass. Still staring at the gown, she didn't see Amy hidden behind an enormous laundry basket. They collided mid-stair; the contents of the basket tumbled down the stairs.

"Wa'ch 't," a familiar voice yelled. Carter was helping Amy gather up the linen. "Oh, mornin' Miss Neale. Best get out o' the way."

Anna quickly moved downstairs. Fiddling with the cuff of her blouse, she stood in the doorway deciding whether she should enter the staff dining hall.

Mr. Blaine's soft voice whispered in her ear, sending a shiver of pleasure down her spine. "Miss Neale, try to look busy." He gave her a cheeky grin as he placed a large tray of eggs and ham and steaming porridge on the

Welsh dresser. "As you can see, mornings are extremely busy. Give me a hand and set the dishes out for the staff breakfast. The plates are stored in the Welsh dresser. It will impress Mrs. Banks."

Anna placed the plates on the table just as Mrs. Banks entered. She nodded her approval.

"Mr. Blaine, are we ready for breakfast?"

"Yes, Mrs. Banks. Miss Neale is finishing the table." Giving Anna the now familiar wink, Mr. Blaine went back to the kitchen as the rest of the staff came in for breakfast.

Mr. Pickles' office had a gentleman's smell to it: the sweet lingering aroma of cigars with the sharpness of a spirit, probably brandy, mixed with the muskiness of leather and wood. Papa's study smelled like this, she thought. It was strange to be in a room without windows. Some natural light filtered in from the lobby but most of the light came from electric wall sconces and table lamps, casting menacing shadows around the room.

"Have a seat, Miss Neale," Mr. Pickles indicated an overstuffed leather chair. He walked behind the large, highly polished mahogany desk and took his place opposite Anna. The bulky chair engulfed her, uneasiness gripped her as if the oversized arms held her captive—she thought she might suffocate. Remembering the embarrassing fainting spell, she immediately sat up straight and looked directly at Mr. Pickles. He looked taller and sharper today. His monk-style bald head had been carefully barbered, leaving one side long enough to comb over the barren patch in the centre. She had a sudden urge to giggle, imagining the wind blowing the long strands of hair above his head, giving him a rooster look. As though Mr. Pickles could read her thoughts, his hand went up to his head smoothing his comb-over. She quickly averted her gaze to a wall of bookshelves.

"Are you interested in reading?" he asked.

"Yes, very much, Mr. Pickles."

"Huh!"

Not knowing if the response was meant to convey approval or disapproval, Anna continued, "I am quite taken with Mr. Rudyard Kipling's writings. Uncle Bertie, with whom you are acquainted, gave me…" Anna stopped.

The electric light threw sinister shadows across his pointy face. Red spots erupted on his neck. Like a panther stalking prey, he leaned forward, his long skinny body stretching across the desk, his hot breath wafting on her cheeks. She feared his long pointed nose might impale her to the chair.

"Miss Neale, you are here to work, not read, and you will refrain from any reference to my acquaintance with your uncle. You may be here as a favour to your uncle, but that does not mean you will be treated with favouritism. Bertie mentioned you were high-spirited and too intelligent for a woman. Too much spirit and intelligence is unbecoming," he scoffed. "I expect you to do your job and do it well or you *will* be dismissed. *Do you understand?*"

Now towering over the desk, his hands left steamy prints on the polished desktop, as he pushed himself back to his chair. His ferret eyes pierced into Anna. She gulped, not daring to move or speak. Tears burned at the back of her eyes, hurt by Uncle Bertie's betrayal, calling her *too* intelligent for a woman. The words would not leave her head; the tears grew closer to the surface. Mr. Pickles voice began sliding into the background when suddenly he lurched forward across the desk and a burst of hot breath hit her face. "Pay attention, Miss Neale!"

Pushing her thoughts and tears deep inside, she sat up as straight as the chair would allow. "Yes, Mr. Pickles."

Forcing herself to focus, Anna listened to Mr. Pickles review hotel protocol and describe her duties. She was not to be the hotel's front desk clerk as Uncle Bertie had implied. Her main duties were as Mr. Pickles' secretary: typewriting, shorthand and operating the telephone. Mr. Lytton, whom she hadn't met because he lived out, was the front desk clerk. Anna's front desk duties would be limited to early mornings, late evenings, and Sundays. Struggling to stifle her emotions, she shifted in the chair. A muffled knock on the door caught her attention.

Mr. Pickles pulled out his gold chain and fob, flipped open the watch, grunted and said, "Enter."

"Good morning, Mr. Pickles." A short, portly young man, dressed in a grey pinstriped suit, entered the room. He looked shiny—his black, overly greased hair shone as glossy as his black patent shoes.

"You are precisely one minute late, Mr. Lytton."

"Yes, sir, my apologies." Unperturbed, he bowed to Mr. Pickles, and looked over at Anna, who was now standing.

"Miss Neale, may I present Mr. Lytton, our front desk clerk. He will instruct you on all matters related to the front desk, and the operation of the telephone exchange." Consulting his gold watch, he added, "At precisely fourteen hundred hours you will report back here. Dismissed!"

"*Yes, sir!*" replied Mr. Lytton, who looked at Anna to do the same.

Anna managed a weak, "Yes, sir," while trying to determine what time fourteen hundred hours would be in regular time.

Standing at the front desk, out of Mr. Pickles' hearing range, Mr. Lytton said, "He was a sea captain; he still thinks he's at sea, and he treats us like his crew. There are days when I half expect him to come in with a parrot on his shoulder. I am tempted to respond with, "Aye, aye, sir!" A wide grin framed the lower portion of his round jovial face, and his contagious laugh passed easily to Anna, releasing the intensity of the last hour.

"Oh, fourteen hundred hours translates to two in the afternoon. Now, Miss Neale, let's get to work."

A large tiered crystal chandelier hung in the centre of the opulent hotel lobby. Each crystal reflected prisms of coloured light on the walls and polished brass fittings. The Hotel Register, a large, tan, leather-bound book lay prominently on the polished mahogany reception counter. An elegant silver pen with matching inkwell sat to the side. Anna sensed the grandeur and prestige through her fingers as they moved over the soft leather and the gold embossed hotel crest in the centre; each page was edged in the same gold. A wall of mahogany cubbyholes hung behind the reception counter. Each numbered cubbyhole held the corresponding guestroom key, plus any messages or letters waiting for absent guests.

Anna picked up the registration procedure quickly. She found it quite exhilarating to speak with the guests as they registered. But she failed dismally with the telephone exchange. She consistently plugged in the wrong telephone lines, upsetting the guests as they answered strange calls, or found no connection. Mr. Lytton's patience was running thin and his quick temper, a side that Anna had not yet experienced, was about to explode.

The perspiration beaded under her hair, making her curls tighten and her fingers sticky. Her nerves were getting the better of her. The complicated telephone exchange was like training an octopus. *This is impossible,* she thought as the plug slipped in her sticky finger and landed on the board in the wrong hole.

A gruff voice said, "The salmon's good t'day Bill, should please the toffs. 'Ow much does y'u want?" Horrified, Anna heard a refined voice answer, "Do you know who you are speaking with young man? This is Lady Thornton. Now get off my telephone line immediately." A loud laugh came from the confused fishmonger. Stunned, Anna stared at the exchange board, trying to figure out what to do. Mr. Lytton snatched the plugs from the offending sockets, and slammed them in front of Anna, his jovial disposition snapped.

"You stupid girl!" he exploded, his face turned from red to purple. "Move away from the telephone exchange this minute. I shall be obligated to report your conduct to Mr. Pickles."

He continued to berate Anna, having forgotten he was in the very public hotel lobby. Anna ran to the staff quarters banging the door. She kept running down the passageway until a blur of white and a pair of strong arms caught her. No longer able to contain her pent-up tears, they released in torrents.

"Hey! What happened?" a soft male voice whispered.

Anna looked up to see a pair of brilliant azure-blue eyes staring at her. "Mr. Blaine, I… um…" Taking a quick breath, she blurted out, "I don't know what to do. I'm going to be dismissed."

Bill Blaine led her down the hallway, through the back door into the courtyard. She sat on the bench, grateful for the fresh air. He pulled a pack of Woodbines from his pocket.

"Smoke?"

"No, no thank you."

He lit a cigarette, took a long drag and exhaled slowly. "So what upset you so? You only just arrived, so I doubt they will dismiss you."

Anna explained about her frightening meeting with Mr. Pickles, how Sophie hated her, and her difficulty with the telephone exchange and the final straw when Mr. Lytton lost his temper. He listened attentively, but the amused curve on his lips was not the reaction she expected.

"Now I understand," he responded, smiling. "I was ordering salmon this morning, and Harry, he's the fishmonger, kept talking about being connected to Lady Thornton." His smile turned to a hearty laugh. No longer offended, Anna smiled, seeing the funny side of the situation.

"Anna... may I call you Anna?" She nodded. "My advice is to go and freshen up, have some luncheon, and apologize to Mr. Lytton. Anna, I have to go... Chef will be looking for me. Oh, and the name is Bill."

"But he should not have said those things in front of the guests," Anna pouted.

"Perhaps you are right, but he reports to old Prickly-Pickles. You did make a mistake. Mr. Lytton takes his duties seriously. Upsetting an important guest of Lady Thornton's stature is a serious offence. And, he is your senior."

"I suppose you are right," Anna conceded.

"Be humble, Anna. You are no longer Papa's little girl. We'll talk later."

"How dare you!" Ignoring her, Bill stubbed out his cigarette and walked through the backdoor.

"Papa's little girl, indeed. He doesn't even know me."

Deep inside, she knew Bill was right. If she didn't mend her ways, she would face dismissal. And it had nothing to do with the telephone exchange although she would have to apply herself in order to operate the stupid thing.

First, she tidied her hair and, taking Bill's advice, she went to meet Mr. Lytton.

"Mr. Lytton, I am most terribly sorry for upsetting Lady Thornton and for causing you such distress." Anna bowed her head. "I don't know what came over me. I am sorry I ran off." Staring at her shoes, she waited for his response. She shuffled her feet slightly, hoping it would shake off the feeling of awkwardness. Being humble did not come naturally to Anna.

"The incident with Lady Thornton should not have happened. It is my responsibility to make sure that *all* our guests receive excellent service. When that doesn't happen it reflects upon my abilities as the front desk clerk. I have spoken with Lady Thornton and explained that today was your first day. She has graciously accepted my apology.

"You should not have run off banging the door. That was most unbecoming for a young lady and quite unacceptable in The Sackville Hotel. But, I do concede that I acted a little harshly. I accept your apology." He smiled. "Mr. Pickles does not need to know about this."

"Thank you," Anna said, feeling as though she had just dodged a bullet and matured ten years.

"I understand; it is your first day." Mr. Lytton smiled. Anna matched his smile. "Gather your sensibilities and be ready to report to Mr. Pickles at fourteen hundred hours."

Anna could hardly feel her feet touch the ground as she walked to the staff-dining hall. She wasn't going to be dismissed and the awkwardness had disappeared. She felt different, more confident, and she liked the feeling.

Striding into the staff dining hall she helped herself to some cold mutton, fresh bread and a hot cup of tea. She was still annoyed by Bill's comment, but he had invited her to call him Bill. His unusual eyes, fair hair, and kind smile appealed to her. Pulling her shoulders to her neck, she could still feel the warmth of his strong arms. She dismissed the thought of romance. The Sackville was to be an opportunity for adventure. Deep in thought, the quarter-hour chime startled her—only fifteen minutes before presenting herself to Mr. Pickles.

Three

Bill and Alex

B ill eased around the kitchen door. He hoped Chef had not missed him, but before he could get to his station, a chilling roar reverberated vociferously off the surrounding sterile white tiles: a marked disparity to the warmth and pleasant aromas emanating from the oversized Aga cooker. The casual kitchen chit-chat stopped, waiting for Chef's roar to subside into recognizable words.

Chef Louis, as English as the King himself, had adopted a fake French accent that fooled nobody. He had trained in Paris—or so he said. However, his culinary prowess, second to none, resulted in The Sackville Hotel's world-renowned reputation for excellent cuisine. But, like most chefs—predisposed to perfection and of a Continental temperament, whether adopted or real—he had a short, cruel temper, of which Bill Blaine was habitually on the receiving end.

"Monsieur Blaine, zee chickens pour le coq-au-vin prepare d'emselves?" His sarcastic tone ended on an unnaturally high note. His white chef's coat pulled taut around his ample girth and his chef's hat added several inches to his already tall frame. The thickness of his neck, undefined from his round puffy red face gave him the appearance of a flashing beacon, currently aimed at the cutting table. Several naked birds lay on the

27

scrubbed wooden surface; their necks and heads hanging over the edge, swinging like grotesque, novelty pendulums.

"No, sir. Yes, Chef!" Bill said, making no attempt to excuse his absence. He swiftly gutted and dissected the chickens, aware of the kitchen bustle returning to normal following an audible sigh of relief that, this time, Chef's outburst had been short.

Chef was a hard master but Bill rarely complained. His passion for cooking and the culinary arts matched Chef's and he considered it a privilege to be an apprentice to such a talent.

Once the preliminary preparations were completed for the guests' dinner, Bill began to prepare high-tea for the staff which brought his thoughts back to Anna. *I wonder how she is getting along with old Prickly-Pickles?* He liked Anna and smiled as he relived the feel of her warm body and heard her indignation when he had called her "Papa's little girl." He almost laughed aloud, recalling the episode with rough old Harry and Lady Thornton. He admired this spirited young woman who was undoubtedly heading for trouble. In an instant he realized he wanted to be her protector and wondered why she was having such an effect on him.

Jolted back to reality by Mrs. Banks' voice, Bill tried to compose himself. "Mr. Blaine, are you unwell?"

"No, Mrs. Banks, I am quite well," Bill replied, frowning at such an odd question. Then he became conscious of the heat radiating from the open oven where he was standing, staring, not at the large roast of mutton bubbling in the pan, but through the side window that looked directly onto the bench where he and Anna had their last conversation.

"You look very flushed. Are you sure you aren't coming down with a fever?"

"I assure you I am only flushed from the heat of the oven, a little distracted… um!" Embarrassed, Bill let his words fade.

Mrs. Banks left the kitchen and Bill's thoughts wandered yet again. His first impression of Anna reminded him of his mother. Both women were feisty, stubborn and had airs and graces: albeit, his mother's airs and graces were genuine. Lady Margaret, as Bill's mother was once known, was the youngest daughter of the Earl of Klyne. She had eloped with the stable manager, Thomas Blaine, Bill's father.

Bill appreciated the finer points of etiquette and grace passed on to him by his mother. He pictured her eyes, the same azure-blue as his own, full of tenderness, and yet even as a child he had sensed a shadow in those eyes, perhaps a yearning for the life she had rejected for the love of Thomas Blaine. That same love had given him a loving home instead of nannies, governesses and boarding schools.

Raised by his parents, mostly his mother, Bill had attended the local school, where he and his best friend, Alex Walker, had spent their school days. Their friendship had started even before school. They met at Alex's father's shop, John Walker's Kilts and Tailoring, on Princes Street in Edinburgh, Scotland. Bill's father ordered the jockey and stable livery at John Walker's shop.

As their fathers talked business or more often discussed their mutual interest in horse racing and gambling, the mischievous boys became bored. Always the prankster, Alex habitually charmed himself into and out of trouble. Bill, the quiet, practical, deep thinker lived contentedly in Alex's shadow—one complementing the other—and the two became inseparable at an early age. Alex's mother expressed an uncharacteristic fondness for Bill because of his mother's social status. Petunia Walker's airs and graces were far beyond the social status of tradesman's wife.

The boys, now grown young men, both studied the hotel business after leaving school. Bill, quiet and creative, chose cooking. Alex, with his natural charm, and an uncanny ability to instinctively know what people needed, studied all aspects of the hotel service. Still the prankster, this childhood attribute would often get Alex into trouble and on occasions it was annoying and inappropriate. Bill hoped, but was doubtful, that Alex had mended his ways.

Bill had begun his apprenticeship with Chef Louis in April. Although they had applied at the same time, Alex had to wait until the end of June before starting his position as a headwaiter.

As boys, they had constantly talked of travel and adventure, and as young men, they considered the hotel business to be a perfect medium to provide jobs while they explored England and the Continent of Europe. Bill had his sights set further afield to the Colonies of Africa, India, and America. He rarely spoke of his ultimate desire to live in America. Amy's voice brought him abruptly back to the present.

"Mr. Blaine, what shall I put out with the tea?"

"There is some sponge cake on the Welsh dresser and there are biscuits in the cupboard."

The staff meals were also Bill's responsibility. The staff took their tea break when duties allowed, usually between the guests' afternoon tea and staff high-tea. It was a welcome fifteen-minute break between luncheon and high-tea and the last opportunity for the kitchen and dining room staff to relax until after the dining room closed at eleven o'clock.

Having wasted considerable time daydreaming, Bill was annoyed that he would not have time to join the staff for tea—a missed opportunity to talk to Anna. He peered into the staff dining hall but could not see her. Maybe Mr. Pickles had not allowed Anna her break. He heard the baize door open and turned to see Anna walking towards him.

"Mr. Blaine, Bill, thank you for your advice. Mr. Lytton accepted my apology. I am grateful to you."

"I hope I wasn't too harsh. How was your afternoon with Mr. Pickles?"

Anna sighed and shrugged her shoulders. "I am not sure." Bill waited for her to explain, but she simply smiled and said, "But I am certainly more accomplished at shorthand and typewriting than operating the telephone."

Bill wondered why she had hesitated and opened his mouth to ask when a roar came from the kitchen. "I have to go," he said, giving Anna a beaming smile and the customary wink.

Chef was unrelenting and kept Bill working until late that night. He didn't see Anna again until breakfast the next morning, but she hardly said a word and he saw little of her for two weeks.

Alex was due to arrive today and Bill had arranged to have time off in order to meet his friend's train. Chef hated his staff taking time off and had worked Bill to the very last minute. What should have been a leisurely twenty-minute walk to the train station became a fast sprint in the unusually hot, humid afternoon sun. Sweating profusely, Bill collapsed onto an ornate wrought iron bench, just outside the waiting room on Platform 4.

The vibrating platform heightened Bill's anticipation to meet his best friend. The rhythmic clanging of the engine as it snaked around the bend reminded him of Alex's constant prattle and mischievous ways. Bill stared into the carriages, trying to see his friend's face, but the faces were a blur until the train finally slowed to a stop. Immediately doors opened, porters shouted and the hissing locomotive gave one last blast of steam, obscuring Bill's view of the alighting passengers. He moved down the platform, standing on tiptoe. Alex's height and shock of red curly hair made him easily recognizable from a distance. There he was, stepping out of a carriage two hundred yards away, looking as dapper as always in a dark suit that his father would have tailored for him for his new venture at Bexhill-on-Sea. A modern, broad-brimmed hat that he held just above his head seemed to hover as he bowed to offer a lady assistance with her luggage. Bill smiled at the typical Alex gesture. He absent-mindedly brushed his hands over his own not so crisp trousers, conscious of his damp shirt sticking to his back.

"He hasn't changed a bit," Bill said quietly to himself and began waving frantically. "Alex!"

Alex looked up and waved back. Bidding the lady goodbye and picking up his own bag he headed towards Bill. The men embraced, slapping each other on the back, shaking hands and both talking at the same time. Bill eagerly reported the goings-on at The Sackville, with considerable emphasis on a beautiful girl named Anna. Alex chattered on about news from family and friends in Edinburgh. The animated pair walked out of the Bexhill Central Station towards the Promenade, quite oblivious to the darkening sky. Thick black clouds crept over the horizon and wiped out the sunshine as large drops of rain began to bounce off their shoulders.

Glancing upwards, Bill said, "Looks bad, follow me. There's a public house just round the corner." Bill's words were drowned in an enormous clap of thunder, and none too soon they pushed the door open of The Fisherman's Nook, as the rain came down in buckets. Alex shivered; the light from the open door threw shadows over his tight, anxious face.

Bill frowned. "Storms still bother you?"

"Och, no' much, just give me a jolt, now-an-ag'in. No' to worry, I'm pretty much over it, still think of the wee lass once in a while." Alex's brushed his hand over his face. "The sweetest sister... if only I hadn't... the lassie was only fifteen...."

"Alex, it wasn't your fault. You could not have known that a vicious storm was brewing or that Meg would catch a chill that would lead to her death. No one did, she was young and healthy..."

Alex interrupted. "I no want to talk about it. Let's eat!"

The proprietor, nicknamed Nosey, was a chubby man with a bulbous red nose, which was known to turn purple by the end of a particularly busy evening. He greeted Bill warmly. The Sackville staff was well known in this pub. Alex and Bill settled down to a plate of hot steaming mussels, fresh crusty bread and a pint of ale.

"Tell me about this beautiful lassie, Anna," Alex demanded with a cheeky smile. "I think you're quite smitten with this lady."

"I hardly know her." Bill cleared his throat. "She arrived a couple of weeks ago. She is quite lovely, golden brown hair with curls often escaping from the pins, and delightful blue eyes." Bill grinned as he visualized her running down the hall. "She is strong willed, stubborn and somewhat spoilt, and is finding it difficult to fit into hotel life."

"Lass sounds like trouble," Alex said, frowning with a puzzled look. "Will ye no introduce me?"

"Hands off!" Bill shouted, with much more force than he intended. "You may be my closest friend but this lady is special. I want to get to know her without you charming her away from me." Bill laughed and playfully punched Alex on the arm, attempting to dispel his unexplained reaction.

All too aware of Alex's charm, Bill wanted to defend his liking for Anna.

Most women couldn't help themselves as they fell for this handsome, redheaded Scotsman. Bill rarely acknowledged his blonde hair and unusual eyes as good looks. He was self-conscious of his shorter stature and quiet demeanour. Women interpreted this as elusive and shy, certainly no match for Alex's natural magnetic charm and flamboyance.

On the surface, and frequently to outsiders, they seemed to be unlikely friends. Bill had always accepted Alex's popularity and was content to be the studious one of the pair. In the past, Alex had chosen their female companions—but Anna was different.

Feeling merry after consuming several pints of ale, they left the pub. Mr. Pickles did not approve of the servants frequenting pubs or indeed, of drinking alcohol at all. Bill suggested they walk the Promenade until their heads were clear of ale. They walked in silence, enjoying the strong gusty wind. The sound of the waves echoed as they pounded onto the beach. The storm had passed and the rain subsided, leaving a turbulent sea and a pleasant coolness to the evening.

Bill opened the back door of The Sackville. The aroma of sizzling beef filled the warm air. Not wanting to be coerced into the kitchen, Bill rushed by the open door into the staff-dining hall. Sophie Romano, the sole occupant, stared pensively into a cup of tea.

"There are some late diners. I wish they would come down for dinner so I can finish turning down the beds."

"Miss Romano, Sophie, is our head-housemaid and this is my closest friend, Mr. Alex Walker. He is about to take up his position as headwaiter here at The Sackville."

"Charmed, to make ye acquaintance, Miss Romano," Alex said as though he were addressing a princess.

She looked up from her tea and giggled. "Pleased to meet you, Mr. Alex Walker."

Bill had never seen her look demure, let alone giggle. Hiding his amusement, he attempted to break the charm by asking, "Sophie, has Mrs. Banks retired for the evening?"

"Yes, I think she is in her sitting room and Mr. Pickles retired to his study at six o'clock, as usual." Her stare was fixed on Alex as she spoke.

"Alex, I will introduce you to everyone in the morning. Chef will also want to meet you. However, now is a very busy time in the kitchen, so we will leave that until tomorrow too."

Bill yawned and caught a muffled yawn from Alex as well and led the way to the staff sleeping quarters. At the top of the service stairs, facing Mrs. Banks' bedroom, Bill stopped.

"That is Mrs. Banks' bedroom, her sitting room is downstairs. To your right are the women's quarters and to your left the men's." Bill hesitated, eyed Alex with concern, and continued with a serious tone to his voice, "*Never*venture into the women's quarters."

"Sounds very serious," Alex said with a grin.

"Alex, this *is* serious! It's grounds for dismissal."

"Och, believe me, I may like flirting with the lasses but I am no likely to jeopardize my position here. I understand. By the way, I notice you called Sophie by her Christian name but introduced us formally. What's the protocol?"

"Always be formal in the guest areas, but most of us use our first names in staff quarters. Superiors always formal."

As headwaiter, Alex was privileged with a small room to himself. Like most of the staff bedrooms, it was nestled in the eaves of the roof. Bill stepped in and Alex followed, automatically ducking his head. Alex's height was ill-suited to the sloping ceilings. Before calling it a night they agreed to meet in the staff-dining hall before breakfast; the introductions and Alex's orientation would follow.

Closing his bedroom door, Bill was pleased to see he was alone. Not as privileged as the headwaiter, he shared his larger room with one of the bellboys. Bill gave a long, pleasant sigh. It felt good to see his friend again. He was pleased to have news of home. He wasn't exactly homesick, but he worried about his mother, and whether his father was gambling. He felt sad wondering if he would ever see his grandfather again. He missed the old man's stories of the Boer War. He had taught Bill many military manoeuvres with his toy soldiers. Little lead replicas of battalions and cavalries, fighting battles in faraway places. Places Bill had resolved he would visit one day. It was rare that Bill won a battle or even out-manoeuvred his grandfather with military strategy. But toy soldiers had taught him patience and concentration, which served him well when playing chess—where he frequently beat the old man. He wished Alex played chess but Alex couldn't sit still long enough to concentrate. Bill lay on his bed, thinking of Anna. He had only seen her briefly and there had been no opportunity to talk. He wondered how she was getting on with the secretarial work and, of course, Mr. Pickles.

Bill, an early riser, started at five o'clock, giving him time to prepare the staff breakfast before his day began. He heard Sophie, also an early riser, speaking with Amy in the corridor. It was Amy's job to rouse the staff at five every morning.

A large tray of hot steaming porridge rested on Bill's shoulder as he entered the staff dining hall. Anna had adopted the task of setting the table for breakfast to help the kitchen staff. Delighted to find Anna alone, he stuttered shyly, "How are you?"

"I am well, thank you."

"How are you doing with the front desk and the telephone?"

"I like working on the front desk and I am getting much better with the telephone, but I spend most of my time with Mr. Pickles." She looked away.

"Anna, is something wrong?" Bill saw anxiety in her face. "Anna what has..."

"Sorry, am I interrupting?" Alex said.

"No, of course not. Alex, I would like you to meet Miss Anna Neale, our new assistant desk clerk and secretary to Mr. Pickles." Feeling the heat flush feverishly from his neck to his face, he prayed that Mrs. Banks did not appear. "And Miss Neale, this is my closest friend, Mr. Alex Walker. Alex arrived yesterday from Edinburgh."

Alex bowed. "I am pleased to meet you, Miss Neale. Bill has told me much about ye."

Anna looked startled. "He has?" She quickly composed herself. "Bill has shown great kindness towards me. My first days here have been difficult."

The conversation was cut short as the staff came in for breakfast. Once the meal was over, Alex met with Mr. Pickles for his orientation and Anna took up her post at the front desk until Mr. Lytton arrived. Bill hustled into the kitchen before Chef lost his temper. He had a challenge today as the lunch menu included quenelles of salmon, a delicate dish, which Chef had entrusted to him. He felt good today, flattered that Chef finally trusted him and impressed that Alex had not tried to charm Anna. Then he remembered the anxiety on Anna's face. He suspected Mr. Pickles, the prickly bastard, had upset her. He wanted to find a way to meet Anna so they could talk and preferably before Alex used his charm.

Four

Friendship

A t precisely thirteen hundred hours on Saturday afternoon, Mr. Pickles pulled out his gold watch, grunted, and left the office. He would not return, unless there was an emergency, until Monday morning.

When Anna had asked Mr. Pickles about time off, he had screwed up his pointy nose, glared at her through his ferret eyes and replied, "You take time on Saturday afternoon, after I leave, but only if Mr. Lytton does not need you," knowing full well that Anna would be needed at the front desk when the four o'clock train came into Bexhill Central.

Mr. Lytton stayed late one or two evenings a week, giving Anna some time off, but too late to go out. The few precious hours on Saturday were the only daytime hours she had to explore Bexhill-on-Sea and most of all walking on the beach and touching the waves.

Within minutes of Mr. Pickles' departure, Anna stepped out of the back door into the bright sunshine. She swung her arms out and twirled around, lifting her face towards the warm sun. She passed the bench in the courtyard and immediately thought of Bill, who she had only seen in passing since Alex's arrival.

Quite a handsome fellow, Alex Walker. *A bit full of himself,* she thought.

37

It had not escaped Anna that most of the female servants were falling all over him. Such charm did not interest her, perhaps because she had no interest in marriage. Bill, she liked.

Talking to Bill was like talking to Charlie, although she couldn't help noticing that her heartbeat quickened when she was near him, and he often showed a slight flush when they bumped into each other.

The seagulls screeched above, soaring and swooping. She leaned back, her hand on her straw hat, a smaller and more suitable hat than her blue one. Anna envied the seagulls and their freedom. She moved her gaze to the horizon and almost stepped into the path of an automobile. The loud blast from the horn made her jump backwards. The driver of a hansom cab had to rein his horse tight as the loud horn and chugging engine caused the horse to rear dangerously. Both drivers shouted out to each other, ignoring Anna, who made a quick run across to the Promenade and down the steps to the beach.

The pebbles crunched under her boots, the unevenness putting her off balance as she picked her way towards the water, avoiding deck chairs and families sitting on blankets. Someone yelled and she turned to see a young man rapidly approaching the water, pulling a white wooden hut, about the size of a privy, perched on wheels. She could see these huts from her attic bedroom. They provided privacy for changing in and out of bathing attire. Curious to see the occupant, she followed the hut to the water's edge.

First a lady's head, wrapped turban-style in a navy and white scarf, peered out of the hut and then she ventured onto the steps. Wearing a loose-fitting tunic of navy blue with white trim around the sleeves and yoke; a small portion of bare leg showed from beneath navy blue pantaloons that ended below her knees. Hurriedly, the lady joined the young men and women bathers. The wet fabric clung immodestly to their bodies. Anna wondered what the cool water would feel like on her body but she could never wear such unbecoming bathing attire. The men's suits were tighter than the women's and it embarrassed her to see the male contour, something she had not witnessed before. She felt her cheeks flush and deflected her gaze to the water.

The pebbles had turned to sand at the water's edge and her heels sank as the waves lapped at the toe of her boot. She lifted her skirts as high as she dared, wishing she could take off her boots and stockings and feel the sand between her toes and the sea wash over her bare feet. Pulling her skirts tight around her knees, she squatted down, trailing her fingers through the cool water, amused by the feel of the waves. Daydreaming of faraway sea adventures, she didn't see the larger wave rolling in until it washed over her boots and caught the hem of her skirt. Anna jumped up, laughing, enjoying the moment. Her feet remained remarkably dry, but the water had wicked along the threads of the fabric and her wet skirt slapped uncomfortably against her legs as she walked to the pavilion to find a café.

The waiter showed her to a small, round table overlooking the sea and she ordered Earl Grey and buttered scones with strawberry jam. And there he was—Bill Blaine, leaning on the railing looking out to sea. He hadn't seen her, and she wasn't sure whether to call out, or wait until he saw her. Before she could decide, the waiter arrived. As he bent down to place the tray on the table, the wind caught the edge of the tray, almost spilling hot tea over Anna. She gasped; the commotion attracted Bill's attention.

"Good afternoon, Miss Neale," Bill said. "We seem to have a habit of meeting in a crisis." He smiled, staring from Anna to the vacant chair.

"Mr. Blaine, how lovely to see you. Please, won't you join me?" Anna's fingers went to her hair, which she knew was curling untidily from under her hat.

Bill called the waiter over and asked for a second cup and saucer and cake to go with the scones. "Fresh air makes me hungry," Bill said. Anna wasn't sure if he was talking to the waiter or her. She smiled.

"I am surprised to see you. Is Saturday your day off?" Anna asked, pouring the tea.

"I was about to ask you the same thing." They both laughed. "You go first."

"Mr. Pickles leaves at one o'clock on Saturday, giving me a few hours before the afternoon train arrives."

"Me too, Saturday luncheon is quiet. Chef allows me to prepare a cold meal, which is served by the dining room staff. I get a few hours off. I can't believe my luck that we have time off together. What would you like to do?" Bill blushed. "Oh, forgive me, I am being very presumptuous."

"I would like to spend the rest of the afternoon with you. I want to explore and be adventurous."

"I'm not sure what adventure there is along the Promenade, but we could use our imagination. Can you see the ship on the horizon?" Bill pointed out to sea.

"Yes. I wonder where it sailed from, India or Africa or the Spice Islands?" Anna's eyes lit up and Bill stared at her. She self-consciously tucked one of the wayward curls into her hat.

"I like the way your hair curls around your face," Bill said, his cheeks turning even pinker. "You are full of excitement today. I have been worried about you. You seemed unhappy. Is Mr. Pickles difficult to please? He seems to be a hard taskmaster."

A shadow passed over Anna and she hesitated. "Mr. Pickles is demanding and precise. My father is an accountant and precise, so I should be used to it, but Mr. Pickles makes me feel uncomfortable." She stopped. "Do they really call him Prickly-Pickles?" She giggled.

"Why does he make you uncomfortable?"

"He has strange mood swings that puzzle me. One minute he's angry and mean and the next he lowers his voice and gives me a smile, but it's an unpleasant smile." Anna wondered if she could tell Bill about how he walked towards her as though to touch her, and then tersely stepped away. Could she tell him how she felt a dark, sinister sensation sweep through her body every time he approached her desk?

"I'm surprised Prickly-Pickles smiles at all. It must be hard working so closely with such an unpleasant man." Bill's head went to one side, waiting for a response.

"It's nothing, my imagination gets the better of me sometimes," Anna took a deep breath. "Let's talk about Spice Islands and far off places. I want to travel the world like my uncle. He used to tell my brother and me wonderful stories about India and other romantic places.

"My grandfather told me stories about Africa, mostly his experiences in the Boer War. His stories fascinated me."

They finished their tea and walked along the Promenade, talking and laughing like old friends. Anna related Uncle Bertie's stories and Bill remembered his grandfather's tales until it was time for them to return to The Sackville.

Anna felt as though she was walking on air. Her cheeks glowed from the sun and the wind. *What a wonderful afternoon,* she thought. The front desk was quieter than expected, allowing Mr. Lytton to leave early, trusting Anna to manage the desk for the rest of the evening and all day on Sunday—his day off. Although not quite alone, as Miss Jenkins, a local lady, came in every Saturday and Sunday to assist at the desk and answer the telephone. With no secretarial duties during weekends, Anna devoted her time entirely to front desk duties.

Sunday morning, Anna woke before sun up, too excited to sleep. Today she was the front desk clerk. She decided to wear her best white blouse with the intricate pleats and lace down the front, her blue pendant sat nicely between the rows of lace, and complemented her blue skirt from her travelling suit. Pinning her hair with more care than usual, she sighed with satisfaction.

"How could you let me sleep in?" Sophie hissed through clenched teeth, jumping out of bed. "If I'm late, it's your fault." Before Anna could answer, there was a knock on the door. "Its 5 o'clock, Miss Romano." Amy's voice announced. "Ur... I'm up, thanks, Amy."

"Why are you up so early? Going somewhere?"

The sarcasm bothered Anna. She liked Sophie, and so did most of the other staff but her meanness towards Anna was unsettling; visions of Dorothea filled her mind. Anna decided to confront her.

"Sophie, why don't you like me?" She sounded braver than she felt, and the immediate silence, made her think that maybe she should have kept quiet.

Sophie was making her bed and stopped, holding the blanket in mid-air.

She turned, her brow furrowed under her ebony hair, her brown eyes wide with surprise. She looked directly at Anna.

"I don't know. Actually, I think I do like you. You remind me of me, when I first started here. You see, I was like you, full of myself, but I didn't want to be here. My family fell on hard times and being too young to find a husband, I had to find work." Tears filled Sophie's eyes, she took a deep breath. "It meant a lot to me when I was promoted to head housemaid and given my own room. Then you came along with your fancy clothes, airs and graces, reminding me of my family. On top of that I have to share my room with you and," Sophie paused and Anna saw a little smile. "I was jealous when I saw that you too had a tiny waist." Simultaneously they both burst out laughing.

The ice was broken. Rather than being enemies, it appeared that they had much in common. She wanted to know more about Sophie and her past, now that she felt compassion instead of resentment.

George, the night porter, snoozed in his chair near the lobby entrance. His head bent to one side, pushing his dark green cap over one eye. He gently snored through fluttering lips. The rest of his body seemed to be at attention, his white-gloved hands neatly placed at the side of his immaculate, double-breasted, dark green, great-coat with polished brass buttons and a neat red cord around the sleeves and collar—The Sackville's livery. Anna tiptoed into the lobby, the thick Axminster carpet muffling her steps. She quietly passed his chair to reach the reception counter. It was early, and he wouldn't be expected to unlock the front doors until seven o'clock unless someone rang the bell.

Anna checked the leather-bound registration book, making sure that no late arrivals had checked in during the night. She then cross-referenced the entries with the keys in the cubbyholes. Odd, she thought, Lady Thornton's cubbyhole had several letters in it. Normally the bellboy would deliver messages and letters immediately upon receipt. If the guests were out, they would pick up letters and messages with their room-key upon their return.

"Morning, Miss Neale," George said, standing and brushing down his coat while clearing the sleep from his throat with a self-conscious cough. "I best get the door unlocked. You's up early."

"Good morning! George…" Anna hesitated, "Lady Thornton has letters in her box. Do you know why they were not sent up?"

"Yeah, the bellboy said she wouldn't come to the door. She's a strange one. Spends her summers here but rarely leaves her room. Other guests complain that dog of hers yaps, and she has a parrot that squawks. Says she's in mourn'n', although you'd not think it, if you heard her yell; a right bark she has. Rumour has it that her husband were drowned in the Titanic."

Anna looked up from the register. "I saw her at the train station the day I arrived. I know what you mean. I heard her barking orders to the poor porter." The memory of the grand lady dressed in black, the yapping Pekingese and the enormous black hat with its grotesque feathered tentacles, made Anna feel ill at ease.

"You might see her today; she goes to church Sunday morning. I'm off to get mi'self some kip, mi wife'll have mi breakfast ready."

Irritated, Anna slammed the register closed muttering, "This was going to be such a great day. The first time I am truly in charge and grand Lady Thornton will spoil it." Anna pouted and stamped her foot in anticipation of a reprimand or confrontation with Lady Thornton.

"G'd morning, Miss Neale." Alex's deep baritone voice filled the lobby. Anna, aware of her actions, hoped he had not seen or heard her little tantrum.

"Good morning, Mr. Walker. What are you doing in the lobby?" Trying to hide her own embarrassment, she sounded righteous. "Dining room staff should be using the service door. If Mrs. Banks catches you, you'll be in trouble," Anna scolded.

Alex leaned on the reception counter. "Ye look lovely today, lassie. Och, those wee blue eyes sparkle when ye'r angry?"

"I am not angry!" Anna was intending to sound incensed by his comment, but her ridiculous and involuntary smile said otherwise. He was flirting with her. "Mr. Walker, don't you have work to do?"

"Fair lassie, I am but ye humble servant. I shall nay tarry to the dining

43

room." He bowed, Shakespearian style, his white apron touching the floor.

Anna couldn't help herself, and burst into laughter. Another voice came from behind, responding to Alex's drama.

"Be gone, my lord Don Juan, for this fair maiden be mine," Bill was laughing as hard as Anna. The contagious laugh spread to the young bellboy and the doorman.

It had surprised Anna, how easily Alex and Bill had drawn her into their friendship. Late in the evening they would sit talking in the staff-dining hall long after the others had retired. When they could all get time off together, they went to the cinema, often making fun of the pianist as the music rose and fell in tempo, attempting to follow the film, but was quite often out of sync with the action.

It wasn't difficult to see the strong bond of friendship between Alex and Bill, a bond that would be hard to break. Anna had never experienced such a friendship, but she realized that, even in a short space of time, she had bonded with both men. Such friendships, she thought, had the propensity to become fragile.

"Mr. Walker! Mr. Blaine! To your posts, immediately! I will speak with you later," Mrs. Banks shouted, her voice and stance that of a stern teacher. She turned towards Anna. "Miss Neale, concentrate on your work." Anna saw the duplicity—the harsh teacher, the warmth in her eyes, and the touch of a smile at the corner of her lips. Anna directed her attention to the guest register. Mrs. Banks was still standing at the front desk. Anna looked up, not sure what to say.

"Is something wrong, Mrs. Banks?"

"No! Not at all. But take my advice and be careful around those two gentlemen. Romance between the staff is not forbidden, but it is frowned upon."

Anna felt uncomfortable and guilty. She wasn't sure how to respond and decided to change the subject. "Mrs. Banks, there are several messages here for Lady Thornton. I asked George about them and he said she wouldn't answer the door. What should I do?"

"I will ask her maid and let you know. Lady Thornton is one of our regular summer visitors. She can be demanding, but her bark is worse than her bite. Her husband drowned in the Titanic last year and she is in mourning." Mrs. Banks leaned towards Anna and quietly said, "She fancies herself as a mourning queen and, like Queen Victoria, I doubt she will ever come out of mourning. Not because she is heartbroken like the Queen, but because as Lord Thornton's widow, she can command sympathy and attention while enjoying a considerable fortune."

It was astounding to Anna that Mrs. Banks would confide this information to her, and that she addressed her by her first name. "Anna, if anything troubles you, either with Mr. Pickles, your work, or unwanted advances from members of staff, please come and talk to me. If Edith had come to me, she would still be here."

"Thank you, Mrs. Banks." Anna wondered how to interpret these comments. She remembered the staff reaction to Edith's name the first day she arrived. Mrs. Banks disturbed Anna with unexplained looks of concern at the mention of Mr. Pickles. Was Mrs. Banks aware of Anna's discomfort and uneasiness around Mr. Pickles? Should she say something? No, she thought. Mrs. Banks was just being kind in a general way. It was now obvious to Anna that Mrs. Banks cared deeply about the welfare of the staff. But she was puzzled by the secretive references to Edith.

The morning was going well. Anna coped easily with the front desk duties. Alex and Bill had scurried off to their duties, somewhat intimidated by Mrs. Banks' reprimand. Just as George had predicted, Lady Thornton ordered a carriage to take her to the Sunday Service at St Andrew's Church. The ornate brass lift gate opened, clanging and clattering as it concertinaed to the side, allowing the imposing black figure of Lady Thornton to march into the lobby. Her face was so heavily veiled that she had difficulty walking and needed her maid to guide her to the carriage.

So engrossed in the charade, Anna didn't notice Mrs. Banks approach the desk again. Her presence in the lobby was unusual. Most of her duties were in the staff quarters or in the guest suite, except in the absence of Mr. Pickles and Mr. Lytton, then Mrs. Banks was in charge.

"Miss Neale, Lady Thornton's lady's maid has asked that you deliver her messages when she returns from church."

"Of course, I'll have the bellboy take them up, when she returns."

"Lady Thornton has requested that you deliver them personally."

"Me!"

"Is there a problem?" Mrs. Banks frowned.

Anna swallowed hard. "No, of course not, Mrs. Banks."

Mrs. Banks left the lobby. Anna tried to concentrate on her work but the thought of coming face to face with Lady Thornton was too distracting. For the next hour and a half, she did little but move papers around, with one eye on the front entrance.

Finally, the guests returned from church and the lobby soon became crowded. Gentlemen in morning suits and top hats congregated in groups, discussing politics and news. The scent of lavender and rosewater emanated from ladies dressed in the highest of fashion. The taffeta and silk skirts swished as they moved and the feathers and ribbons that adorned the hats fluttered softly as heads bobbed in gossip and chatter—a picture of opulence.

Anna's heart jumped into her throat at the familiar bark. "Out of my way!" The crowd parted, and Lady Thornton marched through the centre to the lift. Turning towards the front desk she barked again, "Girl, bring my letters now!"

"Yes, Lady Thornton," Anna managed to squeak out, while emptying the cubbyhole of its contents.

Anna's knees trembled as she knocked on the door of Suite 305. The maid, Miss Barclay, ushered her inside, the Pekingese yapping at her feet. She had never been inside any of the guest suites before. A crystal chandelier hung from the ceiling in the entrance. Beautiful chintz chairs in pastel blues and pinks furnished the parlour. At one end of the room, stood a large rich dark mahogany table with matching chairs and a sideboard. At the other end of the room by the window was a roll-top desk. The wooden slats were rolled up, showing evidence of abandoned letter writing. Sunlight streamed through open French doors, which led to a tiny balcony—decorative, but quite non-functional. The matching chintz curtains swayed gently, the breeze filling the room with the fresh scent of the sea. Lady Thornton reclined on a chaise-lounge, her wide, hooped—somewhat old fashioned, black skirts spread neatly across her lap contrasting with the pastel shades of the chaise giving her complexion a pallid look of illness. Without the veil and the large black hat, she didn't look at all fearsome. Her dark brown hair, peppered elegantly with grey, was neatly pinned in elaborate twists and curls, and held securely in place with a large, intricately carved tortoiseshell comb. Anna's fear abated and she observed this sad and vulnerable lady with compassion.

Just as Anna began to relax, the silence was broken by a high-pitched and a very loud voice. "Get out! Get out! Pretty Anna! Get out!"

Anna gasped and flung her hand to her chest, staring at Lady Thornton, but soon realized that the voice was from behind, and not human.

"Stop that Polly!" Lady Thornton barked.

"Pretty Polly, Polly get out!"

Anna quickly composed herself and stifled a giggle. The strange voice was, of course, the parrot Anna had seen at the train station. Its cage was hanging on a gold stand immediately behind her. Lady Thornton's face lit up and she began laughing. "Polly's vocabulary is very limited. Anna was the previous owner's name. And why Polly says, 'Get out,' we don't know."

"Come child, sit and chat to an old lady," she said, pointing to the chair opposite her. "I have wanted to meet you ever since you connected my telephone to the fishmonger. What is your name?"

Anna's face flushed to a bright pink at the mention of the telephone mishap. Her insides were doing flip-flops and now she was nervous. She cleared her throat to steady her words. "Anna Neale, m'lady. I am sorry about the telephone. It was my first day and the exchange is very complicated. Mr. Lytton tried to teach me. I am much better now and even better at typewriting." Anna stopped, aware that she was rambling. "I have your letters, m'lady," Anna said as she handed them to the maid. "If that's all, m'lady, I must return to the front desk. I am alone on Sundays."

"Oh, very well." Lady Thornton wafted her arm, dismissing Anna, but before the maid opened the door she added, "Typewriting? I would like you to write some letters. Barclay will come and get you when I need you."

"Yes, m'lady." Anna didn't know what else to say. She ran down the stairs to the lobby, wondering what she should do. It would be hard to fit any more work into her already busy days.

Five

Mr. Pickles Makes His Move

⟨⟩❦⟨⟩

T rue to her word, Lady Thornton requested Anna's services as a typewriter. Mr. Lytton was only too pleased to accommodate the request of his most prestigious guest. It reflected well on his front desk management abilities. Less than enthusiastic, Mr. Pickles gave his consent as long as Anna's absence did not inconvenience him. It was agreed that Anna would tend to Lady Thornton's correspondence on Tuesdays and Fridays, from one o'clock until two o'clock, during his luncheon break. A typewriting machine and a small oak table were sent up to Suite 305.

At first, Anna had difficulty seeing this grand lady without the ominous black feather tentacles. Anna would get flustered, waiting for Lady Thornton to bark her displeasure or give unrealistic orders. But neither actually happened.

On Friday of the second week, Miss Barclay opened the door and asked Anna to join her ladyship in the dining room. Anna stared at Miss Barclay. The perspiration was pouring down her back. Finally, it had happened. Lady Thornton was displeased.

Miss Barclay pulled her sleeve and whispered, "Don't look so worried. She really likes you, and if she likes you, she is very kind."

Anna mouthed, "Thank you."

"Barclay, is that Miss Neale at the door?"

"Yes, m'lady."

"Oh, Miss Neale, come and have luncheon with me."

Anna didn't know what to say. The table was set for two and the sideboard was laden with food. A delicious aroma rose from a silver chaffing dish. A plate of cold lamb and some of Bill's quenelles of salmon sat to the side, and a spice cake for sweet.

"Barclay told me that you are not able to have luncheon the days you come here. I decided we should luncheon together."

"Thank you, m'lady, but I don't think I have time to eat."

"Nonsense! Sit down please."

At the thought of dining with Lady Thornton, Anna appreciated her mother's lessons on the finer points of table etiquette. Anna gave Barclay a quizzical look as she served the luncheon. How did her ladyship know that Mr. Pickles had disallowed Anna's lunch break on Tuesdays and Fridays? The quenelles of salmon were delicious, she must remember to compliment Bill, and the spice cake was exquisite—had Bill known she was dining with Lady Thornton and did he know spice cake was her favourite?

The typewriting luncheons became a routine. Anna and Lady Thornton looked forward to their time together. Anna was no longer afraid of the grand old lady, whose bark, as Mrs. Banks had said, was worse than her bite. Even Polly stopped telling Anna to "get out" and Princess, the Pekingese, curled at Anna's feet as she worked.

Lady Thornton talked about her husband, and the horrors of the sinking Titanic and losing him in the freezing waters of the North Atlantic Ocean. She had a flare for the dramatic that captivated Anna. Anna talked about her friendship with Bill and Alex, insisting that romance was out of the question. The threesome was too important, she explained.

"We have so much fun together. Saturday afternoons we go to the beach and then for tea at the Pavilion, and sometimes to the cinema. Alex makes us laugh and Bill, the deep thinker, makes us look for opportunities. I adore them both and they adore me, it's a perfect friendship, romance would spoil it."

Lady Thornton remained silent, her slightly raised eyebrows indicated she wasn't convinced, and if truth were known, neither was Anna. She had seen, but chose to ignore, the signs: the loving looks, the gentle touch, and the signs of rivalry between best friends. And it had not escaped her how her heart missed a beat when Alex touched her arm or when Bill comforted her after a bad day. She told herself it wasn't possible to love both men, in a romantic way, so it had to be a friendship.

A mutual understanding grew between the two. Anna filled a void in the old lady's lonely life; estranged from her only relative, her son Darcy, who she rarely mentioned. Anna found it curious she never referred to him as Lord Thornton. Was he not the heir to the earldom? Any inquiries on the subject deepened the lines of anguish on Lady Thornton's face and sadness or anger, she couldn't tell which, cast a shadow.

On the Friday of the August Bank Holiday weekend, Anna noticed the letter she was typing was addressed to a friend in India. The typewriter machine keys bounced with excitement and she began to babble, "Did I ever tell you about my Uncle Bertie who travels to India? Actually he travels all over the world; he's even done business with Red Indians in North America, and last year he was in South Africa."

"Yes, Anna, you have, many times. You admire your uncle," Lady Thornton sighed.

"I have dreamed of travelling ever since I was a child. My brother, Charlie, and I loved to listen to Uncle Bertie's stories."

"It's not easy for a young woman to travel. Have you considered how you would travel, and with whom?"

She looked up from the typewriter. "I had never thought about that."

"Well, I think it would be prudent to do some thinking, but for now please get on with my letters, it is nearly two o'clock."

It troubled Anna that she couldn't answer Lady Thornton's question. How was she going to travel? How would she find adventure? Women did go to India or North America and even deep into the jungles of Africa, but not many went alone. Society did not approve of independent women.

51

Those who did venture to travel alone were seen as brazen.

Unexpectedly, Anna felt the pain of disappointment in the pit of her stomach. She was foolish for not having considered her options. A woman who travelled alone had courage and means to afford travel and, if unmarried, she would be chaperoned by relatives. Anna had none of these fundamental requirements. Her heart sank as it became apparent that her lust for adventure was no more than a dream. But dreams did come true. Her fingers instinctively brushed the blue pendant as she thought of Uncle Bertie's words, "Follow your dreams and never let anyone destroy them," and she resolved to find a way.

Perhaps marriage was not a bad thing after all? But where would she find a husband with the desire and wealth to travel? Potential husbands in her sphere of acquaintances were the Thomas Tolfords of the world, which would sentence her to life managing a household. No, marriage was not the answer.

Work began early on the busiest weekend of the year and, with a fully booked hotel, it would be late before the work was done. Saturday morning started by encouraging departing guests to checkout early so the chamber maids could clean the rooms and Anna and Mr. Lytton could prepare for the afternoon arrivals. The lobby buzzed with bellboys and porters carrying trunks and bags to waiting carriages and hansom cabs led by impatient horses, most heading for Bexhill Central Station.

A be-goggled gentleman wearing a fashionable tweed jacket, flat cap, and a rakish scarf flung around his neck, strapped brown leather suitcases to the back of a Morris Oxford two-seater automobile. In contrast, a serious, stiff-looking chauffeur bowed ceremoniously as he closed the rear door of a large Daimler. The noisy, chugging engines filled the portico with petrol fumes, which mixed with the smell of horse droppings. Anna screwed up her nose as the odour began to permeate into the lobby. By noon, most of the guests had departed. Anna left Mr. Lytton checking the keys and returned to her desk.

Mr. Pickles, a creature of habit, reconciled the accounts every Saturday morning, and once the accounts were completed, he dictated the weekly report to Anna. *Business must be good,* Anna thought, noticing that the corner of his mouth turned up slightly. Almost a smile, it was a rare expression for Mr. Pickles. Although the office was quite large, the massive bookcases, the large mahogany desk and overstuffed leather chairs left little space for Anna's desk, which was pushed into a corner. She sat with her back to Mr. Pickles, an arrangement that suited Anna well, as she hated looking at his mean, pointy face. He made her feel uncomfortable, even repulsed, when he stared.

"Miss Neale, close the door please."

She stopped, turned and faced him, just as he licked his lips and smiled, a wicked, twisted smile. She stepped backwards, a reflex reaction. Her instincts told her to run. From what, she did not know.

"I think the door should be open in case Mr. Lytton needs us."

"Close - the - door!" Mr. Pickles shouted much too loudly, but he recovered quickly. "These financial records are confidential. I would like you to come over here and check these numbers."

Anna hesitated, and inched her way towards the door, dread filling her chest. She had a choice: if she ran she would be dismissed, if she gave the door a gentle push, it might not close completely, she pushed gently. Her pulse pounded in her temples as she took a timorous step towards the big mahogany desk. Her hand on her stomach, she felt sick; instinctively she now understood—he wanted to touch her.

"Mr. Pickles, I think perhaps I should see if Mr. Lytton needs any assistance. It has been a busy morning and..." Looking into his cold, cruel ferret eyes, she dared not say another word

"I said, *come* and look at these numbers!"

Anna stopped at the side of the desk. He grabbed her arm and pulled her to his side, pointing to the ledger in front of him. Anna had no choice but to move closer to him, in order to read the ledger. She froze. His hand had moved from her arm to her skirt. Bile rose in her throat as the intense heat from his hand spread into her thigh. She looked down at the ledger on the edge of the desk. To her horror, she saw his hips thrust forward and the bulge in his trousers kept moving and growing larger. It was grotesque; she didn't understand what was happening. Terror consumed her.

An involuntary scream escaped from her lips as she felt his hand slide over her hip to the front of her skirt, and up to her blouse, his fingers creeping between the buttons. The top of his head leaned against her bosom, his comb-over strands were wet, his breathing was heavy and emitting guttural sounds as he began thrusting his hips. She jumped away from him, knocking the desk lamp over. It bounced off the desk and dropped to the floor with a loud thud!

The baize door burst open.

"What is going on?" Mrs. Banks stood at the door.

Mr. Pickles quickly composed himself and sat up straight, but he did not stand to greet Mrs. Banks. "Cr... um! Everything is fine, Mrs. Banks. Miss Neale knocked the lamp over while looking at the ledger."

"That will be all, Miss Neale. Pick up the lamp, please. Mr. Lytton needs your assistance at the front desk." Mr. Pickles' voice trembled slightly.

"Yes, sir," Anna whispered. She was shaking all over and she could not bring herself to look at Mrs. Banks. She felt ashamed.

The lobby was relatively quiet between noon and four o'clock on Saturdays. Mr. Lytton was ready to leave for lunch when Anna appeared from the office. "Miss Neale, what is the matter? You look distraught, are you ill?" Mr. Lytton's face expressed genuine concern.

Anna took a deep breath trying to keep her words even and hold back tears. "Oh, you know Mr. Pickles, I knocked the lamp over and that displeased him."

"You don't look well. Why don't you leave early today? Miss Jenkins can take over until I get back from luncheon. I was going to ask you to come back early this afternoon, we have many guests arriving on the afternoon train. That will give you some extra time. Perhaps you need to lie down. You really don't look well. I could ask Miss Jenkins to stay until this evening."

Mustering as much strength as she could to stay calm, she managed to say, "Thank you, Mr. Lytton, that won't be necessary. I would like to take luncheon early and I will be back for half-past three." The kindness in Mr. Lytton's voice made Anna want to cry.

The tears began spilling gently down her cheeks as she walked towards the staff dining hall. Hearing voices, she realized everyone would be eating. There would be too many questions and she needed to be alone. Turning around in the passageway, Anna bumped into Mrs. Banks.

"Pay attention Miss..." Without finishing her sentence, Mrs. Banks guided the weeping Anna into her sitting room.

"Whatever is wrong, Anna?" When Anna didn't answer, Mrs. Banks continued, "Does it have something to do with the commotion in Mr. Pickles' office today?"

Anna crossed her arms and wrapped them snugly around her trembling body. The tears escalated to sobs. Her words were not making sense. Mrs. Banks gently laid her hand on Anna's shoulder.

"Whatever he did to you, you must tell me," Mrs. Banks blurted heatedly and added, "And I'll make sure it never happens again. I will call for some tea. That will calm us both."

"Anna!" Sophie said when she arrived with a tray, anxiety creasing her face.

Mrs. Banks shook her head to silence Sophie.

"But, Mrs. Banks, Anna and I are friends, and I have never seen her like this." Sophie searched Anna's face for an explanation. Anna turned away from Sophie's gaze.

"Anna is not feeling well. Miss Romano, would you check that the maids have finished the second and third floor bedrooms? I will stay with Anna for a while." Sophie glanced over her shoulder as she closed the door. Anna gave Sophie a tearful smile.

The hot tea calmed them both. Anna had stopped sobbing, but quiet tears continued to roll down her cheeks. She felt violated and dirty. She was afraid to tell Mrs. Banks about the bulging trousers because she didn't understand what had happened or what she had done to cause such an attack.

As though reading her mind, Mrs. Banks said, "Please believe me, Anna, you did nothing wrong. Did Mr. Pickles try to touch you?"

Anna's cheeks blushed scarlet as she nodded 'yes.'

"He has done this before. He focused his attention on Miss Jenkins after Edith left, but Miss Jenkins is betrothed and her fiancé threatened Mr. Pickles. But Mr. Pickles had an explanation and nothing more was said. However, Edith was a different story; I tried to talk to her but she wouldn't listen." Mrs. Banks paused as a wave of sadness passed over her.

Anna listened intently at the mention of Edith again. "Mrs. Banks, tell me about Edith, please. There seems to be a shroud of mystery around her."

"Edith was your predecessor as Mr. Pickles' assistant, older than you and perhaps more familiar with the ways of men. Flattered by Mr. Pickles' advances and favouritism, she construed them as romance. Interpreting the secrecy as a way around hotel policy, Edith was convinced he would leave his wife and court her openly. When she became with child, Mr. Pickles denied all, accusing Edith of being a loose woman and blaming one of the stable boys for her condition. Both of them were dismissed." Mrs. Banks gulped back emotion, her voice shaking. "And there was nothing I could do. The truth that Edith was carrying his child could never be proven. He had ruined three lives!"

Mrs. Banks held onto both of Anna's hands and stared intensely. "And I will not let it happen to you. So please, tell me what happened in the office today?"

Anna still thought she had done something wrong. Her mother had told her about what married people did in the privacy of the bedroom and because of it, sometimes babies happened. Mr. Pickles' behaviour wasn't like that and they certainly were not married. But, if Edith thought she was going to get married, maybe that was different. She was confused and Mrs. Banks seemed to know the answer. Anna held on to Mrs. Banks' hands and began to tell her how uncomfortable she felt near Mr. Pickles. She then related exactly what had happened in the office that morning.

"What he did was wrong. He wants to seduce you in a perverted way. You did *nothing* wrong. Edith mistook his lust for love. What he does is not love, it is sick and abnormal. But, he is a man, and the most powerful man in the hotel. He makes his lies believable, and he is not averse to fabricating untrue stories as an explanation. Nevertheless, he knows that I am watching him, and that makes him guarded, but if we complain he knows he has the power to dismiss both of us."

Anna's hands covered her face as she realized the enormity of the situation. Her tears turned to anger; anger for Edith and her child and the poor innocent stable boy and anger for her own situation. Mrs. Banks saw the change in Anna and was hopeful that Edith's demise would not be repeated.

"I have to get back to check that the suites have been prepared properly, so I must leave you, Anna," Mrs. Banks said, looking at the clock on the mantelpiece. "We have many new guests arriving today. Stay here and rest for a while, it is private. I will come by later."

"Would you tell Mr. Walker and Mr. Blaine that I have a headache and I won't be joining them for tea today?"

Alone with her thoughts, a shudder rippled down her back as she thought of Mr. Pickles' fingers on her blouse, and what might have happened if Mrs. Banks hadn't come in when she did. She had to use her head and figure out how to deal with the situation. Of course she could hand in her notice, but then she would have to tell the family. Papa would be furious with Uncle Bertie, who had promised that Anna would be chaperoned and safe. No, that wasn't the answer. But, she thought, Uncle Bertie *was* the answer.

Deciding not to wallow in self-pity, she had to make sure it didn't happen again. *First,* she thought, *I have to move my desk out of his office and if he disapproves, which he will, I will threaten to disclose all to Uncle Bertie.* At that moment, Anna made a promise to herself that somehow, some day, she would make Mr. Pickles pay for all the lives he had ruined.

Mrs. Banks interrupted her thoughts. "Anna, it is three o'clock. Are you feeling well enough to go back to work?"

"Yes, I will go and freshen up. I told Mr. Lytton I would be back for three thirty." Anna paused, deciding to tell Mrs. Banks her thoughts. "Mrs.

Banks, I would like your permission to move my desk out of the office. I think it will fit by the telephone exchange." Trying to sound matter of fact, she listened to her own voice and was surprised at the calmness. *Dictation,* she thought, *there is no way round it. I have to be in the office.*

"I'll ask Carter to move the desk for you. You have my permission. But understand that Mr. Pickles will be most upset. I don't trust his temper. Anna, I am afraid for you and your position."

"I have thought about that too. Miss Jenkins was able to stop his advances after her fiancé threatened him. I don't know if you are aware, but my Uncle Bertie is a colleague of Mr. Pickles. If he insists that the desk stays in the office or he threatens to give me notice, I will threaten to tell Uncle Bertie; not just about his behaviour towards me, which would make Uncle Bertie very angry, but also about Edith. I don't think even Prickly-Pickles will challenge that."

"Anna, I think that will work. Please be careful, he's a slippery character, and although he doesn't deserve your respect, it is not a good idea to call him Prickly-Pickles. No matter what happens, he is highly respected by the owners of this hotel, who in turn are highly respected businessmen. Most, if not all gentlemen think nothing of taking advantage of women in their employ and find it quite acceptable to have discreet love affairs, and unfortunately some maids are willing partners. However, gentlemen will usually draw the line at perverted or deviant behaviour, although they are apt to look the other way rather than dealing with the situation."

"I don't think they are willing," Anna said defiantly. "They are afraid to say no."

"Be that as it may, Anna. Be careful!"

Anna ran upstairs to her room, feeling dirty. She needed to wash and change. Tiredness overwhelmed her and she lay on her bed in her petticoats. The afternoon events swirled in her head, events that were going to be difficult to forget. Once again she vowed her revenge on Mr. Pickles.

The bedroom door opened, and Sophie's voice woke Anna. "There you are. Are you feeling better? What happened?"

Anna sat up trying to process why she was lying in bed in her petticoats in the middle of the afternoon. "Sophie, what time is it? I must have dozed off."

Sophie stared intently, ignoring Anna's question. "Did Mr. Pickles do something to you?"

"How did you know? Oh no, does everyone know?"

"No, of course not! Mr. Lytton, mentioned at luncheon that you didn't look well, and then, as you know, I saw you in Mrs. Banks' sitting-room. It wasn't difficult to guess that something was wrong. I thought it had to do with Prickly-Pickles; you see I know about Edith." Sophie took a breath and gave a little cough. "He tried touching me once." She shuddered. "It's easy for me to stay out of his way, but you have to work with him."

"Sophie, it was awful. But I don't have time to talk. I have to get to the desk. I promised Mr. Lytton I would come back early. Is it three thirty yet?" Anna looked at Sophie's worried face. "I am feeling better now, honestly. Don't worry, we'll talk later." Anna opened the cupboard door and grabbed a clean blouse. "Alex and Bill..." Anna hesitated, "Do they know?"

"They are worried about you and Bill was looking for you, but I doubt they know anything. I didn't tell them and Mrs. Banks wouldn't say anything."

It was almost four o'clock when Anna got to the front desk but Mr. Lytton just smiled.

"Are you feeling better, Miss Neale?"

Anna nodded, apologized for her tardiness, and hurriedly greeted an arriving guest. It was the busiest day she had ever experienced at The Sackville. Neither she nor Mr. Lytton had time to take a break. It was ten o'clock before all the new guests were settled and Mr. Lytton could leave for the weekend. As soon as George arrived at his post, Anna went into the staff dining hall to make some tea. The kitchen still sounded busy. The dining room would be open late. Aware that Bill was suspicious of Mr. Pickles' actions, she didn't want to face him. Although Anna had always implied the difficulties were related to her typing or the telephone, Bill

59

never seemed satisfied with her explanation and she didn't know if she could hide the truth from him.

Six

The Desk Incident

Monday morning was tense. The hotel was full and many of the guests had brought their own, often demanding, servants, which always caused friction. Mrs. Banks had one anxious eye on Mr. Pickles' office door and the other on the difficult guests' servants, especially the ladies' maids, who would try to take advantage of the hotel staff. Chef screamed at Bill about meddling servants and impossible food requests. Anna busied herself setting the staff breakfast table, trying to quell her nerves. In two hours' time, Mr. Pickles would know her desk had been moved. Taking a deep breath for confidence, she vowed to arrest his ardour and stand firm.

Mr. Lytton arrived early, relieving Anna of the reception desk duties and enabling her to answer the constant stream of telephone enquiries; trivial questions about the dining times and maid service. The hour chimed from the grandfather clock and filtered through the baize door as it opened. It was precisely eight o'clock, and Mr. Pickles had entered his office. She waited for the office door to open. Nothing happened.

The keen early risers started telephoning about the historical sites of Bexhill. The Sackville Hotel catered to the wealthy and privileged, who had a macabre fascination with the bad boys of Bexhill—the notorious

61

smugglers. Tobacco and alcohol smuggling from France to the Sussex coast was known to have been a lucrative business for the village during the early part of the 1800s. Other guests were more interested in renting deck chairs or bathing huts for a quiet day at the beach. The telephone provided a welcome distraction for Anna. But every time she glanced at her desk, she stuttered her answers to the callers and turned towards Mr. Pickles' office, almost losing the connection and having to repeat herself. Her anxiety was galloping, while the seconds ticked by in slow motion.

First came a muffled, "Miss Neale!"

Mr. Lytton looked over at Anna with a nod and reassuring smile. "You are safe."

The door vibrated and Mr. Pickles' voice exploded. "Miss Neale! What is this all about? You moved your desk!" Mr. Pickles glared at the position of Anna's desk.

"Miss Neale, you will return your desk to my office immediately." Red blotches began to erupt on his neck.

Anna gulped, fear deafening her ears. She steadied her voice and said, "I prefer my desk here, Mr. Pickles. I am closer to the telephone exchange and I can see the reception desk should Mr. Lytton need my assistance."

The red blotches multiplied at an alarming rate. One erupted on the end of his pointy nose, and then, they began popping up under his comb-over. Anna couldn't contain herself any longer, and had to stare at her feet while she stifled a giggle, trying to remove the nervous grin that had planted itself on her face.

"What is so amusing Miss Neale?" Before she could answer he roared, "Are you disobeying me? Move your desk, THIS MINUTE!"

Anna quickly composed herself and stood as tall as her five-foot four-inch frame would allow. "Uncle Bertie telephoned me yesterday. He asked after your well-being, and bid me to send his regards." Her hands were behind her back with her fingers tightly crossed, hoping the lie did not show. "I was telling him how much more convenient it would be to have my desk near the telephone exchange, and he thought you would agree. Mrs. Banks agreed. Mr. Lytton is pleased that it will allow me to attend to the guests more quickly, should he be rushed." Anna had no idea where these words were coming from. She could say no more, her amusement having turned back into fear. Her knees trembled and her head spun.

Mr. Pickles was scarlet, his body rigid. Anna detected a slight flinch, followed by a shadow of fear in his cold black eyes. He turned abruptly and slammed the office door behind him without saying another word.

"Well done, Miss Neale." The words came from Mrs. Banks, who unbeknownst to Anna, had joined Mr. Lytton at the reception desk.

The talk of 'Anna's desk incident,' as it was referred to by the staff, took some time to settle down. Although the staff was not told why Anna's desk had been moved, the rumours were rampant, and those who had known Edith's story soon made the connection. Anna refused to discuss the issue with anyone, which unfortunately caused resentment from some staff. Mr. Pickles became vengeful towards everyone, not just Anna. He made no more inappropriate advances towards her, but she did have to endure his ferret eyes leering at her when she took shorthand. She was aware that the anger he felt towards her for humiliating him would never dissipate. It was only a matter of time before he would reap his revenge.

Outwardly, Anna recovered from the incident with confidence and maturity, but inwardly the scars were deep. A trust had been violated and it was going to take her a long time to recover. She found herself pulling away from Bill. He asked questions, wanting details. It would be humiliating to look into Bill's beautiful eyes and see ridicule and mistrust. She couldn't bear the thought that Bill might think she had encouraged the evil man. No matter how hard she tried, deep inside she could not shake the thought that she was at fault. How could she explain to Bill that, at this moment in time, she couldn't trust any man, even him? She constantly sensed those dirty fingers creeping along her blouse. It wasn't fair to Bill and she knew it, but she still felt the shame. Mrs. Banks and Sophie—the only two people she had confided in—tried to reassure her that the shame belonged to Mr. Pickles. Alex didn't ask questions. He avoided the situation, teasing her about having been promoted from the back stage of Mr. Pickles' office to front of the house. This bantering suited Anna; it was easy to be with Alex.

By the end of September 1913, most of the summer guests had vacated The Sackville and returned to London, leaving the resident guests and a few stragglers. Lady Thornton didn't leave until mid-October. On the day before her departure to London, Anna spent extra time finishing the last of the correspondence.

"I shall miss your company," Lady Thornton said, staring out of the French windows, closed against the autumn chill. Anna stood up and moved to her side following her stare and pointing out to sea.

"Look, there's a large grey ship in the English Channel."

"Yes, I believe it is the new battleship, HMS Queen Elizabeth. She was launched from Portsmouth only yesterday. There has been much in the newspaper about the Royal Navy's new battleship and I think there are more to come."

"Battleship," Anna repeated, envisioning the sea full of cannon fighting ships. "Does this mean war in Europe?"

"Nothing to worry about," Lady Thornton said with a strange wariness in her expression. "Europeans tend to be temperamental. Germany is squabbling with her neighbours again. And, well…" She paused, "Britain is obsessed with protecting her coastline. The Irish home rule situation is far more worrying. Now, there is a strong possibility of civil war."

That was the first time Anna became aware of the tension building in Europe. She had heard guests talk and the staff gossip, there were stories in the newspapers, and much speculation about the unrest in Ireland, but only a little about Europe and much of that was social gossip about the various Royals, both in Europe and at home. Europe was so far away, it would hardly affect Britain, Anna thought, and certainly not in her world in Bexhill. However, whatever the reason, a battleship in the Channel was ominous.

During the quietest time of the year, October to May, the Sackville employed a skeleton staff; at busy times the workload was heavy, but mostly it afforded more free time in the evenings, and an extra day or half day off for the permanent staff.

The staff dining hall became a regular meeting place and resulted in a kinship between the foursome—Sophie had joined the threesome. Companionship was the key to surviving winter in a dull, dreary and bitterly cold seaside town. The blithe life had been sucked out of the buildings and streets, leaving only shadows of the summer gone by. The sea swell rolled, dark and grey, anticipating the next storm. Leaden grey clouds heavy with moisture moved sluggishly across the sky, disappearing into the swelling sea; there were always more clouds to follow, some dark and black ones would open with torrents of rain. The howling northwest gales brought thick rain, driving sleet, and sometimes cold, blinding, snow.

The attic bedrooms were freezing cold, and Sophie and Anna's room was the coldest. Ice formed lace patterns on the window, the water froze in the washstand and the wind penetrated through the roof into every corner of the room. Getting undressed was swift and thick flannel replaced thin cotton nightgowns. Anna was grateful for the soft woollen blanket her mother had sent, but in the worst of the winter, the weight of the heavy horsehair blanket provided much needed extra warmth. Both Anna and Sophie pulled the covers over their heads, their feet resting on ceramic hot-water bottles. Too cold to talk through chattering teeth, they shivered under the blankets until they were finally warmed enough to fall asleep.

The staff dining hall was always kept cozy and warm with a flaming fire in the grate and plenty of hot tea, coffee or cocoa on the dresser. Any spare evening time was spent huddled around the fire, chatting or reading and sometime playing games or cards. Anna spent much of her time reading. Mrs. Banks had loaned her Rudyard Kipling's books. She and Bill swapped books and spent many hours discussing authors and titles.

On one such evening, Bill, sitting at one side of the fireplace reading, uncrossed his legs, and placed his book, *Plain Tales from the Hills*, a collection of Kipling's early stories, on his knee. He stared affectionately at Anna. If she had been looking, she would have seen how he yearned to touch her, but she seemed oblivious to his attention. She was reading the novel, *Kim*. Her feet tucked underneath her skirts, she rocked slightly, her wayward curls bouncing gently to the rhythm of the rocking chair. Bill stood up and picked up the poker to stir the fire and add more coal.

Anna closed her book and said, "The poverty in India makes me sad. I don't understand it and I don't remember Uncle Bertie talking about it."

Anna's innocence was endearing, her naivety utterly charming. He smiled tenderly. "There's poverty everywhere and it's not always visible. I think you have to see a country with your own eyes. There are some terrible places in Edinburgh and London, but most travelers don't see that side of the city. Bexhill was designed as a seasonal home for the privileged and is quite sheltered from poverty."

Anna had noticed his tender look. She felt his warmth, his gentleness, and she knew how much he cared for her, and she desperately wanted to reciprocate. She just couldn't, not yet. But the memories were fading.

Bill smiled and, for the first time in weeks, she returned his smile and he saw a glimpse of the old Anna. He stepped over to her and gently brushed a curl from her forehead and this time she did not flinch.

"Anna, I have something to say..." Anna opened her mouth to speak and Bill gently pressed his fingers against her lips. "Please, Anna let me say what I have to say. I love you with all my heart. Will you marry me?" Anna face did not tell him what he wanted to hear. He quickly added, "It doesn't have to be now. We can wait. I am a patient man. Once I am a chef, we can travel. We could go to India. I'll find work in a big hotel and I'll look after you and..."

Anna put her hand up to stop him. "Bill, no, it can't happen. I don't want to get married. You are my best friend, please don't spoil that." Anna's mind flashed back to bulging trousers and creepy dirty fingers. She wasn't worthy of Bill.

Bill crumpled into the chair. "I don't understand. You are slipping away from me. Is it Alex?"

"No! Of course not. Why would you think that?" she protested, perhaps too strongly. She couldn't deny she enjoyed Alex's light hearted company.

"Believe me. I don't want to marry. You know the domestic life terrifies me. Travelling to India excites me, but not as a wife." Lady Thornton's words, "It's not easy for a woman to travel alone" contradicted her rationale.

She felt pity for Bill. His disappointment showed in his slumped shoulders. Wanting to soften the blow she added, "Perhaps in a couple of years, by the time you are a chef, maybe things will be different, but not now."

He didn't answer. His shoulders rounded and, slowly taking measured steps, he mumbled, "Good night Anna," and walked out of the room.

Anna scrutinized the coals as they turn to orange embers. Her thoughts drifted from Bill to Alex, travel to marriage. What did she really want? The grandfather clock chimed midnight and she wearily climbed the stairs to her room. Sophie was already sleeping.

December brought life back into the hotel. The Christmas tree in the lobby stood two stories high, every branch laden with glass baubles, red bows and twinkling tinsel. Every evening, Christmas carols filled the air. The guests joined the choir with the popular hymns and the chorus of others, the halls hummed with Christmas spirit. Chef prepared traditional Christmas fare: beef, pork and capon, sweetmeats, mince pies, brandy soaked fruitcake, buttery shortbread, candied fruits and much more. The pantry overflowed as did the wine cellars.

Christmas at home in Rugby paled when compared to the abundance at The Sackville, but no amount of grandeur could replace the love and excitement of Mother's Christmas. She felt strange not to be home. Christmas in the hotel was lavish, but different and impersonal—she missed Charlie and Lou guessing what might be in the gift boxes. However, looking after a hotel full of guests with a skeleton staff left no time to reminisce, and she was soon caught up in the festivities.

By the sixth of January, little Christmas, and traditionally the day the Christmas decorations were packed away for another year, most guests had scurried back to London. The inclement and predictably stormy weather did not encourage long stays. The Sackville quickly returned to its winter quiet, much to the relief of the exhausted staff.

Saturday afternoon, the first free time since before Christmas, the foursome planned a trip to the new cinema, but that was not to be. Mother Nature boiled up a raging storm, the winds so strong it could blow the strongest of men from their feet. The angry, turbulent waves broke over the Promenade and flooded the streets taking anything in their path out to sea as they receded. The staff closed, bolted and secured windows, doors and hatches. The kitchen, laundry room and storage areas were vulnerable to flooding—especially the cellar. Anna assisted George in securing the front entrance as the driving rain and sleet forced its way under the portico. The wind rushed through the cracks, rattling the frames with its persistence to get inside. Once the doors were locked and secure, Anna stood watching the storm escalate, invigorated by its fury. Alex came in from the dining room and stood beside her.

"Storms are powerful to the extreme; masters of nature, which man cannot control." There was a strange passion in Alex's voice. She turned to face him and saw an intense expression of agony. Wanting to ease his distress, she moved closer, but stepped back, sensing she was intruding into a dark and painful place. A piece of debris banged against the glass and for a split second she expected the glass to break and her reflexes pushed her back towards Alex. He slid his arm along her shoulder and she felt every inch tingle with warmth. His mood changed as he gently pulled her towards him and she rested her head in the hollow of his shoulder. She felt safe. But glancing around the lobby, she pulled away hoping no one had noticed.

"I am going to the staff dining hall for some tea," she said to nobody in particular.

Entering the hall, she saw that Sophie and Bill were sitting at the table, the chessboard between them. "Bill is teaching me to play chess," Sophie announced proudly.

Bill smiled at Sophie. "And she is learning fast. If she keeps this up, she will soon surpass the teacher."

"Chess is boring, I have better things to do," Anna said, placing a cup on its saucer a little too hard and regretting her sharp words. She poured tea, keeping her back to Sophie and Bill. They were laughing and involved with each other, paying no attention to Anna. She had a strong desire to smash every cup on the Welsh dresser—what was wrong with her? Bill patiently explained the chess pieces to Sophie. His words irritated Anna and a pain stabbed her inside. She wanted Bill for herself. *But,* she thought, *only a few weeks ago, I rejected him.* Muddled and confused her thoughts went from Bill to Alex. What had just happened with Alex in the lobby? She placed her tea at the other end of the table and opened her book, pretending to read.

Struggling with her emotions and puzzled by her reactions, she searched for answers. Her encounter with Prickly-Pickles had left scars. Scars that made her afraid of getting too close and Bill wanted to get closer. Alex had become more attentive; he teased her and made her laugh. He took her to the theatre; they walked along the beach in the wind, watching the waves crash to the shore. Alex made her forget, feel happy and carefree, it was impossible to be serious around Alex."

Alex's voice came from the passageway, "The storm is easing. I think it's stopped raining."

Anna put her book down and said, "Alex, let's go and walk in the wind."

Leaving Sophie and Bill to their chess game, Anna and Alex set out along the water-soaked Promenade, laughing as they splashed like children in the puddles. Anna began running and Alex chased her, they laughed into the wind until Alex caught up with her, grabbed her and kissed her full on the lips and she did not stop him.

"Alex," and words failed her.

He kissed her again and held her, whispering in her ear, "Marry me, Anna."

"Alex, stop fooling around. I don't want to marry anyone, not yet."

Alex laughed and lifted her off her feet. "One day I *will* marry you, Anna Neale." They walked back to the hotel in silence.

Anna was afraid of falling in love and afraid of losing her chance at independence. She wondered how this could have happened; friends, Bill and Alex, both in love with her, and her own feelings were in shambles for both men. She didn't want romance and definitely not marriage. She liked the threesome friendship.

One year ago on this very day, Anna had started working at The Sackville. She stood at the reception counter, waiting to welcome the guests arriving on the afternoon London train. The front entrance door flew open and in marched Lady Thornton, her black dress swooshed as it swept the floor; Princess yapping at her bosom as she approached the desk. The black hat, slightly smaller than last year, had no veil and deep lavender flowers, and smaller, fluffy black feathers had replaced the black tentacles of prey. Miss Barclay, carrying the birdcage, stood patiently waiting by the lift.

"Good afternoon, Lady Thornton. Welcome back to The Sackville," Anna said with formality and affection. "And welcome, Princess," Anna's voice softened as she greeted the Pekingese in Lady Thornton's arms.

Lady Thornton signed the register, raised her head and smiled warmly. "I think Princess is happy to see you, Miss Neale. Suite 305, I presume? The typewriting machine and desk are in place? I am anxious to start my correspondence."

Anna thought her face looked drawn and pale, even paler than she remembered. The lines around her eyes and mouth were deep with anxiety.

"Yes, Lady Thornton, everything is ready for you." Anna frowned. "Are you well, Lady Thornton?"

"Yes, quite well thank you, just tired from the journey."

"Please call if you need anything."

She watched the ornate brass gate clang shut and Lady Thornton disappear as the lift rose to the third floor. The scene reminded Anna of how she had grown since that spoilt, arrogant young girl wearing the oversized, completely inappropriate blue hat had walked into The Sackville.

The season of 1914 was beginning much the same as the previous year, except under Mr. Lytton's tutelage and guidance Anna had mastered her front desk duties with speed and proficiency. Mr. Lytton was proud of his assistant. Mr. Pickles remained formal, but even he was aware that Anna's secretarial and organizational abilities were excellent. In spite of the show of appreciation, Anna never let down her guard.

Fear of Anna's reprisal had quelled his carnal desires towards her on the outside, but the banal yearning showed in his tiny ferret eyes as they followed her around the lobby and office. On occasion, she caught him licking his lips and consciously brushing past her a little too close. Repulsed and terrified, she grappled with the memories, living in fear that he might try again. She suspected he was satisfying his perverse hunger with another unsuspecting female, but she didn't know who; he was clever and cautious.

Among Anna's many talents, she had a way of calming irate and unreasonable guests and easily resolving their problems. She never lost her temper and would have the guests smiling and content in a matter of minutes. Mr. Lytton admired this skill. Although he was a kind man who took pride in his work, he did have difficulty controlling his temper at times.

Saturdays were always the busiest afternoons, but Anna sensed something different about this late June day. A mixture of overly excited and ill-tempered guests alighted from hansom cabs, carriages and automobiles that queued under the portico. Chaos loomed over the lobby and reception desk. Mr. Lytton's complexion had a red-purple tinge, a warning sign, as he tried to appease a cantankerous lady and gentleman who had had a particularly disagreeable journey.

Pretending she needed some assistance Anna asked, "Mr. Lytton, might I ask you to check this booking."

"Certainly Miss Neale, if you would attend to Sir Walter and Lady Rhodes."

Anna quietly moved to face Sir Walter. "I understand you have had a very long and tedious journey. I am sure Lady Rhodes is anxious to rest. How can we make you more comfortable?"

Sir Walter grunted, standing tall and stiff, his dress uniform likened him to a life-sized toy soldier. "Perhaps a bottle of brandy would ease your discomfort, Sir Walter?"

He still did not reply but his face lost its severity. He bowed his head slightly towards Anna, which could have been construed as some form of acknowledgement. Lady Rhodes' many chins concertinaed into her short, round body and gave the appearance of a barrel topped with an overly decorated flowered hat; her pursed lips could have secured a cork. Anna placed her hand across her mouth trying to conceal a wicked grin.

"Lady Rhodes, I shall have our head housemaid bring you some tea and I will ask Chef Louis to prepare some fresh scones with strawberries and Devonshire cream. Perhaps you would enjoy Chef's chocolate cake?" Anna lowered her voice, "It is one he only makes for special guests."

"That is very kind of you Miss Neale, thank you," Sir Walter said.

Anna called the bellboy instructing him to escort Sir Walter and Lady Rhodes to their suite. Mr. Lytton gave Anna a grateful nod. Once the guests were settled, Anna turned to Mr. Lytton and said, "What's happening? The guests seem on edge today."

"I think the assassination of Archduke Franz Ferdinand is unsettling them, although it is hard to say what impact his death could have on us." Mr. Lytton had a keen interest in anything that was military. His father had served in the African Boer War and there was an intense pride and patriotism in his family.

"Assassination!" The word shivered down her spine. "How could such a terrible thing happen? Who is he anyway?"

Mr. Lytton gave a sigh and spoke quietly, "He is the heir apparent to the Austria-Hungarian Empire. Miss Neale, believe me, Prime Minister Asquith is far more concerned about Ireland than any quarrels the Europeans may have with each other. Britain is quite safe for now."

Seven

Nothing is Fair in Love and War

S till awake at midnight, Anna stared at the ceiling. Mr. Lytton's words repeating in her head, "Britain is safe." She wanted to believe him, but her intuition told her otherwise.

Sophie opened the door, sniggering. "I almost beat Bill at chess tonight."

"I don't know what you see in that game. Or is it Bill, and not the game?" Anna replied, teasing Sophie to cover up the pain of her jealousy.

"Maybe some of both." Sophie yawned. "I'm tired. Good night, Anna."

Sleep evaded Anna most of the night. She thought about how she had welcomed Sophie's friendship and even accepted, perhaps reluctantly, the foursome. She couldn't deny that her rejection of Bill had allowed their friendship to grow. She hadn't expected Bill to let her go so easily. Pouting, she pulled the covers over her head and muttered, "See if I care! Alex is far more fun."

The four had planned to enjoy their last free Saturday afternoon before the summer rush started at the beach. Anna and Alex prepared to leave early, but Bill and Sophie were engrossed in another chess game.

"You two go on ahead. We'll catch up when our game is finished," Bill said staring at the chessboard.

Alex ushered Anna outside, having no qualms about taking advantage of

Anna's rejection of Bill. She had made it blatantly clear to everyone that Bill was a friend. Whether he believed her or not, was immaterial. Alex was preparing to win Anna's affections.

Alex borrowed two bicycles and took Anna along the coastal trail of the Bexhill smugglers. They rode to Galley Hill, where the Martello Towers once stood—the lookout tower for the Coastguards waiting to spot smugglers.

A gentle sea breeze pushed puffy white clouds across a blue sky and rustled through the tall, swaying sea-grass that sprang from the sandy cliff. They sat on the top of the cliff, holding hands, gazing across the English Channel. Alex's talent for drama coupled with his interest in local history made him a great storyteller. His deep, hypnotic voice and animated expressions implied mystery and suspense even before the story began. Anna listened, staring into his eyes, mesmerized.

"Anna, imagine the coastguards huddled in the Martello Tower, over on the cliff." He pointed to where the tower once stood. "Waiting under cover of darkness for the first splash of the smugglers' dory landing on the beach. Biding their time to pounce on the unsuspecting smugglers and confiscate the illicit cargo." Alex took a breath, building the suspense. "But the organized and cunning smugglers easily outsmarted the coastguard. Years of smuggling had taught them to see in the blackest of moonless nights and to be stealthy, nimble and silent. They beached the dory and unloaded the contraband, passing it along the trail, from man to man to man to waiting carts. By the time the smugglers' movements alerted the coastguards, the smugglers had an army of men lining the trail. Batsmen, armed with heavy wooden bats to be used as weapons for the sole purpose of injuring, or even killing, anyone who got in the way, including the coastguards."

Anna and Alex laughed, envisioning the poor coastguard with the impossible task of out-maneuvering the smugglers. Alex's eyes riveted to Anna's. He stopped talking and gently pulled her close to kiss her tenderly on the lips. Anna, incapable of resisting, drifted into his arms, allowing herself to return the kiss. Neither said a word. Suspended in time, they stared at the horizon, listening to the breeze.

Alex spoke first. "The Channel is full of ships today, but those are not smugglers' dory's. They look like battleships."

"Those grey ones with the turrets are battleships," Anna replied, anxious for normal conversation to counteract the warm sensuality that Alex had triggered and was now rippling through her body. "Do you think there will be a war?" She hesitated. "Mr. Lytton says Britain is safe, but I am not so sure that is true."

"No." Alex touched her hair. "Don't fill your pretty head with such thoughts."

She smiled, as his touch sent a pleasant tingle down her spine, not in the least prepared for what he said next.

"I love you, Anna. Will you marry me?"

"Alex, are you teasing me? If you are, it's not funny." As the words came out of her mouth, she saw the love in his expression—he was serious, more serious than she had ever heard him before.

Startled by his question and by her immediate reaction—to say yes, she began twisting long blades of grass in her fingers.

"Alex, I have told you before... I don't think I want to get married... yet." Anna jumped up and ran towards the bicycles. "I'll race you back to the hotel."

Completely out of breath, Anna and Alex opened the back door. After tidying her hair but still flushed from pedaling, Anna joined Mr. Lytton at the front desk.

"The fresh sea air suits you, Miss Neale. You are glowing," Mr. Lytton said with a smile. "Lady Thornton has requested that you resume your duties with her correspondence on Tuesday."

"That is good news. Mrs. Banks said she had some kind of fever. She must be feeling better."

Tuesday at noon Anna knocked on the door of Suite 305. Barclay greeted her with a warm smile and showed her into the dining room where she joined Lady Thornton for luncheon.

"Lady Thornton, it is good to see you again. Are you feeling better?" Anna didn't think she looked at all well.

"Yes, thank you. Dr. Gregory thinks I caught a chill on the journey. Travelling becomes more difficult as one gets older. But you are young and wouldn't understand. How was winter in Bexhill?" Lady Thornton asked, briskly changing the subject.

"Bleak and stormy most of the time. I have never experienced such violent storms and I found them quite invigorating, but Alex seemed strangely upset."

Lady Thornton raised a questioning eyebrow, "Alex? What happened to Bill?"

Anna blushed. How did she know about Bill? "We are all friends, Alex, Bill and Sophie—my roommate. We spent time together during the winter." Anna did not want to talk about her thoughts and feelings. She moved quickly to the typewriter. "I had better start your correspondence. How was London?"

"Thwarted by a different kind of storm. I don't know what the world is coming to, it is changing, and I don't like change." There was a petulant edge to her voice. She frowned, her nose wrinkled, recalling unpleasantness.

Anna looked up, "Is something wrong m'lady?"

"London is terrible. I don't feel safe anymore. The factory workers are militant, violent and talking about strikes. The suffragettes are marching for votes for women, getting arrested and imprisoned. Why women want to vote is beyond me. Sylvia Pankhurst has been on another hunger strike and my own son has become involved with one of her acquaintances." Her voice quavered and she dabbed a white lace handkerchief against the corner of her eye. "It is unbecoming for women to behave in such a way. The country is out of control and so is my son."

Surprised by her candid words and obvious hurt and anger towards her son, Darcy, Anna remained silent.

Dramatically raising her hand to her forehead she sighed. "Lord

Thornton would know what to do but his bones are at the bottom of the cold Atlantic Ocean." She paused for effect. "But Darcy would not take heed of his father's words. No matter how hard I tried, Lord Thornton always found his sons lacking."

Anna smiled at the drama. However, drama aside, Lady Thornton did not look well. She lay prostrate on the chaise–lounge. Princess curled on her lap, both dozing fitfully, paying little attention to Anna punching the typewriter keys. The reference to sons, plural, had not escaped Anna. Lady Thornton only ever spoke of Darcy. What was the story and how many sons did she have? Anna instinctively disliked Darcy—a spoilt brat who showed no respect for his mother. However, his romantic involvement with a suffragette redeemed him somewhat; a keen follower of the Pankhurst family, Anna admired their fight for women. Her personal ambition for independence prompted her to read what she could in the newspapers.

Anna had assumed Lady Thornton to be an advocate for women's independence. To hear her disagree with women having the vote was disappointing. And yet she had encouraged Anna to follow her dream of travelling, or had she? Anna remembered the day she had asked how she was going to travel, and the implication that she needed money or a husband and, preferably, both.

She wondered; was marriage really, such a bad thing? Alex's proposal jumped into her mind. Some women married quite successfully. Perhaps Lady Thornton's referral to Darcy's acquaintance with a suffragette had more to do with a mother's concern for her son and the likelihood of a bad marriage. Engrossed in her imagination, Anna unwittingly stopped typing.

"Miss Neale, if you have finished, that will be all for today. Please ask Barclay to help me to my bed."

Alarmed Anna asked, "Should I ask Mr. Pickles to call the doctor?"

"No! Barclay will take care of me. I just need to rest."

Anna left Suite 305, giving Barclay instructions to call her if she needed the doctor.

As the summer progressed, there was a heightened sense of gaiety among the guests. They were loud, boisterous and demanding. Anna detected an undercurrent of tension and it frightened her a little. She mentioned her fears to Mr. Lytton. He agreed the atmosphere was different, but considered the blame to have more to do with the heat. July was hotter than usual.

Exhausted after a chaotic day, Anna didn't feel like being convivial in the staff dining hall tonight, so she climbed the stairs to be alone in her room. The open windows on the landing gave a nice cross breeze, but a wall of heat hit her as she opened the door to her attic bedroom. She immediately flung the window open and changed into a light cotton nightdress. The cool cotton and the gentle sea breeze felt refreshing on her skin. She lay on top of her bed, falling asleep immediately.

A woman cried out and woke Anna. She looked across to Sophie, who was in a deep sleep. Anna sat up, her pulse beating faster and faster. The cry was her own, the nightmare frightening, as arms had pulled her in different directions. She had cried out, telling them to stop and leave her alone.

She was dripping with perspiration, The attic bedroom was stifling and the breeze that had lulled her to sleep had disappeared, leaving the air heavy. Wide awake, she squinted at the bedside clock—two in the morning. Her legs felt like lead as she walked through the thick air, hoping to get a breeze from the open window. Sitting at the desk, staring into the blackness of night, she wrestled with her own conflicts; Alex was getting too close, and Bill was moving further away. *Am I pushing Bill away?* she wondered. Sophie had confided in Anna about how much she loved Bill. She had even asked Anna if she thought Bill loved her.

Anna was in turmoil; telling the world that Bill was a good friend, but deep inside she was jealous of Sophie's affections for him. How could she feel this way towards her friend? Was she in love with Bill and Alex at the same time? She loved them all and she wanted things to stay the same, but that wasn't possible. She knew someone was going to get hurt.

A brief flash of light changed her focus. She stared intently and a silver sliver of light escaped from behind a black cloud, breaking the darkness, and a beam of shimmering silver settled like a beacon on the dark water as a full moon appeared. She held her breath at what the light revealed.

A fleet of battleships sailed silently northwards in the English Channel. Ghost ships, moving fast and with purpose, the only light coming from the white iridescent wake caught in the moonlight. A rush of wind forced its way into the attic bedroom and blew the clouds back over the moon, plunging the Channel back into blackness. Sophie was now standing silently next to Anna.

Anna looked at her and said, "Did you see what I saw?" Speechless, Sophie nodded.

The wind howled and the rain splattered in through the open window but they left it open, to feel the fresh coolness. The short storm cleared the humid air. Anna and Sophie, both stunned at what they had witnessed, sat on their beds.

"Do you think this means war?" Anna asked.

"No. I think it was those battleships that steamed past the Royal Yacht, saluting the king last week. Admiral Rothman, on the third floor, he's retired, but he was all excited about the Royal Navy exercise at Spithead, the king being there and all." Sophie paused. "Maybe they're going back to wherever they came from."

"Yes, you could be right, but it seems strange that they would sail at night like that." Anna yawned. "It's three o'clock, only two hours before Amy wakes us up."

Nobody else had witnessed the fleet of battleships and nothing was mentioned in the newspapers. Sophie and Anna were beginning to think they had witnessed ghost ships after all. Anna suggested Sophie ask Admiral Rothman.

At teatime, Sophie rushed into the staff dining hall, beckoning to Anna to follow her outside. They sat on the bench by the back door. Sophie could hardly contain herself.

"Anna, this is exciting. Admiral Rothman was shocked when I told him about the battleships. You should have seen his face. Apparently nobody was supposed to see those ships. I was right. They were the ships that sailed before the Royal Yacht, and you were right too, as they were sailing undercover of night with no lights so as not to alert anyone that they were being moved to a secret place. He wouldn't tell me where."

"Sophie, this means trouble. It may even mean war. I have such a bad feeling about it."

"It's alright. Admiral Rothman said the Royal Navy was conducting a training exercise and there is nothing to worry about. But he did say that we were not to tell anyone what we had seen."

"If there is nothing to worry about, why is it secret?"

"Anna, stop worrying. Come, let's have some tea. I think Bill has made us a Victoria sponge cake."

Anna did worry, and for good reason, as was proved only a week later. Early, before six, on the morning of August 5th, 1914, Anna was surprised to find a grave looking Mr. Pickles and Mrs. Banks in the staff dining hall, instructing Amy to tell all the staff to stop what they were doing and assemble immediately. Something of the utmost importance was to be announced.

A tearful Mrs. Banks herded the hushed, anxious staff through the door. People were pushing and complaining as the room filled to capacity, the hush now a low nervous chatter. Mr. Pickles stood at the head of the table looking pale and extremely grim. Whatever he was about to say was so momentous it took him several minutes to compose himself sufficiently to speak.

Taking a deep breath, he paused and looked over to Mrs. Banks, who brushed tears from her cheeks and, in a rare gesture of support, she moved to his side. Both stood tall with an air of solidarity.

"It is with great sadness that I have to announce that Britain is at war with Germany. Prime Minister Asquith made the declaration near midnight last night, August 4th."

There was a collective intake of breath, a low, almost inaudible murmur, and the shushing of shuffling nervous feet followed by complete silence as the gravity of Mr. Pickles' words were processed.

Shocked, but not surprised, Anna's intuition sensed an impending darkness. Not just the war, which was terrifying in itself, but the transformations it would bring. In the few brief seconds it had taken Mr. Pickles to make the announcement, Anna had changed, grown up, and instinct told her that nothing would ever be the same again.

Over the next several weeks, the hotel began to resume a normal routine. The guests continued their holidays. The gaiety had become even more exaggerated, as though laughing and playing would make the war go away. Other than an increased presence of military uniforms as black tails were exchanged for officers' uniforms in the dining room, it was hard to imagine that there was in fact a war going on. For the most part, hotel life went on as usual. The young maids reeled in giggles at the handsome uniformed young men. Young men of all classes talked excitedly about signing up to serve their country. Patriotism was high. Parliament put Irish Home Rule to the side to deal with the war. Labour unrest died down as strikers found war more appealing, and even the suffragettes temporarily dropped their causes; most of the population united to fight for Britain. The recruiting offices were overwhelmed with eager volunteers, which included many of the hotel's male staff members.

The season at its height with several more weeks of bookings, Mr. Pickles' mood darkened with frustration. He was faced with managing the hotel with mostly female staff. Having neither respect nor confidence in women, he relied heavily on Mr. Lytton's succour. But James Lytton's loyalties were for his country, not Mr. Pickles or The Sackville Hotel. The air was thick and heavy the day he marched into Mr. Pickles' office. Anna was engulfed in the leather chair, taking shorthand.

"My notice, Mr. Pickles!" he said, placing an envelope on the mahogany desk. Standing to attention, his chest puffed with pride and a slight smile. *He's enjoying this,* Anna thought, realizing he had not seen her in the chair. Anna stood up.

"I'll come back later, Mr. Pickles."

"My apologies, Mr. Pickles. I had not realized Miss Neale was here."

Mr. Pickles grunted and opened the envelope.

"I have been offered a commission in the 9th Sussex Battalion and I will be leaving at the end of the week."

Scarlet as a tomato, Mr. Pickles finally found his voice and bellowed. "How could you leave now? I need you here, Mr. Lytton. I will not allow this."

"Mr. Pickles, my country needs me a great deal more. In case you haven't noticed, we are at war. Saturday is my last day."

Mr. Lytton's face was purple with rage. He turned and marched out of the office, past Anna's desk to the reception counter. Anna feared he would lose his temper and say something he might regret. She walked over and placed her hand on his sleeve.

"Congratulations on your commission, Mr. Lytton."

Facing Anna, he said, "I probably should have expected that reaction. Miss Neale, you will have to take over my duties."

"Oh? I don't know if I can do that! Take over *all* the front desk duties." Anna's thoughts were racing. This was a dream come true. But in the face of reality, she questioned if she could handle the responsibility.

"Miss Neale, you are as good at this position as I am. You have been a good apprentice and learned well. It is time for you to take over. Mr. Pickles may be difficult but he needs you. Don't forget that."

"Thank you for your kindness, Mr. Lytton. I am sure I can do the work." Anna smiled. *Yes,* she thought, *I can do this.* Realizing one of her dreams was about to materialize, her Cheshire cat grin spread from ear to ear; her excitement palpable. She would be the front desk clerk—or would she? Her jubilation shadowed by doubt, she looked at Mr. Lytton, adding, "Mr. Pickles won't be happy promoting me to the position. Do you think he has someone else in mind?" She couldn't trust Mr. Pickles and her added responsibilities reminded her that she would be forced to spend more time with him.

Mr. Lytton looked at her kindly. "Who? Everyone is off fighting the war. He has no choice." He leaned toward her and whispered, "He would never admit it, but he knows how good you are. It would be foolish to attempt to replace you."

Anna beamed with pride. The compliment from Mr. Lytton touched her deeply. "I'm going to miss you very much." And, she thought, his watchfulness; knowing he was only a few feet away when she took dictation was a great comfort.

"Anna, you are a strong young woman. Don't be afraid and never let him see your fear. He learned his lesson and I doubt he will ever try to touch you again." It was then that she realized Mr. Lytton had known all along what had happened in the office that day.

Euphoria permeated everything and everyone as the young men enlisted and started military training. Both Alex and Bill were caught up in the frenzy and talked of enlisting, but Mr. Pickles, terrified of losing more staff, persuaded them to wait.

A carnival atmosphere fuelled by patriotism and a desire to protect filled the air. Marriages increased at an alarming rate. It all seemed for the best as reality set in and the impact of war began to weigh heavily on those left behind.

Anna poured a cup of tea and lifted the pot gesturing towards Sophie. "Tea?"

"Yes, thank you." Sophie sat at the table putting her feet up on a spare chair. "I'm tired. Another maid quit for the munitions factory today. How are things with you since Mr. Lytton left?"

"Like you, busy. Old Prickly-Pickles is even more demanding but I love the work, greeting the guests and organizing everything, not that Pickles appreciates it. He watches me as I move around the office. He gives me the creeps."

"Be careful, Anna. Don't ever be alone with him."

"I always keep the door open and now Miss Jenkins is here most days. I only take dictation when she is here."

"Oh, did you hear that thin little parlour maid is getting married on Saturday? Her fiancé is leaving for France next week."

"I expect she thinks it is one way she can support him while he's at war. I'm not sure how I feel about that. I never want to get married.

The drudgery of all that domestic stuff scares me but I admit the war has changed things."

Sophie closed her eyes and sighed. "I think it's romantic. Soldiers should have someone to come home to. It's patriotic."

"With a hint of glamour," Anna added, amused at Sophie's explanation. "But I do agree that in the face of war, marriage takes on a different meaning."

Bill walked in, uncharacteristically agitated and slammed a copy of *The Times,* on the table.

"The casualties are staggering according to this report. The politicians say the war will be won by Christmas, quite different from this report. I am not sure what to believe."

They all bent over *The Times,* newspaper. Shock was apparent from the short breathless comments. The euphoria of early August had plunged into an abyss as they all thought about the implications of war.

By October the empty hotel felt eerie, even ghostly. Bexhill was changing as the Cooden Camp, only a mile or so up the road, filled with young men training for war. The public houses and streets filled with soldiers making merry before being deployed to the Continent. But on this particular Saturday, the streets were deserted—a storm was brewing from the north.

Anna and Alex walked along the empty beach, watching the wind whip the waves into thick whitecaps. Anna tied her hat under her chin but it still blew into the nape of her neck, secured by the bow. Holding hands, they laughed as they jumped the waves breaking on the breakwater. Alex was getting wet and Anna's skirt was soaked. Alex pulled Anna to him and they kissed, a long kiss, oblivious to the rising tide until Anna felt cold water wash over her feet up to her ankles. She screamed in delight. Alex kissed her again, whispering in her ear, "I love you. Marry me?"

Alex's arms intertwined around her making them as one, the calm in the centre of the storm as the wind howled and swirled around them. Wanting this moment to go on forever, Anna didn't answer. Alex broke the spell. Pushing them apart, he dramatically knelt on one knee and shouted, "Anna will you marry me? I have decided to enlist in the army. Please marry me."

Anna didn't answer, she was not sure she had heard him correctly.

Alex stood from his kneeling position but the drama continued. "I can't go to war unless I know you will marry me. I am going to walk into the sea and I will keep walking until you say yes."

Anna watched in disbelief as Alex slowly waded into the sea, the stormy waves knocking him off balance.

"Alex, don't be a fool, you will get soaked," Anna called after him, laughing. She was used to his teasing and pranks, but this was making her afraid. He was going too far. He kept walking, the water was now up to his thighs. White caps curled on top of a wall of water; the waves expanded. Horrified to see two big waves taller than Alex's six-foot three-inches rolling towards him. She screamed as first one then the other smashed into him sucking him under the water.

"Yes, I will marry you, please come back."

Minutes passed. No sign of Alex. Another wave came rolling in and smashed on the breakwater. As it receded Alex's head popped up. Anna began running towards the water yelling, "I will marry you. You fool, Alex!"

He managed to get his footing and held onto the heavy wooden breakwater and waded towards the shore.

The panic was now in Alex's voice as he saw Anna trying to reach him. "Stay there, Anna. You'll get wet."

Anna couldn't hear him over the roar of the waves. She yelled again even louder, "I'll marry you, you fool!"

The words were carried off on the wind, but now they were in each other's arms. Dripping wet, they walked towards the Promenade, laughing as Alex squelched with each step. He stopped to empty the water from his boots. Anna was shivering; her skirt and coat were soaked.

Suddenly Alex wailed, "Meg. What have I done? You'll catch your death of cold." The jocular mood instantly switched to horror.

"Alex what is wrong? I am fine, if rather wet." She shivered again as the gale force wind blew around her skirts, thunder and lightning filled the air and the skies unleashed a deluge of rain.

"Meg darling, I must take you home and get you warm." He scooped her up into his arms and ran along the beach to the Promenade.

"Alex, what is wrong? Put me down." Anna wrapped her arms around his neck, clinging for dear life. Anna's cries unheard, Alex kept running. He kicked the back door of the hotel open and ran right into Mrs. Banks who was talking to Bill.

"What, on God's green earth, happened to you two?"

"Mrs. Banks, we must get Meg warm quickly or she will die."

Anna's voice had an edge of fear. "Alex, put me down, now! I am wet, not an invalid and who is Meg?" Her face flushed with embarrassment as she looked at Mrs. Banks. Only then did she notice Bill standing in the shadows. She looked away, avoiding his stare but not before she saw something emotional pass from Bill to Alex.

Alex's vacant eyes darted from Bill to Mrs. Banks to Anna before staring into space for a brief second. He sucked in a laboured breath, exhaling slowly, allowing his body to relax and quickly find words of explanation. "We were walking on the beach and a rogue wave caught us by surprise, and when the storm broke we were caught in the rain."

Mrs. Banks opened her mouth to reply just as the back door blow open, the rain pounded on everything inside as well as outside and the gale blew Carter through the door. Carter appeared to be dripping as profusely as Alex.

"Miss Neale and Mr. Walker, go and change your clothes before you catch your death. And, Carter, go and dry off by the fire."

That night, Anna swore Sophie to secrecy and confided in her all that had happened on the beach, including Alex's strange reaction.

"It was as though he was in a complete daze. He stared into another place. He scooped me up as though I was a child and ran...." Anna hesitated. "He was terrified of something."

"That is so romantic," Sophie said, practically swooning.

"Sophie, it wasn't like that. It wasn't me he was carrying. It was someone else. He called me Meg. When we bumped into Mrs. Banks, he said 'we must get Meg warm, she's going to die,' and then he seemed to realize who

I was and where we were."

Aware of sounding somewhat strange, Anna told Sophie about the proposal and that she had accepted. They giggled like schoolgirls, making wedding plans. Sophie expressed her affection for Bill and hoped he would propose marriage. The thought of Bill marrying Sophie gave her a jolt of reality as she grasped the magnitude of what she had done. She had made her choice—Alex over Bill. Deep inside she felt a wound, was it hers or Bill's? She had always known how much her rejection had hurt Bill. She recalled the look that had passed between Bill and Alex and guessed its significance.

Eight

Bill's Demise

"Monsieur Blaine, zee porreege?" Chef yelled. "'ow you... English say... lumpee." The fabricated French accent sounded ridiculous and Bill wondered why Chef couldn't speak normally.

In no mood to placate Chef's eccentricities, Bill grabbed the oversized wooden spoon and thrust it into the thick, lumpy porridge. Anger pulsated through his hand and the porridge bounced and plunged in deep craters like molten lava. He dug the spoon in deeper, twisted it and slammed it on the side of the pot. He swore under his breath at Chef, all the time knowing that Chef was not the source of his anger. He was afraid to admit the true source—Anna and Alex were in love. Alex had done it again, scooped the woman he loved right from under his nose, and he had let it happen.

He spooned the too thick, but now lumpless porridge into bowls for the staff breakfast. A soft lilting tune floated into the passageway as he carried the tray into the staff-dining hall. He'd never heard Anna sing and his anger vanished into the softness of her voice. He watched as she set the table. Her face glowed and her eyes smiled. She looked up, her curls more wayward than usual. The glow disappeared and her eyes changed as she stared at Bill. Did he detect sadness or guilt? He couldn't be sure.

But, now he was certain, something had happened between them and they were afraid to tell him—he didn't need words. He knew. Anna had accepted Alex's proposal. The pain stabbed his heart. He almost dropped the tray and steadied himself on the Welsh dresser, the hurt and betrayal devastating.

"Alex told you?" Anna said.

"No… it's obvious. I saw it in your face." He stared at her through a bubble, his vision distorted by tears. Unable to verbalize the words out loud, he allowed them to ramble in his head. *How could you do this to me? I loved you and trusted you. I gave you time and waited patiently.*

"I thought you were courting Sophie," Anna said, pouting in a way that Bill had not seen since those early days. "Alex was going to drown, I had to say yes."

"Alex tricked you." Bill's breath caught in his throat. "I have to go."

A crying kitchen maid flew past Bill as he entered the kitchen. Chef was bellowing something about kippers. *I can't take this anymore,* thought Bill. *I'm going mad.* He took one look at Chef, daring him to continue his abusive words. Chef scoffed but said nothing.

Bill didn't join the staff for breakfast but went outside to smoke a Woodbine. He sucked the cigarette hard and blew the smoke into rings and watched them float into nothingness, wondering where he had gone wrong. He had given her the space and time she had asked for, expecting her to change her mind about marriage, which she had done, but not with him. The fool that he was, he had pushed her into Alex's arms and welcomed Sophie's friendship. He couldn't deny his mistake. He had wanted to make Anna jealous. He dropped his cigarette, stamped on it and twisted it into the gravel, imagining Alex's head or Anna's. No, not his precious Anna; his own stupid head for being such a fool. Sitting on the very bench where he had first comforted Anna, he put his elbows on his knees, covered his face and wept.

Hearing the back door open, he wiped his face on his apron and took a deep breath. Mrs. Banks approached the bench.

"Mr. Blaine! Whatever is the matter with you? You look ill." She placed the back of her hand on his forehead. "You have a fever."

"No, I'm fine." His voice was thick and nasal. He could feel the puffiness in his eyes and heat from his flushed face. Bill had not cried so hard since he was ten years old, when he fell out of the tree house, breaking his arm. He remembered being embarrassed then, and now he was mortified.

"To your bed, Mr. Blaine. I don't want the staff coming down with fever. You need rest and fluids. I will send some honey and lemon up shortly." About to protest, Bill realized Mrs. Banks had given him the perfect excuse to explain away his current condition, and a day in bed without Chef yelling at him sounded inviting.

Mrs. Banks, fearful that Bill's fever would spread through the staff quarters, had confined Bill to his room without visitors. She had even moved his roommate to another room. He welcomed the solitude, allowing him to wallow in his grief. He mulled over the idea of leaving Bexhill. In spite of Chef's yelling, he was the best. Finding another apprenticeship equal to this one at The Sackville would be difficult. Enlisting in the cavalry might be an option. His experience with horses and riding would bode well and he thought that would make Granddad very proud.

He smiled at the fond memories of playing toy soldier games with the old man, and was reminded of his grandfather's courage and bravery. "What would Granddad tell me to do?" The words came to him as if the old man was standing next to him. "Never retreat, face your enemy and fight for what you believe in." Never retreat, he thought. Running away was Bill's weakness. Even with toy soldiers he would retreat, hence Granddad's words. Face the enemy. Who was the enemy, he wondered. His best friend or the woman he loved? He could fight neither Alex nor Anna. Could he fight for his country? Enlisting, he thought, would still be running away, and he needed to face the consequences of losing Anna.

I will never stop loving Anna and although it might take a while to forgive Alex, I must try, Bill thought. He wasn't the kind of person to seek revenge and he should do the right thing and wish them well. This last thought stabbed at his heart. Would it ever stop hurting? He pulled the cover over his head just as the bedroom door opened and in came Mrs. Banks with a glass of hot lemon and a headache powder.

"How are you feeling, Mr. Blaine?"

Bill sat up quickly. "Much better, thank you. I think the fever has gone."

Mrs. Banks placed the back of her hand on his forehead. "Um, you feel hot." Bill felt vulnerable with the thermometer sticking out if his mouth. Mrs. Banks fussed about tucking the covers and fluffing the pillows. After five minutes she removed the thermometer and frowned. "I'm surprised. Your temperature is normal, but you don't look well. I will check you again in the morning. Chef will have to manage without you for a day or two. Now take these powders, drink the lemon while it is hot and rest." She gave Bill a quizzical look. "You know, I thought Mr. Walker or Miss Neale would be the ones to catch a chill from the soaking they got on Saturday."

Bill winced at the mere mention of their names but felt it wise to keep quiet. Mrs. Banks didn't miss a thing and he wondered how much she knew or deduced from the activities of the last two days.

Bill woke the next morning, feeling more like himself. Mrs. Banks brought him breakfast and was relieved he had no temperature, but insisted he stay in bed.

A knock on the door startled him from his thoughts.

"Yes," Bill called.

The door opened slowly and Sophie's head peered around it. "I hope you are decent? I have brought you lunch."

"Sophie, it is nice to see you. Mrs. Banks must have decided I am not going to infect the whole hotel," he said, laughing. "Come and talk to me. I am getting bored." Bill fiddled with the buttons on his nightshirt and pulled the covers up. It was highly irregular for a woman to be on the men's side of the hallway, let alone in his room. Sophie sat in the chair, her hands clasped on her lap as though she was taking tea in the drawing room. He'd never really noticed how her dark ebony hair shimmered, so different from Anna's golden brown curls.

"You are looking quite well, but sad," Sophie said, looking down at her hands. "Did you hear the news about Anna and Alex?"

91

Bill felt the now familiar jab in his heart. "Cru... m, yes, it's... good news."

"It must have been a shock, the proposal and all being so sudden."

"No, I think I saw it coming. Anyway, I have my beautiful chess player and I think I would like to get to know her a little better." Bill gave her a wink, the same wink he used to give Anna. "So what's been happening while I've been imprisoned in my room?"

"The hotel is quiet but everyone is busy as the stable boy and another bellboy have enlisted and did you know Mr. Lytton has a commission in the cavalry? He leaves on Saturday. Anna tells me Mr. Pickles is furious and Alex is afraid to tell him that he too has enlisted. He goes for his medical next week and then he has to wait for his papers before he can start training."

"Yes, he told me he was going to Cooden Camp on Friday."

"We have a new guest, Mr. Darcy Thornton, Lady Thornton's son. Anna says he's weird. Friendly with the staff but quite rude to his mother. He has a lady joining him next week. Lady Thornton doesn't approve. She's a modern lady and a suffragette." Sophie giggled as she picked up the now empty tray. "And..." she continued heading towards the door, "Miss Barclay told Anna that she's an American. Isn't that exciting?"

Bill resumed his duties on Tuesday morning and, as might be expected, Chef deliberately made his life difficult—punishment for taking two days off. Bill took the yelling and abuse in stride and coped by throwing himself into his work. He even managed to act normally around Anna, although the yearning inside him took some hiding. He hadn't seen much of Alex and suspected he was avoiding him.

Chef had been impossible all day. Bill felt on edge. He had burnt the caramelized onions and over-cooked Sir Walter's steak. He needed solitude, and finally, after dinner was served, he managed to sneak out for a smoke. The only light in the dark courtyard came from the kitchen window shining directly on the bench, making everything else as black as a rabbit-hole.

The voice came from the dark, "May I join you?"

Bill's heart missed a beat. "Who's there?" His eyes strained. First he saw the orange glow and then he smelled a cigar, which preceded the outline of a tall, slim gentleman.

"Forgive me. Name's Darcy Thornton. I was enjoying the evening air when I saw you exit from the back door."

Bill immediately stood up. "Good evening, sir! May I attend to something for you?" Bill felt awkward. It was unusual for a guest to approach the staff in this way. "Perhaps you took a wrong turn, sir. This is the service entrance."

"No wrong turn, just curious. Are you the chef? I must say the food is fabulous here."

"No, sir. I am apprenticed to Chef Louis."

"Well then I expect you do all the work. I will compliment you anyway."

"Thank you, sir. Would you like something now, sir?" Bill frowned.

"No, I enjoyed a robust dinner tonight. The steak was perfectly succulent. Sir Walter apparently was displeased and complained loudly."

"Yes, sir. I am afraid that was my mistake."

"Rubbish. Sir Walter has a temper. Probably displeased with his ugly wife."

The conversation being inappropriate, Bill thought it best to make his excuses and return to the kitchen. "Excuse me, sir. I have duties to attend to in the kitchen."

"Of course. What is your name?"

"Blaine, sir. Bill Blaine."

"Well, Bill Blaine, I hope we meet again."

Bill nodded. "Yes, sir." What a strange encounter, Bill thought as he walked into the kitchen. He remembered his mother teaching him that everyone, no matter what his or her status, deserved respect. Was this gentleman treating him respectfully? Servants and gentry should know their place and understand the consequences if they crossed the line.

Although they had been a happy family, Bill knew his mother had paid the price of crossing the line by marrying the stable manager. But Mr.

Thornton had different airs—superficial—and Bill considered his motives to be questionable.

Saturday afternoon, Bill and Sophie planned to go to the cinema. There was an awkward moment when they met Alex and Anna unexpectedly in the hall. Sophie assumed they were all going to the cinema as usual. Bill tugged at her sleeve as a reminder that things were different now.

"We're catching the omnibus to Eastbourne to do some shopping," Anna said, grinning from ear to ear.

Bill guessed they were going to buy an engagement ring and quickly guided Sophie towards the door. "Come, Sophie. We'll miss the start."

By the time Anna and Alex returned, Bill and Sophie were into a game of chess. Sophie teased Bill as she took his king. Bill concentrated hard, but Anna's giggles distracted him and Sophie won the game.

"Sophie, would you excuse us please? I would like to speak to Bill… alone." Alex said with an uncharacteristically serious look on his face. "I believe Anna has gone to her quarters. You might like to join her. She has something to show you." Alex looked towards Sophie but avoided Bill. Sophie squeezed Bill's hand and left the room.

"Alex, you don't owe me an explanation. We are grown men," Bill said calmly, but was thinking, *I don't want this conversation. Alex is supposed to be my best friend and yet he stole my girl. I want to forgive him, but how can I?*

"Bill, you are my best friend and I want you to be the first to know. Anna and I are officially engaged. We bought the ring today." Alex beamed for a second until he saw Bill's anger pulsating in his temples.

"I know you are angry. I wouldn't expect anything else. I tried not to fall in love with her. I thought you loved her too, but when you started courting Sophie, I thought it was fair game to court Anna. And then it just happened. If it makes you feel better, she turned me down several times."

"You tricked her, Alex. Always the dramatic! Threatening to drown so she would say yes. That's bizarre behaviour, even for you. She had turned *me* down, saying she didn't want to get married, so I let her have some time. Sophie is a friend, a chess partner. I might have known you would interpret our friendship as courting. It served your purpose." *And mine,*

94

Bill thought, feeling guilty for betraying Sophie. "I should have known better. You've done this before, but this time I told you, hands off. You knew how much Anna meant to me. I can't find a way to forgive you and that makes it worse, because now I have lost my friend."

"Bill, I am sorry. I cannot imagine not having your friendship. I need you and so does Anna. I enlisted in the army last week. I am waiting for my papers to start training and Anna will need a friend. Let's shake hands. We've had differences before but always managed to come to an agreement."

"Not this time. And I can't believe you still want me to pick up after you. You decided to enlist and leave Anna alone. Well, not this time. I won't be there… I can't. It hurts too much."

"You'll get over it and you can court Sophie. She really likes you."

"I'm through, Alex. I hope you and Anna have a very happy life." Bill's forehead was running with sweat, the anger bubbled to bursting point as he pounded up the stairs. Sophie stood at the top of the stairs, her dark hair loose around her shoulders and her brown eyes full of love and caring. Bill felt his anger dissipate and suddenly he wanted her comfort and understanding. He was afraid to speak and walked by her but Sophie followed him.

"Sophie, stop. This is the men's quarters."

Then they heard Mrs. Banks' door open and they both froze.

"Mr. Blaine, Miss Romano, may I suggest you finish your conversation in the staff dining hall and let the rest of us retire peacefully?" Mrs. Banks closed her bedroom door making no reference to the fact that Sophie was standing well inside the men's quarters.

Bill poked the fire in the staff dining hall and placed a few pieces of coal on top of the still glowing embers. They, mostly Bill, talked late into the night. Sophie listened and comforted him until he felt more like his old self. Back in his room, Bill was painfully aware that he had decisions to make. Would he have to leave Bexhill? Leave the work he had strived for? Leave Anna, and mourn the loss of his best friend? He didn't want to leave. When Alex left for the army, life would be easier. But Anna would be vulnerable and that would put him in a compromising situation.

Life at The Sackville went on as usual. More staff enlisted or took on lucrative positions in the factories. Untrained and often unsuitable replacements took over. Things were not as efficient, but they managed. Bill watched Anna smile and show off her sapphire ring. She ignored him and there were awkward moments when they met and avoided eye contact. Chef yelled until his ears vibrated. He played chess with Sophie and they went to the cinema together. She filled a void with her warmth. Perhaps in time their friendship would become love. He sighed, knowing that for as long as Anna drew breath that wouldn't happen.

Bill could not take it any longer and decided to retreat from The Sackville and enlist. He took the omnibus to Eastbourne and requested a post in the cavalry. His horsemanship held him in good stead and contingent upon passing the medical on Saturday he was accepted. Granddad would be proud, he thought, and on this occasion he would forgive the retreat as he headed to battle.

Chef Louis roared at Bill for leaving early on Saturday afternoon. Bill took pleasure in ignoring Chef's rants and headed to the doctor's surgery. The waiting room smelled of disinfectant and old dust with a pungent overtone of excited male. The worn wooden chairs, all occupied, chaffed the wooden chair rail. Those without seats stood, cloth-cap, trilby or homburg in hand, talking nervously, while others, pale-faced and anxious, leaned against the faded green wall staring through the animated crowd. Nearly an hour passed before Bill's name was called. The examination was fast but thorough and finished at Bill's feet.

"I'm sorry son but I can't pass you with those feet."

"What's wrong with my feet?"

"Flat as a pancake. No good for marching and you have a nasty skin infection. I'll give you some salve for that. You wouldn't last a week in the trenches."

Astounded, Bill walked along the Promenade, clutching the jar of foot ointment and wondering what he had done to deserve such misery. He opened the back door and Chef's roar that never ceased greeted him. He turned back into the courtyard and lit a Woodbine. To his surprise, Mr. Darcy Thornton, legs outstretched, sat on the bench, a cigar hanging from his lips.

"Good afternoon Mr. Blaine. Come join me. You look as though the world is coming to an end."

"My world has…" Bill said, mostly to himself. "I have lost the woman I love and the cavalry just turned me down. *Flat feet*. Can you believe that?"

"Have you thought of leaving The Sackville? You could travel to America. I plan to return to Chicago. It is a terribly modern city. Last summer Belle and I watched a carnival parade down State Street; everyone wore gay costumes, rich, poor, it didn't matter. Horses and carriages walked along the trolley tracks.

"There are restaurants and theatres on every street corner. On Randolph Street there is a restaurant that can seat five hundred people at one time. The cake counter alone stretches twenty feet or more. I go there after a night at the theatre. With your culinary talent, you could find a chef's position in any restaurant or hotel."

Bill listened intently. Perhaps America would be a way of escaping. The thought excited him and for a second or two he forgot about Anna, Alex and The Sackville.

"It might work for people like you, Mr. Thornton, but it takes money to do those things and I have none. I dream of travel and adventure and one day I will go to America." Bill's thoughts turned to sadness about the travel plans he had had in his youth with Alex and, more recently, dreams of travelling to India with Anna.

"On an apprentice's wage it will take years to save that kind of money. May I suggest you look for a chef's position in another location? If you're interested, I could give you an introduction to The Grand, in Eastbourne."

And that was all it took. Two weeks later, The Grand offered Bill the position of head chef. Even though he had not finished his apprenticeship, his reputation and the fact that there were no qualified chefs available won him the position. His annual income would be more than double, allowing him to save for America.

Aware that managing a large kitchen in wartime with poorly trained staff and wartime rations would present many challenges, Bill decided he could rise to the challenge and accepted the appointment. It would mean long hours, but hard work would fill the emptiness and maybe he could stop hurting.

Mr. Brown, The Grand's general manager, spoke to Bill as an equal, nothing like the mean, pompous Prickly–Pickles. An amiable man, Mr. Brown made pleasant conversation as he gave Bill a tour of the hotel.

The more Bill saw, the more excited he became. The kitchen was twice as large as The Sackville's and better equipped. Chef Louis would positively salivate over such a modish kitchen. Speechless, Bill viewed the suite that was to be his accommodation. A lighted fire warmed the sitting room, a green velvet chair stood beside the fireplace. No more freezing in a windswept attic. An oak desk stood in front of a large window that overlooked the sea. No sloping ceilings with window alcoves. Even Alex could stand there without stooping. He immediately regretted the reminder. An archway led into an equally well-furnished bedroom. *Pure luxury,* he thought, *but I probably won't spend much time here. I will be a good master and work alongside my staff—quite the opposite of Chef Louis.*

He planned his exit from The Sackville carefully. He intended to leave on Saturday's noon hour omnibus to Eastbourne, before anyone realized he had resigned. He had two letters to write. The first would be his resignation addressed to Chef Louis. He'd leave it to Chef to notify Mr. Pickles. Bill smiled as he visualized Chef's rant followed by Mr. Pickles' outrage. The second letter would be to Anna and Alex.

He knew it was cowardly, but he couldn't face them. Sophie, he thought, deserved an explanation. Under different circumstances he probably could have returned her love. He would miss her friendship and her chess challenges.

The grandfather clock struck eleven o'clock as Bill entered the staff dining hall. Sophie sat at the table, the steam from her tea wafted towards Bill as she blew on it.

She smiled. "Hello. Bill, you look as though..." Sophie stopped. She stared at his bags on the floor by the door.

"I have something to tell you." Bill saw her eyes moisten. This is going to be hard, he thought. "Sophie, I have resigned. I am leaving Bexhill on the noon omnibus."

"Where are you going? Can I come with you?"

"It's better that you don't know where I am. You deserve more than I can give you."

"At least let me visit. We can play chess or go to the cinema." Bill gently pressed his finger to her lips and brushed the tears from her cheeks. "Sophie, you are a wonderful friend and I cherish you, but I cannot love you in the way that you want me to. It is better if we don't see each other again." Bill felt his heart crack as he understood Sophie's hurt and he hated himself.

"I wish things could be different." Bill handed her his chess set. "I want you to have this. You were a good pupil and you play as well as the best. Find someone deserving of you and beat the pants off him."

She smiled a weak, tearful smile and clutched the chess set with one arm, flinging the other around his neck kissing him on the cheek and then the lips. "Goodbye, Bill Blaine. I'll always love you. Now go..."

He picked up his bags and walked out of The Sackville for what he thought would be the last time.

Nine

Turmoil and Marriage

〜⚬⚬⚬〜

Chef roared, flinging his large girth into Mr. Pickles' office. Anna's pencil snapped on her notebook and she shrank deeper into the leather chair. She dared not move; garlic gas engulfed her as this hulk stopped only inches from her face.

"Ma'm'sel… it is because of you… you harlot!" He held an envelope in his fist and raised it above Anna's head. The words stung and, afraid he would hit her, Anna squirmed out of the chair.

Mr. Pickles stood up from his desk, tall and pompous, his eyes wide at the action unfolding before him. Anna cringed at the look of disdain in his black eyes. He grabbed the front of Chef's white coat in his fist, pulled him with remarkable strength and pushed him into the chair, Anna had just vacated.

Chef's face had hues of purple with sunken brown eyes and blue lips that were opening and closing without sound; his tall chef's hat balanced sideways on his tiny head. His anger, second only to the rage that exuded from Mr. Pickles, precipitating the eruption of the all-telling red blotches that popped above his stiff white collar and up to his grey comb-over. The scene was farcical and had Anna not been so scared, she might have laughed aloud.

"Silence!" Mr. Pickles wagged his finger at Chef and without moving he said, "Miss Neale, attend to the front desk and close the door behind you."

Anna ran out of the office and leaned on the closed door, her hand on her chest. Miss Jenkins left her telephone post and approached Anna with an inquisitive look. "Are you all right, Miss Neale?"

Anna took a deep breath. "Yes, Miss Jenkins. Chef had one of his fits and directed it at me. It was unsettling." Anna wished Miss Jenkins would go away. The whole incident had brought back memories. She had seen the same flash of vengeance and hatred cross Mr. Pickles' face but today she had understood it. Fear twisted in her insides. She jumped each time Chef roared or Mr. Pickles shouted, pounding on the desk. Her head flipped to and from the office door and the reception counter; she tried to stop, but she feared the beasts would turn their attack on her.

It was more than an hour before Mr. Pickles opened the office door to the lobby and Chef returned to the kitchen. Making no reference to the incident, Mr. Pickles did what he did every Saturday at thirteen hundred hours. He pulled out his gold fob from his waistcoat, checked the time, gave a nod towards Anna and said, "Good day, Miss Neale. We will continue the correspondence on Monday."

Still shaken, Anna asked Miss Jenkins to take charge while she met Alex in the staff dining hall. At first, she felt relieved to see Sophie alone at the table. She wanted to tell her about the morning events. Sophie stared at the wall, her arms wrapped around Bill's chess set. It was only then that Anna heard her sobs and saw her red eyes and wet cheeks.

"Sophie, whatever is wrong?"

Sophie looked up at Anna, flaming with anger. "It's all because of you. And now he's gone. I hate you, Anna Neale!" Still clutching the chess set, Sophie ran through the door.

Bewildered, Anna sat at the table trying to make sense of what had just happened—first, accusations from Chef and now Sophie. She turned and smiled as Alex entered but his face was drawn and worried.

"Alex, what is it? I don't understand."

Alex gently circled his arms around her. Holding her close, he lightly kissed her hair and rested his chin on her head. "You haven't done anything wrong. But I know why everyone is upset." Pulling his hand free, he lifted his apron and took an envelope from his waistcoat pocket. "This is the answer."

"That's Bill's handwriting…" Anna's words trailed off, as she recalled the envelope Chef had in his fist and Sophie clutching the chess set. "It's Bill isn't it?"

"Yes. Bill has left The Sackville." Alex began reading the letter.

> *Dear Alex and Anna,*
>
> *I have resigned my position at The Sackville and will have departed by the time you read this. I have accepted a post as head chef at a hotel outside of Bexhill. It is a great opportunity. I have chosen to keep the location of my new position secret. I would prefer not to be contacted. I think you both know why. I will miss you both and The Sackville but it is better this way. I wish you both a happy life together but I can no longer be a part of it.*
>
> *Perhaps time will heal enough for us to meet again in the future, but for now I must break the ties.*
>
> *Affectionately,*
>
> *Bill*
>
> *P.S. Anna, please be kind to Sophie. She will need a friend.*

Tears rolled down Anna's face, no sobbing, only a continuous stream of heart-rending sadness. Each tear seemed to represent a misguided action on her part that had washed him away, and how the ripples had affected so many others, especially Sophie. Alex pulled Anna closer and she embraced his warmth and comfort. Her thoughts were confused, nothing made sense. Here she was wrapped in the arms of the man she loved, weeping at the loss of another man's love.

The whole hotel mourned the loss of the likeable Bill Blaine. Most assumed that Chef Louis' temper was the cause. Chef Louis took no responsibility for Bill's departure, finding it easier to blame Anna. Sophie barely spoke to Anna for weeks. She tried to comfort her, and Sophie's rejection hurt. Even Alex seemed distant. He missed his friend and Anna wondered if he had guessed the depth of feeling she had for Bill. She scoffed at the thought: it didn't matter to Alex—he had won. Alex had put the ring on her finger, not Bill.

Alone with her thoughts, sipping tea, Anna revisited the events of the last few weeks. She felt sadness for Bill and sympathy for Sophie who didn't deserve to be jilted. Bill had made that decision and it was hardly Anna's fault.

"I shall put all this behind me. I am going to marry Alex and that's the end of it," she said aloud, voicing her capricious thoughts—Anna's way of censoring the hurt and her attempt to defray any feelings of guilt. She felt resolute and no sooner had she decided to share it with Alex than she heard his voice.

"Did I hear my name? Who are you talking to?"

"Thinking aloud, there's no one here." Anna turned to face Alex her smile faded when she saw darkness.

"Alex, what is it?"

He pulled an official brown envelope from his pocket and handed it to Anna. "I report to Cooden Camp for training on Monday."

"Cooden is not far, it's still in Bexhill and the omnibus goes there. I can come and visit or we can meet at The Fisherman's Nook like all the other servicemen. In the summer we can go to the beach and walk along the Promenade. It'll be okay." The words tumbled out of Anna.

"Anna, stop! I don't know where they will send me after training." Alex took Anna's hands and kissed them gently. "Anna, let's get married now."

"But... but... we only just got engaged. Shouldn't we wait for a while?"

Being engaged was fun but marriage was final. Fear of losing her freedom gripped her insides. Images of the invisible wife, scrubbing, cooking, and children hanging from her skirts flashed across her mind—terror struck her.

"Once I have finished training I will be sent overseas and then who knows what will happen? Anna, if we are married and I am killed in action, you will be taken care of by the war department."

Anna felt the colour drain from her face, leaving her sick and faint—too much had happened. The thought of losing Alex to war was more than she could handle. The world faded and she felt Alex's arms catch her and then nothing. She woke abruptly as smelling salts shot up her nostrils and Mrs. Banks placed a wet towel on her head while berating Alex for scaring the poor girl half to death.

Christmas celebrations had a muted, unnatural feel. The Sackville looked festive with its large Christmas tree and copious red bows, baubles and lights, but it was short on staff and guests, there was no choir to sing carols and even festive food was in short supply. It felt superficial. Nobody was sure how to celebrate with a war raging only a few miles away across the Channel.

Anna had only seen Alex once in three weeks and he had not written about Christmas leave. To make things worse, the postman had not brought either a parcel or a letter from home, which worried her.

She missed her family at Christmas; baking with Lou and Mother; the secret talks of adventure with her dearest Charlie, Father's cheery face when he poured the ginger wine, Uncle Bertie's special gifts and stories from faraway places. She smiled at the antics they would get up to playing charades. Her mother's soft voice, singing *O Come All Ye Faithful*. Just thinking about it tightened her throat; she felt sad and alone, standing in the hallway outside Suite 305.

Princess's yapping snapped Anna out of her daydream and back to reality as Miss Barclay opened the door. Anna bent down to pet Princess and, as she stood up, she came face to face with a stunning young woman, her blue-grey eyes dancing with the brown curls that had been cut short around her face, a tortoiseshell slide holding one side in place. Anna stared. She had never seen a woman wearing a cravat. It was navy-blue satin and not at all masculine. It tucked under the collar of her simple, creamy coloured blouse and into the slim waistband of the matching skirt; the hem several inches above her ankles. Anna liked her immediately and surmised the lady to be Belle Tully. Lady Thornton's disapproval was quite obvious, no introduction was forthcoming and barely a civil smile. Miss Tully excused herself, giving Anna a friendly grin as she left the room.

"Miss Neale, I have decided to host a little Christmas soirée to celebrate my son's visit and I need you to write the invitations," Lady Thornton instructed as Anna entered. "I am going to rest. Barclay will take them to the afternoon post when you are finished."

About halfway through the guest list, Anna sensed a presence looking over her shoulder and turned to see Mr. Darcy Thornton watching her.

"Please, don't let me interrupt. I am fascinated with the speed at which you can use the typewriting machine. You absolutely must meet Belle. She's from Chicago, in America. She too is an independent woman and works for a living. Are you a member of the suffragette movement?"

"Thank you, sir. And no I am not a member of the suffragette movement." It wasn't exactly a lie, she thought. She did support the suffragettes, but knowing Lady Thornton's views on the subject, she thought it prudent to be vague.

He continued speaking to Anna as though she were his equal, which made her uncomfortable. But, Anna thought, he is proud of having caught such a prize as Miss Belle Tully.

"Belle is a social worker for the Children's Protection Association in Chicago. She determines the welfare of children, the poor little blighters whose mothers can't take care of them and drunken fathers who abscond—or something like that. Mother of course does not approve. Belle has marched through Chicago with the suffragettes. I do admire her."

Anna had no idea how to respond to this litany about Miss Tully. She suspected part of the attraction was little more than rebellion to discomfort his mother. Anna already felt an admiration for Miss Tully and envied her freedom and adventuresome life, but it was not her place to agree or disagree with Mr. Thornton.

Lady Thornton appeared from her boudoir, having changed into a rich burgundy afternoon dress, which suited her dark colouring. She glanced at Anna and pursed her lips towards Darcy.

"Darcy, dear... leave Miss Neale to complete her task. I am sure she has no interest in Miss Tully or the suffragettes." Her head gave a flip of disapproval. Anna wasn't sure if it was for Miss Tully, Darcy or herself. She handed the completed invitations to Miss Barclay and waited for further instructions.

"Miss Neale, you appear somber today. I hope my son did not offend you."

"Oh no! It's the time of year. I always miss my family at Christmas."

"Is your fiancé getting leave?"

"I don't know." Anna felt her throat constrict as she held back tears at the thought of being alone on Christmas Day.

"Loneliness can be cruel," Lady Thornton said, staring into a distant past. "Perhaps you could ease your melancholy with your friend Sophie?"

"Sophie has never forgiven me for Mr. Blaine's departure." Anna coughed an attempt to push away the emotion. "Even the guests have no Christmas spirit. Everything is so different this year."

"War changes everything. I am fortunate to have one of my sons here this year. It is hard to celebrate when sons, brothers and husbands are away fighting. We must make the best of it." Lady Thornton took Anna by the hand and with rare compassion she said, "Believe me, Anna, things will get better."

In spite of Lady Thornton's words of encouragement and the excitement of planning the soiree, Christmas of 1914 seemed predisposed to be a miserable time for Anna. Alex's letter telling her he could not get Christmas leave arrived two days later, and on Christmas Eve a parcel arrived from Rugby and the reason for the delay was made clear.

Charlie had enlisted in the army and they were afraid to tell her. He was already in the trenches in France. Anna's heart pained at the news. Her mother's letter said he had promised to write when he could and she was not to worry. Everyone was in good health. Lou had a new beau and there might be a wedding.

Typical Lou, Anna thought, she had to do better than Anna. Uncle

Bertie had arrived from India but he would not be returning until after the war—sailing the oceans was too dangerous.

Her mother had wrapped the presents in tissue paper and tied them with red bows. Anna laughed, pretending she was at home with Lou and Charlie, shaking the packages trying to guess the contents. Joy turned to gloom when she realized she would open the presents alone.

The parcel contained her mother's spice cake, (Anna's favourite) and a Rudyard Kipling collection of stories from Papa. Anna kissed her fingers and placed them on the inscription, *with love from Papa*. She felt the softness against her cheeks of the woolen blanket from Mama and admired the lace handkerchiefs from Lou. She smiled affectionately at the blue crystal bracelet that would match her pendant from Uncle Bertie. She sighed; all the people she loved were so far away. Except, she thought, there was Sophie.

Anna resolved to win back Sophie's friendship and without another thought, she knocked on Sophie's door—the diminishing staff and superior responsibilities had entitled them to single rooms. Anna closed her eyes and started speaking as she heard the door open.

"Sophie, I miss you. I am sorry Bill left, but it wasn't my fault. And... I do not want to take the blame for his decision." Taking a deep breath, she opened her eyes and looked right into Sophie's smiling face.

"What took you so long? I miss you too and I know now that it was Bill's decision to leave." Sophie put out her hand and they hugged and cried, both happy to have their friend back. Comforting each other, they celebrated Christmas.

Anna's status at The Sackville had risen dramatically over the winter. Mr. Pickles' expectations of Anna were augmented by the mass enlistment of male staff and maids who resigned for more lucrative positions in nursing or the factories. The Sackville staff was now made up of disgruntled staff who were either afraid to enlist and considered cowards or had been turned down on medical grounds.

Anna tackled her duties and added responsibilities with excellence. The front desk ran efficiently because of her organizational skills. She managed the staff with fairness and empathy, and had a reputation for soothing unhappy, argumentative staff and appeasing disgruntled guests.

Mr. Pickles had added the dining room waiters to her duties and Mrs. Banks had asked her to monitor the parlour maids. They were really too young to be in the guest salons but with the staff shortage, she had no choice if the rooms were to be kept clean. Anna had drawn the line when asked to assist Chef with staff problems. The shortage of basic supplies and quality ingredients coupled with incompetent staff had not improved Chef's disposition or his roaring temper. Kitchen maids came and went like a revolving door. Her answer was quite clear—Chef Louis must mind his temper and learn to manage his own staff and Mr. Pickles was best suited to deal with Chef.

Spring blossomed and so did Anna. She bubbled with confidence, revelling in liberation and achievements far beyond her expectations. If decorum had allowed, she would have whistled and danced as she worked. She threw heart and soul into each task—even Mr. Pickles' dictations were tolerable. Her new-found confidence allowed her to let her guard down. His deviant behaviour was kept at bay, at least from Anna.

Mrs. Banks' motive for asking her to keep an eye on the maids had more to do with Mr. Pickles than their work. At only fifteen-years-old, Amy, now a parlour maid, was responsible for cleaning the lobby, front desk and Mr. Pickles' office. Anna insisted Amy clean the office before eight o'clock in the morning, thus avoiding Mr. Pickles.

The busyness kept her from worrying about Charlie in the trenches and avoiding setting a date for her upcoming nuptials. Her doubts about the married life grew in strength as did her ambition to do something useful and work at things she excelled at and enjoyed. No matter how much she loved Alex, she doubted she could be a good wife. Trying to ease her doubts, Sophie explained that all brides got cold feet and it was normal. Anna disagreed; she didn't feel normal.

On St Patrick's Day 1915, the daffodils bent their heads in the sunshine and a bright blue sky greeted Alex on his first day of leave. Anna had arranged for Miss Jenkins to take over the front desk for the afternoon and evening.

She held her stomach to hold her feelings in check. So many feelings fluttered about her insides; the love she felt for Alex overflowed, mixed with excitement and fear all at the same time.

"I've made tea," Sophie said, placing the tea tray on the table in the staff dining hall. "Don't worry, I'll leave when Alex gets here."

"No, stay and have tea with us. Alex will want to say hello."

Anna felt conscious of her modern dress. Emulating Belle Tully, she had added a blue cravat to her white blouse to match her best skirt.

"How do I look?"

"Stunning," Sophie replied.

"I have to agree," Alex's deep voice came from the passageway.

Tears of happiness filled Anna's eyes as she feasted on this tall handsome man regaled in full uniform. "Alex!" she said, running into his arms. All her fears and doubts were suspended as she clung to him and kissed him. He cupped her face and she felt the roughness of his hands as he kissed her again and again and held her tight, his chin on her head. The coarse wool serge of his uniform prickled her cheek. She sighed with contentment.

"Cr... um! Should I leave or shall I pour tea?" They laughed.

"It's good to see you looking well, Sophie." Alex smiled, "It's like old times except Bill is missing. Has anyone heard from him?"

"No, at least I haven't," Sophie, said. "But Amy saw him on Grand Parade in Eastbourne just last week. He said hello and hurried off. She thought he went into The Grand Hotel."

There was an awkward silence. Anna wondered why Sophie had omitted to tell her that Bill had been seen. She didn't want to talk about Bill and pushed it out of her mind.

Rosy-cheeked and a little lightheaded from the glass of sherry before and wine with dinner at The Fisherman's Nook, Anna bounced into the empty staff dining hall as the grandfather clock struck ten, bursting to tell Sophie of her wonderful day. But Sophie had gone to bed. Disappointed,

Anna laboured quietly up the stairs. Her news would have to wait until tomorrow.

The March wind started to howl through the cracks in the attic window. Anna shivered as she gazed at the iridescent caps on the waves—a storm was brewing. Climbing into bed, she pulled the soft blanket to her chin, wondering if there was a storm brewing inside her. She loved Alex so much she thought she might burst with happiness. But when he talked about setting the wedding date, a door slammed shut in her mind, followed by the panic of being trapped.

She compared the euphoria that propelled her around the hotel as she administered her duties and felt the satisfaction of accomplishment. She could easily support herself as a career woman doing what she wanted to do; albeit, she might be alone, unloved, and unable to travel.

Aware that neither the life of independence nor that of a wife would give her what she wanted, she wondered if there was a way to combine the two. She fell asleep, dreaming of marrying Alex and sailing off to faraway lands, working independently in hotels, renting rooms that would be their temporary, blissful marital nests. Alex's arms were holding her tightly when suddenly a black shadow swooped upon them and whisked Alex away. Anna stood alone, terrified, feeling the darkness of evil and there was no trace of Alex. She screamed and shouted, "Alex, come back!"

Her shoulders shook and she heard a voice. "Anna, wake up. You are having a bad dream." Anna opened her eyes.

"Sophie, it was so real. Something black and evil took Alex away." Anna sat up and took a deep breath and to her embarrassment saw a collection of maids in nightdresses and shawls staring at her. Mrs. Banks arrived, telling everyone to return to their rooms. Anna assured Mrs. Banks she had just had a bad dream and was quite well.

The image of Alex disappearing haunted Anna. She kept asking herself the same questions. What did the dream imply? Would he be lost to her if she didn't set the date or was it punishment for wanting autonomy? The worst and most terrifying thought of all, was it a premonition that Alex may not return from the war?

On Sunday morning, Mrs. Banks kindly allowed Anna and Alex to use the privacy of her sitting room before Alex went back to Cooden Camp. Amy had stoked the fire; the cheerful flames licked the back of the fireplace and filled the cozy room with warmth. They sat at the little round table, two cups of tea going cold between their linked hands. Anna described the dream in detail.

"Alex I am so afraid of losing you."

Alex beamed as his hand gently stroked her cheek. "Anna, my darling. I could never leave you. I have every intention of coming back from the war, and in one piece. I'm sorry the dream scared you, but it was just a dream."

"Alex, I do want to marry you but I want to be independent as well. If I agree to set the date can I be both? Is that possible? Can you be open-minded?"

"Yes, of course Anna, while I'm in the army I expect you to keep working at The Sackville."

"And when the war is over?"

"I hope to get my job back. We'll work together and save some money so we can get a place of our own—maybe start a family." Alex smiled.

Anna did not.

"I am not sure I want children." Alex looked crestfallen. Anna quickly added, "At least not right away. We could travel and see the world. Explore the places Uncle Bertie talked about. Red Indians in Canada or elephants and tigers in India."

The coals spit and crackled, breaking the silence as they both stared at the hypnotic flames in the fireplace.

Alex took a deep breath. Still staring at the flames he said, "I too would like to travel. I can see us leaning on the railing of a big ship, gazing across open seas with a full moon blessing our love, just like they do in the movies."

"Do you mean that, Alex?"

"Yes, I promise. But I want to get married as soon as possible. Anna, it is important to me to go into battle knowing that you are my wife. After the war, we will take our first adventure. It will be our honeymoon and we will have something to dream about while I'm away. I will have to come back from the war to keep my promise. Now come here and let me kiss you."

Charm had won her over and dispelled her doubts. Anna believed, because she wanted to believe, that she could have it all.

"June fifth," she said. "I would like a June wedding. Can you arrange leave for that day? I will write to my parents; you write to yours. I'll ask Sophie to be my bridesmaid."

"I don't think my parents will come. My father can't leave the shop and Mother will expect nothing less than a society wedding—sorry, but that's my mother, not me. I will write. Do you think it would be too much to ask Bill to be my best man?"

"Of course not. That would be perfect. It might even encourage Sophie and Bill to get together." Anna hoped she sounded positive, but in truth she felt apprehensive for more reasons than she was willing to admit. "I think we should wait until everything is settled before approaching Bill, and we have to find him first. Perhaps you should have someone else in mind in case we don't find Bill or he refuses?"

Alex returned to camp. Anna, with Sophie's help, made wedding preparations for a simple wedding at the Registry Office in Hastings. She decided a new dress was out of the question. She chose her favourite midnight blue travelling suit, her best white blouse with the lace collar and her big blue hat, which had not been out of the hatbox since her arrival—definitely more appropriate for a wedding.

Alex's parents sent their regrets, as expected. Anna's father had given his permission for the marriage, so Alex could apply for the license—Anna would not be twenty-one until July—but her mother had been vague about whether they could make the journey. Charlie, as far as she knew, was still in France and she had no idea if he had received her letter. But she felt uneasy about whether her parents would come. "I'm being foolish," she said to herself, "Father has always been there for me. They are waiting for final travelling arrangements."

Ten

Wedding Surprises

ophie took it upon herself to locate Bill. Amy's report of seeing him entering The Grand Hotel in Eastbourne was a good start, and with only a few enquiries she quickly discovered Bill Blaine did indeed work there. Both Sophie and Alex wrote to Bill but neither received a reply.

Alex had uncharacteristically accepted the army discipline quite well but was now showing his frustration. He wrote to Anna that he had been denied leave to see Bill but he had a plan to sneak out of camp tomorrow evening, and if he had time, he would call on her.

"He's a fool," Anna said to Sophie, showing her the letter. "If he gets caught, he will be court-martialled and all leave will be cancelled and we'll have to cancel the wedding."

Anna's reply instructed Alex to stop his folly. When he did not call, she assumed he had heeded her words, but then worried that he had been caught.

Was the wedding still on or was he in the brig? Two days later, she received bad news. Alex's optimistic letter explained he had indeed been caught leaving the camp. But he told her not to worry, everything would work out. His commanding officer was a reasonable chap and would understand. She was angry with him for being so stupid and impulsive. If it were so important to have Bill as his best man, then she would go to Eastbourne and visit him.

Saturday afternoon, Anna caught the omnibus to Eastbourne. She had told no one, not even Sophie. Typical of April, the weather sprinkled a light rain as she walked along Grand Parade, rehearsing what she would say. The Grand Hotel looked very grand, she thought, walking to the back entrance. A maid answered. "I would like to see Mr. Bill Blaine, please." The maid looked her up and down. "I'm his sister, Mrs. Anna Neale, visiting from Rugby." Anna kept her gloves, on hiding the fact that she was not wearing a wedding band.

"I'll ask if Chef will see you. You'd better wait inside in the dry."

Anna's heart raced out of control when Bill appeared from the kitchen. Speechless, she stared at a man haunted with sadness. Guilt knotted her stomach; she wanted to take him in her arms and comfort him.

A deep frown wrinkled his brow. "Anna, is something wrong?"

"No, but I have something to ask you. Is there somewhere we can talk?"

"Yes, I can take my... married sister... to my sitting-room." The familiar wink took her breath away and she was not at all sure she could do this.

"They treat you well here." Anna surveyed the suite with awe.

"Anna, it is good to see you. How can I help you?"

Anna relayed her wedding plans, adding Alex's stupid scheme of leaving the camp without permission in order to ask Bill to be his best man.

"That sounds like Alex. Going AWOL is a very serious offence. I am flattered he went to such lengths, but I cannot do as you ask."

"But—" Anna started to speak but Bill motioned her to be quiet.

"Hear me out, please. I miss you both very much, and I miss Sophie. My life is empty without you all. I thought being head chef here would fill the void. But I feel useless serving the wealthy and privileged in a fancy hotel as young men fight for our country. I experienced the white feather a couple of times and that was humiliating. These women do not understand, I am not a coward. I tried to serve my country, but the cavalry turned me down."

114

"Why?"

"I have flat feet. No good for marching was what the doctor said."

"You must be disappointed."

Bill shrugged his shoulders. "Whether I would be able to face your wedding, I cannot say. I will forgive Alex in time. I miss him and as his best friend I should be his best-man."

"So why don't you say yes?"

"I can't. I found a way to serve my country. I joined the Merchant Navy as a cook, and I sail for North America on the morning tide."

"Bill, that is dangerous. Even Uncle Bertie has stopped sailing to India with the German U-boats..." Anna's words trailed off. "Will you write?"

"If I can, but don't worry if you don't hear. I will be sailing to strange lands." The memory of the discussions of Rudyard Kipling's India and adventures to strange lands, although uppermost in both of their minds and showing in their faces, went unsaid. Bill escorted Anna from his suite to the service entrance.

"Be mindful of Alex. He is a charmer and manipulates to get his own way. If ever you need me..."

Anna stopped him mid-sentence. "How will I find you?"

"I will find you, and I will write when I can." He kissed her on the cheek and wished her well.

Boarding the omnibus for Bexhill, Anna found herself looking over her shoulder, searching for something. As the omnibus bounced along the coastal road she felt a mixture of loss, guilt and sadness, because she understood the significance of Bill's decision. She had lost something precious and it must always stay lost if she was to marry Alex.

Alex appeared at The Sackville on Sunday morning. He had two hours of legitimate leave to reassure Anna his leave for the wedding had been reinstated. She did not ask how. She told him of her encounter with Bill, but Alex had already moved on and his army pal, Private Hamish Duncan, a fellow Scotsman, had agreed to be best man.

Monday, the busiest morning of the week for dictation, Anna picked up her Pitman notebook, ready for the onslaught of letters. She surmised

Mr. Pickles spent his days off inventing reasons to correspond. Anna had noticed an increase in correspondence from Kendrick Hotels Ltd, Mr. Kendrick in particular. The Company was concerned by the low occupancy rate and resulting revenue decline and seemed to be holding Mr. Pickles accountable, which did not seem fair under the current economic circumstances. Her momentary lapse of concern for the man was obliterated when Amy hurried past looking terrified. Mr. Pickles' smug face sneered at Anna.

"Ah, Miss Neale, good morning. Please, take a seat."

Anna tried to concentrate on the shorthand but her mind kept wandering to the frightened look on Amy's face. Had Mr. Pickles made advances towards little Amy? Remembering that the office door had been open, she was hopeful that nothing too unpleasant had happened. But the office had an atmosphere of dread, fear and oppression. She brushed it off, berating herself for being over sensitive.

"Miss Neale, you seem distracted this morning. I think your impending nuptials or perhaps the thought of frolicking in the bedroom with your red-headed Scotsman has gone to your head." Mr. Pickles leaned forward, pinning her with his ferret eyes. "I could give you some guidance."

Anna jumped up from the chair. "Mr. Pickles! Please mind your manners!"

Mr. Pickles inclined his head and with a smirk, apologized and continued dictation only to be interrupted by Miss Jenkins.

"Excuse me Mr. Pickles but there is an urgent phone call for Miss Neale. I believe it is her father."

Anna ran to the telephone exchange and picked up the call. "Papa, what's wrong?"

At first Anna thought she had misheard, the line crackled and his voice sounded far away. But she had heard correctly and he repeated his words, "Anna darling, I am sorry but the family cannot come for your wedding. Your sister is getting married the same day. The reasons are complicated. Your mother has written a letter explaining the details." The line crackled and buzzed even louder, Anna couldn't comprehend what her father was saying. Anna held the mouthpiece closer to her lips and shouted, "Papa, are you ill? Is it mother?" She pressed the earpiece harder to her ear.

"No, no we are all quite well. But, I am heartbroken to miss my little girl's wedding. Your mother's letter will arrive tomorrow. Goodbye, Anna." And the line went dead.

Anna stood by her desk in disbelief. Lou had done some awful things in the past, but planning her wedding on the same day was the worst thing she had ever done. Lou had always been jealous of Papa's affections towards Anna; this would be the ultimate punishment for both of them. The letter arrived in the morning post.

Dearest Anna,

By the time you read this letter, you will have had a telephone call from Papa giving you the bad news that we are not able to attend to your wedding. You must have wondered why I had not written sooner. All I can say is that in the weeks since you wrote informing us of your wedding date our lives have been upset.

Papa and I were so excited for you, although we have never met Mr. Walker in person. Through his letters and phone calls, Papa found him to be a gentleman and very caring of you. We were looking forward to making his acquaintance. We had started to make plans for the journey to Bexhill until your sister gave us the devastating news.

I am so ashamed. Lou is with child. The father is her fiancé, which is a blessing. The wedding plans have been rushed forward, and the only available day for all concerned had to be June 5th. We could not wait until mid-June, risking that she would already show. As it is, I am bracing myself for the onslaught of snide remarks and catty counting of the months when the baby is born 'premature.' Mr. Laughton is a nice young man, a few years older than Lou. He and his widowed mother own a farm just south of Rugby. I think he will make Lou a good husband. Please try not to be too angry with Lou; believe me, she is suffering great humiliation.

Papa and I thought we might come and visit you during the summer for a holiday before Lou's confinement. The doctor says the baby is due late October. I will be a grandmother and you will be Aunt Anna. Even under the circumstances, I can't help but be a little happy.

Dearest Anna, please have a wonderful wedding day. Papa and I send our love and blessings and we will celebrate with you in the summer.

Your ever affectionate
Mother

In spite of her mother's explanation, Anna didn't fully understand why Lou's wedding date had to be the same day, June 5th. But knowing Lou, and how humiliated she would be, gave Anna some satisfaction. She had to admit she had a difficult time imagining Lou being loose with her affections. "My prim and proper sister is a dark horse," Anna chuckled.

"What is so humorous?" Sophie smiled and added, "You are a strange lady, Anna Neale. You looked as though a tragedy had happened when you started to read your letter and now you are laughing."

Anna was telling Sophie about her sister when Amy joined them at the table. Amy looked pale, tiny and innocent.

"Amy, is anything wrong?" Sophie asked.

Anna asked, "Amy, did something happen in Mr. Pickle's office this morning?"

Amy burst into tears. "I didn't do nufing wrong…" She took a breath, "I were dustin' Mr. Pickles desk… and 'e put 'is 'and on mi…," she said shaking with sobs. Anna gathered her in her arms and held her tight. Amy lifted her head still clinging to Anna. "Then…it were awful… he took mi hand…put it on 'is trousers…and then 'e ripped the lace on mi apron pushin' 'is hand inside."

Amy's tears flowed copiously until Anna's blouse was quite wet. Anna gently moved her to the rocking chair. It was then that she noticed Mrs. Banks standing in the doorway.

"Mrs. Banks perhaps you could take Amy to your sitting room?" Before

Mrs. Banks could reply, Amy panicked and through more tears shouted, "I didn't do nufing wrong."

Mrs. Banks spoke gently, "I understand, Amy. You did nothing wrong. We'll have some tea and you can tell me what happened."

Mrs. Banks and Sophie rearranged Amy's schedule. Sophie would chaperone her for the daily chores and the office would have a good cleaning on Saturday after Mr. Pickles departed for the weekend. He wouldn't dare stay late and upset Mrs. Pickles. It was amusingly apparent that he was afraid of his wife, which explained why he lived at the hotel during the week.

That morning, Mr. Pickles arrived early and challenged Anna as to why Amy was not cleaning his office. "Mr. Pickles, Amy is fifteen years old, a child. And you're…" Anna felt the anger surging inside, but knew it would be unwise to use the word *deviant*. She hesitated and then continued, "… your harsh behaviour frightens her."

Anna watched the red blotches erupt from under his stiff collar. Had she gone too far? He could easily dismiss them all.

"I see, and when will the housekeeping be conducted in my office?"

"On Saturday. It will not inconvenience you as you will have retired for the weekend." Anna grinned, seeing a look of disappointment on his evil face.

Having put Mr. Pickles in his place, Anna had a feeling of satisfaction as she returned to the front desk. The usually bare polished mahogany counter contained a large box with a fancy blue bow on the top. On further examination, she saw that it had come from Selfridge's in London and the attached card was addressed to Miss A. Neale. She looked around the lobby for signs of who had put it there. The bellboy smiled. "It's for you, Miss. A messenger brought it while you were in Mr. Pickles' office."

Anna smiled back and checked the card again, but the only words on the card were "Miss A. Neale, The Sackville Hotel Bexhill-on-Sea." She stared at the box. Excitement, not unlike Christmas, welled up inside her. Her fingers held the ribbon and she pulled gently watching the bow loosen and finally fall off the box. Tissue paper scrunched and a rich blue fabric became visible as she opened the lid. Anna gasped!

The box contained a dress and another card lay on the top. She dared not take the dress out of the box here at the desk, but she felt the softness of silk and saw a blue so rich it took her breath away. She closed the box carefully and opened the card, immediately seeing the words, *Affectionately, Lady Thornton.* The card simply read: *I trust this special dress is to your liking. Please accept it as a wedding present.* She quietly slid the card and box underneath the front desk counter.

That evening, Anna invited Sophie to her room and showed her the box and card. Carefully she unpacked the dress and tried it on. The sleeves and yoke, trimmed with lace, were a creamy white. The V-shaped bodice fitted gently into Anna's small waist. The skirt hung softly above her ankles with a shorter embroidered over skirt. The soft, rich blue silk shone in the light, lifting the blue from Anna's eyes as she relished in the beauty of the dress.

She opened her jewellery pouch and added her blue pendant and bracelet. Reaching into the wardrobe, she pulled out her hatbox and put on her big blue hat, and to her delight it matched perfectly.

The day finally arrived, Saturday, June 5th, 1915. Anna wondered if all brides felt uneasy just before their weddings. Marriage was so final. She missed Mother and dearest Papa. It seemed odd to be getting married without family present. She thought of how much she loved Alex but wondered if she could trust him to keep his word. Would she find herself tied to the domestic life?

Her head spun with her own thoughts and too much advice from others. She longed to talk to Uncle Bertie. She twisted her fingers in the velvet ribbon at her neck and the blue crystal felt cold on her skin. She gave a shiver. A forewarning, she thought, but a forewarning of what?

Alex had promised travel and adventure after the war, but Bill's warning words, "Be mindful of Alex, he is a charmer and manipulates to get his own way," were louder, and had planted a kernel of doubt. She dismissed the words with defiance and decided that she could be strong and quite the match for Alex.

Lady Thornton insisted on lending Anna her automobile and chauffeur for the journey to the Hastings Registry Office. Anna and Sophie travelled together. Anna felt elegant in her new dress; the fabric floated as she moved, complemented by her lovely big blue hat. Mrs. Banks had given her a bouquet of pink and white roses. She smiled as a mix of nerves and excitement swirled inside her. With Sophie at her side, the beautiful bride stepped into the contrastingly austere waiting room. An anxious-looking Alex and Private Duncan stood up from the old wooden chairs. Anna almost swooned. Alex looked so handsome in full uniform. Their eyes locked as the only two people in the room. Everyone else became silent and invisible to them.

"Och... Anna, I'm speechless. You are the most beautiful lassie I have ever set eyes on. I love you." Alex slowly bent his head under her hat and gently kissed her cheek. Filled with so much love, Anna thought she might burst. At that moment, Anna wanted nothing more than to be Alex's wife.

"I love you so much Alex, and you look very handsome. I am the luckiest and happiest woman in the world."

An elderly gentleman announced it was five minutes to ten o'clock, and time to go into the courtroom. The judge would begin at ten sharp. Anna turned towards Sophie, noticing that there were two gentlemen in the room, one in full officer's uniform and the other wearing a lounge suit, over a rather bright striped waistcoat and red bow tie.

Her heart exploded as she screamed, "Charlie, I don't believe it, I'm dreaming!" The bouquet dropped to the floor as she flung her arms around him. She screamed again, "Uncle Bertie. How did you get here? When did you get here?" She turned to Sophie and Alex, "Did you know about this?" Anna began to cry. "You are here for my wedding. I missed everyone so much and now you are here. I am so very happy."

"Cr... crum... we must not keep the judge waiting," said the elderly gentleman.

The short, simple marriage ceremony was conducted in a dull wood-panelled courtroom. The sun beamed through the narrow windows as dust floated and tobacco smoke swirled in the shafts of light.

The judge stood before them, reciting the marriage vows in a monotone; the words, overused of late, lacked passion. But he did smile when he pronounced Anna and Alex man and wife. Once they were outside, Charlie took photographs with his Brownie camera. They all squeezed into Lady Thornton's automobile and travelled back to The Sackville.

Chef Louis, with some considerable persuasion from Mrs. Banks, had laid on a Wedding Breakfast and all the servants were invited to join them, including Miss Barclay. Anna would have liked to invite Lady Thornton but protocol did not allow it—she promised to visit later.

Anna radiated happiness and Alex strutted with pride, chatting to the staff he had once worked with and conversing with Charlie and Uncle Bertie. Quite suddenly, a roar came from the kitchen and all conversation stopped. Anna's heart missed a beat and she glanced towards the kitchen fearful of what might happen next. Chef Louis walked slowly into the staff dining hall carrying a beautiful two-tier wedding cake.

Chef smiled and said, "Pour vous, ma cherie! Congratulations!" With great continental flourish, he kissed Anna's hand and turned to shake Alex's hand. Chef motioned for them to cut the cake and handed them a knife, telling them to make a wish. Uncle Bertie held a bottle of champagne, his thumbs popped the cork and everyone cheered, toasting the bride and groom. By two o'clock the party had come to a close and the staff returned to their duties, including Sophie. Mrs. Banks retired to her sitting room, leaving Anna and Alex alone with Charlie and Uncle Bertie.

"How did you two get here? I expected you to be at Lou's wedding but I am so happy. You made my day so wonderful." Anna pulled them together and put her arms around both Charlie and Uncle Bertie.

"Father insisted. He is angry and extremely displeased with our sister. Of course her condition is a great disappointment, but I think it will be a while before he forgives her for planning her wedding the same day as yours. Father was not convinced it had to be that way. Mother is worried about her reputation and wanted the wedding as soon as possible. To compromise, Uncle Bertie suggested that we came to Bexhill. Two family members at Lou's wedding and two at yours."

"And I got the best part of the bargain; my favourite brother and uncle. How long can you stay? I can find you a room here. Mr. Pickles is off at the weekend, and the hotel is half empty. Mrs. Banks has arranged for Alex and me to stay in one of the suites until Monday morning."

"I had hoped to see Pickles," Uncle Bertie said.

"Uncle Bertie, Mr. Pickles is not a nice man. He is inappropriate with the young maids."

"He always did have an eye for the ladies."

"It's a great deal more than that. His behaviour is quite deviant. But I don't want to talk about that now. Please tell me how long you will be here."

Charlie squeezed Anna's hands and said, "I am sorry, Sis, but we have to get the five o'clock train back to London. I have to join my regiment in France on Monday. They gave me special leave for your wedding. We'll stay in London tonight at Uncle Bertie's club and I cross the Channel tomorrow."

The bride and groom walked Charlie and Uncle Bertie to the Bexhill Station. The train rumbled alongside the platform, doors banged, the whistle blew, and steam bellowed as it chugged away. Alex and Anna stood on the platform waving until the caboose disappeared and the tracks fell silent.

Anna felt a lump in her throat but she couldn't be sad, not today. They spent all evening walking along the Promenade holding hands and watching the sun dance on the sea until it began its slow descent towards the horizon. Reaching The Sackville, they walked in through the normally off limits front door. George smiled and bowed, holding the door open. "Good evening, Mr. Walker. Good evening *Mrs. Walker*." Anna grinned from ear to ear as she heard her unfamiliar name. The big brass gate clanged shut on the lift. The pair, quite oblivious of their surroundings, rose to the third floor for their two-day honeymoon. Alex carried his bride over the threshold of Suite 312, kissed her tenderly and laid her on the bed.

Eleven

Alex at War

‿◌‿◌‿

Somewhat self-conscious, Anna took up her duties on Monday morning, having walked Alex to the omnibus station for the early trip back to Cooden Camp. Her lips were sore, her grin seemed permanent, and the thought of the past two nights' frolicking in bed with Alex made her cheeks glow. Her mother had implied that the goings on in the bedroom were a wife's duty. She had not alluded to the pleasures it might bring.

Anna looked forward to Alex's letters. He wrote to her every day; sometimes twice. Three weeks after the wedding, Alex wrote that the 12th Battalion Royal Sussex Regiment were to move to Detling Camp near Maidstone in Kent. Anna had prepared herself for the day Alex would be shipped overseas. It had not occurred to her that the battalion would be moved to another camp, too far away for the short visits they had enjoyed from Cooden. In fact, Alex's two-day leave prior to moving to Kent in July would be the last until after the completion of training.

The mounting chaos in the capital, fuelled by rumours of German Zeppelin airships raining bombs from the sky and precipitated by the first terrifying attack in late May, had frightened Londoners. The middle and upper classes escaped to their country homes, and those who didn't have country homes took refuge in small, seaside towns like Bexhill. Anna questioned the wisdom of Bexhill being a safe haven. The North Sea and parts of the English Channel were full of German planes above and U-boats below. Bexhill was not immune to the war. Anna witnessed several explosions from her bedroom window, albeit many miles to the north. She read enough in the newspapers to know that the U-boats were targeting ships delivering supplies and troops to France. The thought tied her in knots thinking of Charlie; she had not heard from him since her wedding.

The Times reported daily of the sinking of merchant ships with loss of life. The Royal Navy had no defense against the submarines and the Admiralty was at a loss. She wondered about Bill. Had he escaped the U-Boats? Lady Thornton had assured her that the Germans would not attack a ship destined for America because they were afraid of drawing America into the war. Anna tried to take comfort in this information but she couldn't understand why he had not written, and she wondered where he was and if he was well.

Kendrick Hotels Ltd. expressed their pleasure at the increase in revenue. Mr. Pickles took full credit, as if he personally had brought each guest to The Sackville. Anna and Mrs. Banks had their work cut out to keep the guests content. Operating a full hotel with a skeleton of inexperienced staff was a challenge, but for Anna it was a blessing as it filled the lonesome days and nights without Alex, and limited any morbid thoughts about Charlie and Bill.

By November 1915, a full year after Alex had enlisted, the battalion had moved several times and finally settled at Witley Camp, in Surrey. Alex's letters were not nearly as frequent and quite often very short. Sometimes he sent postcards, which had space for only a couple of paragraphs. The postcards were photos of the camp and the surrounding rolling green hills and farmland of Witley. She liked the postcards, imagining Alex in these surroundings made her feel closer to him, but the short, infrequent letters annoyed her. At times she felt neglected. Alex didn't seem to care about her anymore.

This had been a long day, the guests were demanding and the staff quarrelsome. The last straw, her friend and confidant, Sophie, had announced that she was leaving to train as a nurse. Anna felt abandoned, tired and worried. She stared into her tea and closed her eyes, desperately trying to feel Alex: hear his voice, smell his smell. She imagined running through the green hills of Surrey laughing, kissing and holding hands.

Mrs. Banks voice startled her. "Penny for your thoughts?"

"Oh, Sophie just told me her news and I will miss her very much. It made me think of how much I miss Alex. It's a long time since I had a decent long letter."

Mrs. Banks handed her an envelope. "Maybe this will cheer you up. It came in the afternoon post."

"Thank you, Mrs. Banks, thank you."

Anna looked at the envelope. "Mrs. A. Walker," she said aloud, clasping the letter to her chest. She could feel her heart beating; each beat pulled his love from the letter into her heart. She wanted to cry.

"It will not be read by itself, Anna." Mrs. Banks smiled and left Anna to read her letter.

> *My dearest, darling Anna,*
>
> *Thank you for your letters. I read them every day. I hope you liked the postcards. I know they are short, but I thought you would like to see where I live. I have the night off tonight. Most of the lads went into town but I wanted to write you a long letter while I can, and it's hard to find time when I am always so bloody tired.*
>
> *The training schedule is brutal; we are up at 5 am to start exercises. After breakfast we are on parade. By the time we finish at night we are exhausted, and after our tea we sometimes have night exercises and after that we just roll into bed, more tired than you can imagine.*
>
> *I had no idea it would be so hard. If it rains, we march in mud and water with heavy kit bags on our backs. The sergeant tells us to get used to it because the trenches at the front are stinking quagmires. He*

doesn't mince words. The grub is okay: beef and mutton stew and lots of lumpy mashed potatoes and cabbage, which as you know I don't like, but after a day's marching I'll eat anything and there is lots of it. I am keeping well, a few blisters on my feet, but we march with or without the blisters, so I get used to it.

The lads are friendly, most of them from Eastbourne. Some have joined us since Cooden and there are a lot of Canadians here. They have the American drawl, but they get quite uppity if you call them American. Apparently there is a difference. We usually get one day off a week and some evenings.

There's a gym where we can learn to box and some of the lads are quite good and the matches can be quite exciting. We go into Witley on Saturday nights to the pub. After a few pints it gets a bit noisy. Hamish, Private Duncan, is as bad with practical jokes as I am so we make a good team. We pulled a few pranks on the unsuspecting Canadians, but I can't tell you as you might be upset with me. But we are careful and the laughs ease the tension.

Some people have no sense of humour, but I can charm myself out of most situations. Some of the blokes have trouble holding their drink and the locals don't like that, but the publican is happy to take our money. I guess this sleepy little town feels as though they have been invaded with the influx of soldiers and there must be hundreds maybe even thousands of soldiers here, and more arrive every day.

Lorries roll through the town constantly, filling the streets with dust when it's dry and mud when it rains The engines are noisy and spew exhaust fumes into the clean, fresh country air. The shopkeepers are happy to see us and the economy is booming, but I think the noise bothers them and some soldiers are not very respectful, particularly if they have had a pint or two. The sergeant gets tough on some guys and a few find themselves in the brig.

I miss you, Anna darling. They keep us busy so the time goes by fast, but I miss Cooden. It was nice to be able to meet at the Fisherman's Nook or stroll down the Promenade. How's everyone at The Sackville?

Old Prickly-pickles behaving himself? You said the hotel was busy. I think that is good but a lot of work for you. How are you managing? Are you still typewriting for Lady Thornton?

They keep telling us the training is nearly over and that means I will get some leave before we ship overseas. I hoped it might be Christmas, but now they say it will be February. I am looking forward to being a real soldier. The training can be tedious. Three more battalions shipped out this week.

I miss you and wish I could feel you in my arms. I have your picture, the one Charlie took at our wedding, in my breast pocket close to my heart. Anna, you are so beautiful. Even the lads here tell me how lucky I am to have such a good-looking lass. Keep your letters coming and forgive me if I don't write as often.

Your loving husband,
Alex

Anna read the letter over and over. Now she understood why he hadn't written and she felt guilty for thinking he didn't care. Christmas would be lonely, but then the hotel bookings indicated little time for anything but work. She gave a chuckle, wondering what pranks Alex and Hamish had got up to. He sounded like the same old Alex, and although his pranks and teasing sometimes made her angry, today she loved him for being Alex.

Anna tried not to think about his next leave. It frightened her as it meant he would be heading into the war. He never talked of the dangers, perhaps he was trying to protect her, but Anna read the newspapers. She sensed the propaganda only covered up the truth. The casualties, both dead and wounded were high. She had a sense that the war was not going well.

She read newspapers and overheard conversations, only to find contradictions, even between experts. More confusion for Anna as she read about the rift in the Pankhurst family. She had idealized these strong women in her teens because they fought for women. Anna had followed their activities and supported the suffragette movement.

Now they were divided: Emmeline and daughter Christabel supported this terrible war, but the other daughter, Sylvia, continued to fight for women and exposed some truths about the war in her newspaper, *The Woman's Dreadnought*. Anna believed Sylvia's reports on the war more than she did official news reports.

Rudyard Kipling's son, John, had been reported wounded and missing, but Mr. Kipling continued to write and support the war, confident his son would return. Lady Thornton often spoke of the war with a tone of authority from a political point of view. It seemed the leaders could do no wrong. In her opinion the Germans would be defeated and everything would go back to normal.

Anna questioned her rationale as none of her family fought this war. Darcy had returned to America and would most likely stay there. Lady Thornton could not possibly understand how Anna worried about her brother fighting in France and Bill sailing in U-boat infested seas and Alex soon to be in the trenches. However, it had occurred to her that Lady Thornton had talked of her sons, plural, but she only ever spoke of Darcy. Perhaps there was another son fighting a war, but if so, why did she never speak of him?

The Southampton docks, full of soldiers, resembled a swarm of bees. Some meandered towards the ship, carrying their kit bags over one shoulder and an arm around a sweetheart. Others walked single file up the gangplank into the hive of the ship. The band played marching and uplifting tunes. Anna tried not to be sad. Alex looked handsome, his eyes bright with excitement. She shivered and Alex pulled her closer.

"Are you cold?"

"No. It's a beautiful day, unusually mild and sunny for the beginning of March. You should have a smooth crossing." Her words sounded empty but she could think of nothing else to say.

The ship gave a loud blast of steam.

"I think it is time for me to go," Alex said sweeping Anna into his arms and giving her a kiss that curled her toes. "Bye, my darling. I'll be home soon."

Anna felt the warm tears flow like a gentle summer rain, quiet and persistent. He kissed her again and wiped her cheeks. She watched him disappear into the ship and waved at nobody in particular as it sailed into the English Channel, destined for Le Havre and, after that, only the army knew where he would land.

She shivered again, feeling scared and remembered someone telling her that a shiver meant someone walked over a grave. Was it Alex's grave? That night, Anna sat up in bed, hugged her pillow and tried hard to feel Alex's warmth, but her cheek only felt the wetness of her tears. She prayed for his safety and speedy return.

All her tears spent, and for the sake of the guests and staff, Anna smiled and went about her daily duties with positive zeal. Today she had received a letter from Charlie, which lifted her spirits. The letter was postmarked Rugby; he must be at home she thought, ripping the letter open.

Dearest Anna,

Sorry I have not written but war is not conducive to letter writing, and as you know I am not diligent at the best of times. I have a few days' leave before being shipped to an undisclosed destination. I am excited about this posting as I was chosen to lead a small company of men on a secret mission, in fact I don't even know what the mission is or where it might take me. It reminds me of our childhood, of how we planned adventures together. I am explaining this as my whereabouts will be classified and I can neither receive nor send correspondence. Please do not worry, I am probably safer than most soldiers. I think Father is quite proud, but Mother is afraid for me.

How is Alex? Does he write? Letters take a long time from the front, but bad news travels fast, so try not to worry if you don't hear from him; it means he is well.

Our sister has settled into married life and our baby nephew, Robbie, is quite handsome as babies go. But I am sure Mother has written about her grandson. She survived the embarrassment of the premature birth quite well. Lou is lucky as her husband has been saved from the war. Providing food through farming is considered essential to the war effort at home.

Be happy for me, dearest sister, I will be safe and home soon. The war is coming to an end.

Your loving brother,
Charlie

Letters from Alex were short and infrequent. At first they came from France and he sounded excited about going to the front and fighting a war. The letter she received after they reached the front, somewhere near the River Somme, said little about the conditions except that the dugouts and trenches were wet and the food unimaginable—they ate only because they were so darned hungry.

Alex sounded downhearted; there wasn't even a hint of a joke. Anna had heard stories about the trenches: mud and putrid water, rats as big as dogs scurrying over dead bodies. *The Daily Mail* reported the enemy's barbaric use of poisoned gas.

Alex wasn't saying much, each letter the same as the last one, but Anna filled in the blanks. The last letter from Alex said the battalion was on the move and they were headed to somewhere in Belgium called Ypres. He sounded quite cheerful and told Anna he thought he was getting a promotion and that he was looking forward to the move. However, he complained about the weight of his kit bag and other paraphernalia attached to his uniform making it difficult to march; the latest addition was an ugly gas mask.

He wrote: *Equipment clatters and clangs in rhythm with left right, left right, sounding like an out of tune marching band composed of men that have landed from outer space, men with big glass eyes and a nose like an elephant's trunk. Just the sight of these marching ghouls will make the Germans retreat in terror.*

Anna laughed as a bit of the old Alex shone through with his description of the battalion marching.

Anna had been comforted by the return of Alex's sense of humour, but now many months had gone by without a letter and she worried, sensing dark shadows. All was not well.

A sad faced young boy in a post office uniform walked up to the reception counter. "Telegram for Mrs. Walker."

Anna stared at the buff coloured envelope, the words "On His Majesty's Service," printed across the top. The boy handed it to Anna, turned and left without waiting for a tip or reply. The only words she saw jabbed into her heart, "wounded and missing." She just stared at the word *missing* and remembered John Kipling was wounded and missing, and his father had said publicly that his son had only been wounded on the battlefield and had not perished. In the heat of battle, the War Office had lost track of him. Anna consoled herself that this must have happened to Alex.

A telegram for Anna caused a barrage of questions from The Sackville staff. She didn't want to talk about it. She brushed it off, saying that Alex had been wounded, omitting the missing part, and that she would know more soon. She had to believe he would soon be home.

Anna kept busy but on high alert for Alex's return, her heart missing a beat with every postman's visit, and relaxing as she sorted the mail into the cubbyholes and there was no official letter with her name on it. Almost two months later, a letter, smudged by April showers, appeared with Anna's name on it in a stranger's handwriting but not from the War Office and postmarked Brighton.

> *Dearest Anna,*
>
> *Yes, my darling, it is me, but I am not able to write at the moment and a kind lady volunteer is writing as I dictate, as you write for old Pickles. I am sorry that you must have been frantic with worry after receiving the War Office telegram. I was wounded in Passchendaele,*

as was Hamish, and we spent some time in the field hospital before they brought me here to Brighton. Hamish was not so lucky and he didn't make it.

My injuries are as a result of mustard gas. Although not as bad as some of the lads, it is not pleasant and terribly painful. The gas affected my eyes, but it is only temporary. The doctor is hopeful that my sight will come back. I expect to be here for some weeks. I am allowed visitors. Do you think you could come and visit? Brighton is not far from Bexhill. I have to go now as Mrs. Fox needs to help other soldiers.

I love you and miss you my darling. Please don't worry and write soon.

Affectionately,
Your loving husband,
Alex.

Anna walked on air. Alex was alive. She replied to the letter immediately, telling Alex she would be there on Saturday. She arranged for Miss Jenkins to work the whole day and Anna caught the early morning train to Brighton. She expected to be visiting a hospital, but when she arrived at the address, it was a large private house. She rang the bell and a maid answered the door.

"Excuse me but I think I have the wrong address. I am looking for Lieutenant Walker."

"You have the right address, Miss. Lady Ursula has allowed part of her home to be used as a convalescent home for the soldiers. When they are well enough to leave the hospital they are sent here to convalesce. Please come this way."

Anna followed the maid who directed her into a large wood-panelled room with hospital beds set in rows only a couple of feet apart. Ashen-faced young men lay motionless, eyes staring ahead. Others dressed in uniforms sat on the edges of their beds. Some leaned on crutches that supported them where limbs were missing, white bandages wrapped around mummified heads and burnt faces, the glow of a cigarette protruding from unseen lips. An occasional cry of agony punctuated the muffled conversations. Cigarette smoke hung heavy around the beds as it failed to ease the underlying anxiety of war, injury and loss. Anna's eyes were riveted to the scene. Overcome by sorrow, she stopped, afraid to look for Alex. A cheerful nurse came to greet her and gently took her elbow. "Is this your first time here?"

"Yes. I am Mrs. Walker, here to see Alex Walker."

"Lieutenant Walker is doing well but you may find his appearance changed. The burns are getting better, but some are painful. He will be so pleased to see you. He talks about you all the time."

She led Anna into a smaller, brighter room, three walls housed floor-to-ceiling bookshelves still full of books, and the fourth wall had large windows that opened onto a garden. The flowerbeds were mostly dormant, but Anna spotted a clump of white snowdrops nodding their heads, promising spring. There were only six beds in this room.

The nurse said, "Our special patients are placed in here. It is quieter and they can get more rest."

Anna stood at the end of his bed, her eyes wide with horror. Alex's eyes were swollen almost shut, only a slight slit near his bottom eyelid. His face was drawn and thin; scaling yellow skin peeled off his cheeks, his red curls frizzy. His hands, yellow and brown and covered with sores, lay at the side of his stick-like body. Anna gasped, the nurse gently placed a hand on her forearm and whispered, "It looks worse than it is; he's going to be well again soon."

The nurse went to the side of the bed. "You have a visitor. I'll see if I can find some tea."

Anna took a deep breath and sat on the chair close to the bed. "Alex, it's me, Anna."

Alex's lips smiled and in a weak whisper he said, "Anna, your voice is music to my ears. How I missed you. I love you." She could hardly hear him and pulled the chair up closer. "Don't be scared, my vision is getting better. I can see a little bit—I can see your beautiful face and those bouncy curls, just as I remembered." He sighed and took a slow breath. "My throat is sore so I have to whisper. Why don't you do the talking?"

The nurse brought tea and helped Alex sit up. Anna talked about The Sackville until he fell asleep. She sat with her hand on his arm, as his hands were too painful to touch, and she watched him sleep. The doctor explained that he had been exposed to mustard gas, which had caused painful blisters. The healing process took time, but he would heal. They said his sight and his voice would return slowly but it would be several weeks before he would be fit for active duty. Anna felt terror in her heart at the thought of Alex going back to the war.

Alex made a remarkable recovery, and two months later he was discharged from Lady Ursula's convalescent hospital. After a couple of days' leave he was sent back to Kent for training before being sent to once again fight the Germans in France. It was a sad parting. Alex seemed confident the war would soon be over, but Anna was terrified he would be wounded again, or even worse, killed.

Twelve

Mr. Pickles' Revenge

While Alex battled the Germans, Anna fought her own battles at The Sackville. The occupancy rate had begun to decline and bookings for the summer of 1918 were slow. Mr. Pickles would not acknowledge the decline and continued to revel in the success of past years, which had boosted his ego completely out of proportion. Anna, privy to the accounts and correspondence from Mr. Kendrick, who she had suspected did not like Mr. Pickles, detected a note of concern regarding his performance.

Between Mr. Pickles' insecurities and Chef Louis' bad temper, there were always waiters threatening to leave or kitchen maids in tears. The final straw was when Mr. Pickles accused the maître d', Mr. Filmore, of mismanaging the dining room. Having spent most of his working life running dining rooms in some of the best hotels in London, he was understandably offended and threatened to return to London.

Furious with this latest maître d' outrageous attack on the staff, Anna flew into Mr. Pickles' office, slammed the door behind her and demanded he apologize to Mr. Filmore.

"Mrs. Walker, you forget yourself. The last I heard, I am head of this hotel. It is *you* I should dismiss for insubordination."

Anna's anger calmed down. She had acted impulsively and she knew better than to challenge Mr. Pickles' authority. She had become quite apt at resolving issues without confrontation. But the thought of a chaotic dining room and complaining guests, which Mr. Filmore had so eloquently put an end to, had made her panic, and now she was feeling a different kind of panic. She had not only challenged Mr. Pickles' authority, but her foolishness had placed her alone and at his mercy. She glanced over her shoulder towards the closed office door—panic pounded in her temples.

Afraid she might scream, she held her breath and then, as slowly and as calmly as she could, she said, "Forgive me, Mr. Pickles. I spoke in haste. It will be quite difficult to replace such an experienced maître d'. The guests are impressed when they learn he managed the dining room at *The Savoy* in London; indeed, many guests frequented The Savoy and remember his excellent service."

"Hum... The Savoy you say..." Mr. Pickles said no more, but Anna knew that she had appealed to his ego and had won. Anna turned to leave, her eyes on the closed door that seemed to be miles away, under her breath she whispered, "Dear God, please let me escape."

"Mrs. Walker! There is still the matter of your insubordination. What shall we do about that?" His tone gripped Anna with fear. She slowly turned to face him, taking a slow step backwards. His ferret eyes stalked her, the tip of his tongue licked his grinning lips with minacious hunger. "Now you must be missing your husband's night time comfort. You enjoy it, don't you?"

She turned and leapt for the door but Mr. Pickles jumped in front of her, letting out a wicked cackle. Her heart thumped out of her chest, she tried to speak with authority but she could only squeak, "Mr. Pickles, this is inappropriate."

"Anna, my dear," he said softly, stroking her hair. She pulled away and slapped his face. He staggered back, cackled again and grabbed her arm. Red blotches erupted four and five at a time.

"Ah! So innocent little Anna likes it rough. I'll show you rough." She could feel his thumbs on the top of her arms, digging into her flesh as he shoved her hard against the bookcase. He splayed his legs, leaned back and with knees bent he thrust his pelvis into her, pinning her against the bookcase. Releasing his grip on her arm, he pulled at her blouse until the buttons ricocheted across the room.

Terrified, Anna tried to move. The bookshelves dug into her back, but she felt no pain. To her horror, she felt his fingers groping to unbutton his trousers and one knee shoved briefly between her legs, forcing them to part. His face repulsed her, she dropped her stare, his white linen was now visible and gradually his organ protruded. He fumbled under her skirt. She tried to scream and he let go of her skirt and smacked his hand over her mouth. All the time thrusting, each thrust pressed the wooden shelves into her back.

The books began to fall off the shelves. He didn't seem to notice; his eyes were glazed, his rapid, hot putrid breath blowing in her face. His hand frantically grabbed at her skirt until he managed to pull it above her waist, his body thrusting uncontrollably. Frustrated to find a petticoat, he began fumbling again.

Books were flying and one hit Anna above her eye. She screamed at the top of her lungs, and with all her strength she lifted her knee and lunged upwards as hard as she could. He fell to the floor, writhing in pain. Anna ran to the baize door just as George came through the office door from the lobby.

"Get out!" Mr. Pickles yelled.

Anna ran upstairs to her room; relieved that no one had seen her. Her back hurt and she felt blood trickle down her face and drip on her torn blouse. Too angry to cry, Anna vowed she would have him locked-up. She felt dirty, used and violated. Pulling off her torn blouse, she stepped out of her skirt and threw them both on the floor kicking them under her bed. Her hands trembled as she dabbed the cut with her handkerchief. Her head spun and she sat on the bed as her legs gave way, eyeing the washbasin, thinking she might be sick.

There was a knock on her door. "Anna, it's Mrs. Banks, can I come in, please?" Without waiting for an answer, Mrs. Banks opened the door and sat beside Anna. "What did he do to you?"

Anna's stomach retched as she repeated what had happened. Mrs. Banks took a wet cloth from the washstand and gently wiped the blood from her face and held it on the cut to stop the bleeding. The coolness felt soothing. Anna took some deep breaths and the retching settled, but her head hurt.

"How did you know?"

"George heard you scream and sent Miss Jenkins to find me, while he went into Mr. Pickles' office. He saw you leave and found Mr. Pickles with his trousers round his ankles lying in a pile of books, groaning."

The image of arrogant Mr. Pickles in such a preposterous position brought a weak smile to Mrs. Banks' face. Anna laughed hysterically, the hysteria released uncontrollable sobs and the tears flowed. Mrs. Banks held her tight and gently rocked her until the tears subsided.

"Anna that is a deep cut. I think you should see the doctor and take the rest of the day off."

"I can't. Lady Thornton is expecting me. I am feeling well enough now and typewriting her correspondence isn't taxing. I would rather keep busy."

"I know you are strong, Anna, but sometimes you're too strong for your own good. You need rest."

Anna took a clean blouse and skirt from the cupboard. "I must keep busy. I don't want to be alone," she said as her trembling fingers tried to button up her blouse.

Mrs. Banks sighed. "But first let me dress that cut before you get blood on your clean blouse."

After a cup of tea and before attending to Lady Thornton, Anna forced herself to stop shaking and firmly planted one foot in front of the other so she could walk into the dining room to persuade Mr. Filmore not to leave his position at The Sackville. Not surprisingly, Mr. Pickles had left for the day. She wrote a note for him, which said that Mr. Filmore had reconsidered and would not be leaving.

Anna's head began to spin and she tasted bile as she reached the threshold of his office. Placing the note on his desk she grabbed the corner, terrified she was going faint. Holding her breath, she willed her head to stop spinning so that she could retreat from this evil office.

Anna was too shaken to fear Mr. Pickles' reprimand for reinstating Mr. Filmore but she feared his vengeance. She was aware that he could not tolerate humiliation, and she had humiliated him in front of staff.

Standing at the door of Suite 305, Anna grabbed the doorframe, her head felt as if it was full of cotton. Miss Barclay opened the door and gasped, seeing the black-purple bruise and blood soaked dressing covering an egg shaped swelling on her forehead. Anna couldn't remember knocking on the door and jumped back when the door opened causing her to lose her balance. Miss Barclay grabbed her arm to stop her from falling.

Steadying herself she smiled. "It's all right Miss. Barclay, I stumbled over an electrical cord near the bookcase in Mr. Pickles...." Anna stopped, shocked at the terror of just saying his name. She coughed. "And some books fell off the shelf, as you can see a particularly large book landed on me. I'm just clumsy."

Lady Thornton did not believe Anna's story and immediately called Mrs. Banks, instructing her to call Dr. Gregory, the hotel's physician. Upon his arrival, he was shown into Mrs. Banks' sitting room where he examined the lesion on Anna's forehead.

"It is a deep cut. I will need to suture it."

Dr. Gregory distracted Anna with conversation. "The book must have fallen with great force. Mrs. Walker, are you sure it was a book? Is there something you are not telling me?"

Anna swallowed hard. Dr. Gregory had thick grey hair and kind empathetic eyes with a reassuring smile. He reminded her of Papa, and she thought she could confide in him.

"I can assure you it was a book, Dr. Gregory, but there is more. If I explain the circumstances can I trust you will not repeat it to anyone?"

"Mrs. Walker, I am bound by doctor-patient confidentiality. Rest assured I could say nothing without your permission."

Anna retold the events of the day, breaking down at times and having difficulty explaining the more intimate details. The doctor listened attentively without interrupting her, although at times Anna detected shock and disgust on his face. When she had finished, he asked if this had happened before. She continued and told him about the first time it had happened and her suspicions about other maids, including Amy and the secrecy around Edith. At the mention of Edith, Dr. Gregory did interrupt and he looked sad. "I remember Edith, and I always suspected some wrong doing, but she was too frightened to say."

"Did he hurt you anywhere else?"

"My arm hurts where he grabbed me and my back is sore from the bookcase, but that's all."

"I would like to examine you."

"Doctor, he didn't... you know... my petticoat saved me." Anna said, feeling her cheeks redden.

Dr. Gregory smiled, "That's alright, but I would like to take a look at your back. Would you be more comfortable if I asked Mrs. Banks to come in?"

"Thank you, yes."

Mrs. Banks helped Anna take off her blouse. She flinched when Dr. Gregory touched her skin. It was only then that she saw a large bruise on her chest where he had ripped her blouse and her arm shone with four finger-sized bruises. The evil of this violent man terrified her. She began shaking and the room spun like a spinning top. Dr. Gregory's words were slow and hollow as he called Mrs. Banks. When she came to, Mrs. Banks had a cold cloth on her head and in spite of the large blanket that wrapped her in a cocoon, she couldn't stop shivering. Dr. Gregory was holding her wrist while studying his gold watch.

He glanced at Anna. "Mrs. Walker, you have had a great shock and I am ordering complete bed rest for at least two days. Take these powders in warm milk three times a day; they will help you stay calm. Mrs. Banks, keep her warm and she is to have a light diet until her digestives have settled."

Anna didn't argue. She felt most unwell, her head throbbed and she felt dizzy. She wanted to get into her bed.

It was three days before Dr. Gregory would allow Anna to get out of bed and another day before she returned to her duties. He wanted to report Mr. Pickles to the authorities, but Anna refused. She told Dr. Gregory the rumours and talk about Anna's accident among staff would be enough to make Prickly-Pickles behave himself for a while.

She didn't truly believe her own words. Pushing her fears to one side, she reassured Dr. Gregory that she did intend to report him, but not now, as it would put her position and Mrs. Banks' in jeopardy. When the time came, she would call upon him to disclose her injuries and in the meantime she and Mrs. Banks would be diligent about protecting the young maids.

Miss Jenkins had taken Anna's place while she recuperated from her ordeal. A look of unmistakable relief filled Miss Jenkins' face when Anna appeared, ready for work.

"I am pleased you are feeling better, Mrs. Walker. It has been quite a challenge keeping up with your work."

"Is Mr. Pickles in yet?" Anna dreaded facing him. She felt her stomach tighten and just saying his name prompted her skin to crawl. "Has…" she stopped to steady her voice, "has he been difficult, Miss Jenkins?"

"He spends most of his time in the office, talking to himself, pretending he is on the telephone. When he gives dictation, he paces up and down the office or around his desk. He is always in a bad mood and loses his temper over nothing and then forgets what has happened. I think he is losing his mind." Miss Jenkins leaned over and touched Anna's arm. "I'm sorry," she added. Anna struggled to keep her composure, forcing her lips to smile. "Miss Jenkins, when he asks me to take dictation do you mind sitting as close to the office door as possible?"

Standing at the reception counter, Anna's eyes jumped from one person to the next and her voice trembled when talking to guests. She couldn't remember ever being so frightened, but she knew she had to face him and learn to work with him.

Mr. Pickles arrived promptly at eight. Anna couldn't breathe as he nodded and walked into his office. The day went by as though nothing had happened, except he was overly formal. He did seem agitated and paced while he dictated correspondence. Anna decided that the only way to cope was to keep her distance and return the formality.

The war escalated. The Germans captured more French territory and *The Times* reported they were getting dangerously close to Paris. Reports of Spanish flu spreading through the trenches scared Anna. She worried for Alex's safety but his letters were cheerful and full of optimism.

He wrote about the American troops arriving by the thousands, big burly lads, with large-brimmed hats and the deepest drawl he had ever heard, and they were afraid of nothing. The last line was more than Anna could hope for and she read it many times. *The war has changed in favour of Britain. It will not be long before I'm home.*

But the war raged on for two more months until finally the Armistice was signed on November 11, 1918. As soon as the news reached The Sackville, Mr. Pickles and Mrs. Banks called all the staff together to make the joyful announcement. The cheering and clapping was a sharp contrast to the sadness of the only other gathering of this nature, in August 1914. The armistice precipitated change. Many guests returned to their homes. Lady Thornton decided to open her London house and even staff decided to move on, including Mr. Filmore, who gave a week's notice, taking his chances in London rather than enduring any more unreasonable outbursts from Mr. Pickles or Chef Louis.

The day Mr. Filmore departed for London, Alex walked into The Sackville. Anna couldn't believe her eyes as she feasted on the tall, handsome, redheaded Alex, albeit tired, weary and somewhat thinner. But that didn't matter. She was back in his arms. That same day she received word that Charlie had arrived in Rugby, tired but unharmed.

Panic stricken at the thought of having no maître d', Mr. Pickles offered Alex the position, a welcome promotion for Alex. The Sackville's staff accommodation did not include married quarters, so under the circumstances, Mrs. Banks gave Anna permission to live out and Mr. Pickles had no choice but to allow Alex the same privilege.

The married couple settled on two ground-floor rooms. There was a small, cozy parlour, with a round table, two ladder-back chairs and two old easy-chairs with faded floral cushions. The threadbare carpet was a dirty brown with the pattern long gone, but a large bay window made the room bright and cheerful—a palace to Anna and Alex.

The bedroom contained a double bed, a wardrobe and a dressing table. Anna giggled as she walked sideways around the bed to get to the wardrobe. The rent was cheap and it was a five-minute walk to The Sackville. Mrs. Bromley, the landlady, a kindly, robust woman, also provided meals for her lodgers. Alex and Anna declined most of the meals as they usually ate at the hotel. Alex moved in that day, but Anna waited until Saturday. They spent the next few days packing their belongings; Alex's civilian clothes had been stored in Anna's cupboard. It took several trips to move everything.

Finally, on Saturday afternoon, Anna took one last look around the attic bedroom she once shared with Sophie, smiling at the memories. Five years ago Sophie had almost thrown her out, but ultimately they became close friends. She took one last look at the dancing stars sparkling on the waves and sighed. She would miss the view and she thought how she had grown since Bill called her "papa's little girl". The quickening pace of her heart surprised her as she wished Bill could be part of her new life. Wondering if he had survived the war, she closed the door.

A honeymoon weekend ensued. Although married three years, they could count on one hand the number of nights spent together. Anna was ecstatic with happiness and content that their life together would start tonight at Mrs. Bromley's.

Watching Alex undress, Anna noticed the scars from the mustard gas and his rippled ribs. So happy to have him safely home, she hadn't seen the torture in his once bright eyes or the physical frailty in his once strong body. War had altered him.

"How are you feeling?" Anna asked as she snuggled beside him. He put his arm around her. "I am battle weary, tired and happy. You can't imagine how many nights I fell asleep, pretending you were in my arms, and here we are together again." He kissed her on the forehead. "What's that?" His fingers traced the scar on her forehead.

Anna stiffened, a memory long hidden surfaced. Almost overcome with panic, she quickly willed the memory to go away.

Alex pulled her closer. "Anna, what's wrong?" Hearing the tenderness in Alex's voice, she relaxed. She didn't want to lie, but she didn't want to tell the truth and spoil the night. She decided on a half-truth. Lady Thornton hadn't believed her but hopefully Alex would and anyway she did intend to tell him, but not tonight.

"I tripped on the electrical cord and fell against the book case in Mr. Pickles' office. Several books fell off the shelf and the corner of one very large volume fell on my head, cutting my forehead. Mrs. Banks called Dr. Gregory, who stitched the cut. He said that the scar would lessen in time."

"Why didn't you tell me?"

"You were in France and it was just a cut and not worth worrying you." Much to Anna's relief, he said no more.

Married life suited Anna; she glowed. Mr. Pickles smirked at her. Anna surmised the smirks were to remind her that he was waiting for his chance but, with Alex home, he dared not say a word. Her confidence returned, she excelled at her position and they were saving money.

Alex told her every night how he liked being married, having their own place to escape to, which made old Prickly-Pickles bearable. He did admit to being unsettled at times and his violent nightmares worried and alarmed Anna, but Alex said they would pass with time.

She wanted to believe him but she had noticed how jumpy he was during the day; the slightest bang of a piece of cutlery falling on the floor and Alex would cower and looked dazed for a second or two. Afraid to admit that something was wrong, Anna consoled herself that it was early days. It was only six weeks since he had left the battlefield. Time would heal, she thought, dismissing her concerns. The restlessness she determined was nothing more than boredom, which would be rectified in time when they began planning their travels to far-off lands.

During the early months of 1919, the hotel was quiet. January to Easter bookings were normally the lowest of the year and not a cause for concern. Mr. Pickles seemed agitated and the correspondence with Kendrick Hotels Ltd indicated concern, not about occupancy but excessive expenditure.

Odd, Anna thought, as expenditure should have been low. Staff wages were low and Chef Louis had been forced to cut expenses through rationing.

Curious, while waiting for Mr. Pickles, Anna browsed through Mr. Kendrick's letters, several had been hidden and she found them in odd places. The accountant had concerns about some substantial sums of money that had been spent on new furnishings. What new furnishings? Anna thought. There was a request for receipts for some vague expenditure marked household goods.

Anna was not an accountant, but she did know something about bookkeeping and either someone had made a big mistake or someone was stealing. She quickly put the letters back and opened her Pitman notebook.

Mr. Pickles' uncharacteristically jaunty stride and his curled, almost grinning lips unnerved Anna. She doubted he would risk attacking her with Alex across the lobby in the dining room. She frowned, wondering what he was up to and she didn't have to wait long for the answer.

Mr. Lytton walked into the office. "Mr. Lytton, it is nice to see you. I hope you are well?" Anna smiled, hiding the shock she felt at his appearance. His once round, jocular face was thin with sunken eyes, his body half the size she remembered as he leaned heavily on a cane. His hand trembled when he reached out to shake her hand.

"Mr. Lytton will be resuming his duties as front desk clerk starting on Monday morning. Mrs. Walker. You will assist except when you are working with me. Your salary will be adjusted accordingly but, as you are married, your husband can take care of you now." Mr. Pickles' words hit

Anna hard. He had cleverly demoted her and there was nothing she could do. The worst part was his look of satisfaction and she wondered how long it would be before he dismissed her altogether.

Anna ranted to Alex that night. Her feelings were divided as she liked Mr. Lytton and was happy to see him back, but Mr. Pickles angered her. He had deliberately demoted her and Mr. Lytton didn't look well enough to work. The part that angered her the most was the reduction in salary, which meant that she and Alex would have to work a lot longer at The Sackville before they could save enough money to leave.

Mr. Lytton struggled with the work, his leg painful from the gashes and shrapnel—Anna covered for him all the time. Mr. Pickles gloated over her demotion but he was aware that Mr. Lytton's injuries prevented him from doing his job properly. He still needed Anna.

Alex and James Lytton became friends. They talked about the war; the friendship was good for both of them. Alex would not talk to Anna about his bad dreams. He told Anna they were too horrible but he would talk to James.

Anna invited James to join them in their little parlour on Saturday evenings. Mrs. Bromley made them a late dinner, and after a pleasant home cooked meal, they sat by the fire; Alex and James enjoying a glass of Scotch whiskey, Anna sipping tea.

"James, I know you have some knowledge of accounting. I would like your opinion. There's something strange going on at The Sackville." Anna confided the strange accounting comments from Kendrick Hotels.

"I too thought something was strange. In the past, as part of my duties, I have been responsible for entering the guest payments into the books. Mr. Pickles said that you had taken over that task."

"No, I have nothing to do with the books. It is the correspondence from Mr. Kendrick that caused me to be concerned."

"I think Mr. Pickles is defrauding the company. If he is claiming expenses for furniture that we don't have, he is either taking the money or furnishing his own home. The vague expenses are most likely small amounts he is taking out of the safe. These are often difficult to trace." James laughed, "Old Prickly-Pickles may have been too clever. I must say I would be delighted to see him fired for fraud. No wonder he is getting nervous. This explains his mood swings and agitation."

"What should I do?"

"Anna, stay away from it. Embezzlers are nearly always discovered. It is possible to cover up the discrepancies for a while, but eventually the auditors will find it. It sounds to me as though Kendrick Hotels are already suspicious. Let them do their work."

"Alex also told me not to get involved. I will stay quiet."

Alex poured them another scotch. "I would like to see that pompous, arrogant bastard fighting at the Somme. The lads would make mincemeat of him. That would teach him a lesson or two." They laughed. It was good to see a spark of the old jovial James and she hadn't seen Alex so relaxed in months.

"I think I will take my book and retire. It has been a long week and I will leave you two to talk war stories."

Thirteen

Anna Plans Her Vendetta

Mr. Pickles arrived before eight o'clock on Monday morning in a foul mood. He ordered Mrs. Banks to have the maids move the lounge furniture to storage. She objected but had no other choice. At ten o'clock a lorry pulled up and delivered new chairs, sofas and tables to the guest lounge. He then informed Anna that, as Mr. Kendrick had graciously agreed to visit The Sackville, she would not be needed in the office today. He informed Chef Louis that they would be taking luncheon in the dining room at thirteen hundred hours. Outraged at such short notice, Chef Louis argued with Mr. Pickles. The two men, well matched, raged and threw insults at each other.

Mr. Kendrick, a tall, distinguished-looking gentleman in a cutaway morning coat and striped trousers, arrived by automobile at noon, accompanied by another gentleman carrying a large leather case. After a curt good afternoon to Anna and James, they went directly into Mr. Pickles' office. The conversation sounded angry, raised voices escalated, punctuated by slaps on the desk. At precisely one o'clock, Mr. Pickles, covered in red blotches, with an expression of a scolded child, led Mr. Kendrick into the dining room, leaving the other gentleman studying the books.

After they had eaten, Mr. Kendrick toured the hotel. The nervous staff found him to be kind and genuinely interested in their work, even asking after their families. He stopped at the front desk and Anna moved from behind the counter to shake his hand.

"Mrs. Walker, I am impressed with your talents and abilities to make our guests comfortable. You should be praised for your work here during the war. I believe it was your efforts that filled The Sackville at times when other hotels were experiencing difficulty." He turned to address Mr. Pickles, who was standing behind Anna. "You are a lucky man to have such an excellent employee, Mr. Pickles."

Anna could not see Mr. Pickles' face but she felt his loathing penetrate her back and he did not acknowledge the comment.

Anna replied, "Thank you Mr. Kendrick, but many other staff members worked as hard. I could not have done it alone."

"Perhaps, but I am grateful to you all the same."

Anna looked at him with complete surprise.

"I see you are surprised. You have friends in high places. Sir Walter Rhode wrote to me, complimenting me on my staff, naming you in particular. Mr. Pickles did not inform you of my letter, thanking you for your exceptional service to our customers?" He turned, giving Mr. Pickles a puzzled look. "I believe women have a lot to offer business. My dear wife works with me in my office and she is a close friend of Lady Thornton who also speaks very highly of you."

Anna could feel her cheeks flush. "It's a pleasure typewriting for Lady Thornton. She has always been kind to me. I believe she will be staying with us for Easter."

Mr. Kendrick concluded the visit with a quieter meeting in Mr. Pickles' office. After the party drove off to London, Mr. Pickles had a look of thunder and glared at Anna; anger erupting his red blotches. She smiled at him, knowing he could do nothing. Now she had the tools to keep his ardour at bay, and when the time came, she believed she would have Mr. Kendrick's support to expose him.

She had not told Lady Thornton of Mr. Pickles' attacks on her, although she may have suspected, especially after the bookcase incident. Anna intended to tell her the full story at Easter, knowing it would be repeated to Mrs. Kendrick.

The next day, James and Anna watched the lorry collect the new furniture and the old furniture was reinstated. No explanation was given. In high spirits, Mr. Pickles continued as usual, which left James and Anna confused and wondering how Prickly-Pickles had explained the discrepancies.

Miss Barclay wrote to Anna to say that Lady Thornton was not well and the doctor had advised her not to travel. They would have to cancel their Easter visit but to book her Suite 305 for the summer. Anna's disclosure of Mr. Pickles' deviant behaviour would have to wait until June.

Two weeks later she received another letter from Miss Barclay to say Lady Thornton had died suddenly of a heart condition. Anna stood at the front desk unable to speak, overcome with grief.

"Mrs. Walker, what is it?" asked a worried looking Mr. Lytton.

"It's Lady Thornton. She passed away of a heart condition."

The death of Lady Thornton affected Anna deeply. She had lost a friend and it surprised her how sad, even lonely, she felt. She sensed her death was bringing The Sackville part of her life to a close. Her mind wandered to her first day on platform four, the big hat with preying tentacles, the squawking parrot and yapping Princess. Lady Thornton had taught her many things, and now she was gone.

Alex's nightmares were getting worse. He often cried out for Hamish and sometimes Meg. Some nights Anna would find him in the parlour, afraid to sleep. She suggested he consult Dr. Gregory. He diagnosed shell shock, a not uncommon illness suffered by soldiers returning from war; time was the healer and the nightmares would lessen in time, or so he said. Anna had her doubts. The war had taken something from Alex—the fun had been driven out of him. He never teased or played jokes anymore. Anna longed for the day to hear him laugh again, and she hoped that would come back with time too.

Anna found herself worrying about many things these days. She had more time on her hands as the hotel was quiet. She counted the summer bookings and was discouraged by the diminishing numbers: far less than last year. She was worried.

Mr. Kendrick's praise of Anna had not improved Mr. Pickles' disposition towards her and whatever explanation he had given Kendrick Hotels Ltd. about accounting discrepancies, they had put an end to any investigation. Anna did not trust this vengeful man; she had thwarted his advances and circumstances prevented him from trying again, but she saw the repulsive desire in his wicked face. Afraid for her position, she had no false illusions. This evil man would do whatever it took to discredit her reputation.

James' health had improved and he fulfilled his duties without difficulty. With bookings down, Anna surmised some staff would have to go. The last thing she wanted was to stay at home in two rented rooms. Alex had promised her travel and adventure, but of late he had been talking about family, and she was not ready. A homely life flashed before her; visions of cooking, laundry, crying babies and sipping tea with shallow conversation bound her into a prison of despair.

"There you are. I've been looking all over for you," Alex stepped into the staff dining room and put his arm around her. "Why so sad?"

"I came down for some tea. Alex, what is going to become of us? The hotel bookings are very slow and I am sure Mr. Pickles will try to dismiss me, and maybe even you. Mr. Kendrick can't run a hotel without guests."

Alex kissed her forehead. "We'll move on, find work somewhere else. Bill and I always planned to take our hotel skills and travel. You and I can do that."

The brief mention of Bill's name gave her heart a jolt and reminded Anna that there had been no word from Bill, not even a postcard, in years.

"Alex, what do you think happened to Bill? Do you think he survived the war?"

"Bill is one of those people who survives everything. I doubt he will ever forgive me for stealing you away from him. I don't expect our paths will ever cross again."

Anna found hope in Alex's words that Bill was a survivor, but she had mixed emotions about never seeing him again.

"Alex, you are a dreamer. If The Sackville bookings are slow, believe me, the other hotels are even worse. You know I want to travel but we don't have enough money."

"I know what will cheer you up, a walk along the Promenade followed by a big plate of steaming mussels at The Fisherman's Nook."

Anna took Alex's hand and they strolled along the beach. The gentle whoosh of the breaking waves, followed by the tinkling pebbles as the water receded back into the sea, soothed Anna's anxiety. The sun felt warm for May, the seagulls wheeled through the blue sky, some reaching for the white puffy clouds. They sat on the breakwater holding hands.

"Alex, what do you want out of life?"

"I am so happy to be alive that I haven't really thought about it. There is so much death and pain in war it gives one a warped perspective on life. I just want to be with you. I would like a house and family. And you, dearest Anna, what do you want out of life?"

"A house and family sounds nice," she hesitated, "but I want to travel first. I grew up dreaming of faraway places. Charlie and I listened to Uncle Bertie's stories. Do you remember promising me we could have both?"

"I do, and you shall have both. For, as long as I am with you, Anna, nothing else matters. Come, let's go and see what Nosey has on the menu today."

Alex ordered drinks. Sitting quietly at a corner table, Anna sipped on her sherry and Alex took big, satisfying swigs of ale. Nosey came over with two big plates of steaming mussels and their nostrils filled with the aroma of hot, fresh out of the oven bread as it was placed in the centre of their table. The fresh air had given them an appetite and the ale loosened Alex's tongue. And for the first time since coming home, Alex talked about the war.

"I know you wonder why I don't talk about the war. Anna, the conditions were unimaginable. We went to the front, proud and prepared to fight an enemy but found ourselves like rats in warrens, no better than the rats that scurried around us. The thought of the stench makes me heave, the sounds sometimes deafening as the gunfire bombarded us and other times the silence played tricks in our heads. We sheltered in dugouts, drank tea that looked and tasted worse than dishwater and yet, we were grateful for the comfort that the hot liquid gave us. We watched our friends get blown up, bodies missing limbs. If they were still alive, they writhed in agony after a shell had found its mark." Alex stopped, struggling to fight back tears.

Anna gulped. She had read of the battle scenes, but to hear Alex made it real. She held his hand, small comfort for what he was experiencing. "Alex, I am sorry, those are horrible memories. But you are home now, is there anything I can do to help?"

"Dearest Anna, I wish there was a way to help, but Dr. Gregory says the memories will fade in time. So when I scream out at night just hold me."

"That is easy to do." Anna smiled and squeezed his hand. "Can you tell me what happened to Hamish? You scream his name in your nightmares."

Alex got up from the table. "Let me walk you home, Mrs. Walker. I like the sound of that." The breeze felt cool after the heat of the pub.

"Hamish was a good man. He kept us laughing in the hardest of times and it might have been his practical jokes that got him killed, and I encouraged him. It happened the day of the gas attack."

"Alex, you can't blame yourself," Anna said as Alex unlatched the door.

"If I hadn't been so stupid, Hamish would still be alive. I killed him..."

"I don't believe you." They sat in silence, Anna fighting tears and Alex quietly weeping.

She put her arms around him and led him to the bedroom. They lay in each other's arms. Anna waited for him to continue. Seeing the pain in his eyes, she wanted to stop him but she also needed to know the truth. She hoped that talking about it would ease his pain.

"It was one of those silent times," Alex stopped, frowned and hesitated. "The kind of silence that fills you with apprehension and anxiety. Hamish and I had a reputation of cheering up the lads and breaking the tension. Hamish was fooling around with his gas mask. He hung it over his rifle and edged it to the top of the trench wall, the lads began laughing and we didn't hear the first warning bell. The lookout would tap on an empty shell casing, which sounded like a bell, the signal to put on our gas masks. Hamish's mask stuck on his rifle and by the time he had it on it was too late. That's why his burns were worse than mine and why I recovered and he died."

Anna kissed him and rocked him as though he were a child. "Sh, sh... my darling, shush."

"I will never be a prankster again. It is my foolishness that has killed two people; my sister Meg, because I took her to a parade in the pouring rain and she caught a chill and died, and now Hamish. Sometimes my nightmares get mixed up. Meg has a mask on and Hamish is parading in the rain."

"Alex, you could not have known Meg would catch a chill. She was a healthy young woman and Hamish knew well enough to get his mask on. You are not responsible and you have to stop blaming yourself."

That evening impacted their lives significantly. Alex's nightmares decreased and Anna felt closer to him than ever before. After that one night, he rarely spoke of the Western Front conditions but, he frequently spoke of the good-natured Canadians and the laid-back heavyset Australians who fought beside them. Their stories, Alex explained, occupied many long hours in the grey, muddy, stinking trenches.

"We went on a mindful journey across vast lands that took weeks or months to travel; lakes as big as oceans, frozen seas in Northern Canada or hot deserts in Australia's Outback, contrasted by the lush green rain forests or the colourful coral reefs in a pool of turquoise ocean. These beautiful sights filled our imaginations, allowing us to escape the squalor that surrounded us."

Prompted by Alex's stories, Anna saw her chance of travel. She assured him the stories were true, at least about Canada, as Uncle Bertie had described the same things, but she knew nothing of Australia. They had £150 saved. Alex said that was enough for a passage to Australia; the government was offering cheap fares and land to immigrants. He would ask his father for a loan until he found work. Anna did not have Alex's confidence. She worried about the lack of money but embarking on such an adventure excited her enough to ignore her doubts.

Plans were made. They would give two weeks notice at the end of May, take the train to London and visit Australia House to buy their tickets for the next passage to Melbourne at the end of June. Allowing a month to take a trip to Scotland to say goodbye to Alex's parents, and hopefully they could acquire a loan and visit Anna's family in Rugby before boarding the ship for Australia.

Beside herself with happiness, Anna became the cause of gossip among the staff. Having decided not to disclose their plans until they actually gave their notice, the staff had surmised that Anna's high spirits might be because she was with child. Horrified at this thought, she soon put the rumours to rest and quelled her exuberance.

Anna had one last thing to do before leaving. She would keep her promise to Dr. Gregory and expose Mr. Pickles. Aware that once she departed The Sackville, he would continue his perverted ways with the young maids, she needed to make sure he was dismissed and reported to the authorities, and this she would do with Dr. Gregory's help. Alex had to be kept in the dark until they were miles away from Bexhill. He had no notion of Mr. Pickles' behaviour, and not trusting his reaction, she wanted to keep it that way.

Clutching an envelope, Anna sat in the waiting room. The wooden chairs, floor and panelling on the walls made the room dark. It smelled of Dettol and illness. She shuddered, glad she was here on a different mission. The envelope contained a statement that described in detail the incidents involving Mr. Pickles fondling her and the attempted rape. There was also a reference to Amy and other maids. She would ask Dr. Gregory to describe Edith's demise and add his own report.

The cheeriness of Dr. Gregory's voice calmed Anna's nervousness. "Come in, Mrs. Walker. How are you keeping?"

"I am quite well, thank you. My visit is regarding the… um… matter involving Mr. Pickles. I am keeping my promise that I would allow you to report him to the authorities when the time was right." Anna took a breath. She hadn't realized how difficult this might be.

Dr. Gregory smiled kindly. "Take your time."

"I have written everything in this signed statement. I would like you to read it and add your comments and validate what happened, including Edith's situation. I have a letter to send to Mr. Kendrick also, stating Mr. Pickles' behaviour with me and the female staff. I have given him your name to contact for validation. I have included my suspicions of his fraudulent accounting practices. Finally, I have asked Mr. Kendrick to make sure that Mrs. Banks, Mr. Lytton and Amy are not dismissed by Mr. Pickles. They are good, loyal and hard working employees. The Sackville will need them after Alex and I have given notice."

"You are leaving The Sackville?"

"Yes, Alex and I are emigrating to Australia. But please keep this confidential until after we leave. Is it possible to wait before going to the authorities? Alex does not know about any of this. I am afraid of what he might do to Mr. Pickles. Alex rarely shows it, but he has a violent temper."

"Mrs. Walker, I want to see that man behind bars where he cannot hurt another woman. Send me word as soon as you are ready and I will go to the authorities and press charges."

Anna returned to work confidant that Dr. Gregory would do what was necessary at the right time. Mr. Pickles reprimanded her for her tardiness but Anna didn't care.

"This came by messenger for you, from Boyds and Lambeth." He stared at Anna, waiting for an explanation. Anna said nothing and took the letter. Mr. Pickles continued, "They are prominent solicitors in London. What business do you have with solicitors?"

Anna ignored the question. In spite of her burning curiosity, Anna remained calm. She would not give him the satisfaction of opening the letter in front of him. Pencil poised over her notebook, she waited for him to dictate. He had no choice but to begin. Too distracted, he finished the session early.

Back at the front desk, Anna opened the letter. It was brief and formal, informing Anna that Lady Thornton had bequeathed her a sum of money. Mr. Lambeth requested that she attend a meeting at his rooms in London

157

at her convenience. Anna ran into the dining room waving the envelope. Alex placed the cake plates he was holding on to the sideboard and glanced at the letter. "What is it Anna? I'm busy. Afternoon tea has to be ready in half…" Alex looked up from the letter. "This could answer our prayers. How much is it?"

"It doesn't say, perhaps £100. I was only her typewriter. It was terribly kind of her to think of me and £100 will help tremendously. I'll write and tell them we will call June 18th when we are in London. If we leave on the morning train, we can call in the afternoon, find rooms for the night and save Australia House until the next morning."

Alex gave Anna a peck on the cheek. "Anna. I am so excited. Only two more weeks. Did you give him our letters?" Anna nodded. "I must get back to work. Oh no, here he comes and he *is* angry."

"What is the meaning of this?" Mr. Pickles thrust their resignations in Anna's face and turned to Mr. Lytton. "Are you going too?" Without waiting for a response, he looked at Anna.

Alex spoke first. "Mrs. Walker and I have decided to move on. We plan to visit my family in Scotland and we may look for work in Edinburgh. We haven't decided."

"I will speak with Mr. Kendrick about this."

Anna said, "Mr. Kendrick has already been informed and has received copies of both letters."

Mr. Pickles marched out of the dining room and slammed his office door.

They packed all their belongings, except for two suitcases, and sent them to Anna's parents' house in Rugby. James rallied the staff and they bought a beautiful crystal vase as a going away present, followed by tearful farewells.

Anna cried on the train to London and Alex held her tight. "I'm not sure why I am crying. I feel sad to be leaving The Sackville, but I am so excited and a bit afraid."

"Me too. It had been our home for a long time. I'm here, don't be afraid."

They arrived at Boyds and Lambeth Solicitors at two o'clock sharp and were immediately ushered into Mr. Lambeth's office on the second floor overlooking an open green. Anna's feet sunk into the deep, soft, burgundy carpet. The leather chairs were black and heavy and of an expensive quality, Anna surmised.

Mr. Lambeth was an imposing figure. He greeted them, flipped his morning coat, and sat behind his equally imposing oak desk.

"Lady Thornton expressed great affection for you, Mrs. Walker. She made provision for you just last summer." He turned the document around and pointed to the sum.

"Oh my goodness, three hundred pounds. That is very generous." Anna said.

"No, Mrs. Walker, it is three *thousand* pounds."

Anna gulped. She couldn't comprehend that amount of money. "That is too much. What would I do with it?"

Mr. Lambeth smiled. "I see why Lady Thornton had so much affection for you. The money is yours to do as you wish. I need your signature here." He pointed to the bottom of the documents and handed one copy to Anna with a money draft and a letter. "Lady Thornton asked me to deliver this letter to you."

Anna opened the envelope and cried softly as she read:

Dearest Anna,

In recognition of your loyal service to me as my secretary at The Sackville, I have bequeathed a small amount of money to you. We conversed about travel and adventure many times during our sessions, and I would like you to travel and follow your dreams.

Anna, you made an old lady happy with your kindness. I watched you grow from a girl into a woman. I would have been proud to have a daughter like you.

With my blessing, take your husband and book a passage to somewhere special.

Gratefully and Affectionately,

Lady Thornton

Alex passed Anna his handkerchief and rested his hands on her shoulders. She dried her eyes, folded the letter into the envelope, smiled and asked, "Mr. Lambeth, what happened to Miss Barclay?"

"Lady Thornton provided her with a little cottage on the estate and an allowance, with instructions to take care of the dog, Princess, and I believe there is a bird too. She is well taken care of, Mrs. Walker. It is kind of you to ask."

The next morning, they stood in the queue at Australian offices only to discover that all the ships to Melbourne, or any destination in Australia, were booked for the foreseeable future. Staring silently at each other, they sat on a bench in the main entrance hall, not knowing what to say. Anna's spirits, so high for so long spiralled into despair. She feared she would never recover.

"What are we to do?" Anna saw the same depth of disappointment on Alex's face. His elbows on his knees and his hands cupped under his chin; he stared at the floor and said nothing. There they sat for half an hour.

Suddenly he jumped up and said, "Canada! That's where we'll go." He grabbed Anna's hand and walked into the street. "See!" Alex pointed to a large building across the street. "If Australia doesn't want us, the Dominion of Canada will welcome us."

Anna thought she might burst with excitement and she flung her arms around Alex. "Lakes as big as oceans and mountains reaching the sky!" She laughed and kissed him. "Ever since I was six years old, I've wanted to see those lakes and mountains."

"And so you shall." Alex lifted her off her feet and spun her around.

"Alex, put me down. People are looking at us." Anna looked around and proudly smiled from ear to ear at the disapproving glances from passers-by. Too happy to care, she was following her dreams. He'd kept his promise of travel and something wonderful had happened to Alex. For the first time since the war, the impulsive man had returned

He leaped up the steps and held the door open, waiting for Anna. A tall gentleman in a startling red uniform greeted them. "Royal Canadian Mounted Police, Constable Jones at your service sir, ma'am."

The necessary formalities complete, Anna and Alex left the building. Tucked away safely in Alex's pocket were two 2nd class tickets for the R.M.S. Arcadia, due to sail from Liverpool on July 28, 1919, destined for Halifax, Canada. Late that afternoon, Anna slipped two letters—one addressed to Dr. Gregory, the other to Mr. Kendrick—in the post at King's Cross Station as they boarded the night train to Edinburgh.

II

August 1919 – July 1935

Toronto, Ontario,
Canada

Fourteen

R.M.S. Arcadia

~~~◈~~~

Excitement twitched in every fibre of Anna's body; comparisons from her past unfeasible. The blur of tiny houses and green meadows streamed past the window. Anna, Alex, Mama and Papa, swayed in unison as the Boat Train sped towards Liverpool Docks.

"Anna, I see my bright-eyed little girl sitting before me." Papa smiled affectionately. "Remember riding the train to Lake Windermere for summer holidays? Mama would scold you for fidgeting."

"If Alex was not holding my hand, I would bounce off the seat. I am so excited, Papa."

"Mama, you look so terribly sad. Six years ago you were happy to wave me off to Bexhill, so why so sad now?"

"Bexhill was beside the sea, not across an ocean in another world." There was a frailty in her mother's small frame, the dark green travelling suit had drained the colour from her face and tears shone in her eyes.

"We will write wonderful letters and perhaps you will come and visit one day." Anna noted her mother's concern with surprise. Her mother's affections had always been for Lou. "And you have Lou and little Robbie to occupy your time. Charlie will visit when he is not conducting army missions."

"Anna, you were always the feisty one and Lou the predictable daughter. Your unconventional ways were hard to handle when you were growing up, but we loved you all the more because of them. We will miss you very much."

Anna watched Papa lean over and gently touch Mama's arm. His chest puffed out. "We are proud of you both. You have our blessing to have a wonderful life in the Dominion of Canada. Alex, you take good care of our precious daughter."

Mama took a deep breath and asked, "How was your stay in Edinburgh? Your parents must be sorry to see you leave, Alex. Anna tells me your brother lives in Canada. How will they bear two sons so far away?

"My mother sees herself above us all. She is too busy entertaining her friends for tea or planning dinner parties to notice her sons are overseas. I have become a fashionable icon. Anna's association with Lady Thornton and her subsequent inheritance has become a useful, if somewhat embellished, topic of conversation at her soirées.

"Canada, she is not sure about. Someone told her the country is populated with savages—Red Indians that scalp people," Alex laughed. "My father will miss me as he misses Jim. He was a good father, but he is disappointed neither of his sons took an interest in his tailoring business. He works long hours, either serving in the store or tailoring kilts. I think he uses work to avoid Mother at times. I do worry about him. He is not well. My sister Florence has expressed her concern and his doctor keeps telling him to slow down.

"Florence has not married. She enjoys Mother's lifestyle as much as Mother. After Meg, my younger sister, passed away..." Alex stopped talking. The pain of an unhealed wound passed through his face. "Crum... they became over-protective with Florence, and she has become rather a demanding young woman. Any suitors that my parents presented to her were never good enough for Florence. I fear she will remain a spinster."

"I sympathize with your parents. Mr. Neale and I gave up the task of finding a suitable husband for Anna. She dismissed them all. It was awfully frustrating. Perhaps your sister will make her own choice, as did Anna.

Mr. Neale and I could not be happier with her choice in you, Alex."

Alex blushed and squeezed Anna's hand. "I think Anna found the confines of protocol my mother and sister uphold rather arduous. My dear, free-spirited Anna."

They fell into silence. Anna thought about her stay in Scotland. Alex was right, her encounter with Mother Walker and Florence had not been a happy one. But she liked Edinburgh and most of all she liked walking on the moors.

Alex was always handsome, but in his Stuart tartan kilt, he had walked through the purple heather as though he were part of the land, with a handsomeness that made Anna swoon.

She understood Alex's love of Scotland and she suspected that if they had not already bought the tickets for Canada, he would have found it impossible to break away. Horror struck Anna as she envisioned being sucked into Mother Walker and Florence's world of domestic protocol. Anna expressed an audible sigh of relief at her escape, but the vision remained, her discomfort masked by the clanging train pulling into Liverpool Docks.

The deafening noise of the train releasing steam made it impossible to speak as the family stepped onto the platform. Anna took a breath, expecting the clarity of the Bexhill sea air but coughed instead. The air hung heavy with soot and grime. Varying shades of grey blanketed everything from the sky to the long, plain warehouses and worn wooden planks below her feet. What a depressing place, Anna thought. Alex snapped his fingers for a porter; their trunks and bags were loaded on a cart and the four of them hurried behind the porter. Once in the ticket office, a large warehouse converted for the purpose of registering passengers, the porter pointed to the queue and wheeled the baggage to be loaded on the ship. Anna's excitement tempered as she stared at the hundreds of gabbling people standing in a queue that snaked around the drab building. Leaning towards Alex, she whispered, "This will take hours."

Papa's voice called, "Anna, Alex, over here."

A steward directed them to a much smaller queue reserved for saloon passengers, 1st and 2nd class travelers. Their travel documents and medical certificates were checked. The formalities complete, they stepped out onto the dockside.

Anna took a sudden breath, exhilaration flooded back as she gazed upwards to the elegant R.M.S Arcadia. One of the four White Star Line's largest ocean liners, she towered over everything in the harbour. Anna marvelled at her sleek black body, lined with rows of perfectly symmetric portholes, as though they had been embroidered on the ship's hull. The white bridge spanned its width and two massive orange-yellow funnels emitting a small trail of grey smoke were flanked by four tall masts outlined against the grey sky. The steward escorted them aboard through the companionway to their assigned cabin.

All four squeezed into the small but pleasant space dominated by polished dark wood. Mama sat on the narrow, green brocade couch attached to the side of the cabin. Anna joined her and stared at the two bunk beds opposite, thinking there would be no frolicking at sea on those narrow beds. Papa sat on the chair by the little writing desk while Alex remained standing, his red curls brushing the ceiling.

"Mr. and Mrs. Walker," the steward said, "perhaps you would like to entertain your visitors and take afternoon tea in the Café on deck, or if you prefer to be indoors, tea is also served in the lounge saloon. The ship will be sailing on the evening tide and all visitors must be ashore by five o'clock," He moved towards the door. "Dinner is served in the Dining Saloon at seven o'clock. The electric call button will summon your steward." He pointed to a button beside the lower bunk and then to a brochure on the desk. "The brochure is for your perusal, detailing the ship's activities." The steward bowed and Alex discreetly handed him a tip as he exited the cabin.

The passageways and companionways linking the decks all looked the same and Anna thought she might get lost, but Alex seemed confident and found the Café, where a congenial waiter guided them to a round table surrounded by four wicker chairs.

"This is delightful," Mama said.

The Café was open on three sides revealing a panoramic view of the harbour—the gateway to the ocean.

"It is hard to imagine that beyond that horizon is a whole new world. I am intoxicated by the promise of adventure, discovering new lands and people." Anna wanted to dance a jig right there on the deck.

"Mama, did Uncle Bertie ever feel like this?"

"Bertie's feet never stopped moving as a young boy. He would drag me into his make-believe pirate ships." Mama laughed at the memory. "As he grew older, he talked of nothing else but travelling. You, my dear, take after your uncle. You and Charlie have always had the wanderlust."

The waiter served tea and they nibbled on neat sandwiches, followed by delicious scones with strawberry preserve and a selection of small cakes. The relaxed conversation began to falter, the deck vibrations increased as the time drew closer to five—the ships engines impatient to start the journey. The bugle sounded, relieving some tension and within minutes, a steward began to walk the deck shouting, "All ashore that are going ashore! All ashore that are going ashore!"

Mama clutched her lace handkerchief, dabbing her cheeks. Seeing Anna's tears trickle, she gently wiped Anna's too. Papa never showed emotion, but today she saw him struggle to stay controlled as he hugged the breath right out of her—no words were needed. The steward discreetly waited for the goodbyes to be completed and escorted Mama and Papa to the gangway. Alex held Anna close to him, watching them disappear into the companionway.

Two loud blasts announced the ship's departure. The moorings were let loose, the tugboats and pilot boat inched the R.M.S. Arcadia from her mooring into the harbour. Anna and Alex leaned on the ship's railing, waving to the crowd on the quayside: confetti rained, the crowd cheered and the ship's band played loudly. Anna searched the crowd for her parents, but as the ship moved away the crowd became one mass of miniature people—she waved, anyway.

Holding each other, they watched the Liverpool skyline disappear. The deck became quiet, passengers dispersed and the band moved inside. The engines droned beneath their feet and a cool breeze brushed their faces. She felt a strange mixture of anticipation and trepidation, together with a sense of accomplishment. A trans-Atlantic crossing was an even bigger adventure than getting off the train in Bexhill. Anna sighed with satisfaction as Uncle Bertie's words, "follow your dreams" were materializing.

"Did I keep my promise?" Alex kissed her before she could answer.

Changing for dinner was not required the first night on board. So, still dressed in their travelling clothes, they entered the dining saloon. Several long tables draped in white damask and set with silver stretched the length of the saloon. The meal began with thick oxtail soup, followed by fricassee of rabbit. Alex ate heartily, but Anna ate little.

"Shall we explore the ship? It is quite early and we can unpack tomorrow," Alex said, matching Anna's enthusiasm, which, when he glanced her way, he realized had changed.

"Anna, what is wrong? You look pale."

"I am tired. Perhaps we can explore tomorrow. I would like to rest."

Alex led the way to the ornate brass elevator gates and along the passageway to their cabin. The steward had delivered the trunks and secured them to the sofa.

Anna laughed at the site of the trunks tied to the sofa. "Do they think someone will steal our trunks? I will unpack the necessities. The rest can wait until the morning. Alex, if you would like to tour the ship please do so, I just need to rest."

"If you are sure, I would like to find the smoking room and have a whiskey and maybe a cigar."

Anna closed her eyes, relieved to be lying down and quickly fell asleep. But the cabin door crashing into the bulkhead woke her with a start. Alex stumbled into the cabin. Anna rolled to the edge of the bunk—everything was moving.

"Alex, what is happening?" Aware of a heightening sense of fear, she remembered Lady Thornton's stories of poor Lord Thornton in the icy waters of the Atlantic. "Is the ship sinking?"

"We are sailing the Irish Sea and it is a bit rough. The steward says it is temporary. This is one of the steadiest ships on the seas today. Anna, are you seasick? I have never seen you so pale."

Anna could only nod as she tried to calm her retching stomach and spinning head. Every time the ship pitched or rolled, so did her stomach. Anna was sick all night and finally drifted off to sleep as dawn broke and the sea calmed.

Two days later, Anna still could not eat. Alex called the ship's surgeon. The doctor diagnosed seasickness, as expected, and ordered Jamaican ginger to ease the biliousness and a light diet of bouillon and toast to get her strength back. He suggested she take a walk on deck. The brisk sea air would help her feel better.

Alex took Anna up to the deck and ordered two steamer chairs—wooden deck chairs with footrests. The steamer chairs were lined along the deck facing out to sea, but sheltered from the cool Atlantic wind. They sat down together and the steward placed a steamer blanket over each of them.

"The air has taken the greyness from your face and you look brighter. How are you feeling?"

"It is nice to be out of the cabin. But Alex, I am afraid. What is wrong with me?"

"Seasickness is very unpleasant, but as you get your sea legs, you will feel well again."

"What if this is an omen of things to come? Did we do the right thing, coming to Canada? It's so far away and I'm missing England already. This was supposed to be such an adventure."

"And it will be." Alex stroked her cheek.

The steward interrupted them with a tray of steaming hot soup. Anna took the soup and was delighted that it settled well and warmed her insides. She leaned back, feeling as though she could finally enjoy the voyage. At one o'clock, Alex took Anna's hand and they walked to the Dining Saloon for luncheon. The smell of food retched at her stomach and she quickly excused herself. She wandered into the drawing room, a small pleasant space with chintz chairs and pretty French prints on the walls. The hum of the women gossiping spun in her head and the wafting perfumes tugged at her stomach again. She made a hasty retreat to her cabin. The steward brought her a pot of tea and a piece of spice cake.

Anna smiled and said, "How did you know spice cake is my favourite?"

"It is my job to know my passengers' preferences. I thought it might cheer you up."

"And it has. Thank you for your kindness."

Anna had not thought of Bill since they said goodbye to Bexhill, but the cabin steward's kindness of anticipating her needs, reminded her of Bill and his Victoria sponge cake. She wondered if Bill had his sea legs like Alex. It would be terribly unpleasant to work as a ship's cook feeling as Anna did.

"Madam, may I suggest a visit to the Writing Room and Library? Perhaps some reading would fill your days until you feel well."

Anna ventured to the Writing Room and sat at an empty table well stocked with paper, envelopes and pens.

Dearest Mama and Papa,

Our third day at sea, and this is the first day that I have ventured from my cabin, having spent most of the journey quite unwell. I cannot wait to get to port. I find myself afraid for what is to greet us in Canada. I miss you terribly and I wish I were at home. Alex is not afflicted with this horrible seasickness and is quite well, enjoying the food, which I cannot face; the sight and smell makes me bilious.

I was so excited to be on a ship with a swimming pool, but I feel too unwell to try it. Alex tells me it is wonderful. He spends the days swimming and playing quoits and shuffleboard. After dinner, he joins the gentlemen in the Smoking Room and comes to bed smelling of whiskey and cigars, which further increases my biliousness. We did spend some time on deck in the steamer chairs yesterday. I feel as though he has abandoned me, but that is unfair as he is enjoying the voyage.

The cabin steward is considerably more attentive than Alex and brings me ginger to settle my tummy and cake to cheer me up. Today

he brought spice cake. I don't know how he knew it was my favourite.
I am writing this in a pleasant writing room with similar tables and
wicker chairs to the Café where we had tea. There is a well-stocked
library and I plan to take some books for the remainder of the journey.
I can feel the ship rolling as I write. I hope we don't experience a
storm. I am quite afraid. The waves in the Irish Sea were quite large
but since we sailed into the Atlantic, until now, it has been calm.

  Give my nephew Robbie a kiss and my love to Lou, and Charlie if
he is home. I will write again once we get to Halifax.

  Your affectionate daughter,

  Anna

Anna sealed the envelope, browsed the bookshelves and found a fascinating
Canadian book called, *Anne of Green Gables,* by Lucy Maud Montgomery.
The steward directed her to the Bureau of Information to buy stamps
and post the letter. She felt a pang of nostalgia as she approached the
high wooden counter, not dissimilar to the front desk at The Sackville;
the same rows of cubby holes behind the desk, with one difference, a
metal grill that stood between Anna and the clerk, a security measure
because the Bureau of Information also handled cash and had a large safe
for passengers' valuables.

Delighted to find a little shop on board, Anna bought three picture
postcards of the R.M.S Arcadia. She would send one to Edinburgh and one
to Rugby and save one as a keepsake. Anna felt better. Strolling around the
ship had occupied her mind. She returned to the quiet, pleasant, Writing
Room, to write the postcards. Staring at the third postcard, she wished
she had an address for Bill to tell him of their adventure.

He had said he would find her, but in more than four years there had
been no contact. She didn't even know if he was still alive. Anna moved
to the bookshelves and found her hand resting on the spine of a Rudyard
Kipling book. Tears prevented her from reading the title as a sense of love
and caring tingled through her arm and into her heart. She thought Bill
must be close by, but how could that be? They were in the middle of the

Atlantic Ocean. It would not be impossible, she thought. He too could be sailing the Atlantic. She embraced the warmth and brushing away the tears, she sat at the table and opened the book, flipping through the pages. She recognized it as one of Bill's favourites and smiled at the coincidence. Feeling the ship move, she decided to return to her cabin and replaced the book.

The ship rolled and she stumbled against the bookshelves, several books dropped to the floor, narrowly missing Anna. Her heart jumped into her throat and her fingers traced the scar on her forehead. Terror struck her and she looked over her shoulder, expecting to see Mr. Pickles leer at her. Her stomach began to heave, bringing back a bad memory.

Anna quickly made her way to the elevator, her vision blurred as the brass gates opened. She staggered down the passageway, but the cabin numbers were all wrong. She turned and grabbed the railing as the ship swayed and threw her against the wall. She was lost. Afraid she would disgrace herself as the taste of bile filled her mouth; she pulled out her handkerchief and held it to her face. Supporting herself on the railing, she headed back to the elevator and companionway. Coming round the corner the ship rolled again and she bumped into someone.

"Mrs. Walker! Can I be of assistance?"

Anna dare not remove the handkerchief but hoped the appeal in her eyes would tell him she was lost.

"I will help you back to your cabin. I think you exited the elevator on the wrong deck."

Safely back in her cabin, Anna laid down on her bunk, fully dressed. The cabin steward pulled a blanket over her. "I'll fetch you some Jamaican ginger. I have sent one of the stewards to find your husband. He will be here soon." He checked that the steamer trunks were fastened. "I am afraid we are running into a bit of bad weather." Seeing the panic on Anna's face, he hastily added, "It will be over very soon. There is nothing to be concerned about."

Anna ignored him. Although the impending storm was cause for concern, the flash memory of Mr. Pickles' vicious attack had been both surprising and frightening, especially coming so close to the vivid image of Bill. It made the whole episode a source of trepidation. Anna thought hard to find a connection but there was none, at least nothing she was aware of. During the not so pleasant stay in Scotland with Alex's parents, Anna had scoured the newspapers every day for news of Mr. Pickles' arrest—not a word. It made her feel uneasy and question whether or not Dr. Gregory had, as promised, reported Mr. Pickles' crimes.

The steward tapped on the door, carrying a steaming cup of ginger tea. Anna marvelled at how steadily he walked through the cabin. Concentrating on quelling her boiling stomach and trying to focus on swallowing the hot tea, she felt the velvet ribbon tighten on her neck. Petrified she was going to choke or worse, be sick, she quickly untied the pendant and laid it on the side table.

She stared at the smooth blue crystal thinking of Uncle Bertie's love of travel and adventure, and her own quest for independence. The things she had held so close were drifting away in the constant motion of the ocean; her energy depleted, she hadn't the strength to hold on. Another bout of seasickness kept her in the cabin for the remainder of the voyage.

On August 4, 1919, the R.M.S Arcadia sailed into view of the Nova Scotia coastline. Alex insisted Anna come on deck to get a glimpse of the Dominion of Canada, their new land.

"Isn't this wonderful?" His demeanour bubbled with enthusiasm.

Anna no longer cared, giving an unconvincing nod and thinking how grateful she would be to set foot on dry land. The ship docked at the Halifax Ocean Terminal, Pier 21.

They were guided along the gangway to a long converted warehouse not unlike the one in Liverpool. But, unlike Liverpool, the air felt clear and fresh, the sky was a brilliant blue and the sun warm on their faces.

After the formalities, the porter escorted them to the train bound for Toronto, the Ontario city that they would call home. Concerned for Anna's health, Alex arranged for them to make the long journey in the comfort of 1st class accommodation.

The rhythm of the train lulled Anna to sleep, and she slept until almost noon the following day. She woke to strange, cramped surroundings, even smaller than the ship's cabin. She looked for Alex. In spite of the long sleep she still felt tired, weak and definitely not herself. Her great sea adventure had been demoralizing. She wept.

The compartment door opened and Alex bounced in. "You are awake, but I see tears."

"A little melancholy, that's all. I am feeling much better. I believe I am a little hungry."

"Do you feel well enough to go to the dining car? I have been exploring and had a good chat with the maître d'. It is quite an experience, working on a passenger train. I think someday I might apply for a position on the trains."

Jim, Alex's brother, and his wife Abigail met them at Toronto's Union Station. They took a taxi to their small two-bedroom apartment on Dundas Street. The men hauled the steamer trunks up to the second floor apartment and into a tiny bedroom that belonged to Jimmy Jr., Alex's two-year-old nephew, who would sleep with his parents. These cramped quarters would be their home for the next few months.

Fifteen

Domestic Harmony Threatens Anna

A nna had nothing in common with Abigail, a small, mousy woman content to answer to her quiet accountant husband and care for her two-year-old son, Jimmy Junior. Quite the opposite of impulsive, charismatic Alex, Jim was several inches shorter, a temperate man who did everything in moderation. The one feature they did share was red hair, but even that was slightly different—Jim's was straight and a darker tone. But there was no denying the brotherly affection between the two.

Anna's thoughts were bland. Her sense of adventure had stalled on the other side of the Atlantic, but Toronto pleased her as much as anything pleased her at the moment. She liked the wide, tree-lined streets and stone buildings, the sense of spaciousness and clean, sootless air. There was always a gentle breeze coming off Lake Ontario and many consecutive days of brilliant blue sky. It lacked the greyness of Rugby or Liverpool but didn't have the charm of Bexhill.

Staying with domesticated Jim and Abigail frightened her though. This was not the life she wanted but what else was there? Alex's enthusiasm for everything Canadian annoyed her. This should have been her adventure and she resented his enthusiasm. She could see how playing with Jimmy

Jr. and relaxing contentedly in Jim and Abigail's family nest pleased him.

By mid-August the mercury had climbed to 98°F. She had not expected the humid heat. The apartment dripped with moisture and at night they tossed and turned, trying to catch a breeze from the tiny window. During the day, attempting to keep the heat out, all the windows were closed and the drapes drawn; the oppressiveness made everyone irritable. The apartment became a sauna.

Anna had to get out of the apartment. "Alex, I would like to visit Lake Ontario."

Alex stopped playing with Jimmy. "That's a good idea. We'll take little Jimmy with us."

"No!" Anna replied somewhat sharper than she intended. "I would like to be alone with you."

The tramcar took them to Lakeshore and Anna's first sighting of Lake Ontario took her back to the first sighting of the sea at Bexhill, except the lake looked like glass. There were no waves sparkling in the sun. Heavy clouds had obscured the sun, the stillness strange and ominous. Alex took her arm and they walked along the shoreline.

"Uncle Bertie said Canadian Lakes were as big as oceans and he was right." Anna felt a spark light inside her.

"Alex, Jim and Abigail are very kind to give us a place to stay, but we need to find our own place and we need to find work."

"I would like to buy a house and then we can settle down. I can find work in one of the many hotels here in Toronto. We have enough money. I can provide for you. You don't need to work." Alex beamed.

Anna stared at the lake. The glass surface had begun to ripple, the sky darkened and a cool wind blew against her face. She felt a storm brewing, both outside and inside.

"Alex, I want the independence a position gives me. I too can find work in a hotel. Mr. Kendrick gave me an excellent reference. I am not sure we need to buy a house. An apartment or rooms would do until we find work. If we intend to explore Canada and find work in hotels, we don't want to be tied down with a house." Seeing his ambivalence, she shouted, "Alex, you promised!"

"And I will keep my promise. Anna, the ocean crossing made you ill. You need time to get well again. It is best that we settle first and get to know Toronto. When you are well again, you will find secretarial work and then we can plan to travel."

BOOM, the air flashed a brilliant white and forks of phosphorescent lightning filled the black sky, plunging into the boiling lake. The thunder vibrated along the shoreline and the trees bent in submission to the gusting wind. White balls of hail bounced on the sidewalk. They ran laughing into the first shop they came to and found themselves in a Chinese restaurant.

A small Chinese man spoke to them in indecipherable broken English, but his wide smile and bowing head translated to welcome as he showed them to a small table. Alex ordered tea. A tiny young woman, dressed in bright yellow satin brocade delicately embroidered with flowers, placed a large teapot and two tiny china bowls on the table. They looked at each other and then to the little woman.

"Tea! Chinese tea." She lifted the teapot and poured a light brown liquid into each bowl. "You try, you like."

Anna picked up the hot bowl and sipped the tea and smiled. "It's lovely. Alex, do try it. It is smooth and has a floral scent."

"You like Chinese tea, jasmine? You eat?" She handed them a sheet of paper.

Anna looked at the list of dishes but recognized nothing and looked appealingly at the woman.

"You English?"

Anna nodded.

"I fix you nice Chinese dinner, special for English, you like." She disappeared into the back room.

"Alex, this is wonderful. I think we were meant to come here."

"Yes. It was odd how we finished up here." Alex frowned as he glanced at the storm outside. "I am glad we are inside. I still have nightmares over storms. I sometimes think I will never get over losing my sister, Meg." He took Anna's hand and kissed it. "I am afraid of losing you and that is why I want to settle in Toronto and make sure you are quite well." Alex appealed to Anna with his green eyes—something she could never resist.

"As long as we can find our own apartment…" Anna stopped. A delicious aroma came from a large plate of steaming vegetables that the waitress had placed on the table with a bowl of white rice and two plates adorned with chopsticks.

The woman proceeded to demonstrate how to hold and move the chopsticks—it looked easy. Anna and Alex began to laugh as they both opened and closed their mouths like goldfish, the food unwilling to stay in the grasp of the chopsticks. Laughing with them the Chinese woman said, "I get forks. You not eat like Chinese."

Once the storm had passed, they said their goodbyes, promising to visit again. Relieved that the temperature had dropped many degrees, they strolled along the lakeshore. Alex stopped walking and brushed her cheek. The warmth of his hand took her breath away, she stood on tiptoe and they kissed. She felt safe and warm as he pulled her close.

The door burst open as Alex put the key in the lock. "Oh, you are safe. We were so worried about you in the storm." Abigail ushered them into the sitting room.

"We are fine. We found a wonderful restaurant and waited for the storm to pass." Alex brushed Anna's hand and tried to link his little finger in hers. "We are tired. I think we'll have an early night."

"I got the scotch out, thinking you might need warming after the storm. Have a night cap?" Jim produced two glasses.

"I think I'll have an early night," Anna said, trying to disguise the alluring smile. "Alex, are you coming?"

Alex hesitated, gave Jim a knowing glance and followed Anna. She had not felt so much desire since the day they moved to Mrs. Bromley's. Impatient to feel his body, she moved her hands inside his jacket. He snickered, feeling the warmth as he opened the bedroom door.

He swooped Anna in his arms and kissed her, kicking the door closed with his foot. The room filled with the heavy breath of desire as Alex laid her gently on the bed and together they began unbuttoning each other until the physical longing reached a fever pitch and clothes went flying.

Their insatiable appetites for each other's love took them through most of the night. Finally, their bodies exhausted, they slept.

Still entwined in each other's arms, Alex woke first and kissed Anna on the cheek. "Good morning." Anna stretched briefly, mumbled something and curled up again against Alex's chest.

"My darling Anna, I love you so much. I've made a decision. I need to find work. You are right. We need our own place."

Anna sat bolt upright. "Do you mean that?"

Alex embraced her. "Of course I mean it."

"Alex, you are right too. Our adventure yesterday showed me there is much to explore in Toronto."

True to his word, Alex took his letters of reference to the Royal York Hotel in downtown Toronto. The general manager complimented Alex on his references but he had no position open. Alex heard similar stories from every hotel he called upon. The situation in Toronto was not dissimilar to Bexhill.

Soldiers returning from the war had filled what jobs were available and hotel bookings in general were slow. Alex even applied for a headwaiter position on the passenger trains. Canadian Pacific and the Royal York were the most promising, but he would have to wait for a position to open up. Patience was not one of Alex's attributes and he did not take rejection easily.

The tension at Jim and Abigail's was becoming intolerable. Alex's temper flared and frequently clashed with Jim. Anna tried to befriend Abigail by asking her to help them set up a home. But their tastes were so different that it became a constant battle.

Abigail's disapproval of Anna's easygoing attitude came to a head. She accused Anna of putting the family in danger because she and Alex had had dinner at a Chinese restaurant. This precipitated an argument, causing Alex and Jim to protect their respective wives and for weeks the couples barely spoke. Mealtimes were particularly awkward until breakfast one morning in late September.

Abigail glanced at Anna. "Anna, you look very pale, are you feeling poorly?"

Anna stared at her toast. "My stomach is upset and I can't eat. I have the same bilious feeling I had on board the ship."

Alex insisted that Anna spend the day in bed and Abigail made her beef broth and took care of her. Several days later Abigail brought her some dry toast and water.

Anna laughed. "Abigail what is this, prison rations?"

"Tell me how you feel. Are you sick in the mornings but hungry at other times? Do you feel strange, not quite yourself?"

Anna swallowed hard as she felt the sickness rising. Abigail soothed her until the biliousness eased. "Take a sip of water and a bite of this toast. It will settle your stomach. I think you are suffering from morning sickness. I think you are going to have a baby."

"No!" Anna felt a sense of dread wash over her. "I can't be pregnant. It's not possible. We are careful." As the words were spoken, Anna remembered the night of the storm. They had wanted each other so badly that they had not been careful.

Abigail put her head to one side. "This is exciting. I think we can be sisters after all. I will make an appointment with Dr. McCarthy. It will be wonderful to have a wee bairn in the house."

"Please don't tell Alex yet." Abigail gave her a sweet smile and closed the bedroom door.

She stared at a branch of red maple leaves brushing gently against the windowpane. She wanted to be that branch on the outside looking in. She wanted the windowpane to shield her from the truth. Abigail's comment played over and over. *I think you are having a baby.* "I can't have a baby," she said aloud. Even the word, baby, plunged her deeper into despair. Deep down she felt the baby growing, and guilt stabbed her insides as her dreams of travel and adventure shattered. Her greatest fears would soon be a reality.

Anna had resisted Abigail's prompting to see the doctor until Alex insisted, his concern for her health reaching panic proportions. Upon their return from Dr. McCarthy's surgery, they found Alex combing the newspaper for work. Anna stood like stone. Abigail spoke with a broad grin on her face. "Anna has something to tell you Alex. I will put the kettle on."

Anna tried to smile. "I am with child… that is the cause of my sickness."

Alex jumped up, grabbed Anna and spun her around. "Anna, this is wonderful news. I'm to be a father. Will it be a lad or a lassie? I am so very happy. Anna, I love you, and at last we will be a family." He kissed her, hugged her and kissed her again. His face glowed with joy and pride. Stopping abruptly, he stared at Anna. "You don't look happy. What's wrong?"

Anna hesitated, her insides churning. She felt faint and gasped for air. She couldn't tell him she didn't want this baby. She meant no harm to the baby but she didn't want the life the baby would bring. Alex did. Her feelings scrambled in her head and she couldn't think. She loved Alex. They had dreams but now she understood they each had different ones. If Alex was aware of her true feelings, and she would never tell him, he would be crushed.

"It's hard to be excited when you feel sick all the time," Anna said, forcing a smile. "Dr. McCarthy said the sickness will pass after the first few months. He cannot be certain exactly when the baby is due as it is very early, and I have to see him again in a month's time. All-knowing Abigail predicts it will be May or June."

"Anna, I have been thinking about what other alternatives there might be for work and living accommodation. How would you like us to operate a store with an apartment above it? It would provide us both with work and a place to live." He pointed to an advertisement in *The Star*.

"It sounds like a good idea. Can we afford the rent? We need a great deal more information."

Abigail came in with a tray of tea and freshly baked scones. She and Alex shared a joyous conversation about wee Jimmy having a cousin and how excited *Uncle* Jim would be. Anna excused herself, feigning tiredness.

The pregnancy had broken the tension in the apartment. Everyone except Anna talked of nothing else. Alex treated Anna like an invalid as the morning sickness continued making her feel most unwell throughout most of the day. It also provided her with a cover for her true feelings about imminent motherhood.

The mid-afternoon sun still felt warm, although the smell of autumn filled the chilled air. Anna's feet crunched through the crispy red and gold leaves that the now bare trees had shed onto the sidewalk. Thankfully, the sickness had settled down to mornings only, and Anna had ventured out alone. She needed to think.

Alex was up to something. She could feel his excitement when he'd left that morning, saying he had a surprise. Alex's surprises were rarely practical, and the secrecy surrounding this one indicated his fear of Anna's disapproval. She had a bad feeling.

Anna took off her hat and coat, hanging them at the top of the stairs. Abigail greeted her. "The fresh air has brought colour to your cheeks."

The outside door opened.

Alex literally leapt up two stairs at a time, into the apartment, waving a folded document in his hand. "Anna, I did it. We have a store and a place to live. We can move in next week when the bank completes the paperwork."

Anna frowned. "Bank? What has the bank got to do with anything?"

"To complete the sale of Kenwood Bakery. Our new home."

Abigail discreetly closed the apartment door, ushered Anna and Alex into the living room and escaped to the kitchen.

"Sale? Alex, what did you do?"

"I bought us a bakery, complete with a baker who will teach me how to bake. Imagine, Anna, *me* baking bread and you can serve in the store and there is an apartment above. We have work and somewhere to live and raise our family. Anna, are you proud of me?"

Anna just stared at him. Seething with anger, she thought her chest and head might explode. Alex had done some strange things but this was beyond all comprehension.

Anna gulped and willed herself to stay calm. "Alex, tell me exactly what you have done and how the bank is involved." Even as she asked the question, Anna knew the answer, but she needed to hear it from Alex.

"I just told you, I bought a bakery with a store and an apartment. Anna why are you so angry? We talked about this."

"We talked about renting. I expected that *we* would make the decision together and..."

Alex interrupted. "I wanted to surprise you. You have been so ill and out of humour. I thought this would cheer you up." Even Alex's pleading eyes did nothing to ease Anna's anger.

"You said you bought it. Where did you get the money?"

Alex looked down at the floor. "I went to the bank."

Anna screamed at him. "Don't be evasive. Whose money?"

"I used the money from Lady Thornton's inheritance." Seeing Anna's taut face, he quickly added, "I had to make a quick decision and I didn't use all the money. Anna, you will love the place; it is perfect for us."

Anna's emotions took over, anger and regret spilled down her face. "Lady Thornton... left that money to me... so we could travel and see the world. Not to set up a family home. At least *she* understood how I felt about—," Anna stopped. Her anger had driven her to say what she never intended Alex to know.

"You don't want our baby," Alex's voice trembled.

Anna watched his face fill with sorrow. He gasped a ragged breath and turned away from her.

"Alex, I am sorry. I didn't mean that. Of course I want this baby and I do want a home. I am angry that you made the decisions without consulting me and spent *my* money."

They had both said things they regretted and forgiveness took time. It was a few days before Anna was willing to view the bakery. She grudgingly agreed that it looked quite nice from the outside.

The shop was situated on a corner, with a yellow and white striped awning over the window with 'Kenwood Bakery' written along the edge. As Anna opened the door, a charming bell announced their arrival. The smell of fresh bread wafted from the hot ovens and a massive mixer whirled in the background. Nick Gunter, as wide as he was tall, waddled his way to the front and stood by the bread shelves, wiping his hands on a white apron smeared with flour and red jam.

"Mr. Walker, come in." He turned to Anna. "This must be the lovely Mrs. Walker." And with continental flare, Nick took Anna's hand and kissed it. Anna immediately thought of Chef Louis and hoped Nick's temperament was more Canadian than European. At least he didn't have an accent.

"We have come to see the apartment," Alex said, guiding Anna through a door at the back and up a flight of stairs. In spite of her earlier objections, she liked the bright, spacious living room filled with sunlight from two large windows. The front window looked onto St. Clare Avenue and had a small window seat in its alcove. Anna walked over and sat in the window.

"Alex, this is a lovely room. I shall buy some cushions for this quaint little seat and curl up and read on sunny afternoons like today."

"We need to find a bookcase for your books," Alex said, smiling. "Anna, it does me good to see you happy again."

The kitchen and bathroom were small but adequate. They walked into the sunlit bedroom. "Oh, Alex this room is big enough for a bedroom suite. No side-stepping around the bed to get to the wardrobe." Anna laughed at the memories of their bedroom at Mrs. Bromley's. The second bedroom was quite small but ideal for a nursery. Anna put her hand on her tummy, and for the first time felt what she thought might be a motherly feeling.

Hurt and still angry over the money and what she perceived as deceit, Anna had to admit Alex meant well. His inherent impulsiveness often got the better of him. She conceded the purchase of Kenwood Bakery was the answer to their situation. But it angered her that the purchase had been made with her money, without consultation or her consent. Alex's name and not hers was on the deed of title. Anna insisted her name be on the deed and Alex agreed. The bank manager and solicitor had other ideas. Financial transactions were conducted in the husband's name. Alex supported Anna and the ownership of Kenwood Bakery was reluctantly changed to Anna's name alone.

The heavy, fancy Victorian furniture did nothing for Anna and the overstuffed leather chairs gave her nightmares. She wanted a cleaner, more modern look and scoured the second-hand furniture stores along Bloor St.

Anna's tenacity served her well and she found two chairs with wooden arms and a simple floral print and a sofa with good sturdy springs but somewhat worn in faded green velvet that could be re-upholstered in a more modern fabric at a later date. Further along Bloor Street, Anna found a rug with a floral pattern that blended well with the chairs and would cover the scratched wooden floor.

At the same store, tucked away in the back room, Anna saw a mahogany sideboard. A little more ornate than she would have liked, but it was cheap and had lots of cupboard space. Browsing through a poky, dirty store, full of junk, she unearthed a small round pedestal table. The surface needed a good polish, but it came with two matching wooden chairs in good condition. Anna gave the owner a look of incredulity at the price, and using her newfound confidence bartered for a ridiculously low price, which he accepted. Abigail gave her some pots and pans and a belated wedding present of a complete set of Royal Albert china for six. Anna appreciated having something pretty and new.

Alex wanted to buy a new bedroom suite. Proud of her bargain finds, Anna disagreed until Alex explained about cockroaches, and living above a bakery they would have to be extra careful. Anna easily relented. The thought of sharing her bed or wardrobe with those ugly little creatures quickly changed her mind.

Abigail took Anna to Eaton's, Toronto's department store. It was enormous and spanned several floors, offering everything imaginable for sale. The elevator took them to the fourth floor. The young operator wore a little round hat fastened under his chin with elastic, a double-breasted brown coat with brass buttons and matching trousers. He reminded Anna of the bellboy at The Sackville as he pulled expertly on the brass lever that moved the elevator from floor to floor. He called out the wares for each floor: ladies' wear- second floor, gentleman's attire - third floor, and then as they reached the fourth floor, furniture, lamps and linens. Anna walked slowly, in awe, and was interrupted by a gentleman in a grey suit. "Good afternoon, madam."

Abigail spoke, "Could you direct us to the bedroom suites, please?" And they were escorted to the far side of the store and handed over to a young assistant.

Anna looked around the floor and quickly found what she liked, a plain wooden dressing table, wardrobe and bedside tables with straight square lines and a matching headboard for the bed. Shocked at the price after her bargain hunting, she reluctantly paid and arranged delivery. The young assistant then escorted them to the linen department where she selected sheets, blankets and pillows, and it was there that she saw the delicate pastel floral cushions.

"Abigail, do you think it would be terribly extravagant of me to purchase three of those cushions for the window alcove?" Anna picked one up and felt its softness.

"Anna, they are lovely. I can see you curled up resting on those soft cushions reading your books. Definitely a good idea; I would take four, two to sit on and, two to rest your back against."

Anna giggled. "I think three will be enough. I will take them."

It took nearly two weeks to get all the furniture in place, but the day finally arrived and they packed their steamer trunks and moved into Kenwood Bakery.

Standing at the bottom of the stairs, Alex announced, "I want to carry you over the threshold. I have a surprise for you!" *Surprise,* she thought, *oh no, what has he done now?*

"Alex, I don't want to be carried over the threshold. What if you drop me? Did you forget that I have a baby inside me?"

Alex took Anna's hand and told her to close her eyes as they walked to the top of the stairs. He guided her into the living room. Her stomach tightened, afraid that the surprise would cause them to have another disagreement. She had enjoyed setting up their first home and a spark of excitement had kindled inside her as she looked forward to being alone with Alex.

"You can open them now."

At first Anna saw only the window seat with the delicate floral cushions, noticing there were four, not three, cushions.

"Abigail told you about the cushions."

Alex look puzzled.

"Cushions? No, next to the window seat."

Anna thought, how sweet it was that Abigail had bought her the fourth cushion. She followed his glance and her hands flew to her cheeks as a wide grin spread on her face. She gasped and said, "It's beautiful, and you even arranged my books." She ran her fingers over the mahogany bookcase. "And this is a new book." She picked up the book, glanced at the author, Rudyard Kipling, and immediately thought of Bill. Ashamed of her thought, she hugged Alex tightly. "Thank you. This is a wonderful surprise." The kiss lingered with warmth, both feeling that they were home at last.

Sixteen

Bill Returns to Bexhill

❧

July 1919, the tugboats skillfully pushed the S.S. Dorset towards the wharf and manoeuvred it into its moorings at Southampton Dock. The massive cranes poised to unload the cargo of tea from Ceylon and spices from the islands. Impatient to step on dry land, Bill Blaine stood on deck, his leather satchel at his feet, and the rising sun throwing pink and orange hues on the drifting clouds. It had taken him four seafaring years, but the time had come. He had to find Anna.

A night didn't go by without dreaming of her lovely face. He dreamt of the wayward curl that escaped from its pins and beguiling smile. He remembered her steely look of defiance and determination when she was challenged, and yet she had succumbed to Alex's charm.

It was late July, four years, two months and one week since he had sailed out of this very port; running away from the pain, regret and loss of so many things. He understood what it meant to have a broken heart. As much as he hated Alex for stealing Anna, he missed his best friend. His pranks and humour had lifted Bill from many melancholy moods. Now he was always sad, and given all that had happened, he should be happy to be alive.

The inconceivable number of lives lost in the Great War at the Somme and Passchendaele where Alex almost certainly would have been fighting. The thought prompted him to ask the question—did Alex survive? Was Anna a widow? The thought of Anna being widowed gave him hope, but his conscience reminded him that for Anna to be a widow, Alex would have to be dead. Ambiguity filled his head. He sensed Alex had indeed survived the war, but he also sensed his premature death. He brushed the dark thought to one side as uncharacteristic thinking—he would never wish Alex any harm. Life had shown him it was time to forgive.

During the war, he had docked in Liverpool or Glasgow but never in Southampton. He had broken his promise to Anna: he had never written. Putting words on paper was difficult. He read all the masters of love, but when he tried to write, the pen stuck in his hand, unable to shape the words.

What could he say? How could he write a letter of friendship when he wanted to write of love? His own words, "I'll find you," rang in his ears. He speculated on what might have happened in the last four years. Had they settled with a family? Strange, Bill thought, impetuous and foolhardy Alex wanted to settle, but he doubted if Anna wanted the same. He remembered all those nights by the fire, talking of travel and adventure; how they'd drooled over Rudyard Kipling's travels. He feared Alex might revert to his manipulative ways, resulting in Anna's unhappiness and *that* he could not forgive. He spoke into the wind, "I need to find them and to know Anna is happy." He had two days' leave, before the S.S. Dorset would set sail for North America on the evening tide of July 26th.

The Bexhill Central Station clock chimed twelve times as Bill jumped off the train. *Noon,* he thought, *a busy time at The Sackville. I'll stop at The Fisherman's Nook for a pint of ale first.*

"'ey, look who's 'ere. Mi! It's good to see y'u, Bill Blaine," Nosey said from behind the bar. "So what'll it be? It's on the 'ouse."

"A pint of your best ale, thanks." Bill looked around the pub. Not much had changed around here, he thought. "How have you been?"

191

Nosey placed a full tankard of frothy ale on the bar. "It's be'n quiet since the end of the war. Cooden Camp kept us busy during the war. A bit 'airy at times, but we did well. This summer has seen a few more 'oliday makers. So what 'ave you bin up to these past years? Lost a bit of 'air I see and had some sun from the look of y'u."

Bill took a gulp of the golden brown liquid.

"I see you haven't lost your touch with the ale, Nosey. The first good drink I've had in four years. Do you still serve those hot mussels?"

"Sure do." Nosey yelled to someone in the back. "Plate o' mussels and bread please, love." He looked at Bill and explained, "Bread's just comin' out o' oven. So Bill Blaine where've y'u bin?"

"I've been at sea. Travelled the world with the merchant navy. I docked this morning in Southampton; first time in four years."

"Not sure I'd like that... all them foreigners. But I guess it beats being in the war?"

Bill didn't like the inference. He had served his country well at sea.

"We saw plenty of action during the war. Dodging the bloody German U-boats was no picnic and many were blown up and we had some close calls. If it wasn't for the brave seamen on the merchant ships, you wouldn't have had food or supplies on your table."

"'ere sorry mate, I didn't mean no disrespect." Nosey disappeared into the back and came back with a steaming plate of mussels.

"It's okay. I guess I'm a bit touchy. But a lot of lives were lost transporting food and supplies and not all civilians understand what we went through on the high seas."

The pub filled up with patrons. Bill finished his lunch and walked along the Promenade, his head full of memories and wondering what changes he would find at The Sackville. He might not know anyone.

Leaning with his back on the railing that separated the beach from the Promenade, Bill stared at The Sackville, deciding whether to enter by the front door and face Anna at the desk, risking the wrath of old Prickly-Pickles or the service entrance at the back, and encounter Chef Louis' rage. He decided he had every right to enter by the front. Besides seeing Anna's face first was preferable to Chef Louis'.

"Mr. Blaine! How wonderful to see you," George said, holding the door open.

Bill looked intently across the familiar lobby, the same brilliant crystal chandelier epitomizing the expectant luxury of The Sackville, the mahogany reception counter just as polished. But the person standing behind it was Miss Jenkins, not Anna. Suddenly, Bill felt out of place. Nobody spoke and an awkward silence filled the lobby until a familiar voice came from the office.

"Did I hear Bill Blaine's name?" Mr. Lytton enquired, walking by Miss Jenkins. "Bill, it is good to see you. Come into my office. There have been many changes since your departure."

Unable to speak, and filled with apprehension about what the changes might be, Bill smiled and followed Mr. Lytton into Mr. Pickles' office. Completely confused, Bill sat in the overstuffed leather chair and watched James Lytton sit behind the desk.

"Where's old Prickles?" Bill said raising an eyebrow.

"Much has happened, and most of it in the last month since Anna and Alex left for Scotland."

Bill's heart sank and his throat tightened. He had not expected to react so intensely. Was he upset or relieved to discover Alex was alive, or disappointed that he would not see Anna?

He shifted in his chair, crossing and uncrossing his legs, clearing his throat, he said, "Alex survived the war, and Anna, how is she?"

James put his head to one side. "You had a thing for Anna. There was a time when we all thought you and Anna..."

"Yes, well, Alex swept her off her feet and I let it happen. He had a habit of doing that kind of thing." Bill surprised himself with the bitterness in his voice. He felt a surge of anger and quickly pushed it out with the rest of the emotions. "You said they went to Scotland."

"Bill, I am sorry to say you only missed them by a few weeks. Bookings at The Sackville have been quite slow since the war and they decided it was a good time to start anew. They talked about going to Australia, but Anna sent me a postcard from London to say they couldn't arrange a passage to Melbourne and were on their way to Scotland. She didn't give an address."

"Alex and I grew up together in Edinburgh. I know his parents well. His father is a tailor and kilt maker; they live above the shop on Princes St. I know where they are so I can give you the address."

"Thank you that would be nice, although I am not good with correspondence. We became quite friendly after the war. Alex and I spent many hours talking about our war experiences."

"Alex survived the war without injury?" Bill asked.

"None of us escaped without injury. Alex had a dose of mustard gas but he was one of the lucky ones and survived. I took shrapnel in my leg, a cavalry man who will never ride again. But I am alive and well. How did you survive the war?"

"The cavalry turned me down and the only way I could serve my country was as a merchant seaman. I am lucky to be alive. The convoys saved us from the German U-boats."

"Bill, come over and have dinner with me tonight? My landlady, Mrs. Bromley, is an excellent cook. I have a great deal to tell you. As you see, I am now the general manager. Mr. Pickles left with great drama a couple of weeks ago. I have work to do, but I finish at six o'clock. Why don't you go downstairs? Mrs. Banks is still here and little Amy. Believe it or not, she is now the head maid. Sophie took up nursing during the war." He laughed and added, "And Chef is as bad tempered as ever. Have a cup of tea and I'll come and fetch you when I am finished here—we can have something a bit stronger later."

Bill exited through the service door. He felt like a ghost floating through the passageway. Memories flooded his mind, but nothing seemed real. He floated to the kitchen, invisible. He stood and watched as Chef Louis barked orders at a young chef, a ghost of himself. He moved into the staff dining hall and caught his breath as he saw Anna's shadow in the rocking chair. Was his mind playing tricks? He pinched his arm to make sure he wasn't dreaming.

A familiar voice came from behind. "Can I help you?"

"Mrs. Banks. It's Bill, Bill Blaine." Bill swung round and put his hand out, although, he would rather have embraced her as he would a favourite aunt.

"Mr. Blaine! Oh my, it is good to see you. What are you doing here?"

Bill related his story of adventures on the high seas. Amy and Chef Louis joined them. He asked about Mr. Pickles but nobody was talking. Bill sensed something sinister had happened. James Lytton joined them as the grandfather clock struck six and he and Bill walked to James' rooms.

As they walked into the sitting room, Bill was overcome with Anna's presence. He could smell her soft floral scent, he heard her laugh and for a split second he thought he felt her brush by his cheek.

"Bill, what is it? You look as though you have seen a ghost."

"Um! I think I have…" Bill said bringing his thoughts back to reality. "Nice rooms."

"I used to rent one room on the second floor, an adequate arrangement when Alex and Anna lived here. I spent many evenings with them. It seemed natural to take these rooms over when they left; inexpensive, comfortable and a delightful landlady, Mrs. Bromley. I couldn't ask for more. You can stay here tonight if you wish. I don't think Mrs. Bromley has rented my old room yet."

Bill felt relieved that sensing Anna's presences was genuine. For a second he'd thought he was imaging things, but now he felt comforted.

James must have sent word to the landlady, Bill thought, because the dining table was set for two. James pulled two wine glasses from the sideboard and poured them each a glass of red wine. Mrs. Bromley brought in two plates of steak and kidney pie covered in rich dark gravy and a dish of mashed potatoes and green beans. Bill savoured every mouthful.

"It is a long time since I have had good, fresh, home cooking. I try to serve the seamen good food, but fresh food soon runs out."

"What prompted you to go to sea?" James asked.

"After I moved to The Grand, I couldn't settle. I wanted to enlist, but the cavalry turned me away. The merchant navy needed cooks and they gave me a ship right away. It was lousy pay, but I didn't care. Mind you, I hadn't bargained for the treatment I would get on board. The cook on board a ship is the lowest of the low, it is considered woman's work and hated by most of the crew—with good reason I might add.

"The food on most ships was, and still is, terrible. I used my cooking skills to give the food flavour and nutrition. Seamen work hard and need a substantial diet. It took about two voyagers before I finally gained some respect.

"The solitude of life at sea suited me. I enjoy the challenge of cooking tasteful meals with the bare bones of ingredients. I have seen spectacular countries and met some unusual and interesting people. During the war, the damned U-boats had everyone on edge. The silent enemy lurking below us; very disquieting."

"I am curious. You mentioned the cavalry. Why the cavalry?"

"I have been around horses all my life and I ride well. I thought it would be a good place to serve."

"The cavalry was perhaps the worst place to be. Those generals who served in Africa, including my father, could not comprehend the terrain or the enemy in Europe. The horrific carnage of horses and men was a direct result of bad decisions by arrogant, powerful men. I am one of the lucky ones. A bit of shrapnel in my leg but I am alive. The reason Alex and I became friends was because of the horrors we had witnessed. Battle scenes of dead, mutilated bodies haunt you forever. We both suffered terrible nightmares," James took a breath. "Every time I close my eyes, I see a muddy face, eyes staring in death. I hear men cry out in fear, shrieking in pain—heads blown up, limbs missing and the horses screaming as they lay helpless in the mud." James stopped to control his voice. "Enough of the war." He coughed, shifting in his seat. "Your sea voyagers sound more exciting."

"At times more excitement than I would have liked. My worst experiences were hurricane and typhoon force storms. Petrified, I watched man against nature, and nature was on the winning side. How the captain kept us afloat as the ship pitched almost vertically and then twisted and rolled with forty-foot waves towering above us, I will never know. After the first couple of storms, you learn to trust the captain, follow orders and, surprisingly, wake the next morning to blue sky."

Mrs. Bromley, red-cheeked and huffing, pushed the door open with her foot and entered, carrying a tray of pudding.

"That steak and kidney pie was excellent, Mrs. Bromley," Bill said.

"Glad you enjoyed it. It was one of Mr. Bromley's—God rest his soul—favourites." She set down a treacle tart and a steaming jug of thick, creamy custard.

"Even I can't cook food like this. It is a treat. Thank you." Bill smiled.

Bill ate two helpings of treacle tart before they moved to the easy chairs. James poured brandy. Content and relaxed they puffed on cigars and sipped the warming liquid.

"James, what happened to old Pickles? It seems there is a big secret nobody is talking about."

"Mr. Kendrick warned the staff that there would be consequences if anyone spoke of the Pickles' incident. He was afraid for the hotel's reputation. I can't be sure of exactly what happened but I am certain Anna had something to do with it. She never mentioned it to Alex or me. I only know the details Mr. Kendrick revealed plus a bit of gossip and some observation on my part."

"What happened? How was the hotel's reputation in jeopardy? I always suspected Pickles made advances to the maids. I think he might have tried it with Anna. Did he cook the books too?"

"All the above. Remember the commotion when Anna moved her desk near the telephone exchange? I think he attacked Anna that morning."

"I do remember and I had the same suspicions, but Anna wouldn't talk about it."

James refilled their brandy glasses. "Anna must have reported him, because after Anna and Alex left for London, Mr. Kendrick's shiny black Bentley pulled up under the portico. He and his accountant marched into Mr. Pickles' office and there was a hell of a row. Mr. Pickles' voice could be heard above the others, "It's all her fault. Now that she's gone, we need to remove Lytton and Banks and that little trouble maker, the maid."

197

I could hear things crashing and breaking. Mrs. Banks came up to the reception counter looking pale and nervous. I thought she might faint. She had heard too. Next thing, I hear sirens and the lobby is full of policemen and a paddy wagon pulls up behind the Bentley. A man in plain clothes introduced himself as Detective Durham from Eastbourne. We are told not to move as he directed the constables to close and lock all the doors. He asks me if I am Mr. Pickles. I shake my head...vigorously I might add, and point to the office. I was *scared*. I had just heard Pickles accusing me of something and now the police were in his office. Guests had gathered on the landing and stairs, asking why the police were in the building. The policeman ushered them back to their rooms. The noise from the office reached a crescendo; Detective Durham boomed over Pickles' pleading voice, which was followed by one loud *thud* and then silence."

James drew on his cigar and blew smoke circles in the air. Bill, mesmerized by the drama motioned to James to continue.

James took a sip of brandy. "The office door opened and Pickles is in handcuffs—if you can believe that—flanked on both sides by policemen. He has a black eye and blood is dripping from his bottom lip; his contorted face is covered with those red blotches. He looked grotesque. I backed away, bumping into poor Mrs. Banks, who had moved close to me. She gasped to muffle a scream. Pickles shouted, 'Let me go, you've got the wrong person. It's that harlot you should be arresting.' He struggled like a weasel; the policemen were more or less carrying him to the paddy wagon. All but one of the constables left the hotel, and Detective Durham was in the office talking to Mr. Kendrick. Mrs. Banks and I didn't quite know what to do when Mr. Kendrick came up to the reception desk and explained that Mr. Pickles had been charged with fraud, among other things."

"*Other things*. Did they say what?" Bill interrupted.

"I'm coming to that," James continued, "He instructed Mrs. Banks to calm the guests and reassure them they were in no danger. He then directed *me* into the office where the accountant was inspecting the ledgers. I don't mind telling you, Bill, I was bloody scared. Detective Durham stood in front of me, giving me an accusatory stare. Mr. Kendrick must have seen the expression on my face and gave me a reassuring smile. Not very reassured, I listened to what he had to say. 'Mr. Lytton, as you have witnessed, Mr. Pickles is no longer general manager and I am promoting you to the position.' It took me a minute to digest what he had said—*me* general manager? Apparently Pickles had been stealing and defrauding the hotel for some time. I had suspected as much because when I came back from the war he wouldn't let me work on the books."

Bill frowned. "Did Anna know about the fraud? How was Anna involved?"

"I am sure she knew. Anna was promoted to front desk clerk while I was at war. She wasn't too pleased when I returned. She told me about some correspondence from Kendrick Hotels Ltd, which led to questions about expenses. But Pickles always managed to cover it up. My first assignment as general manager was to work with Mr. Goldberg, the accountant, to get the books straight. Mr. Goldberg was quite the gossip and revelled in his account of the *other charges.* He told me that Pickles had been charged with a whole litany of crimes including attempted rape, indecent and lewd behaviour, assault and battery, assaulting a police constable and resisting arrest."

Bill felt a cold chill pass over him. He couldn't be sure whether he felt anger or pain at the thought of Pickles touching Anna. He looked at James. "Oh God, I hope he didn't hurt Anna."

"Bill, I wish I could tell you he did not hurt her. Much of this happened while I was in France. I can tell you she was well and appeared unharmed when I was re-engaged as front desk clerk. Her pride was hurt when Pickles took great glee out of demoting her, but there was nothing physical to my knowledge."

"Bill laughed and said, "I can imagine Anna's displeasure at being demoted. How did you stay friends?"

"Anna never blamed me, she accepted it. But I think that it had a lot to do with their decision to leave The Sackville."

"Anna would not take kindly to the humiliation, and she does not forgive easily," Bill said.

"According to Mr. Goldberg, Mrs. Kendrick, who works in the London office and supports working women, told him Mr. Kendrick thought highly of Anna, attributing the success of The Sackville to Anna's efforts and not Pickles'. Mr. Goldberg thought the Kendricks had every intention of promoting Anna to the position of general manager. Displeased and angry when Anna gave her notice, they were convinced that Pickles had forced Anna to leave. A fact that was confirmed by another letter that I believe also came from Anna."

"Did Anna know of the Kendricks' intentions?"

"No. I am sure she and Alex would have stayed, had they known of the prospects. Anna would have done well as general manager. Pickles knew how good she was and that terrified him."

"James, how could Mr. Kendrick have possibly known of all Pickles' wrong doings? I can understand the fraud; his accountants would see that. But the other charges?"

"The second letter insisted on confidentiality to protect the staff and referred Mr. Kendrick to Dr. Gregory. It seems that not only had Dr. Gregory witnessed the results of Pickles' perverted behaviour but had statements, photographs and evidence of wrong doing from hotel staff going back six years. Together, Dr. Gregory and Mr. Kendrick reported the crimes to local police and the higher authorities in Eastbourne. I presume that that is how they managed to coordinate the police raid and arrest. Detective Durham spent much time here collecting statements and evidence. The last time he came, he confided in me that there was enough evidence to put Pickles on the end of a rope, but at the very least he would get life imprisonment. I believe he said the trial is set for early December, and Pickles will stay incarcerated until the trial."

"Hanging is a just reward for such an evil man." Bill shook his head and stifled a yawn. "I think I will take you up on your offer of a bed, if Mrs. Bromley doesn't mind. I have to leave early in the morning to get back to the ship. We sail tomorrow and I need to get supplies."

The ship rolled slightly and Bill's boots clanged on the metal ladder as he ascended to the deck. Mid-afternoon, Bill took a cigarette break from the steamy, confined space of the galley. He liked the solitude of the wide-open ocean. It cleared his head to think. He mulled over all he had learned at Bexhill.

Grateful that his friend Alex had survived the war, he was ashamed of his thoughts that Alex, his rival in love, had lived. He needed to accept it, as he had to accept Alex's marriage to Anna. His desire to be close had not waned, and Anna would remain in his future as his friend.

Black clouds hung on the horizon; an Atlantic storm was brewing. He tried to light a Woodbine. Six matches later, he walked to the stern for shelter. He inhaled the relaxing smoke and stared at the emptiness of the vast ocean. He felt a presence, a sense of peace overwhelmed him. He wasn't alone.

A ship was approaching from behind, black smoke billowing from its funnels and moving at a much greater speed than the S.S. Dorset. Bill recognized it as one of the big trans-Atlantic passenger liners. The two ships spoke with loud blasts from their respective horns as the liner passed the S.S. Dorset.

Bill slowly exhaled smoke from his lungs and felt unexplained emotion enter his body. Watching the liner cut through the growing swell of the Atlantic waves, the image changed. Pale and forlorn, Anna stood before him, holding a book. He reached out to touch her and called into the wind, "Anna, I'm here!" but she was gone. He remembered telling Anna he would always be there for her. Flicking his cigarette butt, he watched the orange tip twist away in the now gale force wind. He shook his head, wondering what had just happened.

Confused and unsettled, Bill strode back to the galley, compensating for the heave and sway of the ship. He had become accustomed to storms and found the small ones invigorating on deck but in the galley he and his shipmates battened down the pots and pans, secured the dishes in the racks, and played catch with loose objects. Over the years, Bill had learned to roll with the ship and continue preparing the food. It was a rare storm that prevented a meal being served to a hungry crew and this storm would be over soon.

Late on August fifth, the S.S. Dorset, heavy with cargo, slowly riding the evening tide, edged through the narrow channel. Entering and leaving port were Bill's favourite parts of the journey. He particularly enjoyed the approach to Halifax; the tiny islands on each side of the channel sat gleaming like emeralds, the massive ship intruding on their tranquility. Bill frowned as they passed Halifax Ocean Terminal, a passenger liner was moored at Pier 21, the name on her stern R.M.S. Arcadia, was loading supplies. Once again he felt besieged with Anna's presence; he felt sadness, but it wasn't his. *It's uncanny,* he thought, *Anna feels so close.* He shook his head to break the intense sensation.

The ship moved in slow motion, revealing a scene he could never have imagined. The lush green turned to black. Shock and dismay overcame Bill, charred naked sticks that were once trees stood in blackened open spaces, rubble where families once lived. Since the Halifax explosion in 1917, they had sailed directly to New York or Boston, he had never seen such destruction. How could anyone have survived? And yet, as they approached the dock, the atmosphere felt upbeat—the phoenix rises, he thought. Determination sprang from the pores of the labour. Saws whined, hammers banged and the smell of fresh cut wood permeated the dock. Shocked by the devastation, Bill was reminded of how quickly things can change. His thoughts returned to Anna and he made a decision—he needed to be near Anna. He would leave the ship when it returned to Britain at Christmas.

Seventeen

Toronto 1919 – Kenwood Bakery

Anna lay in bed, heeding the new sounds around her. The kettle whistled its readiness for Alex to make morning tea, and the hum of the mixer below told her Nick had started baking. She delighted in the raindrops glistening in the streetlight, tapping a cheery good morning on the window. Breathing in the aroma of the new furniture, she pulled the covers up to her face, feeling the smoothness and freshness of the new linen. The clock ticked past five. No stranger to early mornings, Anna flung her arms out of the covers; she wanted to sing from the treetops. And then it struck her how well she felt, no sickness.

Alex came into the bedroom carrying two cups of tea with arrowroot biscuits in the saucers. Placing them on the bedside table, he switched on the lamp.

"Good morning, my darling," he said, kissing her on the forehead. "Tea and biscuits to sooth your tummy."

"It's gone. Alex, the sickness has gone. I feel wonderful today."

"Really! Just like that?" Alex drank his tea and with a mouthful of biscuits said, "I am going to see Nick. I think it better you stay in bed and I will make you breakfast later."

Delighted to be feeling so well, Anna swung her legs out of bed, dressed and went to the kitchen. They said little over breakfast, content to be with each other in their new home. Alex cleared the table, suggesting Anna rest.

"It is wonderful that you are feeling better but I don't want you getting overtired. Why don't you sit in the window seat and read?"

"Alex! I am having a baby. I'm not an invalid, and it is only six in the morning. I want to take a look at the ledgers and accounts. You work with Nick and learn how to bake bread and I will take care of the office."

The office, which was little more than an oversized closet situated next to the back door, was dark and dingy. It had one small dirty window that looked onto St. Clare Avenue. Every surface was covered in a thick layer of dusk, white with flour particles and the cobwebs that hung like white lace in each corner of the ceiling. The desk, a cabinet and two chairs were piled high with papers, pamphlets and unrecognizable samples—it all stood frozen in time. She chuckled aloud. The scene could have come out of a Dickens novel. It had a ghostly, Jacob Marley quality to it.

Nick's voice intruded her thoughts. "Sorry, Mrs. Walker, the office is a bit of a mess. Old Mr. Draper took care of the books and his wife cleaned but since she died and he took ill, no one's been in here. I'm no good at the book stuff."

"Nick, who kept the accounts?"

"No one kept the books after old Mr. Draper left. Young Mr. Draper came by on Fridays to pick up the mail, paid my wages and took the week's takings to the bank. Excuse me, Mrs. Walker, but I have to proof the dough."

Proof the dough, Anna thought, smiling, wondering what exactly happened to the dough when proofed. *But,* she thought, *I'll leave Alex to sort that out.* She found the ledger: a large, long black book, recently used with only a thin layer of dust on the cover. Tucked into the cover were several statements from suppliers. This was a start, she thought, and took the ledger up to the apartment.

Anna was appalled by the poor bookkeeping. At first glance, it appeared the sales did not cover the expenses. Unless they made some drastic changes, the bakery would not make enough money to support her and

204

Alex, let alone a baker. Would the bank extend her credit? She hated the thought of credit. It was such a dangerous route to take. The obvious solution was her inheritance.

Just the thought of using more of Lady Thornton's money evoked feelings of sadness and disloyalty. Following Uncle Bertie's journeys to India or the Rocky Mountains cost money, and with the money spent it would annihilate her dreams. "Follow your dreams and don't let anyone destroy them," Uncle Bertie's words stuck in her throat. Had she already destroyed that dream with a baby on the way?

"Why so pensive?"

"Alex, did you look at the books before you purchased Kenwood Bakery?"

"No, Mr. Peabody, the bank manager, said the business was in good order. I took his word. Why do you ask?"

"The bakery is operating at a loss."

"Don't you worry your pretty head about money. We have lots of money. Nick is an amazing baker. The customers I met today have high praise for Nick's bread. Nick and I make a good team. We'll soon have this place overflowing with customers."

Typical Alex, his head in the clouds, she thought. He had not heard one word of what she had said. His dismissive attitude was irritating, almost to the point of making her angry. But that would do no good. She needed to get to work.

First she must get the office cleaned up. She'd ask Abigail to help. Pleased at having been asked, Abigail arrived the next morning to start the clean-up. By the end of the day, the office had a clean aroma of polish, carbolic and a hint of Dettol. Abigail had wanted to make sure there were no bugs lurking in the corners. The oak furniture shone and the old linoleum floor, cracked and scuffed with wear, was at least clean. People were now visible through the window as they walked along St. Clare Avenue.

Admiring their work, Anna gazed out of the clean window at a dull, grey day. "The dampness and gloominess of November reminds me of home."

"This will pass. November is the most dreary month here. In spite of the cold, most Canadians prefer blue skies and sunshine."

Anna agreed, but having no concept of what Abigail meant by *cold,* she would in the future change her mind.

"I have some lace curtains at home that would fit that window and give you some privacy. I'll bring them tomorrow. Now I must get home for little Jimmy."

Anna sat down behind her desk on a modern captain's chair. Mounted on casters, the chair moved around the desk easily; it also swivelled and rocked. She liked the feel of it and quietly relished being the king of her own castle. The confidence she had felt at The Sackville during the war returned.

She glanced around the office. *I shall enjoy running Kenwood Bakery,* she thought with satisfaction. Two stacks of papers she had deemed important sat atop the desk and she began to read and sort them before filing them in the cabinet. She frowned. Some of these bills did not match the ledger; the bills had all been paid, she found nothing outstanding, but these expenses were not listed. The bakery was not just running at a loss, it was close to bankruptcy. Panic gripped Anna as she thought of the baby. Where were they headed—to the poorhouse? Or were they destined to spend the rest of their lives in a room in Jim and Abigail's apartment?

"Anna. Whatever is wrong?"

"Oh Alex, Nothing. I was studying the accounts and I didn't hear you." Quickly closing the ledger, she forced a smile.

"It's six o'clock. I have closed the shop, and now I am ready for dinner and an evening with my wife," Alex said with his lips on her head. Anna pushed back one of her wayward curls. How could she tell him? Only two days in business and they were on the brink of disaster.

The two stacks of paper on Anna's desk had been reduced to one small pile. She made a list of the bills not listed in the ledger and decided she would introduce herself to the suppliers. The man at the flour mill tried to brush her off and laughed in her face, he could not comprehend doing business with a woman. Anna produced a roll of bills from her reticule and paid for the first order. Insisting on cash-on-delivery, he agreed to supply the bakery with flour.

At Ned's Warehouse, she found Ned more cooperative. Mr. Draper had been in arrears but he explained that the bank had paid all the arrears about two weeks ago. Ned said it was unusual as Mr. Draper always paid cash. He grunted and gave Anna a wry smile when Anna introduced herself as the new owner. But he said as long as the bills were paid in a timely manner, he was happy to do business with Kenwood Bakery. She felt a jolt in her stomach as she smiled her assurance, at the same time wondering if the money would be forthcoming.

On the tramcar heading home, Anna thought about her findings. She surmised the bank manager's loyalties would be with his client, Mr. Draper, and it looked as though the bank had paid off a considerable debt from the proceeds of the sale, misrepresenting the status of the bakery. Furious at being taken for a fool, she would confront Mr. Peabody. She shuddered at the thought. A weedy looking man with a pointy nose, he reminded her of Mr. Pickles; immaculate in dress, stiff high collar, conservative grey waistcoat and black tails, he had made it quite obvious he did not approve of Anna's forward ways. Anna sent a letter to the Bank of Toronto requesting an appointment.

Two days later a letter arrived, inviting *Mr.* Alex Walker to attend a meeting with Mr. Peabody at two o'clock the next day. Anna had signed the letter Mrs. Anna Walker. The dismissal annoyed her, prompting her decision to attend the interview alone. After all she knew more about the accounts than Alex. This was her job, and Mr. Peabody had better get used to it.

Anna opened the wardrobe door, carefully making her choice of appropriate attire. She slipped on a simple white silk blouse and stepped into the box-pleated skirt of a silver-blue wool suit. The waistband uncomfortably tight, she left the top button undone—upset that her tiny waist had already expanded. The fashionable loose-fitting jacket would cover the unbuttoned skirt.

She placed her black velvet, turban style hat at an angle and the blue ostrich feather fluttered as she moved. Finally, she pulled on her black leather gloves, finishing the ensemble perfectly. Not trusting the overcast skies, she picked up her umbrella, and slipped out of the back door. Alex would assume she had gone to Abigail's for tea.

Standing on the corner of Bay and King streets, Anna gazed up at the staunch, impressive building that exuded power and authority. Suddenly she felt like David preparing to meet Goliath. The doorman opened the big heavy doors of the Bank of Toronto. Anna pulled herself up to her full five-foot four-inches height, put her chin in the air and breathed in the stuffy male aroma as she marched down the massive hall. Her club heel shoes tapped rhythmically on the marble floor and men turned and stared while whispering to colleagues. Anna kept walking until she found the reception desk.

"I have an appointment with Mr. Peabody for two o'clock," she said to the stern, excessively thin clerk, who could have been male or female except for the tight chignon on top of her head. Her gender confirmed by her nameplate Miss P. Peabody, the family resemblance unmistakable.

"Madam, Mr. Peabody is already booked at two o'clock."

Anna took the letter from her black beaded reticule and thrust it under the woman's nose. "My name is Mrs. Walker. *I* will be meeting with Mr. Peabody."

Anna was asked to take a seat and Miss Peabody went scurrying off behind a large wooden door. Appearing again within seconds, she held the door open and invited Anna to pass through. Anna froze as she heard the door click behind her. The dark wooden panelled office, stuffed leather chairs and a smirking Mr. Peabody, morphed into Mr. Pickles, he was leaning over to touch her; she nearly screamed and then realized he only wanted to shake her hand. Anna wanted to run, to get out of this office. Fortunately, sanity prevailed. She forced her memories out of her head, took a deep breath and even managed a smile as she politely shook his hand.

"Mrs. Walker, I would prefer to wait for your husband."

"Then you will wait a long time, Mr. Peabody. My husband will not be joining us. I handle the accounts for Kenwood Bakery."

"This is most irregular. What can you possibly understand about money except perhaps how to spend it?" He finished with a raucous *cu-fuf* of a laugh, obviously thinking his remark was clever.

Anna gulped down her temper—dangerously close to exploding.

"Mr. Peabody, the money that you have in your bank is *my* money bequeathed to me in *my name* by Lady Thornton of London, England. If you would rather I remove my money to the Dominion Bank, I will do so today."

Mr. Peabody huffed and puffed but assured Anna that would not be necessary.

"We'll see about that, Mr. Peabody. I have some questions about the accounting prior to my purchase of Kenwood Bakery. There seem to be some discrepancies."

Now it was Anna's turn to smile as Mr. Peabody shuffled in his chair; he gave a few coughs, his index finger pulling on his stiff collar. "Mr. Draper was elderly. There may have been some confusion."

Anna watched him intently, half expecting to see red blotches appear. "My concern is that the bank misrepresented the accounts. I found many receipts dated after the sale of Kenwood Bakery and not entered in the ledger; debt that the Bank of Toronto did not disclose.

Mr. Peabody cocked his head to one side, curled his lips into a placating smile and said, "Mrs. Walker, accounting is very complicated. I would not expect you to fully understand the complexities. I can assure you the bank acted with the utmost rectitude."

"Mr. Peabody, before I came to Canada, I was in charge of managing the prestigious Sackville Hotel in Bexhill-on-Sea. I fully understand the complexities of accounting." Anna crossed her fingers that he would not challenge her on either her position at The Sackville or her accounting experience.

"Commendable, I am sure, Mrs. Walker. What is it you would like the bank to do?"

"I would like the bank to extend Kenwood Bakery credit for a short time, allowing us to cover the undisclosed discrepancies and bring the bakery into profitability or perhaps I could report the unusual accounting to the authorities." Anna held her breath.

"Unfortunately, Kenwood Bakery would not qualify for credit at this time."

Mr. Peabody stood up from his desk and walked to the door. "Now if there is nothing further, I have other appointments. Good day, Mrs. Walker." Anna had no choice but to follow Mr. Peabody to the door. She had been dismissed.

Anna rocked to and fro on her office chair, painfully aware that her reaction to Mr. Peabody had almost been her undoing. How could such long ago memories burst into life as though they happened just yesterday? She could feel the fear, and what if she couldn't control her fear the next time a pseudo Mr. Pickles appeared? She prayed he had been brought to justice. She had thought that reporting him would be enough for her to forget, but she found herself wondering if Dr. Gregory had followed through with their plan. She needed to know if he had been punished, perhaps then she could forget. Writing to Dr. Gregory would be simple, or would it? Alex didn't know about the attack and she was not ready, and might never be ready, to tell him. And, she thought, if I contact Dr. Gregory, Alex would ask questions.

"Anna, you don't look well. Has the sickness returned?" asked Alex from the hallway.

A pang of guilt stabbed her upon hearing Alex's voice, knowing she was keeping a secret. But she couldn't tell him. She had to forget about Mr. Pickles.

"No, I feel quite well."

"So why so serious?"

"Alex, I need to talk to you about something."

The shop doorbell chimed and Alex hesitated. "Of course but Nick has gone home. I need to serve the customers." Alex frowned. "Anna what is wrong? Is it the baby?"

A voice rang out from the shop, "Is anyone there?"

"No, Alex, I'm fine. Go and see to the customer. We can talk about this when the shop closes at six."

That evening Anna proceeded to tell Alex of her findings in the bakery accounts books, her visit to the suppliers and the day's meeting with Mr. Peabody.

"Anna, you should have told me. Don't you trust me?" The hurt was quite clear in his voice. She felt guilty, but sometimes her need to be independent masked consideration for others, especially Alex.

"I am sorry, Alex. I should have confided in you. The whole idea of the bakery was to give us work, compensation, and a place to live. The bakery barely makes enough money to pay Nick's wages let alone pay us."

"It can't be that bad. You worry too much."

"Alex, stop being the optimist. This is serious."

"Why don't you ask Jim to look at the ledger? He'll know what to do."

Sunday, the only day the shop was closed, Anna invited Jim and Abigail over for lunch. It would be the first time she and Alex had entertained in their new home, and they were both looking forward to the afternoon. After lunch, Alex and Abigail played with little Jimmy while Jim and Anna went into the office. Surprised at how quickly Jim went through the ledger, Anna didn't have long to wait for his comments.

"At first glance, Anna, I think I can reassure you that the bakery is a viable business. Your income from sales this first week is more than double that of any previous weeks."

"How could that happen? Although I am relieved to hear we are not bankrupt."

"Here is what I think has happened. It looks to me as though young Mr. Draper did not deposit the full amount of the shop's takings. I suspect he pocketed about half the money. He paid the suppliers enough cash to keep them quiet, which enabled him to make false entries in the ledger. I doubt the bank would know about it until after the sale of the bakery, at which time the bank would be obliged to pay the arrears. Mr. Peabody should have made Alex aware of the situation and he was perhaps embarrassed when you confronted him."

"He was rude and placating. I don't like the weedy little man."

"I understand, but you must understand that bank managers are old-fashioned and they can make or break a business. Threatening him was not a good idea. I deal with Mr. Peabody through my work and I know him well. Anna, you have to swallow your pride and try to get along with the man. The fact that you have considerable money in his bank is good. He will treat you well because of the money. First we have to apologize."

"Never!"

"If you want to learn how to operate a business, Anna, you will have to curb your stubbornness, and there will be times you have to do things you don't like. I will study these books and make sure there are no other discrepancies. Once I have an understanding of your business, we will meet with Mr. Peabody."

Jim found no further discrepancies in the books and he assured Anna that prior to Mr. Draper's illness and his son's involvement, the store made a good profit. Together, they met with Mr. Peabody and the bank did offer credit. Although the bakery was doing well and didn't need it, Jim advised Anna to take it, anyway.

Jim was a good mentor and teacher. Anna learned the finer points of business accounting from him and quickly earned a reputation for bartering and prompt payment among the suppliers. Mr. Peabody reluctantly conceded that, for a woman, she had an astute sense for business.

Alex learned the practical side of the bakery from Nick, who had learned to bake at his father's knee. But tragedy struck the family. His Austrian-born father's heavy accent had ostracized him during the war, resulting in the family bakery falling into ruins, and ultimately the humiliation killed both his parents. Old Mr. Draper hired Nick and Kenwood Bakery thrived on his high quality European breads and pastries until young Mr. Draper took over and the bakery went into a steady decline. Nick's enthusiasm to teach Alex and see Kenwood Bakery rise from the dust showed in his cheerful disposition and hard work.

February was colder than Anna could ever have imagined. She wrapped her thick cardigan around her as she looked through the office window. A veil of white obscured the view of St. Clare Avenue as the snow fell thick and fast. She worried about Alex clearing the sidewalk, yet again. The cold made him cough and wheeze, but the City of Toronto bylaws dictated that residents must clear their sidewalks.

The baby kicked inside her and she wondered if her skirt might be too tight even though it was her loosest skirt and she had left the waistband undone. At five months, she couldn't hide her pregnancy anymore.

At times she felt lonely. There was no one she could talk to about her true feelings and her apprehension about motherhood and her fear of being pulled deeper and deeper into housewifery was closing in on her. And yet, she thought, she had settled contentedly with Alex in their apartment. Being in charge of the business side of the bakery challenged and satisfied her business talents. What more could she want?

Few customers ventured out on such a cold day. Anna had sent Nick home early and Alex was clearing snow outside, leaving Anna to concentrate on the books. The unexpected ding of the shop doorbell startled her as a blast of cold air entered the store.

The mailman stood cold and covered in snow at the counter. "Some mail for you from Scotland, Mrs. Walker."

"You must be very cold. Can I offer you a hot drink?" Anna asked, taking the letter.

"That's kind of you, Mrs. Walker, but I am almost finished and just want to get home."

Anna went back to the office and opened the letter from Alex's father. She found it odd that his father always wrote the letters. In her family, it was her mother and sister who wrote regularly with the family news.

News from Scotland was sparse but welcome:

Dear Anna and Alex,

How happy Mother and I were to hear the news that we are to be grandparents again. I hope Anna is keeping well; a cousin for little Jimmy. How are Jim and Abigail? Do you see them often? Give them our love.

Your mother and Florence are entertaining lavishly and it is hard to keep up with them at times. Thank goodness the shop is doing well. I have more kilt orders than I have time to tailor and sew. Last month I hired someone to help me. It seems to be working out. I get tired easily these days. I must be getting too old to work the long hours.

We had a surprise visitor over Christmas. Your old friend Bill Blaine came calling. His mother died a few months ago while he was at sea. His father, William, and I are still good friends; he took his wife's death pretty hard, so he was glad to see Bill.

Bill came to Edinburgh looking for you. He said he went to the Sackville Hotel in Bexhill in July to find that he had just missed you. Unfortunately, they told him you had moved to Scotland. He did not know you had emigrated to Canada. His ship left Southampton about the same time that you left from Liverpool, both heading for North America. Bill thought you had settled in Scotland and knowing his ship would be docking in Glasgow at Christmas he had planned to surprise you. He was astounded and upset when I told him you were in Toronto. I gave him your address, but he didn't say what his plans were.

Love from Father, Mother and Florence

Anna placed her hand on her chest. She could feel her heart race at the thought of Bill looking for them. But more to the point, she felt relief he was alive and well. Anna thought hopefully that he might write or come and visit. A blast of cold air whistled past Anna's desk as Alex opened the back door. She could hear him coughing and wheezing from the exertion of shovelling snow.

"I will close the shop, Alex. You go upstairs and I'll make you a hot drink."

Anna covered the few loaves of bread on the shelves and took the cash drawer from the till but stopped before going in to the office.

"Alex, what is wrong?" Alex was clinging to the banister leaning against the wall his face the colour of putty.

"I... can't... huh... get my... huh... breath."

Anna grabbed the office chair and pushed it up to Alex and helped him to sit down. She sat on the stairs opposite to him, holding his wet, clammy hands, while willing him to breathe slowly. Sweat poured down his face; she put her hand on his forehead.

"Alex, you are burning up." He stared at her with glazed eyes, wheezing air into his lungs. Thankful that Alex had insisted on installing a telephone, she telephoned Dr. McCarthy. Anna shook with fear at the worried tone in Dr. McCarthy's voice, instructing her not to move him. Alex struggled to breathe. Anna felt helpless and terrified—was Alex going to die?

Dr. McCarthy examined Alex in the chair and sighed with relief. "It's okay. We can move him now. He has bronchitis and we need to get him to bed." Seeing Anna's worried look he added, "His symptoms could have been a heart attack, Mrs. Walker. That's why I asked you not to move him but his heart is fine. His chest is not."

Alex was confined to his bed for a week. Anna applied a mustard poultice to his chest twice a day and sat with him until his breathing became normal. The cough mixture Dr. McCarthy prescribed didn't seem to help and Anna worried that the persistent cough was serious. He needed rest but Anna had difficulty keeping him quiet, let alone in bed. In all the activity, Anna had forgotten to give Alex the letter from his father. When she gave it to him, he was pleased to have news of home but alarmed about his father's health; it wasn't like him to say he was tired or getting old. Anna noticed that he ignored the news about Bill.

Dr. McCarthy confirmed Anna's fears. The damage sustained from the gas attack during the war had weakened his lungs and he suspected the flour dust in the bakery might be an added irritant. He advised Alex to keep out of the dust, which was impossible to do in the bakery. Alex brushed it off, saying he would be fine and everything went back to normal.

Eighteen

Baby Isabelle is Born

A nna welcomed the warm May sun on her face. Her swollen legs were stretched out on the window seat. She leaned on the cushions, trying to read with the book balanced on her large round belly. Everyone told her how well she looked—the glow of motherhood—Abigail's favourite expression.

Anna hated being pregnant and in spite of Abigail she felt fat and ugly, and she did not feel well. Her back ached and no matter where or how she sat, she could not get comfortable. Dr. McCarthy had ordered bed rest to reduce the swelling in her legs but when she lay on her back the baby kicked her ribs until they were sore. She had compromised and agreed to rest on the window seat. Even her book collection did not keep her amused for long.

Forbidden to go downstairs to the office, she worried about the accounts. Jim had promised to drop in on Saturdays and bring everything up to date. Gazing out of the window, she saw Abigail walking towards the bakery and groaned at the thought of an afternoon of Abigail's conversation. It seemed she had assumed Anna's pregnancy had reformed her into God's gift to housewifery, linking them together with more sisterly affection than Anna cared to accept.

Kind and attentive, Abigail just wanted to help. Helping was something she did well. She helped Anna set up the nursery and prepare for the midwife. But Anna desperately needed a confidante, and dear Abigail would never understand how she felt.

"Follow your dreams and don't let anyone destroy them." Uncle Bertie's wise words were slipping away, along with her dreams. Lady Thornton had understood her, and so had Bill, but for different reasons they were both unreachable. She had hoped Bill would write. She secretly wondered if he might visit when his ship docked in Halifax, or even closer in Montreal.

"How are you Anna? I have brought a meat pie for your dinner. I'll put it in the kitchen and pop the kettle on." Abigail's voice came from the hall.

Anna stood up and a sharp pain resonated through her body. Sitting too long, she thought, and paced around the room. Abigail came in with the tea. Another pain shot through her and she winced. "That's the second time today I have had this pain."

"Oh, it's what they call false labour pains. Nothing to worry about. It often happens at this stage. You have what, about four or five more weeks?" Abigail sounded quite confident. "The last few weeks seem the longest. You look tired. Why you don't lie down?"

Anna lay down on the bed, partly because her head ached and her legs and back throbbed, and partly to avoid Abigail's constant chatter. She tried to sleep, but she had several more pains and they were intense. The next pain made her call out for Abigail followed by a plea to fetch Alex and call Dr. McCarthy.

Dr. McCarthy turned to address Alex. "Mr. Walker, your wife is in labour and it is much too early. I am troubled by her swollen legs, which may indicate a condition called toxaemia." He then spoke directly to Anna, "The condition can be serious. I would like you to go to the hospital."

"Hospital?" Alex repeated.

"It's alright, Alex, this is for the best. Now help me downstairs. Dr. McCarthy is driving us in his automobile. I'm ready to have this baby." She tried to smile but stopped as another pain paralyzed her.

The auto swayed and bumped as it flew through Toronto towards the hospital. She felt the urge to push, the pain intense. She wanted to scream but seeing Alex's terrified face, she willed herself to stay quiet. Alex carried her through the big hospital doors and laid her on a stretcher.

Surrounded by white uniforms and faceless people, she clung to Alex's hand. He bent down and kissed her but his tears frightened her. Dr. McCarthy asked Alex to take a seat in the waiting room. He objected, but Dr. McCarthy shouted, panic rising in his voice, "She is in danger. Let us do our job or you will lose both your wife and your baby."

Tears spilled into Anna's hair as she watched Alex disappear. She felt something on her face and then...peace, beautiful peace. She saw faces floating in purple, and white lights swirling in her head and the pain was gone. She liked it here. She dreamed of Alex's red curls, and then Bill's kind face passed by—they both smiled lovingly and in unison mouthed, "I love you."

She felt warm as Papa's hand brushed her cheek saying "Fight... you must fight." Mama smiled and said, "You were always the feisty one." Uncle Bertie floated by saying, "Follow your dreams." Anna felt herself slipping away.

She was tired, oh so tired. Lady Thornton's rich, burgundy dress appeared, one arm outstretched to touch her; the waving black tendrils of her enormous hat beckoned her and then faded away. Anna called out, "It's me, Anna. Tell me what to do. You understand me." But she floated away and a kindly man's face passed before her. "Papa Walker?" she called out, confused as he floated into the light.

Lady Thornton appeared again, a waterfall of tears flowed down her cheeks, surrounding a baby cradled in her arms. "He's safe with me. Anna, stay strong." She merged into the sea of floating faces as they all faded into white light. Anna called out but her voice could not be heard. Silence engulfed her as she felt herself falling, falling, falling, into a deep, black hole.

First she heard voices. Her limbs lay limp and she couldn't move. Her eyelids, too heavy to open, were awash in sadness.

"She's waking up," a stranger's voice whispered.

"Anna! I'm here. You're going to be all right. We have a baby girl."

Anna tried to collect her thoughts. The last thing she remembered was the dream of mixed up faces and the pain, and both were gone.

"Where am I? Alex, I had a dream."

"You are in hospital but you are going to be fine. Anna, we have a baby girl."

"Where is she? Is she all right? The dream, Lady Thornton carried the baby away..." Anna started crying.

Dr. McCarthy entered the ward, giving Anna a kindly smile. "Mrs. Walker, because of birthing complications we sedated you, which caused you to hallucinate. Your baby is doing well. She is very small so the nurses are keeping her warm in the nursery. I will tell the nurse to bring her to you shortly. Now, you must rest."

Alex stroked her hair and smiled but she saw pain. "Alex is something wrong with the baby? I want to see her." Her insides were tight with panic and a sense of grief; there was something they were not telling her.

"The baby is doing well. I will ask nurse to bring her to you, so you can see for yourself. Now promise me you will rest."

Anna relaxed and although she tried to stay awake her eyes would not stay open and she drifted into sleep.

A baby's cry woke her. Alex stood beside the bed, holding a bundle. The nurse helped Anna sit up and he placed the bundle in her arms.

"She is so tiny. I had no idea babies could be this small, but she's beautiful," Anna laughed. "She has her Papa's red curls." The baby kicked and began to cry. The love she felt for this baby was a love so different it filled her to overflowing. *So this is what motherhood feels like,* she thought. All too soon, the nurse insisted the baby had to go back to the nursery. Once again she had a sense that all was not well.

"Alex, is there something you are not telling me?"

Alex cleared his throat. "No, everything will be fine. I will find nurse and see if I can get some tea."

Alex turned and bumped into Dr. McCarthy and guided him away from Anna's bed whispering, "We have to tell her. She knows something is wrong. She will not rest, it is better that she knows."

"What is it?" Anna called out, sitting bolt upright and staring at them both.

Dr. McCarthy stood at the side of the bed. Alex stood close and put his arm around her shoulders to comfort her.

"Mrs. Walker, if you remember, I brought you into hospital because I was afraid you were developing toxemia. I am happy to say toxemia was not the cause of your swollen legs and early confinement. After we delivered your baby daughter last night we realized you were carrying twins. The other baby had no heartbeat. I delivered him with forceps, an instrument we use to deliver babies quickly. The baby boy's heart had stopped; he weighed less than three pounds and we could not revive him."

She leaned on Alex, understanding where the sadness had come from. Lady Thornton's words from her dream made sense. "He's safe with me." She felt calm, a waterfall of her tears spilled into that memory and she felt Alex's tears join hers. No words were spoken, just their thoughts said goodbye to their baby son. Dr. McCarthy discreetly took his leave.

"It is strange to feel sad over a baby we never knew. Alex, I don't want to keep calling him the baby boy. We had chosen names, Isabelle after my mother for our little girl and John after your father for a boy. We will call him John."

"I would like that." Alex looked away. "There is more sad news."

A feeling of dread pulsed through her at the thought of more bad news.

"Jim received a telegram from Scotland this morning… our father died of a heart attack late last night."

Stunned at the news, Anna recalled Papa Walker's face floating by in her dream. "Alex, I am sorry. Such sadness you have endured in one short day. Will you be going to Scotland?"

"And much happiness. I am so proud of you and our baby daughter. I can't leave you and Isabelle. Jim and I have discussed the situation. Jim has the expertise needed to deal with the business and make sure provisions have been made to take care of Mother and Florence. He has booked a passage to Britain from New York and he leaves on the night train."

Alex dismissed his grief with practicalities, but Anna could see the sadness in his face—he had loved his father dearly.

Ten days later, Anna felt quite well and Isabelle's weight had climbed to a healthy five pounds. She was small but strong enough to leave hospital. Abigail welcomed them home: the nursery prepared, the apartment tidy and clean, and dinner in the oven. Anna sat in her window seat gazing onto St. Clare Avenue. How her life had changed since she last sat here. She smiled, surprised at how happy she felt. Perhaps this domestic life was not so bad after all.

Anna's euphoric feeling of motherhood soon waned. Feeding an infant every two hours, day and night, took its toll. At night, if the baby wasn't crying, Alex was wheezing and coughing. Sleep deprived, she worried she wasn't coping. The days were full of laundry; she smelled of sour milk and dirty nappies. She needed to get into the office and do the books. With Jim away, no one had worked on the accounts. Adding to her worries, she received a telephone call from the bank.

A gloating Mr. Peabody said, "Mrs. Walker, your account is in arrears and the bank cannot extend any more credit." Anna panicked. No money in the bank; where had the money gone? Alex said the bakery was doing well.

"Mr. Peabody, I need time to look into the situation." Anna had to shout over Isabelle's crying. "I have my hands full at the moment with my new baby. Mr. Jim Walker was to take care of our accounts during my confinement, but the untimely and unfortunate death of my father-in-law has sent him to Scotland."

"My condolences, but your family affairs are of no concern of mine. I expect the account to be put into good order by tomorrow at five. Perhaps you should have Mr. Walker look after the business and you attend to your family duties."

Anna's anger boiled at Mr. Peabody but she had to attend to her wailing daughter. She assured Mr. Peabody the money would be in the bank by five the next day. Cradling Isabelle, she went to find Alex in the bakery.

"Alex, please tell me the truth. How much money has the bakery made in the last few weeks?"

"More than usual. The week's takings last week were more than double. Nick introduced a new variety of bread. He's still making the maple pie he introduced in April and this week we made a fresh strawberry pie that we can't keep on the shelves. Why do you ask?"

"Because Mr. Peabody just telephoned to tell me we have no money in the bank. Where is the money?"

"Where it always is, in the safe in the office."

"You were supposed to deposit the money every week. Sometimes, Alex, your naivety or lack of thought is exasperating." Anna gave a long sigh, stomping her feet. Isabelle, now on Anna's shoulder, renewed her wailing as Anna flounced into the office.

She counted out over $800 from the safe, relieved that the business was indeed thriving. She immediately sent Alex to make the bank deposit. Anna took Isabelle in the pram to visit Abigail and ask for her help until Jim returned from Scotland. Between them, they established a workable routine.

Jim reported that mother and sister were well and grieving more for their curtailed social life than for the loss of a husband and father. Florence had expressed an interest in coming to Canada, but she would not leave her mother, and Mother had no interest in mixing with savages.

Mother Walker's impression of Canada always made them laugh. For Anna and Abigail, it meant that their mother-in-law was unlikely to take up residence with her sons but with Papa Walker gone, they wondered if she might change her mind.

Kenwood Bakery continued to do well through the summer. Anna managed to find a balance between domestic duties and the business. Alex adored and indulged his daughter, the lack of routine often causing disagreement between him and Anna. The fall leaves turned red and gold and in no time the cold harsh winter blew in with wind and snow.

Anna hated the cold—stubborn freezing temperatures and snow that never went away. Every time Alex cleared the snow from the sidewalk he returned gasping for breath. His skin turned sallow and pasty looking, contrasting the dark circles under his eyes; each breath, already an effort through the flour dust, halted by the freezing temperatures.

Bronchitis struck Alex for the third time in February and Dr. McCarthy suggested they move out of the bakery before the flour dust killed him. At the very least, he should stop working in the bakery. Neither Anna nor Alex wanted to move from the apartment. Managing the bakery was an important part of Anna's life, making the domestic duties bearable, but Alex's deteriorating health concerned them both. Some changes were inevitable.

Anna sat in her window seat, watching the snowflakes hover around the streetlight. Alex coughed and rattled as he poked the fire into a flame of warmth.

"Alex, we have to talk about the future. Do you think it is necessary for us to sell the bakery and move elsewhere?"

"No, I don't want to move. Don't worry, my chest will get better. I will stay away from the flour."

"You can't keep working in the bakery. You heard what the doctor said."

Alex supported himself on the mantelpiece as the coughing reached a climax. Anna said nothing while he pulled air into his lungs and his watery eyes caught hers. He nodded his agreement.

"Do you think you could go back to hotel work? If you were working, we could afford to hire an assistant for Nick."

"Anna, that is the answer. I will find out which of the hotels is hiring."

They switched roles while Alex recovered from bronchitis. He delighted in taking care of Isabelle. Equally delighted, Anna baked with Nick and served customers.

Alex found employment on his first day of searching. In his usual impulsive manner, he did not consult Anna, but came bounding into the office with an excitement that immediately made Anna suspicious. She braced herself for one of Alex's surprises.

"Anna, I am beside myself with excitement. I have found the perfect job."

He looked at her cautiously. "Now don't get upset, it may not be what you are expecting."

"Alex, I have seen that look before. What did you do?"

"I have secured a position as a restaurant manager and I start on Monday."

"That's wonderful news. Where? At the Royal York?"

"Not exactly…" Alex hesitated. "I will be managing the restaurant car on CP passenger trains."

"You accepted a position on the railroad without consulting me?" Anna's thoughts were racing. The railroad meant he would be away from home for days at a time.

"I didn't have time. The general manager at the Royal York Hotel complimented me on my experience but regretted that he had no position open. He advised me to follow the recommendation from Mr. Kendrick's letter of reference and seek a position in management.

"I thought he had dismissed me as he shuffled through some papers on his desk. I bid him good day, but he told me to sit down. Handing me a piece of paper to read, he picked up the telephone receiver. I couldn't believe what I was reading: an opening available on CP Rail. And then I listened to his phone call, 'I have a gentleman sitting in my office who has all the qualities you describe in your letter. May I send him over to meet with you?' He put the telephone back in the cradle and explained to me the position of restaurant manager had opened up unexpectedly in CP Rail's first class restaurant car. He wished me luck and sent me across to the office at Union Station."

Mr. Dryden interviewed me and asked if I could start on Monday. Anna, I am over the moon with happiness. I cannot believe my luck." Alex swung around the tiny office, knocking over the chair in his excitement. He flung his arms around Anna and squeezed her tight. "I have dreamed of this ever since we took the train from Halifax."

Anna's stoic expression and stiff body escaped his notice completely. She should be happy for him, she thought, but instead a fury of resentment built inside her as Alex fulfilled his dreams and she stayed at home.

"Does *your* dream include Isabelle and me?" Her words sounded sharp and accusatory.

Alex looked perplexed. "I don't understand. I thought you would be happy."

"As usual, Alex, you do not think. Your impulsive behaviour is infuriating." She wanted to lash out at him, aware that even in modern 1921 it would be unusual for a husband to consult his wife regarding his choice of work. But, she and Alex were different. She felt dismissed. *He's no better than Mr. Peabody,* she thought.

"The position will take you away from home for days at a time. Who is going to look after Isabelle? You spoil her enough, now she will miss you and I will have to cope with her crying while managing everything else."

"Why are you so upset? We decided together I should look for work outside the bakery. What, did you expect that I tell them that I needed my wife's permission? They would laugh at me. You are being unreasonable."

"Am I? What happened to your promise that even after we married, I would keep working and we would travel the world? Now I am left with looking after a baby, household chores, accounting, serving in the store and helping Nick while you travel across Canada serving and mingling with the elite, putting on your charm with the ladies, and where will that lead? I should have married Bill. He warned me you were a manipulator." Anna stopped, seeing the hurt. She added, "I'm sorry, I didn't mean that."

Alex's red face blended with his hair; he rarely exhibited the typical temper that so often was associated with red hair but today, his temper had flared.

"I have appeased your extraordinary ideas of adventure and independence. We came to Canada, an adventure in itself. We have a shop so you can work. I worked in the bakery until it almost killed me, but you are never satisfied. Yes, you will have to take care of our daughter, but that's your duty as a mother. Now that I have the opportunity to do what I want to do, you are angry with me. Enough, Anna. I am head of this family and it is about time you showed me some respect." Alex stomped out of the office, leaving Anna speechless. She heard the bell ring and the shop door slam. Anna's insides boiled like a witch's cauldron, each emotion splashing up into her throat, the anger having spilled into words she already regretted.

Monday morning, Anna kissed Alex goodbye and wished him luck. They had both regretted the argument, but in spite of the apologies, the words said in anger were irreversible. The unfamiliar goodbye kiss lacked the usual passion, but she saw the passion when he kissed and hugged Isabelle.

He would be on the train all week, accompanied by Mr. Dryden, learning the routine and how things were done in the confined space of a moving train.

Isabelle cried constantly. Whether the cause was missing Papa or the pain of erupting of teeth, it made no difference. Anna had not slept in a week. She brought Isabelle into her bed hoping the comfort would bring sleep to them both, but it did not. During the day, Isabelle rested in her arms while she served customers or worked in the office.

Ten days later, Alex breezed into the bakery full of smiles until he saw Anna's exhausted face. "Anna, whatever happened?"

"Isabelle has not stopped crying since you left." Anna thrust Isabelle into his arms as she marched into the office. She did not want to hear of his wonderful experiences on the train. She resented Alex's freedom and happiness.

Isabelle had stopped crying, falling asleep on Alex's shoulder. He tried to put his free arm around Anna but she moved behind the desk.

"Don't I get a welcome home kiss?"

She leaned forward and pecked his cheek, seeing his hurt expression she tried to smile. "I don't want to disturb Isabelle."

Alex sat in the chair opposite Anna and studied her closely. "What is it, Anna?"

"I'm just tired. There is a lot to do when you are away."

"Would you let me hire an assistant for Nick and take some of the burden off your shoulders?"

"No, that won't be necessary. Abigail has offered to help with Isabelle. I can manage."

Being a martyr and keeping overly busy allowed Anna to mask her fear of being trapped in a life she did not want. She loved Isabelle, but no one understood she wanted more from her life. Her feelings of resentment and jealousy were becoming difficult to mask.

"If you're sure..." Alex broke off, staring at Anna puzzled. "I can at least take over for a couple of days. Why don't we go upstairs? I want to tell you about my trip."

"You go. I'll be up later. I have some things to do."

Aware of pushing Alex away, she sensed a chasm forming between them, afraid it would get deeper and wider if she didn't comply with the traditional role. But she could not and would not comply. Anna told no one of her feelings; there was no one to tell. She put on a brave face, worked hard, ate little and slept less.

Winter turned into a brief spring. Isabelle celebrated her first birthday, and as passengers booked their summer vacations Alex had less and less time at home. By the end of June, the mercury had risen into the high eighties. The lake breeze was still and the wet, humid air hung heavy over Toronto. Anna hated the heat. It drained her of energy. She didn't feel well, her head felt like wet cotton wool and her legs wobbled. She willed them to carry her to her office chair, but as she reached out to grab the wooden arm, it rolled away and her legs disappeared under her.

She lay still, listening to an unfamiliar voice floating in her head. "There, there, dear. You must have fallen on the chair. One of them new chairs on wheels. Dangerous they are. Here, take my hand." Anna couldn't move. Who was this woman spinning in her head? The bell on the door rang and she heard Isabelle's little feet. "Mama, mama!" She must get up, she thought. Then she heard Abigail's voice. "Anna, are you hurt?"

"I found her like that," the woman said. "Heard the chair bang and came to look. I wanted a loaf of bread. Can you serve me?" Abigail stared in disbelief. "Suit yourself, I'll be off. But I need bread for his supper." The woman grabbed a loaf put it in her bag and left.

Abigail scooped Isabelle in her arms and picked up the telephone. "Dr. McCarthy, Anna Walker has collapsed. She can't move or talk. I think she's unconscious. Doctor, she's awful white, what should I…" A deep voice called, "Anna!" Abigail swung around to see Alex bending down over Anna who was beginning to stir. He picked her up and carried her upstairs, laying her on the bed. Anna thought she might be dreaming. "Alex, is that you?"

"Yes, it's really me. They changed my route and I have a couple of days off." Before he could say any more, Abigail brought Dr. McCarthy into the bedroom. He determined Anna had collapsed from exhaustion but warned both she and Alex that this degree of exhaustion was serious. He gave her a tonic to give her an appetite and pills to help her sleep.

"You scared me, Anna." Alex looked at her with more love than she had seen in a long time. "I do not want any argument. We have to find an assistant for Nick."

"I know," she said, not having the strength to argue. "I'm sorry, Alex. I have been stubborn and foolish. Talk to Nick tomorrow. He mentioned his son Henry had finished high school and wants to become a baker. I think Nick was hoping he could work here. I told him we didn't need anyone, but it's obvious we do."

Feeling the comfort and warmth of the bed soak into her back, Anna neither wanted to, nor had the energy to move. She stared into space, wondering what had happened. The bakery had started out so well, and she loved her little daughter and she loved Alex. There were times she felt possessed, she was so angry and resentful. Uncle Bertie echoed in her head, "Follow your dreams." But how? Her inner voice screamed, "and don't let anyone destroy them." Had she destroyed them? Was she blaming Alex and Isabelle? Perhaps it was unrealistic for her to have such dreams.

I can't let them go, she thought, *but I can put them on hold for a while.* Her stubbornness was stupid and dangerous. She had embarrassed and frightened everyone, including herself. She had to adjust.

Although fortuitous that Alex came home unexpectedly, the reason did not please Anna. He had been promoted and assigned to the longer routes going west; a journey that took almost a week, he would be travelling hundreds of miles through Ontario, the Prairies and through the Rocky

Mountains to Vancouver and the Pacific Ocean. Anna wished she could be a part of Alex's journey.

Relieved that they no longer hated each other, Anna kissed him goodbye and wished him luck, knowing it would be two or more weeks before he came home. She promised she would not work too hard. Isabelle locked her little arms around his neck and cried when he handed her to Anna. Finally, she let go and snuggled into Anna's shoulder.

Anna recovered quickly, mostly because of the help that she had previously shunned. Abigail became a second mother to Isabelle. Jim spent some time on the books and Henry started his apprenticeship with his father. The anger had dissipated, but whether the rift would ever heal completely, only time would tell.

She tried to rid herself of the resentment she felt towards Alex as he travelled across Canada, every day an adventure while she rarely set foot beyond St. Clare Avenue. All too often her thoughts wandered to Bill. She missed him, or was it that she missed his validation of her dreams? Years had passed since he went to sea and months since Papa Walker gave him their address in Canada, but still no letter. She wondered if he had settled. Maybe he had found a wife or was he still sailing the open seas? Her thoughts darkened as she imagined his ship wrecked on a craggy coastline in some foreign, barbaric country. No, that couldn't be, she thought. For some inexplicable reason, at that very moment, she felt drawn to him.

Nineteen

Bill Leaves His Ocean Life

J uly 1920, Bill Blaine disembarked the S.S. Dorset in Boston, U.S.A.,
departing his watery life for good. No longer oceans apart from his
beloved Anna, he prepared to start a new life. But why he boarded
that train for Chicago to meet Darcy Thornton instead of Toronto to find
Anna, he could not explain and would always regret.

He bought a one-way train ticket to Chicago and settled contentedly to
enjoy the twenty-four-hour journey. After spending years at sea, staring
at wide expanses of water and distant horizons, broken only by rising or
falling fiery suns or turbulent stormy seas, he feasted on an equally wide
expanse of land. This new horizon was broken by trees and hills. Rivers
meandered through the tapestry of farmland; green meadows with grazing
cows and varying crops that swayed in the breeze.

The train's rhythmic lullaby gave him a good night's sleep and he woke
early, enjoying the many hues of pink and red that painted the clouds and
brushed the top of the trees. A mass of still water mirrored the shoreline
until the far shore faded into the horizon. Lake Erie, he thought, part of
the Great Lakes.

He remembered Anna talking about her Uncle Bertie's adventures on
the Canadian side of these massive lakes. How she would love this train

231

journey. He smiled and banished the thought. He wanted no more rejection from Anna. Now he knew why he was not heading to Toronto. Being in America was fulfilling a boyhood dream, and he abruptly brushed aside any niggling doubts of his new life in Chicago.

He reached into his satchel, which contained a clean shirt, a pair of old trousers and not much more. He hadn't needed much in the way of clothes while at sea. He pulled out a notebook and read, *Darcy Thornton, 21 Lakeside Drive, Chicago.* He smiled and shook his head, putting the notebook in his brown suit pocket. He recalled his unbelievable chance encounter with Darcy in Johannesburg. Bill recollected Darcy's habit of unexpectedly appearing from nowhere when he was at the Sackville, but South Africa seemed an extreme coincidence, even for Darcy.

The S.S. Dorset had docked the day before and Bill was heading for the early morning market to gather fresh supplies for the crew. Passing the passenger terminal, he heard a voice call his name, "Bill... Bill Blaine?" He turned to find Darcy Thornton greeting him like a long-lost friend. No longer a hotel employee, Bill was not constrained by etiquette and welcomed a familiar face. Their short encounter took place while the ship's crew processed the last few first-class passengers.

Darcy was returning to America, where he now lived with his wife, Belle. Bill had had difficulty comprehending this excited, animated man, who he remembered as a rebel, sullen and angry. It had been a mystery to Bill why he befriended a chef's assistant but, obviously, the friendship still stood. He had invited Bill to stay with them, insisting that he write down the address.

During Darcy's proclamation of all things exciting in Chicago, the steward had interrupted, politely asking *Lord*Thornton to board the ship. Bill had given him a quizzical look. Darcy's response had been, "It's a long story; I'll tell you all about it when you visit." That had happened six months ago, and in a few hours Bill would find out if the invitation was indeed genuine and perhaps have the answer to Darcy's new title.

The last part of the journey did not hold Bill's interest and he felt tired and bored with the flat landscape until the train curled around a bend revealing Chicago's skyline. It truly reached for the sky and even from a distance he felt its excitement. Half an hour later, the train clanged along the platform of LaSalle Street Station, hissing and belching to its final stop.

He stood outside the station, hoping for cooler air but sweat trickled down his back—his thick wool suit inappropriate for the Midwest heat. Not quite sure what to do, he looked up and down LaSalle Street. The sidewalks were jammed with people: cowboys, men in dark suits, ladies in soft tea dresses and round hats, Negro porters wheeling barrows of luggage.

The air hung with moisture, seizing the smell of hot, sweaty bodies poorly disguised with perfume and cheap pomade. The noise, a cacophony of activity, was deafening but nobody cared. Hundreds of people rushed around laughing, animated, keyed up for some unseen, exciting purpose.

Bill felt his initial revulsion of smell, noise and too many people too close dissipate and an involuntary smile curved his mouth as he became caught up in the excitement of Chicago. He nodded to two young ladies and found he was staring at T-strap shoes, ankles and shapely legs. The fashions had changed since he had been at sea, and he liked what he saw. Embarrassed, when he realized he was staring, he smiled, expecting a reprimand, but the two returned his smile and giggled as they entered a cab.

A voice from another taxi yelled, "Where you going, mister?" Bill was about to dismiss the man when he realized a cab would take him to Darcy's house.

Bill sat in awe as the taxi weaved its way between automobiles of every shape and kind, with noisy engines and honking horns. He felt claustrophobic as the buildings on each side of the street towered above them. Eventually the buildings diminished in size until they entered suburbia with green open spaces. The taxi pulled up to a large three-story red brick house with bay windows, a porch and a view of the water that he thought might be Lake Michigan. A white wooden fence surrounded the garden, disproportionately small against the tall house. He pushed the gate open and climbed the porch steps. Lifting the shiny brass knocker, he took a deep breath, preparing an announcement, but before he could think, the door opened and a tall, stern man in a black morning coat greeted him.

"Good afternoon, sir," A stiff British voice came from the morning suit but not a muscle moved.

"My name is Bill Blaine and I am here to see Mister, I mean, Lord Thornton."

Bill was shown into a dark drawing room. The darkness took him by surprise until he felt its coolness and saw the drawn curtains shielding the heat of the day. While he was deciding whether to sit on the delicate floral sofa or stand, the door burst open.

"Bill! I don't believe it! It really is you. Welcome, welcome to our humble home." Darcy pumped Bill's hand so hard he thought his fingers might drop off.

"It's good to be here." Bill answered, while having second thoughts and wondering if he had indeed done the right thing.

"Gordon, this is my great friend from Bexhill-on-Sea, where my mother spent most of the war." Darcy turned to Bill, "You are staying, aren't you?"

Bill said, "Thank you. Are you sure it will not be inconvenient?"

"Not at all. Gordon, please ask the maid to make up the guest suite and tell cook there will be three for dinner tonight. Come, we must have a drink to celebrate."

Darcy led Bill into his study, a contrast to the feminine pastels of the drawing room, with dark wood-panelled walls, a heavy polished desk, deep leather chairs and a large glass-fronted wooden bookcase, which sadly, Bill thought, contained few books.

"Rye whiskey. It comes from Canada," Darcy said as he poured two glasses. "Prohibition. Damned inconvenient but as long as you know where to go there is plenty of alcohol to be found. Just stay away from the moonshine. That is rough, even lethal." Darcy handed Bill the glass.

"Tell me, how did you finish up in the merchant navy? The last time we spoke in Bexhill you were at The Grand hotel. Imagine my surprise, seeing you in Johannesburg and only a few months later you are knocking on my door in Chicago."

"There were many reasons I joined the merchant navy but first and foremost to serve my country. After the war, it became an escape. I decided, after our chance encounter, it was time to pursue a different life. I have always wanted to visit America so why not start a new life here and accept your invitation?"

Bill continued to relate his adventures at sea, some humorous, some harassing and many filled with danger. Darcy sat spellbound. Bill felt comfortable talking to Darcy. In the past he had mistrusted him, not without reason. Darcy's behaviour had been erratic. He remembered Anna saying how badly he treated his mother.

Bill did not understand why this toff would want to befriend him, even ignoring the difference in their breeding, although it was not that different. His own mother was a disinherited titled lady. She never forgot her heritage but had an uncanny ability for treating people with kindness, whether gentry or servants. Did Darcy sense his upper class heritage and ability to relate to both classes, or did he just like Bill?

"I admire your adventures and war time U-boat experiences. Conceivably, you may think me a coward. I escaped to Chicago during the war to avoid being killed or maimed." Darcy looked down at his feet.

Bill inwardly agreed his actions were cowardly but chose not to comment. "I'm curious, what were you doing in South Africa, and when did you become Lord Thornton?"

"I have, or had, a brother, Felix, two years my senior, eldest son and heir to both the earldom and Hillcrest Estate. Felix hated the estate and any form of farming. He considered it all a waste of time. When we were young boys, he constantly played with toy soldiers and dreamed of riding into battle.

"The estate sank into my bones and filled me with passion even as a young boy. War games had no appeal to me. Nothing pleased me more than to walk the estate or mount a horse to ride with father's estate manager. By the age of twelve, I knew every nook and cranny, all the tenant farmers respected me. They gave me the nickname, Little Lord Darcy. The summer I turned fifteen, during the school holiday, I learned the economics of estate managing. By the time I finished boarding school, I had a vision of a twentieth century estate—Father had no concept of modernization or profitability.

"I wanted to step into my father's role, but the rules of British aristocracy cannot be changed. Felix would become Lord Thornton and I would be an officer in the infantry, both of us hating our lives. Finally, in 1910, father agreed to buy Felix a commission if he promised to return in three years. I would stay on the estate and help father and take up a commission when Felix came home, except Felix did not come home.

"When the Titanic capsized with my father on board, we telegraphed Felix, expecting him to take up his position as Lord Thornton. He refused and we never heard from him again. Our mother, grief stricken over father's death, built a fantasy around Felix. I hated my mother for not acknowledging my passion for Hillcrest. She treated me as nothing more than a caretaker, waiting for her favourite son to return. Consumed with anger, I rebelled, abandoned Hillcrest and sailed to America, where I met Belle."

"I remember Anna telling me you were not kind to your mother, now I understand why." Bill felt sympathy and had a better appreciation of this complex man. "Where is your brother now?" Bill said frowning. "Oh, that's why you were in Johannesburg."

Darcy topped up their glasses and offered Bill a cigar; he declined and lit a cigarette. "Partly right," Darcy said blowing circles of sweet smelling smoke.

"Checking Mother's correspondence after she had died, I discovered a letter from the War Office reporting Felix as missing, dated March 2nd, 1919, and in May the War office confirmed his death. She told no one of either letter, except her maid, Barclay, who told me that mother was convinced the War Office had made a mistake. Mother died shortly after the second letter, still believing Felix was alive. There was no mistake. I went to Johannesburg to settle Felix's affairs, which is when I met you."

"As your brother's heir, you inherited both title and estate. Why do you live in here and not at Hillcrest?"

"The Estate manager runs it in my absence, which he has been doing since I left in a tantrum almost five years ago. Chicago is Belle's home and we both like it here. Eventually we will have to return to Hillcrest, possibly later this year. Between the changes the war has brought and my neglect over the last couple of years, I have a great deal of work ahead of me to make it viable again."

The study door swung open and three incredibly beautiful ladies walked in. "Belle, darling, look who's here, Bill Blaine." Belle looked confused. Darcy added, "The chef fellow I met in Bexhill and then met again in Johannesburg."

"Oh, I do remember but I don't think we actually met. I remember your friend Anna Neale, at The Sackville Hotel, Lady Thornton's secretary; a delightful young woman. Her Ladyship held her in high esteem. How is she?"

"Anna married several years ago, m'lady, and I believe they now live in Canada." Bill felt his cheeks flushing and a hurt in his chest he did not expect.

"Please, call me Belle. We, Darcy and I, enjoy the more casual American style of life, except for Gordon who joined us from the Hillcrest Estate. Poor Gordon is terribly shocked at times." She laughed and her sharp eyes danced as she glanced at Darcy.

"Please forgive my rudeness. Allow me to introduce my dear friend, Mrs. Julia Castillo and Miss Claudia Castillo, Julia's sister-in-law. Julia and I studied together at the University of Chicago."

"I am honoured to make your acquaintance," Bill said, bowing slightly. He hoped his response was appropriate. His mother's lessons on etiquette were a distant memory and he had been at sea a long time. Belle exhibited a charming rebelliousness that reminded him of his mother. Her simple unadorned dress of a creamy-white blouse, matching skirt and bobbed short brown hair, gave her an air of confidence. She appeared tall, although he doubted she was more than five-foot, three-inches tall

Julia, had a quietness about her that Bill immediately related to. Standing side by side, Belle and Julia were the same height, but Julia's more feminine appearance in a flattering white and floral chiffon dress made her appear smaller. Her fair hair, a little longer than Belle's, fell softly around her porcelain face and distinctive blue eyes shadowed sadness. Claudia stood apart, taller than both women. Her short, thick black curls hugged her head, making her olive Mediterranean complexion glow. Bill couldn't help smiling and staring at her playful brown eyes, enhanced by a cheeky, sensual smile. She wore a green tunic-style dress that gave her the appearance of a coy schoolgirl. But, Bill thought, there was nothing schoolgirlish about this young woman.

His heart was racing. He had an immediate desire to know her better and was delighted when Darcy invited everyone to dine. Claudia flirted with him all through dinner and Bill felt stirrings he had not in years. How he wanted to feel her plump lips and if honesty prevailed, he would have liked considerably more.

Darcy and Belle introduced him to the never-ending Chicago nightlife and underworld. Most of the city ignored any kind of law. In fact, the police and justice system were as corrupt as the lawbreakers. Nobody cared as long as they could drink, dance and have a rattling good time. The speakeasies had come into being with prohibition and were spreading rapidly across the city.

Bill relished the cloak and dagger sensation as he walked down the dirty, dark alley and knocked on the big wooden door. He waited for an eyeball to appear through the peephole to verify his identity, then the door opened and two enormous men in black, with white ties and fedoras escorted him into the club.

He stood in awe as a palace opened up through a fog of smoke and his ears were assaulted with the din of voices, laughter and music. A palatial visual of ladies perched on bar stools, twinkling in sequin dresses, long cigarette holders dodging suitors who drew too close. Feathers and diamantes sprang from curls and bobbed hair.

Through the haze of smoke, Claudia came slinking towards him. There were no twinkling sequins but black fringe swayed in tiers, mirroring her every move as she approached him. It took his breath away and he almost gasped when she kissed him. Feeling uncomfortable, Bill realized that every man within twenty feet of them was staring with envy. Grateful for Darcy's insistent contribution to Bill's wardrobe, he fit in with all the dinner jackets, some black like Bill's, and some white.

"Bill, *darling*, come and join us."

A glass of something appeared in Bill's hand; drinks flowed generously. Drawn into the contagious gaiety, the once quiet, temperate Bill laughed raucously with the crowd. One arm around Claudia, her warmth penetrated his hips as she leaned against him, he turned and kissed a black curl that bent around her ear; he felt her shudder ever so slightly; arousing his carnal desires. How he wanted her, but he must be patient. Needing a distraction, he took Claudia's arm and steered her towards the crowded dance floor.

"Claudia, come dance with me."

The band played *Margie* and they danced. Claudia, graceful and confident, while Bill's two left feet caused them to giggle. Finally, they sat down at an empty table and ordered another drink. Deep in conversation, they didn't see Darcy and Belle enter the club.

"May we join you?" Darcy asked, giving Bill a wink.

"Oh, of course." Bill immediately stood up and pulled the chair out for Belle and as he did, Julia appeared next to Darcy, who did the same. The conversation halted, feet shuffled and a path opened up between the tables, revealing a tall heavyset man of some notoriety approaching the group. His flat, greased hair emphasized his heavy Italian features; its blackness a stark contrast to the white, ill-fitting tuxedo.

Darcy made the introductions. "Bill, may I introduce you to Julia's husband and Claudia's brother, Luigi Castillo." Bill's knuckles crunched painfully as they shook hands.

"Respect, Mr. Blaine… for me and my baby sister. Treat her well, Mr. Blaine, or answer to me. She's done nothing but talk about you and that makes me nervous. I don't want no trouble…" Luigi leaned over; the front of his jacket fell open casually, deliberately exposing a leather gun holster. His breath hot on Bill's ear he whispered. "You hurt one hair on her head and you're a dead man. *Understand?*"

"Oh, stop Luigi, I am a grown woman and quite capable of looking after myself." Claudia laughed. "Bill is a darling man."

Terrified, Bill understood all too clearly and knocked back his drink in one gulp. Claudia stroked the back of his head, pouting her lips. "Ignore him. He's a puppy dog at heart. He's used to protecting his baby sister and hasn't noticed I am all grown up."

Puppy dog, Bill thought. Luigi's closest resemblance to the canine species would be a teeth baring, rabid, pit bull terrier.

Luigi excused himself and disappeared into the alley. Darcy followed, glancing towards Bill. Another door from the alley brought visitors into a gambling den. Darcy gambled frequently and while Bill had enough skill to keep himself afloat, he didn't have Darcy's resources and declined to join them, preferring to enjoy the ladies' company, without Luigi peering over his shoulder.

Each day that passed filled Bill with more excitement and even memories of his youth in Edinburgh with Alex were no match for this city. Here, he didn't have to compete with Alex. The ladies flocked around him, devouring his stories of sea adventure. He was being seduced, not just by Claudia, but also by the City of Chicago.

Years of celibate life at sea had abruptly switched to raging hormones like a young buck with one-dimensional vision. Bill totally ignored the peripheral warnings of jeopardy and its consequences. He wanted nothing more than to stay in this vibrant city and pursue women, especially Claudia.

Claudia's father owned several restaurants in town including, Café Lune, which for years had been and still was the legal front for the illegal gambling den, and more recently their favourite night club, the Lune Speakeasy.

When Claudia discovered Bill was a highly skilled chef, she convinced him that his skills would be a great asset to her father's restaurants. Bill was not so sure, but he did need work and cooking was his work of choice. Claudia made arrangements for the two to meet.

Tony-the-Boss, Claudia's father, was heavyset, like his son, but with considerably less attitude. He had the commanding stance of earned respect. He talked with his enormous hands as though orchestrating his broad Italian accent and conducting his own speech. Black curls similar to Claudia's but tamed with grease, dark eyebrows, and straight, skinny lips framed his round puffy face. His dress was neat: typical shiny suit, dark blue and specially tailored to conceal a weapon. Bill had become accustomed to the bulging jackets and the warnings they contained.

Tony barked a lot of questions at Bill about his upbringing, fixated on his mother having been a genuine lady, daughter of an earl. Bill's connection to the British aristocracy seemed to be a shoe-in and his experience at The Sackville and Grand Hotel clinched the deal. Bill was hired as head chef for the Café Lune at a salary he could have only dreamed of a week ago.

He could barely contain himself upon his return to 21 Lakeside Drive, and bounded like a schoolboy towards Darcy's study, only to have Gordon inform him the master was not home, but would he like to join the mistress in the drawing room, where he found Belle and Julia having tea.

"I have some good fortune to tell you ladies. I have decided to stay in Chicago. Claudia's father has hired me as head chef for his restaurant, Café Lune." Bill glanced from Belle to Julia, both had frowns, which were close to disapproval.

"What's wrong?" Bill asked.

"You do know that Café Lune is a front for a gambling den and the speakeasy? Claudia's father is a small-time gangster and racketeer," Belle said.

Bill laughed. "It seems to me that everyone is into some kind of racket. I liked the guy. He wants a good chef and he's paying me well. I'm looking forward to getting back into the culinary art instead of beans and mash for a bunch of hungry sailors."

"Be careful, Bill. These guys are ruthless and, as a stranger, you are naïve. I regret the day I married into the Castillo family." Julia wrapped her arms around herself, looking straight at Bill. He saw it again, a subtle wave of sadness ripple through the blue-grey of her eyes. Before he could answer he heard Gordon greet Darcy in the hall. A moment later Darcy strode into the drawing room, apologized for interrupting and invited Bill to join him in the study.

Bill told him of his good fortune and of the ladies' warnings.

"Bill, this is a great opportunity. Tony is a good guy, a family man. Yes, he has a reputation for running some illegal businesses, but he's small time compared with most—that's where I get my whiskey. He's smart and runs a couple of legitimate restaurants. Café Lune is one of them, so there is nothing illegal about that side of his business. He will be impressed with your culinary skills. Make his restaurant one of the best in Chicago and he will be forever grateful. Make sure you stay on his good side. Belle is right to be cautious."

Bill moved out of Darcy's house and rented two furnished rooms a ten-minute tram ride to Café Lune on Madison Street. Two weeks later, patrons were lining up to dine at Café Lune and, by Christmas, advanced bookings of more than a week were necessary.

Small time racketeer, Tony-the-Boss had proudly made his mark on Chicago. Everyone in town was talking about his restaurants—the food, the jazz and the ambience—no one could touch them.

Tony Castillo's pride in the restaurant's success and his gratitude to Bill were overwhelming. Bill could do no wrong and he frequently called him 'son,' which did not endear him to Luigi who obviously wanted his father's approval but rarely got it. Claudia pouted and complained that Bill worked too hard. She had become quite possessive and made no secret of the fact that she loved Bill and wanted more; more commitment with not-so-subtle hints of marriage.

Twenty

Dangerous Nuptials

❧

B ill could not be sure when the relationship changed, but he vividly remembered the day it began. It was an exceptionally hot and sticky July evening while dining at the Thornton's. He and Claudia had taken a stroll in the garden, sauntering by neatly trimmed flowerbeds and through the sweet scent of a rose-covered arbour. Well hidden from the house, a small white gazebo appeared overlooking the lake—an ideal trysting place.

A year later, he still remembered that kiss. He couldn't help being aroused as he remembered gently pulling her into his arms, another kiss and as tongues slowly explored, the urgency exploded and they began pulling off each other's clothes; first Claudia ripped off Bill's shirt, then he slipped the straps of her dress down her arms and watched the loose fitting chiffon slide to her feet. She unbuttoned the rest of him and leapt towards him, one leg on each side, pushing him to the ground.

Panting, hot and satisfied, they had lain on their backs laughing, hardly believing what had just happened. The attraction, purely physical, led to many such encounters. But of late, Claudia had slowed down their sexual encounters to love making. The primal satisfaction had become emotional and meaningful for Claudia and she wanted more.

Bill only wanted hot sex. When she called to see him at Café Lune, the slight sway of her walk or the way she provocatively moved her lips, filled him with lust and desire. He was incapable of resisting her advances. His intellect told him he needed to break off the relationship before it went any further and became complicated. It might have already been too late. Claudia had fallen in love. Hurting Claudia would be suicide—Luigi would hurt him pretty bad. Even if he wanted, to and he didn't, he couldn't be sure that her father would approve a marriage. Being his chef was one thing, his son-in-law quite another. If he did agree, becoming Tony's son-in-law would drive Luigi's jealousy to the brink, and he would be signing his own death warrant.

As Christmas approached, the Café was booked every night. Tony-the-Boss made a habit of demanding extra tables for his friends. The maître d' would attempt to turn them away and Bill was called upon to soothe a bunch of Tony's mobster cronies. How Bill wished he had Alex, with his charm and knowledge, as his maître d'. A table was always found, often at the expense of a booked customer. On one such night, Tony arrived alone, asking Bill to join him to discuss the menu for New Year's Eve, which was to be a private party of family, friends and business associates.

"Billy, New Year's Eve, we make a good celebration of der Castillo family success in Chicago. Everybody who is somebody is invited and as der clock chime midnight, Tony Castillo is a somebody, deserving der respect from everybody."

"Is there anything in particular you'd like on the menu?"

"Nah, make a-sure dere's some good juicy steaks." Tony pinched his fingers to his lips, kissing the air. "And some good Italiano dishes, make it der best, Billy."

Café Lune was getting busy; Bill needed to get back to the kitchen and stood up.

"Hold on dere, son; I wanna talk."

Bill sat down slowly, wondering what was coming next.

"My little princess, she talk-a to her mama, and it-a seems she set on marrying you."

Bill gulped and choked on his own saliva. "She is?"

Tony slapped him on the back laughing. "Not'ing to choke over, son."

Bill's thoughts raced around his head. How could he get out of this? What came out of his mouth surprised even Bill. "Sir, I am fond of Claudia and she will make someone a great wife but I have nothing to offer her; no money, no status or property and definitely no inheritance. I have been sailing the world until six months ago and before that I was an apprentice in a hotel."

"I want you as my son-in-law. My daughter, she wants you as her husband. We Castillos get what we want. You break my little girl's heart and you are a dead man." The menacing tone and emphasis on *dead man* rang heavy in Bill's head. Tony narrowed his eyes and stared Bill down and then... a smile burst across his face. "Money, no problem. I see to it she has all der money she needs. I triple your salary. I know all I need to know about you. Your mama was an aristocrat, a British Lady, and der royal blood in you is good enough for me. You treat her good. No gangster for my princess. Dat's settled, son." He slapped Bill on the back, pumped his arm. "Welcome to the family, Billy!"

Bill's words bounced with the last slap. "Th-thank you, sir."

"None of the 'sir' stuff. Call me Tony. You're family. Go and see Carlo Cavaliere on La Salle Street and pick out an engagement ring. Make-a-sure it's a big rock, not'ing but der best for my Claudia."

Bill walked towards the kitchen as casually as his trembling knees and buzzing ears would allow. *Marry Claudia or prepare to meet your maker, Bill Blaine. How could I have been so stupid?* he thought.

Bill busied himself around the kitchen until Tony moved off to gamble. Leaving his assistant in charge, he left Café Lune early that night. Fortunately for Bill—he couldn't face Claudia tonight—Belle had invited Claudia and Julia to a quiet farewell dinner at Lakeside Drive. She was leaving for England the next day to join Darcy, who had returned to Hillcrest Estates to take up his role as Lord Thornton.

245

Bill needed to think and decided to walk to his rooms. The wind blew in off the lake and a light snow swirled in the lamplights. He barely felt the cold, but instinctively pulled his collar up and stuffed his hands in his greatcoat pocket. He felt numb to the cold, his surroundings and his life. He had succumbed to the seduction of Chicago's gaiety and his lust for Claudia, and in so doing he had lost all sense of reality.

Who would have thought that quiet Bill Blaine called a lord his friend, operated a gangster's restaurant and was betrothed to a gangster's daughter? For a brief second Bill smiled, feeling smug, wanting to show Alex what he had achieved.

The smugness quickly changed to shame and fear. He missed Alex's friendship. It didn't seem to matter anymore that Alex had married his one and only love. He yearned to hear Alex tease or see Anna smile as she brushed a curl off her cheek. With Darcy and Belle back in England, his only friend was Julia, but as Luigi's wife, it would be prudent to be cautious for both their sakes.

He pulled his collar up further to shelter the wind, trying to light a cigarette with his trembling hands. He must have walked miles. He no longer recognized the street names and he turned around and walked back where he assumed he had been. He was no closer to solving his problem now than when he'd left the café. One thing was clear: he had no choice—Claudia would be his bride.

Thankfully, it being the busiest time of the year in the restaurant, Bill was not expected to socialize. Shopping and gift buying kept Claudia busy, but the subtle hints about rings made it clear to Bill what she was expecting for Christmas. Bill obliged by going to Carlo Cavaliere's expensive jewellery store.

"Miss Castillo picked it out herself," said a smiling Carlo Cavaliere, placing a small velvet box on the counter.

Bill's eyes must have been like saucers as he looked at the size of the diamond. "I can't afford that."

"Don't have to, it's paid for."

"I can't let my... b... bride pay for her ring. Can you show me something smaller?"

"No, I can't. I was told to give you this exact ring and I want no trouble." Carlo Cavaliere had a scared rabbit look about him. "And if you know what's good for you, you'll give the lady and her papa what they want." Again Bill heard the words, "What they want." And so, with a heavy heart, Bill did as he was told.

On Christmas Eve, he met the Castillo family for mass and ate what he considered to be his last supper at the twenty-room mansion they called a house. As was their tradition, the gifts were opened after Christmas Mass. Bill pulled the ring from his pocket, trying to form his words into a proposal but he couldn't utter a syllable.

Seeing the blue velvet box, Claudia replied to the unsaid words. "Yes! Bill Blaine, I will marry you." She grabbed the box and placed the ring on her finger. Flinging her arms around his neck, she whispered in his ear, "Meet me in the library in ten minutes. I want to thank you properly." Her tongue slid along the lobe of his ear and her hot breath caressed his neck as the hairs on his arms stood to attention. He rubbed his arms harshly. He wanted to resist but lust was persistent.

As everyone admired the ring, Bill took his chance and slipped into the library. A few minutes later Claudia came slinking to his side, teasing with each swing of her hips and finally pulling Bill into her arms. Any resistance he may have had dissolved as he succumbed once more.

Breathless and satisfied, Bill flopped into the leather chair. Claudia sat on his lap and stroked his hair. "I love you, Bill. I can't wait to be married. Let's run off."

"Your parents wouldn't like that." Bill was thinking how he wanted to run off, but not with Claudia—just off, away from gangsters and the deep hole he had dug for himself. He wanted to erase Chicago.

Bill could not get warm. The tightest of windows and doors, or thickest of jackets were no match for Chicago's howling winter wind in late February. It was enough to keep customers at home and a rare sight of empty tables at Café Lune. Julia sat alone, drinking coffee after dining with Luigi, who had abandoned her for the poker table. Julia didn't care as it gave her an opportunity to talk to Bill. Based on their in-law status with the Castillo family, they had bonded as friends.

The kitchen door swung open and Bill moved forward but held back for a second, watching Julia's despondent face as she stared pensively into her cup.

"More coffee?"

Julia smiled sadly. "Thank you, this is quite cold." Bill flipped his fingers towards the waiter and ordered two brandies and fresh coffee.

"Why so sad tonight?"

"Oh, I am disappointed. Luigi has forbidden me to work with the students at the university. My old professor invited me to help the women students a couple of afternoons a week. I was looking forward to getting out of the house. I miss Belle, and since she returned to England, my life is rather boring."

"I don't understand. Why would Luigi stop you?"

"He's afraid I might think for myself. I made a big mistake marrying him."

"Why did you?"

"I ask myself that question every day. I can't answer…it just happened. Luigi swept me off my feet. I was blind. I couldn't see beyond his charm, his money and promises."

Bill gave her a knowing look. "I know what you mean. Once you succumb to the Castillo charm you are trapped for life. I am trying to figure out how I can break off the engagement without meeting with a nasty, painful and maybe fatal accident."

"You know, Bill, it isn't too late for you. We could devise a plan to spirit you away without a trace. The family would be angry for a while, but if I know Claudia, she would quickly find someone else and you would be forgotten."

Bill laughed. "I don't think so. Claudia truly loves me, but more to the point, I doubt I would get out of Illinois before the hoods found me.

Believe me, if there was a way I would try."

Julia looked around to make sure the waiters were out of earshot. "Do you want to marry Claudia and become permanently indebted to Tony Castillo?"

"Claudia is a lot of fun and I like her very much. I'll admit, I willingly allowed her to seduce me. I'm ashamed to say my attraction to her is shallow—lust, not love. She is not the kind of woman I want to marry." Bill's thoughts wondered to Anna, and his heart filled with tenderness. But just thinking of both women in one thought repulsed him and tarnished his memory of Anna.

"Bill Blaine, I do believe you have a secret love," Julia said laughing.

"Yes, it was a long time ago and she married my best friend."

"Oh, I am sorry. Does that explain the years at sea and the new American life?"

Bill nodded. He felt the old Bill from Bexhill briefly surface and, at that moment, he decided not to marry Claudia.

Honourable and honest was the best way to go. Tony-the-Boss would understand, Bill rationalized. He made two separate attempts to tell Claudia he didn't want to get married, and both times Claudia laughed and said he had cold feet. Her mama had told her it was normal for men. If her mama knew of his attempts, so did Tony and Luigi. Honesty was not going to work. Aware of Luigi's watchfulness, he pretended to take an interest in the lavish wedding plans. As the July 2nd wedding date grew closer, Bill could see no way of escape.

Claudia and her mother, and on occasion with Julia's help, organized everything for the wedding. Bill's expertise was required for the menu planning. It had been decided that the Café Lune staff would prepare the food although the wedding reception was to take place at the mansion. The three ladies and Bill met at nine in the morning at Café Lune to discuss the banquet details. Once the menu decisions were made, Claudia and her mother rushed off to the dressmaker, leaving Julia and Bill alone.

Julia quickly switched subjects. "I think I know how you can escape, Bill."

249

"Julia, I have no choice but to go through with the marriage."

"Listen to me. Luigi and Tony are watching you like a hawk right now but once you are married they will relax, especially on your wedding night."

"Julia that's crazy. I think Claudia will notice if I am missing on our wedding night."

"Not necessarily. Where are you staying that night?"

"Claudia thinks it is romantic to keep it a secret."

"Good! You and Claudia can leave the party and go to your secret hotel. Don't forget to tell me where you are," Julia laughed. "But it is perfect that nobody else knows where you are staying. After Claudia falls asleep, with some help from champagne and laudanum, you can sneak out. Make sure the do not disturb tag is on the bedroom door. You'll be newlyweds, so no one will disturb you. I will drive you to Union Station. There is a night train that leaves for Toronto, Canada at midnight."

"Julia, it would never work. How could I be such a cad and leave Claudia on her wedding night? And, if Luigi found out, you would be in terrible danger."

"Don't worry about Claudia. Tony will find his princess an Arabian Prince. She'll be fine. I don't intend Luigi to find out. The only people who know about this are you and I. It is highly unlikely that anyone would suspect you had help. Leave the arrangements to me."

July 2nd turned out to be a miserable day. Ushers stood to the ready, struggling to hold umbrellas as the black Lincoln pulled up to the church. Claudia will be so disappointed, Bill thought, struggling with the guilt, but not nearly as disappointed as she will be tomorrow morning. Bill could barely stand as he stepped out of the car on his trembling legs. Sweat had beaded around his receding hairline, dripping onto his white shirt. His best man, the maître d' from the Café Lune, gave Bill a friendly pat to reassure him he was doing okay. The apparent wedding nerves were a good cover for his intense fear that his impending escape might be exposed. Bill glanced at his best man and for a brief second he saw Alex, and then

Anna's face flashed in front of him. Bill almost dropped to his knees. A strong arm lifted him up and Luigi moved him towards the church door, leaving the best man running to catch up. Bill forced a smile and willed his feet to take a step and all three walked down the aisle to the altar.

Claudia's exquisite white dress and long veil flowed as she walked down the aisle. The whole ceremony and reception turned out to be perfect and, as Julia had predicted, no one noticed the groom. Claudia helped things along by having too much to drink, making it easy for Bill to hustle her off to the secret hotel early. Another celebratory glass of champagne, this one laced with a heavy dose of laudanum and Claudia was out cold. Bill changed his clothes, kissed Claudia goodbye and ran down the emergency staircase. He flung the back door open an audible breath of relief escaped his chest. He almost laughed when he and heard the latch click as the door bounced shut and locked behind him.

The street was deserted. Where was Julia's car? Bill looked up and down the street. His heart, already racing, was now pounding the sides of his chest. He paced up and down past the locked door; afraid someone would notice him and ask questions. He glanced at his wristwatch. She should have been there ten minutes ago. Had something happened? If she'd been caught, heaven knows what Luigi would do to her. He jumped into the shadows as car lights approached, terrified it might be Luigi. The car pulled up to the curb.

"Jump in, we're late," Julia called.

"What happened?"

"Luigi started a brawl because some distant cousin made a nasty remark about Claudia. Tony threw the guy out. I had to calm Luigi and send him off to gamble."

Bill stared out of the back window. "Did anyone see you leave the party?"

"No, I pretended I needed to talk to the kitchen staff about the midnight buffet. I'll be back before anyone misses me."

"Do you think anyone suspects?"

"No, Bill. Stop worrying. Here we are."

Julia handed him a train ticket and his pre-packed bag as they ran on to the platform. She had to shout in Bill's ear to be heard over the bellowing steam. "The ticket is in the name of Thomas Jones. You will be in Canada before Claudia wakes up and realizes something is wrong. A trail has been laid that looks as though William Blaine caught the night train to New York to board the R.M.S. Olympic, bound for England."

Bill stopped running and held Julia by the arm. "Julia, be very careful. Never let Luigi find out you helped me." Bill wished he could take her with him to freedom. "How can I ever thank you?"

Julia kissed him on the cheek, tears drops glistening. "I will miss our friendship. This is goodbye, Bill. You must never contact me again." The train started to move along the platform. He heard Julia shout. "Good luck and be careful," as he began running alongside the train, barely keeping up as it picked up speed. It took him three tries to grab the handle of the train car. A stab of pain shot through his shoulder as it wrenched at its socket, but he hung on, throwing himself onto the metal platform. He looked back along Chicago's Union Station and waved to Julia's lonely shadow, dwarfed by the station clock as it struck the twelfth chime of midnight.

He owed her his life, in more ways than one, and he worried that if ever anyone discovered she devised the plan and assisted in his escape, they would kill her. He rubbed his sore shoulder, thankful it had not been dislocated, and stumbled along the corridor until he found an empty compartment. He fell into the seat, grateful for the rest, yet aware that he must remain vigilant. But, with luck, his absence would not be discovered until morning.

A subtle trail had been laid with clues that Bill Blaine was heading to New York intending to board a ship bound for England. Tony-the-Boss, his father-in-law of twelve hours would have his mobster connections searching the New York trains and ocean liners. If the plan worked, it would be days before, if at all, the search spread to the Canadian border, and by then Bill would be safely in Toronto. He cursed and muttered, "Where I should have been a year ago. Then none of this would have happened."

The train rattled and swayed, plunging through the darkness with urgency and determination to reach its destination. Bill stared at his reflection in the carriage window, despising what he saw. He willed the train to move faster, to widen the gap between him and the last twelve months. By the next day there would be a contract on his head, and that he could live with, but he could not live with this stranger he had become.

His motive for escaping to Canada, beyond running for his life, had nothing to do with the mob. This he had not confided even to Julia. Finding Anna, the love of his life, and Alex, once his best friend, had become an obsession. *That,* he concluded, was his true motivation.

Six years, he thought. *Six long years ago I began running, first to The Grand Hotel and then to the S.S. Dorset. The further I ran, the more I loved Anna. I could have challenged Alex before they married but I allowed her to slip away. I promised Anna I would stay in touch and not to worry, I would find her. But, I never did write and unbeknownst to me, they settled in Canada, long before I made the attempt to find them in Edinburgh. Mr. Walker gave me their address in Toronto, but I still did not write. I ran off, boarding a ship bound for Australia.* He stared at the window, loathing the man who stared back at him and then... the reflection, began to soften and fade; he caught a glimpse of the old Bill. Lights shone on a sign reading Battle Creek. The train slowed, eased and clanged its way along the track and came to a steam-bursting halt.

Dread gripped Bill's body as he looked up and down the station. A man walked to the exit, another ran to the train. A door slammed, the conductor blew his whistle and waved his flag. The train chugged slowly out of the station. A young cowboy sauntered past the compartment, hesitated, but moved on. Bill relaxed, rested his head and slept.

Sensing the rhythm of the train changing, Bill opened his eyes, not sure where he was. He remembered waving goodbye to Julia and travelling through the night. Fear gripped him like a vice, he looked around the compartment—he was still alone. Suddenly he felt more alone than ever before in his life. Knowing Alex and Anna were close by was no comfort. He felt worse. His despicable self could not face them. In daylight, he could not see his reflection, as the train pulled into Toronto's Union Station.

Twenty-One

An Uneasy Reunion

Henry put his head round Anna's office door. "Mrs. Walker, could you give us a hand in the bakery? The queue is out of the door onto the sidewalk."

"Of course, Henry. What are we selling that has drawn such a crowd?"

"Fresh strawberry pie and Dad's new recipe for strawberry strudel. Thought we'd cash in on the strawberry season." Henry puffed out his chest. "The strudel was my idea. It's usually apple."

"Good work, Henry!"

Anna shook her head at the scene. The store resembled a Women's Institute or Quilting Guild meeting and a drone of ladies' gossiping and laughing filled the bakery. All had wicker shopping baskets of various sizes hanging from their arms. Within half an hour, they were sold out of anything strawberry and had orders for the next day.

"Nick…Henry, I am delighted with the sales. Will you save me one of those strawberry strudels tomorrow? Mr. Walker will be home by dinner time."

"Sure will, Mrs. Walker. It might be the last for a while as strawberry season is almost over." Nick turned to Henry, a father's pride written all over his face. "Henry, what shall we bake next?"

The father and son team was a good decision. Kenwood Bakery thrived on a reputation of top quality European breads and pastries and with Henry as an apprentice, the volume had increased, making Anna a handsome profit. The store line-ups had kept the business hopping. On the pretence of recovering her health, she had delegated all things domestic, including Isabelle, to Abigail. But that afternoon she closed her account ledgers early and prepared a special dinner for Alex's homecoming.

Isabelle heard Alex first and toddled from the kitchen calling, "Papa, Papa!" Anna followed to see Alex's long legs stride over the safety gate at the top of the stairs. He looked very handsome, she thought. His face shone as he picked up his delighted daughter and glanced warily towards Anna.

"Welcome home," Anna said, hugging him the best she could with Isabelle between them. His kiss lingered on her cheek.

Anna couldn't remember ever having so much to say or so much to listen to, except perhaps when they had made plans to leave England. She was relieved that Alex was well. He coughed less and no longer wheezed at night.

The conversation was animated as Alex talked about the waiters and the difficulties they had serving food as the train struggled through the Rocky Mountains, and the beauty of Vancouver and the Pacific Ocean. Resentment crept into her mood, but she quickly brushed it away by chatting about the business. She described the store overflowing with customers and how good it was to see the pride Nick had in his son.

Home for a few days, Alex took care of Isabelle and let Anna work. He wasn't due to go back on the train for a week but was expected in the office to attend meetings. Anna surprised herself at how much she enjoyed the family time and there was no doubt about Alex's happiness. Within a couple of days, Anna noticed his cough getting worse. This worried her and, when his wheezing kept her awake at night, she didn't need to be told that he was reacting to the flour dust. She thought some fresh air would do him good and arranged to take the day off on his last day at home. She packed a picnic basket with sandwiches, homemade lemonade and one of Nick's strudels. Alex threw a plaid blanket over his arm and carried Isabelle, clutching her bucket and spade, and they boarded the tramcar down to Lake Ontario. Alex spread the blanket on the beach and they watched their little daughter play.

"What a beautiful day," Alex said, lying on his back, staring at the clear blue sky and feeling the breeze temper the hot sun.

"This is nice, Alex, spending time together. It has been a nice week, having you home. But I have noticed your cough is getting bad again. How long has it been like that?"

"Oh, it's nothing. I must have picked up a cold when I got home."

"Alex it is not, *nothing*. Nor is it a cold." Anna's brow furrowed with worry lines as she reached for his hand. "I expect it's inevitable that the flour dust escapes into the apartment."

"I'm fine. Dr. McCarthy said I was reacting to the flour. It will go away when I am on the train. It must be that clear fresh mountain air."

"Do you think we should move out of the apartment?" Anna asked, hoping Alex would say no. Moving out of the apartment would mean moving from the bakery and then what would she do with her time—household duties.

"We can't afford to move."

Alex's comment was not encouraging. He didn't actually say no, and he didn't acknowledge how important the business was to Anna and to their finances. Maybe that's what he meant when he said they couldn't afford to move, she thought. She poured them a tumbler of lemonade and unwrapped the sandwiches, avoiding the sand that Isabelle had been scattering on the blanket.

"I almost forgot," Alex said. "I think I saw Bill Blaine on Yonge Street."

Anna's heart skipped a beat and she swallowed to control a gasp. "Bill Blaine! What would he be doing on Yonge Street?"

"I don't know and the strange thing is, I think he saw me and deliberately turned and walked away. I would have followed him but I had to meet with Mr. Dryden."

"You must have been mistaken. Why would Bill be in Toronto? And surely he would have contacted us. Your father gave him our address."

"That was a long time ago. Perhaps he lost it. But why would he turn away? You're right, I must have been mistaken."

Isabelle began to cry. "She's tired and it's past her nap time," Anna said, picking her up. The wailing only got louder as she reached for Alex. He cradled her and walked along the beach. She looked so tiny, Anna thought, watching this tall handsome man cuddle his daughter against his chest and kiss her red curls.

"She's asleep," Alex said, gently placing her on the blanket.

They talked little on the tram ride home, tired and content after a lovely day at the beach. Anna's thoughts wandered to Bill. Could that have been Bill on Yonge Street? Why would he avoid Alex? Was he still upset about the marriage?

As they walked along St. Clare Avenue towards home, they saw Henry picking up the sandwich board sign that sat outside the store. He stopped and waited for them.

"I am glad you're home. I wasn't sure what to do after I had closed up shop. There's a gentleman waiting to see you, Mr. Walker. I showed him into the office. I hope that was okay. He said he was an old friend from Scotland. I didn't want to turn him away, but it didn't feel right to let him into the apartment."

"Thank you, Henry. You did the right thing." Alex looked at Anna and shrugged his shoulders. "Could it be Bill?"

Certain her thumping heart could be heard for miles Anna said, "Who else do we know from Scotland?"

Isabelle struggled to escape Alex's arms and ran to Henry, her new friend. She came to a halt upon seeing a man at the office door and ran back, clinging to Alex's leg. Both Alex and Anna stared in silence.

Anna spoke first, "Bill… what a surprise. Alex said he thought he saw you on Yonge Street. When did you arrive in Canada? How did you find us? And, are you still at sea? What are you doing in Toronto?" Anna was babbling. Questions kept falling out of her mouth. He looked older, thinner, and she noticed his hair had receded, but the biggest difference was the bleakness in his eyes. What had happened to him, she wondered.

Alex stretched out his arm and shook Bill's hand and slapped him on the shoulder, saying, "Bill, it is good to see you. How are you and what brings you to Toronto?"

Bill still had not spoken. He smiled, clearing his throat and looking nervous. His eyes flipped from Alex to Anna and then to Isabelle who was still clinging to Alex's leg.

"And this little lady is our daughter Isabelle." Alex picked her up and said, "Say hello to Uncle Bill."

Isabelle whispered, "'llo," and then shyly snuggled her face into Alex's shoulder.

"We live upstairs in the apartment. Come in and I'll make some tea," Anna said, grinning from ear to ear. It felt so good to have Bill here.

"Maybe Bill would like something stronger?"

"No, tea would be nice."

"Well, I'll put the kettle on." Anna's heart galloped and her lips smiled as she glanced from Alex to Bill. She sensed tightness and apprehension. Untold secrets rippled around the room.

Bill and Alex cleared their throats and took a breath to speak at the same time.

Alex politely nodded to Bill. "Please, go ahead."

"No, nothing really, you go ahead."

"It's been a long while," Alex said.

"Yes, for me, many years at sea."

"So you never married?"

Bill mumbled, "No, not really."

Alex looked puzzled. "What do you mean, not really?"

Bill's face tensed as he forced a laugh. "A slip of the tongue. Not many young women at sea and who would want an old sailor?"

An awkward silence was broken when Anna carried in a tray of tea and cookies.

Isabelle said, "Cookie!" and clapped her hands. Everyone laughed, relieved to break the tension. She toddled between them, soaking up the pride from mother and father and the admiration from Uncle Bill.

"She has your red curls, Alex." And staring at Anna he said, "Anna's smile." Feeling the intensity of his stare penetrating deep into her soul, Anna felt a pink flush creep up her neck. She quickly turned and scooped Isabelle into her arms.

"It is time for Isabelle's dinner. Bill, will you join us?"

Conversation became easier over dinner, possibly the wine relaxed their tongues as they chatted and laughed over old times. Alex talked of their trip to Canada and how Anna managed the bakery while he worked for CP Rail.

"So Bill, what have you been doing?"

"Well, I spent the first four years dodging U-boats on a merchant ship and managed to stay alive. I liked life at sea, so I stayed on after the war. Every day was an adventure, different languages and cultures, some friendly, some not and days at sea varied from mill pond calm to waves taller than skyscrapers."

Anna felt her stomach lurch at the thought. "I did not do well at sea. The ship's movement made me ill. How did you manage?"

"I must have a stomach of iron because nothing bothered me at sea but some of the men, like you, had a difficult time. How did you fair, Alex?"

"I had a great time at sea, never missed a meal," Alex laughed.

"The summer of 1919, my ship docked in Southampton and I took the train to Bexhill expecting to find Anna at The Sackville and wondering how you, Alex, had fared during the war. I was astonished to find James Lytton in Mr. Pickles' big office. Did you know that James Lytton is now the General Manager?"

"No. Where did Pickles go?" Alex asked.

"The local constabulary escorted him out of The Sackville in handcuffs, arrested him and transported him to the Eastbourne jail."

"No... never... Why?" Laughing, Alex continued, "Now *that* I would have liked to see. What had he done to get arrested?"

Anna smiled, a look of satisfaction on her face. "I expected that would happen."

Both men gave Anna a quizzical look. "You look like the cat that caught the canary," Bill said.

"I do, and it feels good."

"Did you know about this?" Alex asked.

"No, but I knew about his thieving and devious behaviour. The day we departed from Bexhill I wrote to Mr. Kendrick suggesting he investigate and audit the accounts. He must have done just that."

"You never said anything to me about the letter. Is there anything else you haven't told me?" Alex sounded hurt. He bent down, opened the sideboard and taking out a bottle of Scotch poured three glasses. An awkward silence hit the room as all they looked questioningly at Anna. She shuffled in her chair, feeling guilty for not having told Alex about the scheme she and Dr. Gregory had put together. Originally, Anna had omitted to tell Alex about Pickles' attempted rape, for fear he would lose his temper, and now she decided that neither Bill nor Alex needed to know.

Bill took the glass, sniffing the aroma of good Scotch. "It is nice to have a drink without breaking the law. I spent the last year in Chicago—prohibition. Not that prohibition had any great effect on the availability of alcohol, most of it is controlled by mobsters. The corruption in Chicago is intrinsic. I am happy to be in Canada in more ways than one." Bill gazed into a space only he could see and gave a nervous laugh. Anna saw his body tense. "It was not a good time for me."

"Prohibition here is controlled by the provinces, but you can get a drink in most places. American passengers are always surprised to discover legal wine and liquor on the train. We hear reports of the speakeasies and newspaper accounts of gangsters and guns resulting in mob shootings. Is it really that bad? It sounds exciting but dangerous. Why did you decide to come to sleepy Canada? Not much happens here," Alex said.

"Chicago is a fun city, plenty of glitter, booze, women and music—jazz in particular is great to listen to. But there is a sleazy side. It's not all that it appears. You get sucked in…" Bill hesitated. "It's a period in my life I am not proud of…." Again, his body stiffened. "And for your own safety, the less you know the better."

What an odd thing to say, Anna thought, or more to the point was what he wasn't saying. Anna remembered Bill being a man of integrity but she sensed a dark cloud. She decided to let the comment go for now as she was more interested in hearing about Mr. Pickles.

"What happened at The Sackville, to old Prickly-Pickles?" Anna asked.

"I'll try to relate the story as James told it to me. It was a big scandal. The staff had a great deal of satisfaction seeing Mr. Pickles dragged out of his office in handcuffs."

"I wish I had been there to see that happen. I hated that man," Anna's tongue spat out the venomous words. "He was an evil man. He deserved to be arrested. Tell me more."

"There isn't much more to tell. James said the accountant gossiped that the charges were lengthy including fraud, embezzlement but also grievous bodily harm, including rape." Bill stopped and looked directly at Anna. "And a charge related to a young maid. I thought it might have been young Amy—quite a list. The trial had been set for November, that would be 1919, and rumour had it that he would get the noose. But I heard nothing more."

Just talking about it evoked painful memories and a sense of panic in Anna. But, she thought, the noose would be a fitting punishment. In fact, he could already be dead.

"So you didn't hear what happened then?"

"No," Bill said, frowning and watching Anna carefully.

She needed to move the conversation away from Pickles and changed the subject. "Where are you staying?" Anna asked.

"I have a room at the YMCA. It's comfortable and cheap. I work at the Front Street Diner as a cook."

"Well, that's a bit of a comedown from The Sackville," Alex said.

"I needed a job. It's temporary until I decide if I am staying in Toronto. I must go. I am working the breakfast shift tomorrow. Thank you both for dinner. It was good to see you again."

Bill departed as abruptly as he'd appeared, with no mention of coming again. Anna wanted to see him again and decided she would pay the Front

Street Diner a visit after Alex left for work.

Walking down Front Street carrying Isabelle on a hot July afternoon, Anna appreciated the cool breeze coming off the lake. The door to the diner was wide open and a blanket of heat from the grill hit her as she and Isabelle slid into a booth. Definitely a comedown from The Sackville, but it was clean. The brown upholstered seats had seen better days and the floor was well worn by hundreds of diners over the years. Even at three in the afternoon the place buzzed. Bill was flipping burgers in the open kitchen. A half wall separated it from the restaurant, the counter displayed two plates of steaming burgers and a mass of hot French fried potatoes; not the kind of food Anna was accustomed to. She ordered tea, cake, and milk for Isabelle. The waitress, a sullen, skinny woman of about fifty, almost dropped the tray on the table, spilling some tea. Anna quickly moved Isabelle away from the hot tea and glared at the waitress. Seeing how tired the poor woman looked, Anna smiled. She responded by smiling at Isabelle and apologizing to Anna. "Sorry, Miss. It's been a long day."

"Thank you. That cake looks good. It looks like Victoria Sponge Cake."

"Yes, miss. Our new cook, Tommy, makes it."

One mouthful told Anna that this was Bill's sponge cake, and with it came a flood of memories from Bexhill. She looked up to see the waitress bent over the counter, speaking to Bill and pointing in their direction. She felt her heart skip as he gave a nod and smiled at her.

The waitress handed two plates of burgers to the next table and leaned towards Anna.

"Tommy said he'll join y'u when he's finished this order. Relative, are y'u? He never talks to customers." She gave Anna a suspicious look.

Who is Tommy? Anna thought, but the waitress had moved away before she could ask.

"Hi there! What are you doing here?" Bill sat down on the other side of the booth. Anna had not thought about an excuse to be on Front Street. "Just passing," she said.

Bill raised an eyebrow but said nothing.

"It was good to see you. I have been wondering how you were getting along. By the way, the waitress called you Tommy. She said Tommy made the sponge cake and I would know that cake anywhere, and Tommy didn't make it."

"Here, I am known as Tommy…Thomas Jones," Bill whispered, looking over his shoulder to the next booth. "I left Chicago in a hurry and there are people who might do Bill Blaine harm if they found him."

"Are you in some kind of trouble with the law? That doesn't sound like the Bill I know. I mean Tommy."

"No, nothing like that. I became involved with the wrong kind of people. It's unlikely they will look for me here but I need to keep a low profile for a while. Anna, it really is wonderful to see you again." Bill hesitated. "I have to get back to the kitchen. I will come and visit soon… it's better if I come to see you." He tickled Isabelle under the chin, making her giggle. He smiled and gave Anna the all too familiar wink, his hand lingering on her arm.

Tired, Isabelle whined all the way home, making Anna irritable, but she knew the encounter with Bill was the real cause of her mood change. His last words, "It's better if I come to see you," told her not to visit the café again. Shrouded in secrets, Anna's curiosity wanted to know what had happened that had changed him so much.

Did that include his affections for her? Or was he being a gentleman?

However, there was no denying the wink and she could still feel the warmth of his hand on her arm. Suddenly, guilt flooded her senses and she hugged Isabelle a little tighter and thought of Alex. What was she thinking? Her feelings for Bill could never be more than friendship, and the sadness and regret must stay hidden deep inside her. She did have a happy life with Alex and they did love each other.

During the fall months, Anna saw little of either man. Bill's visits were infrequent and Alex was home rarely and briefly. Alex took on more and more routes with only a day or two between trips. His enthusiasm for the trains, passengers and experiences fed Anna's growing resentment. Anna kept busy looking after Isabelle and the bakery. Nick and Henry were increasing sales daily and with Christmas less than two weeks away, there was little else to think about. And then the telegram arrived.

The boy stood in the office doorway, his arm outstretched with a light brown envelope. "Telegram for Mrs. Alexander Walker."

Anna stared at the boy, glued to her chair. Who would be sending her a telegram? In the few seconds it took her to take the envelope from the boy she thought about her parents, her brother and Alex. Telegrams meant bad news. Taking a deep breath, she tore the envelope open and pulled out the folded paper.

COMING TO VISIT STOP SHIP DOCKS NEW YORK DECEMBER 14 STOP

TRAIN ARRIVE TORONTO 2 PM DECEMBER 18 STOP CHARLIE NEALE.

Anna's face lit up like a beacon, a smile spread from one ear to the other. "Charlie. My Charlie is coming to visit."

"That's nice, Miss. I don' often bring good news," the boy said.

"Nick, give the boy a tip please."

Nick and Henry stood staring at Anna with obvious relief on their faces at seeing her overjoyed. "Pardon me for asking, Mrs. Walker, but who is Charlie?"

"Charlie is my brother and I haven't seen him since my wedding." Anna clasped the telegram to her chest. "I can't believe he will be here in…" Anna looked at the calendar. "In two days. Today is the 12th. He must have sent this from the ship. Oh, there is so much to do."

Anna arrived at Union Station at one o'clock and showed Isabelle the trains and where Papa worked. She went into the office to inquire if they knew when Alex would be back. Mr. Dryden heard her speak to the receptionist and came out of his office.

"Mrs. Walker, I don't think we have met, but Alex speaks of you and this little princess all the time. He is a very proud daddy," he said, smiling at Isabelle. "Is there something I can help you with?"

"I was wondering when Alex's train is due back. I have some wonderful news. My brother is visiting from England, an unexpected visit. In fact, I am here to meet his train from New York."

Mr. Dryden pulled out his pocket watch and said, "You're early. The train is not due until two o'clock, but it is on time. Alex is on the Pacific route but he will be home before Christmas. I'll give him some time off to enjoy his family. I can send a telegraph and let him know your good news."

"Thank you, I would like that." Anna took Isabelle's hand and they walked back to the platform and sat outside the ladies' room, watching the trains. Finally, the New York train rumbled and snaked up to the platform. The bellowing steam frightened Isabelle, who let out a piercing scream attracting the attention of a tall handsome young man in an officer's uniform.

"Anna, I'm here."

Anna couldn't believe it as she stood face to face with Charlie; they hugged and laughed. She stepped back to look at him in his khaki uniform, polished brass buttons, smooth brown leather belt and lanyard, an officer and a gentleman. He looked wonderful and then horror struck. Charlie was wearing a black armband. Who had died? That would explain the sudden visit.

Seeing dread on her face he said, "It's okay. Mother and Father, and Lou and the kids are fine. It's a military thing."

Anna knew Charlie better than anyone; someone or something was not fine, but for now she believed the family was well. She just wanted to enjoy the moment with Charlie. He heaved his kit bag on his shoulder and they walked to the tramcar.

Twenty-Two

Sadness and Justice

C hristmas night, Anna lay in bed, staring at the snowflakes fluttering by the window. She leaned over to Alex at her side and whispered, "This is one of the best Christmases I have ever had." Alex answered with a snort and a wheeze from his dreams. Closing her eyes, she pictured the day's events starting with the morning.

Isabelle pulling the ribbon on her present, more interested in the ribbon than the present, until the baby doll appeared. Anna smiled, remembering how Isabelle had giggled, her eyes wide with excitement as she hugged her new doll. Anna noted with concern how Alex, Bill and Charlie lavished both presents and attention on Isabelle, which fostered Isabelle's tendency to be quite the demanding little princess.

The little sitting room above Kenwood Bakery had overflowed with people, including Nick, his wife Helga, and son Henry—twelve in all. Anna, Abigail and Helga worked to produce a feast fit for kings. How they had laughed, a little tipsy, sipping sherry as they cooked. Alex had unscrewed the kitchen door, supporting it on shelves brought up from the bakery to make an extra-long table. Chairs had been carted from Abigail's and Nick's. Her thoughts wandered to Christmas in Rugby. She wondered where her parents were celebrating. Charlie said they spent a great deal of time at Lou's, so they would be celebrating at the farm with Lou and Robert, and the three boys. She missed them all.

The wind rattled the window and the snowflakes were coming down so fast they blanketed the window in white. Anna pulled the covers up and snuggled against Alex's warm body when a thought struck her... where was Uncle Bertie? The last she heard, which was months ago, he was in India. An involuntary shiver ran down her spine—she had a bad feeling. Charlie had not mentioned Uncle Bertie since he arrived and then she remembered the black armband. He had removed it without any further explanation. She didn't need to be told, she knew: Uncle Bertie had died. *I wonder when he was going to tell me?*

The next morning, Alex kissed her on the cheek and told her to sleep in. The guys would clean up and get breakfast. Anna didn't want to get up because Charlie would confirm her suspicions. It was hard to explain. She didn't feel emotional. Uncle Bertie was where he always was, in her heart. He lived in her dreams of adventure, his stories of strange people and far-off lands. She swung her legs to the floor and opened her dresser drawer, pulling out her blue pendant and held it to her chest, feeling his love and encouragement—Uncle Bertie would be with her forever.

Isabelle, whose cot had been moved into Anna and Alex's room to accommodate Charlie, woke up, demanding attention. Anna couldn't complain. She had slept in too, tired after the celebration of Christmas Day.

The men had worked hard: the kitchen door had been re-hung, the living room was back to normal, except for a few extra chairs and the smell of bacon wafted through the apartment. The men ate heartily while Anna picked at her plate.

"You're not eating, Anna," Alex said.

"I'm not hungry." Anna wondered how they could eat after the feast they had had yesterday.

"Charlie, is there something you are not telling me? You haven't talked about Uncle Bertie. He's dead, isn't he?"

Charlie stopped eating and glanced toward Alex for support. "How did you know? I didn't want to say anything and spoil Christmas. Anna, I am so terribly sorry. Uncle Bertie died of malaria in India in October. But we didn't find out until December. You know Uncle Bertie, always going off somewhere, so Mother never questioned it when she didn't hear from him, expecting him to turn up at Christmas."

"What happened?" Anna's voice trembled. It suddenly seemed final, hearing it from Charlie.

"The details are somewhat sketchy. Mother received a brief letter from the British High Commission in Delhi. 'We regret to inform you that Bertram Charles Bedford passed away on November 10th, 1921.' Father contacted the High Commissioner and was told he had contracted malaria some time ago. It was tactfully explained that a lady friend had been taking care of him. Knowing Uncle Bertie, she was probably living with him. His will was clear and brief. All his possessions he bequeathed to this woman, with instructions that he was to be buried in India, the country he loved.

"Mother was upset. She thought the world of her brother. Father was sympathetic for Mother's sake but had never liked Bertie. Father was happy he had died in India and not brought any scandal to England. None of us understood why it took the authorities so long to notify next of kin but Father decided not to investigate. Anyway, one of the reasons I decided to come and visit was to tell you in person, Anna. I had leave for Christmas and my commanding officer approved some extra bereavement leave. How did you know he had died?"

"It occurred to me that you had not mentioned him, and then I remembered the black arm band when I met you at the station. I am sad, but Uncle Bertie and his adventures will always be in my heart."

"I know what you mean. All those stories he used to tell us when we were kids. That's what he was all about. Through my military service in Africa and India I have actually lived some of them—tales I will be able to tell my niece when she's older. India is a country full of colour and amazing people."

"Stories of the Far East were always your favourite, Charlie. Mine were the Rocky Mountains. He would say, 'Powerful mountains that spring from turquoise lakes and reach beyond the heavens.'" Anna looked at Bill, but dared not say, *the colour of your eyes.* "And, 'Lakes as big as oceans.' Gosh, he must have said that a million times."

"Well, he was right about the Rockies and the turquoise lakes," Alex said. "They are truly as beautiful as people say. Bill, have you been to the Rockies, or perhaps your ocean travels took you to India?"

"No, I have never been to the Rockies. Toronto is as far west as I have been. I did get to India several times, but I rarely saw more than the harbour and dockside. I know what Charlie means about the colours in India. They are so vivid, it's hard to explain. Cheerful, happy is also something I remember about India."

Anna listened, hearing Uncle Bertie's words, "Follow your dreams," over the conversation. She felt a deep wave of sadness. The grief was not for Uncle Bertie, but for the adventures she would never experience. It took an enormous effort to hide the growing resentment she felt towards Alex.

The snow fell all night, although the wind had died down. Anna was pleased that she had decided to keep the store closed on Boxing Day. She sat in the window seat and gazed down at the deserted St Clare Avenue. The sidewalks were a pristine white, even the tracks from automobiles were barely visible. It would not be long before the roads were impassable. Charlie stood at her side, his arm on her shoulder.

"Winter is beautiful here. I don't mind the cold or the snow. I think I'd like to live here."

"I would like that, Charlie. Perhaps you can find a nice Canadian girl and settle down. But what about your military career?"

"I have been thinking of getting out for some time now, and Canada might just be the opportunity I am looking for."

"You, brother, are a dark horse. What else are you hiding from me?"

"Nothing. Well, that's not true, although I am not hiding it from you, I had forgotten about it. The week we received the news about Uncle Bertie, I was checking *The Telegraph* for obituaries and on the front page was this news report on Mr. Ebenezer P. Pickles of Bexhill-on-Sea. Isn't that who you worked for at The Sackville?

"Yes." Anna giggled nervously, "I didn't know his name was Ebenezer. He always signed his name E. P. Pickles, but how very appropriate." She tried to calm her racing pulse. Was she finally going to hear that Pickles had been brought to justice or did he get away with it? She closed her eyes and prayed for justice. When she opened her eyes, the men were staring at her. She gave a half laugh, attempting to ward off any questions that might reveal her involvement. "That is funny. I think his evilness lends itself well to a Scrooge, like Dickens' character."

"It's in my kit bag." Charlie fetched the newspaper. "The headline reads, *Dastardly Mr. Pickles of Bexhill-on-Sea, back in jail for life!*" Charlie read with dramatic intonation. He gave Anna's tense face a quizzical glance before looking down at the newspaper clipping. "Released from prison after serving one year for fraud, Mr. Ebenezer Pickles is to be incarcerated again; this time for life.

"At the time of his original arrest, the crown had insufficient evidence to pursue the alleged crimes. The case never came to trial; a mystery witness had disappeared and another refused to testify. Dr. Gregory of Bexhill-on-Sea told *The Telegraph* he had enough evidence to put Mr. Pickles behind bars but, without the witnesses, the crown could not proceed. After being brutally beaten and left for dead, Miss Amy Peterson, a maid from The Sackville Hotel, finally agreed to testify. Mr. Pickles was charged under the *Offences against the Person Act,* which included rape, causing bodily harm and attempted murder. The judge allowed Dr. Gregory to present photographs and sworn statements as evidence. The eyewitness's statements were corroborated by Mrs. Banks, the head housekeeper at The Sackville Hotel, and left no doubt that Mr. Ebenezer Pickles was the perpetrator and guilty of these dastardly crimes.

"A jury of ten men found Mr. Pickles guilty on all counts. Judge Berkley deviated from his usual impartial address to the court, addressing Mr. Pickles directly. 'Mr. Pickles, you are an evil man. I am sorry I cannot don the black hat, thus pronouncing death by hanging. But you will spend the rest of your living days in jail, and there you will discover what hell you put these young women through. May God have mercy on your soul.'"

Silence replaced Charlie's voice.

Anna could hear nothingness buzz in her ears and her head spun slightly. She had fallen into a lonely vortex. Memories whirled around her, Mr. Pickles' blotchy face came right at her and then poor, sweet little Amy appeared, sobbing silently in her head. Her inner voice wanted to scream, 'I want justice; justice for me, for Amy, for Edith.' Guilt, anger and sadness pulsed, one after the other, through her body. She wanted to feel vindicated, and she thought about him rotting in a prison cell. She wasn't sure she felt the justice she had hoped for, but she did sense its finality—it was over. She felt the lightness of a burden lifted, and the memories and anger finally faded away. The Mr. Pickles incident was behind her at long last.

Bill spoke first. "I always thought he was a mean bully, and I had my suspicions about the maids. I remember Edith leaving in a hurry and the staff gossiped about her climbing above her station and into Mr. Pickles' bed. I was new at The Sackville just as Edith and the stable boy were dismissed. Rumour had it that she was with child and the poor innocent stable boy was a scapegoat." Bill glanced at Anna, who was reading it over again.

Anna sighed. "Prickly-Pickles will not be bothering anyone ever again. Can you imagine those red blotches erupting from his collar and into his face as he was questioned in court?" She laughed hysterically, joined by the others. A look of triumph passed over Anna's face as she realized Dr. Gregory had done his job as promised. The end result meant Mr. Pickles would never walk the streets of Bexhill again. Poor Amy, she thought. I hope it wasn't too bad—it sounded dreadful. She thought she might write to Mr. Kendrick or Dr. Gregory and inquire about Amy, now that it was all over.

"Anna, you worked closely with Mr. Pickles, especially during the war. Did he ever make unpleasant advances towards you?" Alex asked with a stern voice. His brow creased above his nose and his stance full of judgment.

Anna kept reading, keeping her head down, not sure what to say. "Mrs. Banks had warned me about his *strange ways*. Remember the desk incident when I moved my desk out of his office and near the telephone exchange? Well, that was Mrs. Banks' suggestion to keep me out of harm's way." Anna glanced at Bill who looked away and kept silent.

"Why didn't Mrs. Banks report him?" Alex asked.

Anna swung round and glared at Alex; his naïveté astounded her. "He would have dismissed us all without references." She stopped and took a deep breath. "Anyway, after the desk incident I thought he had mended his ways." Anna wanted to move the conversation away from Pickles. She didn't know why she was so averse to Alex knowing the truth, but she had seen the judgment—was the judgment for her or Pickles? Although Bill was aware of Pickles' earlier attacks, he was not aware of the most brutal one that had summoned Dr. Gregory and was the root of the conviction they were reading about.

Life had slowed down after the Christmas rush, and the snowstorm had brought most of the city to a standstill. Bill had returned to the YMCA the following day and the bakery opened for business, but there were no customers. Alex's train had been delayed a day, giving he and Charlie an opportunity to get to know each other. Anna worked on the accounts, catching up on the office work after a busy two weeks in the store.

Alex, now on his way to the Rocky Mountains, would be gone for two weeks. Anna was already beginning to feel the loneliness. But she was determined to enjoy the last day alone with Charlie before he boarded the train for New York and the ship back to England. She scrounged some pastry from Nick and made a steak pie with thick gravy, which was followed by Nick's apple strudel with custard.

"That was delicious," Charlie said, leaning back in his chair. "I am sorry to be leaving you. I will tell Mother and Lou that you are an excellent cook. Mother will be delighted."

"Why? I cook well because I have to, not because I want to and most of the time I leave the domestic work to Abigail. She relishes caring for the children, cleaning, shopping, cooking, all the things I hate doing."

"Considering your dislike for all things domestic, you do your duty well. Alex tells me you have made the bakery a great success. Anna, you should be proud of your accomplishments."

"Alex never compliments me on the business or the home. I am surprised he mentioned it to you. All I hear about are the passengers and trains." Anna could feel herself pouting.

"I know that look. You would give Father that look when you couldn't get your own way." Charlie smiled. "You look forlorn, lost. What is it Anna?"

"I have enjoyed having your company. I am going to miss you. I do get lonely at times with Alex away so much. I am fortunate that I enjoy the work in the bakery."

"Anna, I saw the brightness in your face when we were talking about India and the Rockies. I remember how we dreamed of adventures when we were children. I have fulfilled that dream but you haven't. Why don't you ask Alex if you can go with him on one of his trips west and see the Rocky Mountains?"

"Alex is too busy. He would never think of asking me. And who would look after Isabelle and the bakery? Alex doesn't understand my love for adventure, he never has. He thinks the trip across the Atlantic was adventure enough for me and I was so seasick I couldn't enjoy it. That is where Alex and Bill are different. Bill understands."

"It may be my imagination but I have seen the way you and Bill connect at times. Is something going on?"

Anna felt awkward. Did Charlie know? Had he seen how she felt about Bill? She must answer carefully, she thought "Bill and I are friends, nothing more."

"Anna, this is me, Charlie, you're talking to." He took her hands across the table and smiled. "I occasionally see sadness in you. Are you truly happy?"

"Is anyone truly happy? I enjoy my work. I even enjoy Isabelle and you know how I felt about motherhood. Sometimes, I am afraid of the resentment I feel towards Alex travelling across Canada. I try not to and I am happy for him. At times I wonder if he takes on extra routes just to get away from me although I know part of that is his problem with the flour dust. Recently, he has been moody when he's home and he has terrible nightmares."

"Some of the moodiness and nightmares are from the war. We talked about our war experiences and I understand the nightmares. It isn't you he's running away from; it's the war memories. Alex worries about you, and he made a strange comment to me about Bill still being in love with you."

"Oh Charlie, I wonder if I made a mistake. I have always loved both Alex and Bill, and now I am married to Alex. But there are times I look at gentle, caring Bill and I want more than just friendship. But Bill, the typical gentleman, is keeping his distance."

"And so he should. Anna, you are a married woman with a child. You made your decision. Please don't do anything foolish. Alex is a good man."

"You are absolutely right." Anna cleared the dishes from the table and went into the kitchen. "Pour yourself a brandy. I'll put these in to soak." She leaned on the kitchen sink, watching the bowl fill with water, wondering what it was she did want.

Charlie caught the early train to New York the next morning.

Twenty-Three

A House to Call Home

May 1924. Bill had lodged with Mrs. Love, for the past three years, after leaving the practical but impersonal YMCA. True to her name, she was a sweet old widow who treated Bill as a son, which made her sudden death come as quite a shock to him. Having no obligation to Bill, Mrs. Love's landlord evicted him within days of her death.

Alex offered Bill the couch until he could find something more permanent. Anna took advantage of the situation, suggesting Bill have Isabelle's room and Isabelle could sleep in her room. Alex approved of the idea. Having Bill in the house would be company for Anna and it eased his conscience during his long absences on the rails.

Anna had taken great pride in the bakery's success but she was bored. Hidden deep inside her was a growing bitterness towards Alex's lack of awareness. He couldn't see her need for challenge or her longing for adventure. Bill did, but she noticed he avoided her by working long hours. She felt trapped by the current household and bakery routine. Alex's ambitious predilection for CP Rail had engulfed his life, which left little or no thought or time for Anna. Had she had a crystal ball indicating what the next year had in store for her, might she have elected for the status quo?

Excited to be planning Isabelle's birthday, she put these negative thoughts out of her head. Alex had arranged his route so that he could be home for his little princess. Henry baked a special chocolate cake, decorated it with pink roses and tied a pink ribbon around the sides, with a big bow in the front. Isabelle, overexcited and with the impatience of a four-year-old, was full of questions. When was Daddy coming home? When was Jimmy coming? Was Uncle Bill coming? Anna tried her best to soothe the little girl. Alex had promised to be home at ten o'clock. His train was due early morning, but the clock ticked just past noon.

At twelve-thirty, Anna heard Alex's voice in the bakery and his long legs leapt up the stairs two at a time.

"How is my birthday princess? I have a surprise for you. Come with me." They all trooped down the stairs to the tiny back yard and there was a bright red, brand new tricycle. Isabelle screeched with delight and immediately sat on it, her long legs easily reaching the pedals and her red curls bobbed up and down as she worked at pushing the pedals.

Alex turned to Anna and kissed her on the cheek. "I told you she would love it."

"She certainly does. But Alex, I thought we were going to do this together." Anna felt dismissed.

"I know, but I didn't think you would mind. It was on display outside the store and I just had to buy it and see how she rides."

Always an explanation, Anna thought. She felt hurt but let the subject drop.

"Why were you late? It doesn't take two hours to buy a bike."

"Oh, Mr. Dryden called me in the office and I have some very good news. I am so excited, Anna." He squeezed her shoulders and kissed her cheek again. "I've been promoted. I'll tell you later, after the birthday party."

Exhausted after the day's celebration, Anna sat in her window seat, attempting to read but the words seemed to muddle on the page, her mind bracing for Alex's explanation of promotion.

"She was asleep before I finished *Jemima Puddle-Duck*. She loves that story," Alex said, pouring a Scotch and sitting next to Anna. "It's nice to be alone. Is Bill working tonight? How is it working out with Bill as a lodger?"

"I don't see much of him since he started working at the Royal York Hotel. I am in the bakery during the day and he is at work in the evening. I sometimes wish Isabelle had her own bedroom but other than that, he's considerate and quiet. Not much company as he's rarely here. I still spend most evenings alone."

Alex smiled and Anna detected some relief on his part; as much as Alex had agreed it would be a good idea for Bill to move in with them, his voice had an edge of doubt—an almost undetectable sign of mistrust. Anna wondered if the mistrust was for her or Bill. Alex had nothing to worry about—Bill kept his distance. She had thought his friendship would relieve some of the boredom, but he might as well have been a stranger.

"I can't wait any longer, I am bursting to tell you. I have been promoted to Inspector. I don't know the details, but it will be a big increase in pay and in between assignments, I will have an office at Union Station, meaning I will be home much more."

"That sounds wonderful! Alex, I am pleased for you. Mr. Dryden has recognized your hard work. When do you start?

"Tomorrow, I meet with the committee, and if all goes well, I start training my replacement on Monday, and then I do my own training. Be patient for another month, and then you will see more of me."

Anna found it difficult to be excited. Alex often exaggerated about something new, and reading between the lines she thought the added responsibility would translate to more work not less. But the promotion did sound good.

"We can buy a house, one of those houses on Forest Road you admired. Isabelle can have her own bedroom. If we move away from the bakery and out of the flour dust, I will stop coughing. Isabelle can have a garden to play in. You don't need to work."

Anna was stunned as she listened to Alex. "We have to discuss this. Are you talking about selling the bakery? What about my work here?"

"We can have a nice family life. This was always our dream, to have our own home and garden." Alex laughed. "I might even grow some vegetables."

"Alex, it was your dream, not mine. Yes, a bigger house would be lovely but I don't want to sell the bakery. I want more work, not less. I am not like Abigail. Domestic chores and quilting groups are not fulfilling to me. I want some excitement and even the bakery gives me little of that these days. You have adventure and excitement every time you board a train. I don't. We have talked about this many times and, Alex, you do not understand. I am not like your mother and sister, taking tea with the ladies, entertaining and gossiping. I want my life to have purpose and you keep shutting me out." Anna could hear her voice rising; she couldn't stop. "What do I have to do to make you understand?" Anna glared at him; her anger bubbling up into tears. "I'm going for a walk."

Anna slammed the sitting room door and ran down the stairs on to St. Clare Avenue, tears streaming down her face. Her chest heaved with sobs as she ran and ran, not caring that people were staring. She wanted Alex to understand and to care about her need for challenge and adventure. Breathing heavily, with all her tears spent, she sat on a bench by a little park where she often walked with Isabelle. At that very moment she realized that Alex had never understood. Their dreams would always be his dreams.

"Mrs. Walker, are you ill?" Hearing her name jolted Anna out of her thoughts. A matronly woman with a kind face was speaking to her. She recognized the woman as a regular customer from the bakery.

"No, no, I am just a little upset. It's nothing, my husband..." Anna didn't know what to say.

The woman patted her on the hand. "Marriage is a funny thing and it's those that can weather the storms have the happiest. I says it's give and take, but we woman do most of the giving. And for you young'uns, that can be hard."

"Is it wrong to want more?" Anna looked at this woman and briefly saw her mother's kindness and understanding. She wanted to hug this woman.

"'Course not. But we can't always have what we want, *when* we want it.

Sometimes you have to wait a while. Your man's a good man. Be patient and count your blessings. I lost my man in the Great War."

"I'm sorry to hear that. I almost lost Alex, but I was one of the lucky ones. He did come home." Anna gave a shiver. She had run out without a coat and the May evening was cool. "I must look a sight." She ran her hand over her hatless head and wayward curls, and then down her blue, tear-stained blouse, feeling foolish. "You are right. I should count my blessings. He is a good man."

"Here, I'll walk you home."

Alex was standing outside the bakery, his arms folded, his foot tapping, his face stern. "Where have you been?"

The woman spoke first. "She's upset but she's alright. Now, be good to her." She nodded and walked away. Anna called thank you as the woman headed back up St. Clare Avenue.

"I told you I was going for a walk. Alex, we need to talk."

That night Anna fell asleep surprisingly quickly, only to be woken by yelling and Alex sitting bolt upright in bed. "Alex, you're having a nightmare. Wake up," she whispered. Alex opened his eyes, lay down and went back to sleep, but Anna's eyes would not close again. She quietly slid out of bed, checked that Isabelle had not been disturbed and went into the sitting room.

Sitting in the dark on her window seat, she heard the birds chirping and the night sky was changing from black to dark blue. It must be close to dawn she thought, the promise of a new day. She mulled over the words spoken in the park—"what we want, *when* we want, sometimes we have to wait"—perhaps she needed to be patient. Alex *was* a good man and tonight's talk had been productive, she even thought he had listened to her concerns. She really was happy about his promotion and she hoped that he now understood her aversion to household duties and her need to work in the bakery. Understanding her need for adventure was perhaps expecting too much. He said he understood, but Anna had doubts.

"I would like a nice house," she whispered aloud. "We could afford it with Alex's promotion and the money I've saved from the bakery."

Alex was right. She had seen a nice house in Forest Road. She pictured the gingerbread trim on the porch and gables; the steps leading to a path up to a pretty front door that had a stained glass insert. Isabelle could have her own room. It was only a matter of time before one of his nightmares frightened Isabelle.

Anna tucked her dressing gown around her legs as she pulled her knees up to her chin. *Have I been selfish?* She thought about Alex coughing and wheezing. He seemed to cough no matter what, but she couldn't deny that the wheezing started only hours after he came home and then it worsened the longer he stayed.

Lately she had noticed the black rings under his eyes were getting darker and larger. Alex's health should come first but the thought of living her days as a lady of the house twisted her insides. Perhaps they could do it without selling the bakery and rent the apartment. She could still work in the office. But looking after Isabelle would be a problem without the apartment. As helpful as Abigail had been, she had her own life now that little Jimmy was in school. She thought, *Sometimes we have to wait.* Could Alex wait a year until Isabelle was in school?

The interview confirmed Alex's promotion and the following morning he set off to instruct his successor. Anna reluctantly settled into her routine. Wednesday mornings, she always met with Nick to discuss the orders and supplies needed for the weekend. A note in Bill's handwriting sat prominently on her desk, advising her he would be home for dinner, with a P.S. *If that's all right.* Anna couldn't help smiling at his politeness. The rent he paid included two meals, which he rarely consumed, as he ate mostly at the hotel.

Delighted to have Uncle Bill home, Isabelle kept him busy reading her favourite Uncle Bill stories, which were from Rudyard Kipling's, *The Jungle Book*. Beatrix Potter stories, *Benjamin Bunny* and *Jemima Puddle-Duck* were Papa stories

Curled up on the window seat, Anna smiled as Bill came into the sitting room.

"That must be your favourite spot," Bill said. "I would guess that is where you read. Of course, if you have time."

"Yes." Anna nodded. "I do read here. I have graduated from Rudyard Kipling and really enjoy H. G. Wells. He's a little racy at times." She blushed slightly. "This window seat persuaded me that the bakery was a good thing. Alex took it upon himself to buy the bakery without asking me first. I was angry but it worked out well in the end."

"Alex hasn't changed then." Bill shifted in his chair and cleared his throat. "Anna, is everything all right?"

"Yes," she said, talking to the floor. "Why do you ask?"

"I happened to come home early on Monday night and I could hear you arguing. I turned around and went for a walk. Then I saw you running down the street. I followed you but you were talking to a lady by the park, so I came home. Alex growled something to me at the door and I went to bed."

Hesitating, Anna couldn't find the right words. How she wanted to tell Bill everything. She yearned for the old days in Bexhill; it had always been easy to talk to Bill. He had been so cold towards her of late.

Bill interrupted her thoughts. "I'm sorry. It's none of my business. I shouldn't have asked."

"Alex has been promoted to inspector." The words exploded from Anna. "He wants to sell the bakery and buy a house, fulfilling his dreams of the traditional family and ignoring mine. I want more." She stopped, recognizing the bitterness in her tone and felt a sudden reluctance to confide in Bill. The man she had known years ago was buried deep inside the Bill that sat in front of her today.

He frowned thoughtfully, but said nothing and waited for her to continue.

She took a breath and calmly dismissed the conversation. "Later that night, we talked and I can assure you all is well. Now tell me about the Royal York. Is the Executive Chef as bad as Chef Louis?"

"Yes. Most chefs are arrogant, but this one doesn't have the false French accent or the bad temper... at least not *as* bad." Laughing helped them both relax and enjoy reminiscing about those early days.

That first awkward evening grew into many pleasant evenings due to Bill working the day shift and being home for dinner. Anna enjoyed the company and felt the return of a friendship, although she did sense a stubborn barrier. Anna filled him in about the war years at The Sackville. Bill talked about his years at sea, deliberately avoiding his travels in America. Whenever she mentioned Chicago, the barrier became a blockade, his whole demeanour changed and a terrible fear darkened his face.

The mailman often delivered mail from England. Anna's mother wrote frequently with news of the family but this day there were two letters, one from Rugby and one from Mother Walker in Scotland, a rare occurrence. The old lady mostly ignored Anna, blaming her for her son's departure to live with savages in the Colonies. The fact that her older son already lived in Canada was also ignored as was Jim most of the time.

Anna ripped open the letter from her mother, smiling at the antics of the grandchildren and then frowning near the end of the letter as she read... *your father has not been well, he caught a cold that went into his chest. I didn't want to tell you but Lou insisted, she said you would want to know. The fever broke yesterday and he is feeling much better but the doctor says he must stay in bed another week.*

She felt a knife stab her heart. Whatever was wrong with Papa, it had to be serious. No. Papa can't be ill, but Mother would only write if it were serious. Lou would make a big scene about it. That was it. Lou in her usual fashion had made it seem worse than it was. A cold, Mother had said. That's all. It was a cold. Anna could feel her heart racing with fear. For the first time since they had arrived in Canada, she wanted to be back home to kiss her father and feel his warm hug. She quickly scribbled a reply to catch the afternoon post. By the time the letter crossed the Atlantic he could be quite better or, she dared not think, worse. She questioned if a letter was enough and wondered if she should be making plans to return.

Alex arrived home in high spirits; the new guy was ready to go. Alex would join Mr. Dryden for his training the following morning. Anna told him about her father and he gave a cursory look of sympathy, saying he was sorry to hear that, continuing to espouse the incredible experience of training someone with less talent than himself.

Anna ignored the hurt from his dismissal and raised an eyebrow at his self-adulation. He could bask in his success at least until after Bill had joined them for dinner. The conversation, dominated by Alex as Anna expected, had a friendly tone to it. Bill and Alex bantered about their job experiences and prospects; a glimmer of the old friendship had begun to rekindle. Tired, Anna had decided to retire when she remembered the letter from Scotland. "Alex," Anna called from the bedroom, "there's a letter from your mother on the sideboard. It arrived this morning."

The conversation in the sitting room stopped. Anna assumed Alex had opened the letter and then she heard alarm in his voice as he shouted. "Good grief!"

Lying in bed, she strained to hear more of the muffled conversation as it floated down the hall. She would have to wait until Alex came to bed to find out what was in the letter. Knowing Mother Walker, she probably had a sore toe. Anna's worrying thoughts drifted to her own family and she fell asleep.

She heard coughing, a hacking, and a heaving dry cough. She was dreaming about her father and woke up with her heart pounding. The coughing didn't stop. Then Isabelle started crying. Anna jumped out of bed to console her and only then did she realize that it was Alex coughing.

Red faced, Alex was wheezing and gasped for air. Anna ran to the kitchen to get him water and one of the pills Dr. McCarthy had prescribed. Isabelle sat at his side, tears running down her little face, her speckled hazel eyes frightened, appealing to Alex, while Anna coached him to breathe slowly. Gradually the coughing subsided and the wheezing lessened. Anna propped him up on pillows and the three of them rested together until morning.

Pale and drawn, his breathing still laboured, Anna looked at Alex across the breakfast table. "Why don't you stay home today and call in on Dr.

McCarthy?"

"I'll be fine as soon as I get some fresh air. Remember, this is my first day as inspector. Mr. Dryden and I have a train to catch, and the best cure for me is the cool mountain air. So don't worry, I will be all right." He picked up his bag and kissed her. "Time to go. Anna, you should read the letter from Mother and Florence; they want to come to Canada for Christmas."

"What?"

"We can talk about it when I come home. Christmas is a long way off."

As she waved to Alex, her worst fears were unfolding. Alex's health had to be a priority, as did Isabelle. The apartment above the bakery just didn't work for them anymore and the final straw was a visit from her in-laws. They had to have a house. She thought about Alex's impulsive nature and decided that she must pre-empt any impulsive house buying on his part and start the search before he did.

That afternoon, she walked Isabelle to the park and on the way home she took a detour by Forest Road. To her delight, the house she had admired was still for sale. Her mind photographed every detail. A few stray red tulips and yellow daffodils still blooming bordered the neat green lawn and, in the middle, an oak tree showed fresh green leaves of spring.

The morning sun reflected off the bright-coloured stained glass insert on the front door. Fragrance from the lilac bushes growing at the side of the porch drifted down the path. Anna stood rooted to the sidewalk, mesmerized as a flood of childlike emotions engulfed her. *I want this house,* she thought.

She felt her lips pout as if pleading with her father for a new dress or hat. Smiling, she remembered her big blue hat. How she had pleaded with Papa. *and that,* she thought, *is how I feel at this very moment. I have to buy this house.* Suddenly invigorated, she felt her old zest for life return. The desire for this house abrogated her fear of running a household. The front door opened and a short, slightly portly older gentleman wearing a bottle-green cardigan, the buttons not quite even, walked down the path, leaving the door open. Anna felt the warmth of home spill onto to the porch.

"Is there something I can help you with?" he asked with a curious, but friendly, smile.

Although, Anna was speaking, she didn't sound like herself. "I am sorry for intruding but your house is so lovely and I would like to buy it."

"It is for sale," he said. "My wife died recently and the house is too big for me. I plan to live in an apartment."

Anna filled with compassion. Seeing the wetness of his aging, red-rimmed eyes, she caught a glimpse of the magnitude of his grief. He brushed the back of his hand, child-like across his wet face. "Would you like to take a look inside? Lily, that's my wife, would be upset at the state of the house. She always kept a clean and tidy house. I don't know how. So I apologize to you and to you my, dear Lily," he said looking up to the heavens. "My name is Wilfred, Wilfred Johnson," Wilfred stretched his hand towards Anna.

Shaking his hand Annie replied, "Mrs. Anna Walker and this little lady is Isabelle."

"I recognize you from the bakery. My wife frequented your store regularly. I like Nick's strudels. As good a cook as Lily was, she couldn't match those." He smiled. "Please come in."

Stepping inside, Anna sensed children's laughter. This was a happy house. The slight mustiness came from the closed, unused rooms. Dust sheets covered the parlour furniture; a bright room that gathered the morning sun. Next to it was a large dining room, the dark mahogany furniture thick with dust.

"We have four children so we needed a big dining room. I have no need for it now." They walked across the hall to a small room. "Lily used this as her study when she was teaching. She taught at the local school for many years until her illness." He guided them into a well-equipped kitchen and opened the back door. "I grew all our vegetables and the trees at the end are fruit trees. Lily baked all summer and pickled and preserved all fall."

Upstairs there were four bedrooms and a bathroom. One of the smaller rooms had pink wallpaper with roses, the curtains and bedspread matched. Isabelle jumped on the bed folded her arms defiantly saying, "This is my room."

285

"This room belonged to Christine, my youngest daughter, and she would be happy to pass it on to you."

Isabelle's voice brought Anna back to reality. What was she doing? She had practically told the man she would buy the place.

"Mr. Johnson, the house is lovely, but it is much bigger than it looks from outside and I am not sure we can afford it. I will talk to my husband."

Mr. Johnson patted her arm, "I want you to have it. This house needs a nice family. Bring your husband and we'll talk about the price. He led them into the kitchen and filled the kettle. "Please, stay and have tea with me?"

Whether it was his kindness or Anna's yearning for this particular house, she couldn't say but she found herself sipping tea and telling him their life story, including why they were moving: her need to work, Isabelle needing her own bedroom as they now had a lodger, Alex's coughing and his work with CP Rail. She concluded with the latest news, a possible in-law visit.

"I understand your need to work. There was a time when I didn't understand. My Lily taught me how important it was for her to teach. When the children came along, her mother helped out. Perhaps your mother-in-law would help you. I think this is the perfect house for your family."

Anna finished her tea and thanked him, saying they would be back when Alex came home.

Ten days later, Anna and Alex walked up Forest Road. Her heart missed a beat. The 'For Sale' sign was gone.

"Alex, there is no sign. Did he sell it to someone else?" She felt a knot in her stomach as they walked up the path. Wilfred opened the door. "Come in." He took Alex's hand. "I am pleased to meet you."

"Mr. Johnson, where is the sign? You didn't sell, did you?"

He looked hurt. "No, no! The house is yours. I didn't want to be bothered with people calling."

They agreed on the price, $2,500, which in Anna's opinion was more than they could afford without selling the bakery. Alex had no qualms about selling but, for Anna, her independence was in jeopardy. Conflicted by her need to work and her need for this lovely house, she decided they could not make the final decision until they spoke with Mr. Peabody at the bank.

As expected, Mr. Peabody would give them a mortgage on the Forest Road house but he required a substantial down payment. They would have to sell Kenwood Bakery. One of the most difficult parts would be informing Nick and Henry. They would of course include Nick and Henry as employees in the sale. If the truth be told it was because of these two that the bakery did so well, so any prospective buyer would be foolish not to keep them. They asked Nick to join them in the office.

Alex spoke first, "Nick, we have some interesting news. Anna and I are finding the living accommodation upstairs a little cramped for the family and we have decided to buy a house. Unfortunately, we have to sell the bakery."

Anna intervened. "We will insist that any buyer keep you and Henry..."

Nick interrupted. "I will buy it. I will buy the bakery. Helga and I have been saving up to buy our own store. Baking is our business but Helga kept putting it off. She's afraid she can't do the office work. And we didn't know how to tell you."

Anna and Alex fell silent, hardly able to hear what Nick was saying. Anna quickly honed in on the office issue. "Nick, I can continue to look after the office."

"Mrs. Walker that would be ideal. I will compensate you and perhaps you can teach Helga how to keep the books."

"Of course we will sell to you." Alex stretched out his arm and shook Nick's hand. "It's a deal."

Anna had one of her Cheshire cat grins that filled her with joy and said, "Will you be moving into the apartment?"

Nick hastily added, "I would like to speak with Helga first, particularly about moving. But Helga likes it here. I am sure she will agree."

Anna could not have been more pleased. All their prayers were answered. Everything had fallen into place so easily and quickly. Perhaps too easily, Anna thought.

"Mr. Henry, I have a pink bedroom with roses all over it and you shall come and visit. Mr. Johnson is my pretend grandpa and if you are good, we can share him. I need a grandpa. Mine is across a big ocean." Isabelle stopped to take a breath and looked at her mother. "Can I have a pretend grandpa?" Everyone laughed at her innocent words, touched by her excitement.

Twenty-Four

Mother Walker's Destruction

Anna's enthusiasm at the prospect of moving to 72 Forest Road prompted her to indulge in new furniture. Most of the furniture from the apartment was either cheap or second-hand. The Eaton's bedroom suite that she had thought so extravagant she passed on to Isabelle, replacing it with an expensive Queen Anne-style set.

The old dining table was far too small for the dining room, but would fit in the kitchen now that they had a kitchen big enough for a table. Anna picked out a high quality walnut table and chairs, with a matching sideboard for the dining room. She promised herself she would save for the china cabinet.

The little room at the bottom of the stairs became her office and she bought an oak roll-top desk with little cubbyholes that reminded her of The Sackville to keep her papers neat. Anna loved this little office. She decorated it with prints and her favourite knick-knacks, adding a comfortable chair where she could read and escape.

Nick, Henry and Helga moved into the apartment and the customers hardly noticed there had been a change of ownership. Isabelle played happily in her rose pink bedroom and Mr. Johnson became her adopted grandpa and a family friend. Alex spent most of the summer on the trains and when he was at home, he rarely wheezed or coughed. Even the nightmares lessened.

Bill seemed to be more comfortable; perhaps a bit too settled as a result of the time spent with Anna in the evenings. Anna enjoyed talking about their common interests. She had forgotten how important these things were to her. Alex cared little about books or anything that was not of interest to him, their commonality at this time was the house. Alex loved his new home. Anna suspected it had more to do with her staying at home and devoting her time to household chores, which to her surprise she found a welcome change from the hurried busyness of the store. She suspected boredom would eventually be a problem but, for now, organizing the house and the garden challenged her. Astonished by her own reaction, she was actually enjoying being a housewife.

"Good morning!" Wilfred Johnson called to Anna, who was raking the leaves under the oak tree. "I wondered if Isabelle and I could take a walk to the park?"

"Good morning, Wilfred. I am sure she would like that."

They didn't have to ask. Isabelle jumped over the pile of leaves and slid her hand into his, and off they went. Wilfred looked ten years younger since he had sold the house. Initially, Anna had thought Wilfred to be her father's age but today, she realized he was considerably younger. Anna grinned, thinking of her father and how he would love to take Isabelle to the park. He had written the last letter from Rugby—his way of reassuring her that he had fully recovered from his chest ailment. How she wished it were her parents visiting for Christmas, not Mother Walker and Florence. She knew her mother would never leave Lou, not at Christmas. Perhaps she could persuade them to come in the summer.

The leaves scrunched under her rake and an acorn dropped with a thud. She looked up at the squirrels scurrying up and down the branches, cheeks puffed out with acorns, their little noses twitching with urgency. She leaned on the rake, feeling the golden sun on her face and drinking in the leafy smell and coolness of fall.

A white veil of frost had coated the lawn earlier that morning, a sign of colder things to come and she wasn't just thinking of the weather. Mother Walker and Florence would arrive in a month's time. Her memory of these two ladies scared her. The two weeks they had spent in Scotland before coming to Canada had not been pleasant. Mother Walker ruled the roost with rules of etiquette, many of them hers alone, and all without a hint of emotion. Florence had been spoiled all her life. The only relief had been Papa Walker, a gentle, kind hard working man whose spoils were gobbled up by wife and daughter. Anna often wondered if his only escape had been to die.

Alex's position with CP Rail accorded him some privileges, one of which was first class travel for his close relatives, so his mother and sister travelled in style from Halifax to Toronto, arriving on November 15th, in the middle of the first major snowstorm of the season. Not surprisingly, the train chugged slowly into Union Station two hours late. The manager, showing his respect for Alex's position, came to greet Alex, shaking his hand and nervously escorting him to his mother's compartment. Unbeknownst to Alex his mother had been a difficult passenger.

Alex leaned over to kiss his mother. "Welcome to Canada, Mother. How was your journey?"

Petunia Walker tightened her already pursed lips and pecked him on the cheek. "Dreadful! The worst journey I have ever experienced. I feared for my life."

"I am sorry to hear that, Mother, but I am glad you arrived safely and your journey is nearly over. We have a taxi waiting. There isn't room in the taxi for your luggage. It will be sent separately."

Never having seen a black man before, Mother Walker stared at the porter as he loaded her trunks onto a cart. "Has he been trained?"

"Mother!" Alex said, embarrassed by her comment as he handed the man a generous tip with profuse apologies.

Ignoring Alex's obvious discomfort, she continued, "Is it safe or will he steal me blind?" She huffed, tightening her grip on her reticule. Alex rolled his eyes towards Anna as they waited for the last bag to be loaded.

Mother Walker stood five feet tall and so straight that Anna wondered if she had a broomstick down her back. Her grey complexion blended with her dark grey Wooster travelling suit; the skirt too long for current fashion. The wide high-collared jacket buttoned to the neck dwarfed her face and head, and the black, wide-brimmed hat perched on top gave the impression of a lid too large for its receptacle.

Florence, a few inches taller, kept a few paces behind as a servant might. Her expensive navy blue travelling suit had a more stylish hem length and loose fitting jacket; a rather jaunty blue hat hugged her head, leaving a fringe of dark red curls. Standing beside these two ladies, Anna felt like an orphan in her heavy brown coat, although it did have a fur collar. She had thought it the height of fashion when she purchased it from Eaton's. Mother Walker looked straight to her thick wool hat that she had worn for warmth rather than fashion. Isabelle shrank from the new arrivals and clung to Alex's leg when Mother Walker bent forward.

"Och! So this wee thing is my granddaughter," and that was all she said, her heavy Scottish brogue difficult to understand.

The journey to Forest Road was silent and long, the snow made travelling hazardous. Alex sat in the front with the driver. Anna hugged a frightened Isabelle on her knee with Florence and Mother Walker at each side of her. *It is going to be a long two months,* she thought. Anna already felt the euphoria of her new home escaping into a gloomy sense of anguish, and she thought, *all that luggage for only two people?* Where were they going to store the trunks? She felt Florence shiver. It was cold and neither of them had winter coats. Pleased that she'd had had the foresight to bring blankets, she pulled the blanket tighter around Florence and leaned towards Mother Walker. But the rebuff of her glare made Anna pull back. Mother Walker folded the edge of her blanket precisely, muttering to Florence not to make a fuss.

Anna had a feeling that the taxi ride had set the tone for her in-laws' visit. She consoled herself with the knowledge that in mid-January—she wasn't sure of the exact date, and it would be impolite to ask—their lives would return to normal.

But, as Mother Walker settled at 72 Forest Road, Anna was thrown into double jeopardy, her deep fears—housewife and servant. She had hated the short time she had been in service and her life now was worse than any maid's. Neither Mother Walker nor Florence lifted a finger in the house. Alex was never home and Bill left earlier and came home later.

Anna cooked, cleaned and did the laundry, although she did insist that Florence do her mother's ironing. And in fairness to Florence, she had little time to do anything but her mother's bidding. Florence managed to steal a few minutes to play with Isabelle. This surprised Anna but the two got along well. She noticed that little Jimmy enjoyed playing with her too. In that moment, Anna felt sorry for Florence. Had she had the opportunity, she would have made a good mother.

Electrified, would be an apt described of the household and by mid-December, ten days before Christmas, the tension was building. Snide remarks sparked sarcasm instead of conversation. Isabelle, feeling the tension, reacted by throwing tantrums. Mother Walker sat primly in her wingback chair, her grey hair expertly coiffed into rolls and curls that took Florence an hour or more to dress. Her round, almost protruding, hazel eyes surveyed the emotional chaos. Anna detected a smirk on her scrawny face. The same smirk Anna had received when she had forgotten the butter knife or jam spoon, or worse, the day Anna served a special treat of poached salmon only to be berated for not having the proper fish knives and forks.

The special dinner for Alex's weekend off was spoiled by a constant chatter of how the cutlery would always smell of fish and she would never be able to eat with them again. The hurt Anna felt that day had less to do with the unjust reprimand and more to do with Alex's reluctance to defend her.

When she could no longer hold back the tears after a scathing comment about Anna's inadequacies as a wife, she excused herself from the table. Standing in the hall, calming her quickening temper, she overheard Alex apologize to his mother for Anna's behaviour. It was Bill who followed her into the kitchen putting his arm on her shoulder to comfort her. The warmth of his arm took her by surprise and the humiliation took her back to Bexhill. She wiped her tears and laughed.

"Remember when you told me I was Papa's little girl?"

"Yes, I do. And right now, Alex is behaving like a mama's boy. Anna, you have to talk to him about how his mother is treating you. This can't go on. You are exhausted."

"Bill, I'll be fine, it's only for a few more weeks. Now, we had better get back before she starts talking about us." Their eyes met, seeking the once familiar affection.

Anna escaped to her little office for two hours of an afternoon while Mother Walker took a rest and Florence played with Isabelle. Sometimes Wilfred would call to take Isabelle outside to build a snowman or go ice-skating at the park. Isabelle insisted that Auntie Florence went too, leaving Anna time do her bookkeeping work for Nick.

Wintertime in Canada, especially in Ontario, was not a good time to entertain guests. And this year, not only had winter started early, but it was colder than usual. After the Christmas festivities, which were far from festive in the Walker household, Anna decided to cheer everyone up with a cocktail hour.

Cocktail parties were all the rage: a new style of a social event popular in America, lasting about an hour and usually held before lunch or dinner. Inviting friends and neighbours, she thought this might impress her mother-in-law and perhaps the invitations would be reciprocated, encouraging Mother Walker to make some friends. Anna had long thought that Mother Walker's melancholy and resulting bad temper was related to the lack of social interaction. Her life in Scotland had been all teas and soirees.

The event started well. All the ladies dressed in cocktail attire, glittering dresses not as formal as evening wear, and the gentlemen wore dark suits. Petunia Walker held court, enjoying the attention, willingly accepting compliments on her long silver gown and swept up hair adorned with flowers and long black feathers—a Victorian apparition.

Alex feasted his eyes on his beautiful Anna wearing a pink, sequined cocktail dress, the hem sexily above her knees and a long string of pearls around her neck. "I love you, Anna Walker. Watch out tonight," he whispered in her ear. His smile ignited a spark intensified by his gentle kiss. Before she could respond, a loud bellow ricocheted across the room.

"Alex!" Mother Walker cleared her throat and in a quieter tone said, "My glass is empty." Every head in the room turned. She smiled, nodding her head and coyly placing it to one side, pleased that the attention had re-focused on Petunia Walker.

Wilfred innocently asked, "How are you enjoying your stay in Canada, Mrs. Walker?"

"It is the most godforsaken country I have ever set foot in." Her hand shook as she raised her glass, to what, nobody could tell. "Only idiots would... crum... tolerate the weather. I expect to die of frostbite." Raising her voice even louder and smiling at her audience, she continued, "The place is only fit for... crum... polar bears and Eskimos." Leaning back in her chair, she smirked and bowed.

Wilfred's kind heart attempted to ease the tension and humiliation by laughing, making a joke of Mother Walker's comments, although the righteous expression on her face gave no hint of humour.

"Mr. Johnson, Canada... will never be a proper country.... While... it's...," she coughed, "run by colonials and..." she wagged her finger at him, "savages." The room went silent, but not Mother Walker. "That Ma.. Mac... King fellow is a bit strange for a Prime Minister." Fortunately, this last recitation was hardly decipherable between slurred words and rolling Scottish R's.

Alex whispered to Anna, "I think my mother is drunk. I'll take her upstairs. Can you ask Florence to come and help me?"

Anna nodded, stifling a giggle. The prim Petunia Walker was tipsy. Tomorrow they would get an apology.

Mother Walker carried on as though nothing had happened and no apology came. Anna had thought of having a tea afternoon for the old lady, involving no alcohol, but decided she was too embarrassed to expose her friends to another tirade. Besides, if her calculations were correct, they would be returning to Scotland soon. Time to get the trunks up from the basement. Anna wondered exactly when their ship would be leaving Halifax. She must remind Alex to book the train. Anna could already feel the relief of having her home and family back to normal. Her spirits lifted with renewed resolve to be kind to Mother Walker and Florence. Poor Florence had become a slave to her mother. Anna had seen a different side to that spoiled, subservient daughter. Florence could be warm and kind. She loved children and Isabelle adored her Auntie Florence. Canada had shown her it was possible to have more. Anna suspected that she would find it difficult to settle back to life in Scotland.

The January wind howled, penetrating through every window and crack in the house. The central heating barely kept the chill off. Alex had lit a roaring fire in the sitting room and everyone huddled in the one room to keep warm. Conversation with Mother Walker was never fluid and usually arduous, but tonight Anna decided to be cheery.

"I had a letter from my brother, Charlie, today. He will have served ten years in the army come this spring and has decided to settle in Canada after he is discharged. Alex, he wondered if you could help him find work."

Alex thought for a moment. "Did he say what kind of work? There might be something at CP Rail. Do you have any ideas, Bill?"

"During the summer months, there are always positions open at the Royal York or one of the other hotels. It would be fun to have Charlie here."

Mother Walker sat up even straighter than usual. Fixing her gaze on Bill, she shuffled slightly, her expression tense with concentration, a movement you would expect to see from a cat preparing to pounce on its prey. Anna thought the old lady had been waiting for such an opportunity.

"Are you planning on moving elsewhere to make room for Charlie? And, if so, you can make room for me. I will have your bedroom. Sharing a room with Florence has been most unsatisfactory. It is time we had our own rooms. Charlie will have to find alternative accommodation."

"Mother Walker, you will be back in Scotland by the time my brother arrives. I doubt he will be here much before the summer. Should you decide to visit again we will make you and Florence comfortable, I promise."

"Visit? Is that how you feel about me? Your poor, widowed, mother-in-law—a visitor? This is *my* home!" She snivelled, placing a white lace handkerchief to her dry eyes.

A heavy quietness descended on the sitting room. Anna felt terror strike deep in her soul. Alex deliberately stared at his feet like a scolded schoolboy. Anna now knew why there had been so many trunks upon their arrival. Mother Walker and Florence were here for good and Alex had known this all along.

Completely unaffected by the awkwardness in the room, Mother Walker continued, "Alex, when can I expect to move to my own room? If not Bill's, then Isabelle's"

"Mother, we need to think about this. Perhaps we could convert the little room downstairs."

"That's nothing more than a cupboard. I couldn't possibly move in there." She hesitated. "But Florence could."

Anna bristled. "No! Alex, that is my study. I need the privacy and quiet to work on the Kenwood Bakery accounts."

Already trying to absorb the fact that these unwanted visitors were permanent, as was her unwanted role of maid and servant, Anna was horrified that Alex would even think of taking away her nine by nine piece of heaven where she could escape and be herself.

Mother Walker stood up and announced, "That settles it. Florence will move her things to the study and I will stay as I am."

"Sit down!" Anna commanded. "Nobody is sleeping in my study and neither Isabelle nor Bill are giving up their rooms. It was my understanding that you were visiting for two months and then returning to Scotland." Anna glared directly at Alex, her face strained with anger. Alex and his mother had threatened all that was dear to her and a compromise was no longer an option.

"If you want your own bedroom, Mother Walker, you had better ask your son to help you find a suitable apartment. I might suggest with maid service because I am no longer willing to provide you with such service, and while I think about it, neither should Florence. She too should have a life of her own." Breathlessly, Anna continued. "Of course you could go and stay with your eldest son's family, Jim and Abigail, and destroy their lives. Abigail is a much better cook and housekeeper than me. Perhaps you would find less to criticize there."

The room fell quiet, Anna had never spoken like that before and she felt quite strange and pleasantly vindicated. Florence cowered behind her mother's chair and Alex made no attempt to agree or disagree.

The exchange had become personal and Mother Walker's face had greyed, her eyes stony cold, her voice mean with hatred. "Perhaps my son should know why you do not wish Mr. Blaine to move out of this house. You think an old lady does not see how you steal glances and whisper behind her son's back? You are a loose woman, harlot. Maybe it is you who should find another place to live."

Tongue-tied, Anna looked to Alex for support but none was forthcoming. The old lady had sown a seed of doubt, re-opening a rift between Anna and Alex that had long since healed. Was she trying to push Anna out of her own home? Alex shrugged his shoulders, his silence speaking volumes.

Bill's voice called from the hallway. "I will be staying at the YMCA until I can find suitable rooms." His coat was buttoned up against the cold, his hat pulled over his ears and his gloves in hand, holding a bag.

Anna's head started spinning. This was a nightmare. She turned to Alex, appealing to him to do something—to stop Bill from leaving, to defend her and put his mother in her place. But what she saw was uncertainty even mistrust. His mother's damaging words had been well aimed.

Alex stepped into the hall and slapped Bill on the back. "I think it's for the best, old boy. You're doing the right thing."

Misery overcame Anna. Her head would not stop spinning and she felt sick. Her limbs would not move and her lips could not utter a word. Her eyes spoke for her as they went from Bill to Alex and then Mother Walker. Anna filled with horror as Mother Walker's lips curled, gloating over the scene with a macabre satisfaction. A cascade of tears flowed over Anna, flushing away the anger and falling into a pool of deep despair. Willing her legs to walk, she began to climb the stairs and, taking a fleeting look over her shoulder, she saw the hurt in Bill as he stepped through the front door. Her heart cried out. She wanted to follow him, fall into his arms and hear him say everything would be all right. But it was Alex who stood at the bottom of the stairs, cold and disparaging.

"I'm sorry," he said, the compassion in his voice surprised her but instead of comforting her, he moved towards the sitting room. "I had better go to Mother. You'll feel better in the morning."

Anna threw herself onto the bed and buried her face in the pillow. There was no hope left, nothing to hold on to. Her deepest fear had materialized and its mistress was the worst kind—a vindictive mother-in-law. Feeling the cold, she rolled off the bed, washed her swollen face, pulled on a flannel nightdress and found a dry pillow. Her ribs hurt as she slid under the warm eiderdown.

The pain in her heart was more than she could bear. Dry tears welled inside, leaving a deep ache for all that was dear to her. She yearned for comfort and kindness, for Bill's gentleness or Papa's protection. That's it, she thought, I should take Isabelle and go home to Rugby. Hearing Alex climb the stairs two at a time, she curled up on her side and closed her eyes.

Alex carefully lifted the covers and lay on his back. Anna could tell by his breathing he was wide awake. She heard him take a deep breath. "Anna, is it true what my mother said about you and Bill? Is there more than friendship between you?"

Anna stayed curled up with her back to him. "Can you not see that your mother is driving us apart? You know Bill is a friend to both of us. He helps me around the house doing chores you either can't or won't do. He keeps me company of an evening when you are away." She heard the despondency in her monotone voice. "Your mother has driven your friend from this house." Anna rolled onto her back. "She has no respect for me. Alex, you have to make a decision as to who is the lady of this house. I am prepared to take Isabelle and move back to England." Where she had found the strength to say these words, she did not know, but she felt so empty it didn't matter what she said.

Alex pushed himself up on his elbow and grabbed Anna's arm, forcing her to look at him. Her vision blurred from her puffy eyes she saw Alex's temper rise and quickly fall. Releasing his grip, he said, "Anna, please don't leave and *I beg* you, don't take Isabelle away."

Anna turned on her side, her back towards Alex. "The choice is yours, Alex."

Twenty-Five

What Goes Around Comes Around

O ther than including Mother Walker at meal times, Anna stopped waiting on her and they rarely spoke. Alex moved her into Bill's old room and Anna reluctantly accepted that he would never tell his mother to leave. But she held the wild card. He was terrified she would carry out her threat of leaving with Isabelle. When his mother complained her room was dirty or Florence had to do her washing, Alex defended Anna and offered to hire a maid. She surmised this was his compromise to making a choice between the two women.

Anna and Alex had called a somewhat shaky truce. Neither had seen nor spoken to Bill since that stormy night in January. The everyday operation of the household had a palpable undercurrent of tension but, for the most part, it ran smoothly, and by the time the snow had melted and daffodils were blooming it had taken on the appearance of normalcy.

Daisy had a great deal to do with the house running smoothly. She was just a snippet of a girl of sixteen, not quite an orphan, but no father, and a mother who had fallen on hard times. Daisy took up her position of maid enthusiastically, working hard, doing general chores and helping Anna in the kitchen. Always a willing girl, she found time to do Mother Walker's bidding and the old lady had taken to her quite well.

Every morning, Anna walked to the bakery to do her accounting work. The relaxed and comfortable atmosphere at the Günter's was a pleasant change from 72 Forest Road.

"Good morning, Mrs. Walker," Henry called as he spun the handle, unwinding the awning over the bakery window. "It promises to be a warm day. Ma's in the office."

Anna greeted Nick as he pulled a batch of steaming bread from the oven and walked to the back office where Helga was staring at the books.

"Good morning, Anna. I don't know if I will ever understand debits and credits."

Anna had offered to teach Helga how to enter the daily accounts. "You will. It's not nearly as daunting as it looks. Shall we start with coffee?"

"Good idea, I have some upstairs. I just made it for Nick and Henry."

Anna sat at the dining room table, enjoying the view of St. Clare Avenue and remembered how safe and comfortable she had felt sitting in the window seat. How simple their lives had been then.

"Penny for your thoughts?" Helga asked as she placed a tray of coffee on the table. "Are things still bad at home?"

"No. Since we hired Daisy, things have improved. She's a good worker and even gets along with Mother Walker, which allows Florence to relax a little. Florence spends much time with Isabelle. I am surprised that the old lady doesn't object. Speaking of Isabelle, I must ask Nick about a birthday cake. It's hard to believe she is turning five."

Helga took two big cups of coffee down to the bakery and Anna went into the office. Hearing the store bell jingle and Isabelle's voice, she stepped into the store.

"Mr. Henry, did you know I am going to be *five*?" She held up her hand, spreading her fingers apart.

"Does that mean I have to bake a cake?"

Isabelle jumped up and down. "Yes, of course you do."

"Isabelle, mind your manners," Anna reprimanded.

"Hello, Florence. I am pleased to see your mother allowed you out early today." Anna then saw Wilfred in the doorway. "Wilfred, I didn't see you there. Good morning."

Florence flushed a little. "Daisy took Mother her breakfast this morning and she said she would dress herself. I told her Isabelle and I would take a walk. It's such a beautiful day." Florence's flush deepened. "And I met Wilfred who was admiring the tulips."

Wilfred bought a loaf of bread and an apple strudel and the three waved goodbye, Florence held Isabelle's hand and Anna noticed Wilfred slip his hand into Florence's other one as the three walked down St. Clare Avenue. Anna and Helga went back to the office.

"Helga, am I imagining things or is there romance in the air?"

"I think you're right."

"How exciting. But he must be fifteen years older than Florence."

"Does that matter?"

"No. He is a kind gentleman and Florence deserves some happiness. I dread to think what will happen when Mother Walker finds out."

Helga laughed. "Perhaps she will go and live with them if they marry and leave you and Alex alone."

"I can't see that happening. I hope they keep it a secret."

The family and the Günters gathered to celebrate Isabelle's birthday on the following Sunday. Upon Isabelle's insistence, Alex had invited Uncle Bill. The Günters crept in the back door and Henry surprised everyone as he carried a fairy castle cake, complete with dainty sugar fairies, into the dining room. Five flaming candles stood on the castle turrets and a drawbridge perched over a moat of blue icing. Isabelle screeched with delight. Relieved that the attention was on the cake and Isabelle, Anna had a strong desire to look over at Bill, but she dared not take the risk. Mother Walker never missed a thing. Anna hoped that she had not noticed how Florence and Wilfred stole glances throughout the afternoon. As pleasant and calm as the afternoon had been, Anna could not shake off a feeling of dread. Unnaturally quiet, the scheming old lady was up to something. Anna tried to open a dialogue, finding praise for Mother Walker.

"Isabelle is delighted with her new dress. Such a lovely and generous birthday gift, Mother Walker. The hem needs shortening, otherwise she would have worn it today." Anna crossed her fingers telling such a lie. Isabelle hated the frilly old-fashioned dress and had refused to wear it.

"Good. At least she will have one respectable dress."

"Isabelle is fortunate to have a generous grandmother and aunt. It is delightful to see her get along with her Aunt Florence so well. Don't you agree?"

"Florence seems to be getting along with too many people," Mother Walker said, fixing a stare on Wilfred.

"Isabelle looks upon Wilfred as a grandfather. She is lucky to have him in her life." Anna wanted to steer her mother-in-law away from any hint of romance between Florence and Wilfred but she suspected it was too late.

Petunia Walker clasped her hands in her lap, shifted, adjusting her broomstick back, to sit straighter. "Contrary to what you might think of me, I am not a fool. That man has designs on my daughter. He is a widower and too old. You yourself just commented that he was like a grandfather. It's unseemly."

"He's not that old. I just meant he is a gentleman and kind, and Isabelle likes him." Annoyed with herself for speaking of Wilfred as a grandfather, Anna thought this was not going to end well.

"Be that as it may, if my daughter doesn't come to her senses then I will do it for her." She gave Anna a scathing glare and continued, "I would be obliged if you would refrain from meddling in affairs that do not concern you. Your flawed judgment in matters of the heart is not wanted." The stay in Canada had softened Mother Walker's rolling R's and Anna had no trouble understanding every word.

Under her breath Anna whispered, "Witch, you should be burnt at the stake." It was Anna's turn for caustic looks as hatred bubbled to the surface. Holding her tongue, she busied herself cleaning up the dishes. Mother Walker retired to her room.

It had been the briefest of springs, the weather heating up in early June.

Most of the household welcomed the heat after a long winter but Mother Walker now constantly complained about it being too hot. The complaints grew in intensity as the humidity joined the heat in July and August. Expecting a drama or crisis to emerge at any moment, Anna walked around the house on eggshells. But nothing happened. Even Bill's occasional visits were tolerated without comment.

Isabelle was to start school in September, keeping Anna occupied buying school uniforms, satchels and supplies. Excited for his daughter, Alex behaved like a kid himself. This milestone in their lives brought the family together and Anna began to relax too.

The school year always commenced on the Tuesday following Labour Day. Alex enjoyed the holiday weekend at home, extending it one more day so he could accompany Isabelle to her first day of school. After seeing their daughter settled in her classroom, Anna went on to the bakery and Alex went home. That afternoon, Helga finished the accounts and Anna went home early.

Entering the house by the back door she heard Alex shouting. She stopped and listened, realizing she had walked into a heated argument between Alex and his mother. She heard the edge to his voice, barely controlled. Alex was losing his temper.

"You told me all father's money had gone and that you and Florence were destitute. You came here, disrupted our lives, abused our kindness and now you want me to finance your return to Scotland. It has been a strain on my finances to support you here. Mother, I cannot support you in Scotland."

Anna stood motionless in the hall staying out of sight. Her heart jumping for joy hearing the words 'return to Scotland.'

"When I wrote to you, the funds had been depleted. It seems that the bank omitted to inform me of the proceeds from the sale of the business, which the bank suitably invested. When I enquired recently, I was told the funds were considerable."

"I don't believe you, Mother. You are not a foolish woman and the bank manager would have been obliged to keep you abreast of your financial situation." Alex's voice quivered. "You came here under false pretences and I will not forgive you for that or the way you treated my wife. I felt it my duty as a son to give you a home."

"Oh, that's what you call it? Not much of a home to me. Anyway, Alex, there is no debate. Florence and I are returning to Scotland and I have asked Daisy to come with us."

"Have you asked Florence about this? She seems happy here and Daisy is in my employ, not yours." Anna jumped back into the kitchen as Alex started pacing in the sitting room.

"Florence does as I tell her and I need Daisy's services more than you."

"Can you afford to pay for three passages to Scotland? Where will you live?"

"Mr. McDonald has sent a money draft from the bank and he made the arrangements for the passage. It is all paid for and the ship leaves Halifax next Tuesday."

"Mother, why such a hurry? What are you concealing?"

"I am not happy here. The weather is inclement and I have no intention of freezing through another winter. My friend Bertha Forbes has offered us accommodation until we find something suitable. At least I am welcome there."

The grin on Anna's face reached from ear to ear. She went to the back door, opened it and slammed it shut so Alex would know she was home. Just to make sure she called. "I'm home. Would anyone like tea before we pick up Isabelle?" As she expected, no one answered. She could hear shuffling and whispers. Alex came into the kitchen, red faced and agitated.

"I have something to tell you. Let's go for a walk."

They walked slowly through the park to the school. Alex told Anna what she had overheard. He was hurt and angry, and perhaps for the first time, he had seen his mother as a vindictive, manipulative, self-serving woman.

The trunks were all packed and Mother Walker and Florence boarded the night train to Halifax. Florence couldn't stop weeping. Wilfred had ended the romance without real cause and Anna knew the old lady had something to do with it. She hugged Florence and tried to reassure her that one day she could return. Poor Florence dissolved into more tears, prompting Mother Walker to scold her for sniveling. Alex had made no attempt to change his schedule to see his mother off. In fact, Anna thought he might have deliberately been in Vancouver the day she departed. Daisy declined the offer to join them in Scotland, preferring to stay with Anna.

Anna never told Alex she'd heard him lose his temper with his mother and how much it had meant to her that, at last, he had defended her. She wished he would say the words to her, but he never did. His way of showing he was sorry was to allow Daisy to stay, freeing Anna of the domestic duties. Now Anna had a different problem, that of boredom. She had nothing to do. Helga had taken over the daily bookkeeping at the bakery, Isabelle was in school all day and Alex seemed to take on more and more work and longer trips. Anna had too much time on her hands.

Daisy had become part of the family and Anna decided that she was quite capable of taking care of Isabelle after school while Anna worked as a hotel receptionist in the afternoons. She began her job search by inviting Bill for dinner, asking him to inquire at the Royal York on her behalf. During dinner he agreed to introduce her to the general manager if she agreed to help him find suitable rooms.

The accommodation at the YMCA was adequate at best. Anna was playing with fire but it seemed silly for Bill to rent rooms elsewhere when he had a perfectly good room at 72 Forest Road and half of his belongings were still packed away in the basement. Two days later, Bill loaded a suitcase and a box of books into a taxi and moved back to his old room.

Having not told Alex of the new arrangements, truthfully because she couldn't reach him, and secretly afraid he would say no, Anna had rationalized that his mother had depleted them financially and they could use the extra money, and better it be Bill than a complete stranger.

Alex arrived home after a particularly arduous trip; difficult passengers and incompetent staff and what, on this occasion, had led to firing one of the supervisors. Seeing his pale, drawn face, Anna greeted him with a loving hug. He kissed her holding on to her almost as tightly as Isabelle was holding on to his leg trying to get his attention.

"Papa, it's Halloween tomorrow, come see my costume. Aunt Abigail made it." Alex bent down and hugged his excited daughter. Isabelle slipped her hand in his and led him to the dining room. A white costume with feather-covered wings lay across the table.

"See," Isabelle pointed to the duck like head. "She has a scarf just like Jemima Puddle-duck."

Alex smiled. "What a wonderful costume. I can't wait to see you wear it. Perhaps you can wear it tonight when we read the Jemima Puddle-duck story. That's if Mummy says it's okay." Anna nodded her approval.

The front door opened and Bill walked in. "Alex, good to see you. How are you?"

"Tired but otherwise fine thank you. Are you staying for dinner?"

There was an awkward moment. Bill looked at Anna and she cleared her throat as she often did when she was nervous. "Alex, I didn't have a chance to tell you that Bill has moved back into his old room." Without waiting for a reply Anna said, "Why don't you two take a seat in the sitting room while I prepare dinner."

She listened carefully from the kitchen and although she could not hear all the words, the conversation appeared to be quite amicable. The three spent a pleasant evening together. The colour had returned to Alex's face after a good meal and good company but he had been coughing and Anna suggested they retire early.

Lying in bed, feeling the warmth from each other's bodies, Anna snuggled close as Alex wrapped his arms around her, and she succumbed to the warmth of his kisses, her body melting into his as they made love. Content and tired, they lay close, talking about small everyday things. Anna took the opportunity to mention her thoughts of working.

"Now that Isabelle is in school, I thought I would look for a receptionist's position."

She felt Alex's body stiffen. "Why would you want to do that? I can provide for you."

"Alex, I need a purpose in life. I enjoyed my work at The Sackville and the bakery. I would like to do something like that again."

Alex gave a sigh and dismissed her. "I'm too tired to talk about it now."

Disappointed he had not supported her, but not surprised, she decided not to discuss it further. He had not exactly said no, which meant if she did find work she would not be totally disregarding his wishes.

He stroked her hair, gently twisting the golden brown curls. "Anna, do you love me?"

"Of course I love you. Why do you ask?"

"Why didn't you tell me Bill was moving back?"

"How could I? You were somewhere between Vancouver and Calgary and I didn't think you would mind. We could use the extra money. We have the room and I would rather have Bill than a stranger. Bill needed somewhere to live other than the YMCA."

"You once told me you and Bill were *just friends*. He helped you with odd jobs around the house and kept you company when I was away. Is that still true?"

"Yes. Bill is a gentleman and your friend. Are you still upset about what your mother said? That was nothing more than your mother being vindictive and I think you know that."

Alex kissed her and held her tight. "Never leave me, Anna." He closed his eyes and began snoring within seconds.

Anna lay awake for some time, perturbed by something she heard in Alex's voice. She found herself questioning and wondering if it could be fear or jealousy. Did he have cause for jealousy? How honest was she being about her feelings for Bill? Was it friendship or was it more? She had always loved them both, and on more than one occasion she had asked herself if she had made the right choice. The answer was never clear.

Calm, quiet Bill was the one who kept his distance, although the attentive glances did not escape Anna. Bill wasn't a fighter. He accepted life for what it was. It was as though he had won the consolation prize of friendship, allowing him to stay close and be a protector, leaving Alex with the prize. She could not deny that she enjoyed Bill's company and he supported her need for independence, her interest in literature and travel. *Perhaps*, she thought, *I am lucky and have the best of both men.*

Alex got up first, made Isabelle breakfast and took her to school. Anna came downstairs as the postman delivered the mail. There were two letters, one from her mother and the other from the Royal York Hotel. She assumed the latter was in reply to her inquiry. She ripped the envelope open wanting to read it before Alex returned. It was brief, inviting Anna to meet with the manager at two o'clock the next day. Hearing Alex's long stride, she pushed the letter in her pocket and was reading her mother's letter when he entered the kitchen.

"Who's the letter from?"

"Rugby. Mum's chatter about the grandchildren. Little Robbie has a cold and it sounds as though she has been helping Lou. Charlie was home last month, getting his papers ready to come here."

"I thought you ate breakfast with Isabelle?" Anna said as Alex started frying bacon and egg.

"No, I was waiting for you. I thought we could eat together. The train leaves at two this afternoon. Vancouver run, so I have to leave shortly," Alex said, pouring coffee for them both.

Anna wanted to ask him about going to work again and she really wanted to tell him about the letter but she was afraid he would say no and they would have an argument.

"Hey! Don't be so sad."

"I'm not sad. I need something to do." Anna was hoping he would suggest it was okay for her to look for work.

"Why don't you talk to Wilfred and volunteer your time at the hospital? He's worked there for years. He must know people."

Anna decided not to argue and gave a vague nod, eating intently. She considered volunteer work to be beneath her expertise and something ladies did to occupy their time, the kind of scene she vehemently avoided. The letter from the Royal York was the answer and she decided she would tell Alex after she had secured the job.

Anna was finding it difficult to remain calm as Alex packed his bag and finally caught the tramcar to the Union Station. It was almost noon and she didn't have time to telephone the Royal York before picking up Isabelle, so it would have to wait until after lunch. She finally called at two, but the manager was in a meeting and would return her call as soon as he could. It was the following morning before he called and Anna could confirm her appointment for that afternoon.

After trying on almost everything in her wardrobe, Anna decided on a simple black suit for the interview. She had thought The Sackville to be a very grand hotel but the Royal York exuded culture, wealth and a cosmopolitan atmosphere. Stepping out of the swivel doors, she suddenly felt nervous and thrown back in time.

The reception counter, twice the size of The Sackville's, had three clerks attending to guests. Anna noticed they were all in uniform and all very young ladies. With her experience, Anna thought she was perhaps needed to supervise the reception desk. Bill had not said anything, but she thought his recommendation had added to her suitability for the position, although she didn't quite know which one. The gentleman who escorted her to his rather sparse and less than elegant office was not the general manager but his assistant, Mr. Engle, a pleasant man, small of stature and impeccably dressed in a black suit.

"Please take a seat, Mrs. Walker. I read your letter with interest." He pointed to the open letter on his desk. "For a woman, your experience is astounding."

Anna handed Mr. Kendrick's letter of reference across the small desk. "I think this will confirm what is in the letter. During the Great War, I was in charge of not only the front desk but also the dining room and some housekeeping staff." Anna felt confident as she remembered her best days at The Sackville.

"Your experience is commendable, but it was six years ago. Do you have any more recent hotel experience?"

"Not hotel experience but I do have business experience. My husband and I owned a bakery until recently and I managed the bakery and have extensive accounting experience as a result."

"Um… a bakery. Perhaps not quite the experience we are looking for. You are married, Mrs. Walker?"

"Yes, but…"

"Children?"

"Yes, one daughter. But she is in school and well looked after. My home responsibilities would not interfere with my work." Anna did not like the change in tone that the interview was taking. "Mr. Engle, I noticed when I came in that the front desk clerks are young and perhaps in need of guidance and tutelage by someone older and more experienced. I was only nineteen when I began work at the Sackville and I was fortunate in having an excellent tutor and mentor and…."

Mr. Engle interrupted Anna. "Mrs. Walker, we do not need a tutor, but as you observed our front desk clerks are pretty, young, and unmarried ladies, who I have personally trained." His face strained, he forced a smile. "The only position I have at the moment is for a front desk clerk. Your experience, even though it is six years old, over qualifies you for the position and undoubtedly your responsibilities to your husband and daughter would pre-dispose you to being unreliable." His words crushed Anna. She had never expected her experience and accomplishments to work against her. Her earlier confidence had turned into anger and resentment.

"I can see you are upset, Mrs. Walker, and had you come to me with Mr. Kendrick's recommendation immediately after leaving The Sackville, I would have been honoured to employ you at the Royal York. Might I suggest you look for volunteer work? Your experience would be of great value to some organizations and it would allow you to look after your family."

Dangerously close to saying something she would regret, Anna stood up and through tight lips she said, "Good day, Mr. Engle."

Incensed by his placating attitude, Anna marched out of his office through the hotel lobby and onto the street. She wanted to scream. The whole experience had shattered her confidence.

Anna's broken ego prevented her from telling anyone of her experience and it festered in her mind. She regretted not having applied for work when they had arrived in Toronto. She hated Alex for persuading her that she didn't need to work. All she could think of was how different things could have been. She imagined herself working at the Royal York and, by now, she would be managing those pretty young ladies. Instead, she had no interest in her life and she was acutely aware that she had never felt so unhappy.

It was Wilfred who noticed the change in her and, although she never told him the whole humiliating story, he gleaned enough to realize that she needed a new purpose in life. He persuaded her that volunteer work could be gratifying. He recommended she try helping out at the hospital information desk where he worked. So disengaged from life, Anna didn't care what she did and conceded that volunteer work would at least fill in some time. She laughed at herself because that was the very reason she had refused to become involved in the past.

It pleased her to be out and about meeting new people but her heart was not in it. It only gave her a reason to get up in the morning. If Wilfred worked the same day, they often took their lunch breaks together in the cafeteria. On one such day Anna asked Wilfred what had happened between him and Florence.

His shoulders sagged. "Florence deceived me."

Frowning with disbelief Anna said, "That is not possible, not Florence. She can be petulant, even manipulative, but not deceitful."

Wilfred continued, "I intended to propose to Florence and did the gentleman thing and asked Mrs. Walker's permission for her daughter's hand in marriage. She told me I was too old for Florence and that I would ruin her young life. She said Florence had a young suitor in Edinburgh and they were returning to plan her wedding. Florence had never mentioned anyone else to me. I considered her omission to be deceitful. We had talked about marriage and setting up home here in Toronto. I felt used, nothing more than a convenient distraction. I was very angry and told Florence I didn't want to see her again. I am sorry, Anna. I know she is your sister-in-law. Honestly I couldn't believe it but when they left for Scotland, it confirmed the truth."

"And you should not have believed it. Florence has no suitor, nor has she ever had a suitor in Edinburgh and she is not married, nor has she plans to marry. It was Mrs. Walker who lied to you, not Florence. She was afraid you would take Florence away from her."

Wilfred paled. "Oh, Anna, what have I done? I never asked for an explanation nor did I explain to Florence why I ended the courtship. If I had, she would have been able to deny her mother's story. How could I have mistrusted her?" Wilfred stared at his uneaten ham sandwich. "I saw the hurt and surprised confusion when I told her, but anger clouded my judgment."

"It's not too late. Write to her and tell her what happened. She loves you, Wilfred. I think she will understand." Anna leaned across the table, smiled encouragingly and touched his hand.

"I am too old. I must be fifteen years her senior. She deserves a young man. Mrs. Walker is right to be concerned."

"She deserves the man she loves. The only way she will find happiness is if she marries you. Age has nothing to do with it."

Wilfred raised his eyes, a glint of hope shone through and turned into a smile. "Do you think it is possible? Shall I write to her?"

"I do think it is possible. Write to her and tell her you love her, but I suggest you allow me to write the envelope, because if Mother Walker sees your handwriting Florence will not get the letter."

Wilfred and Florence penned their romance through the winter and, by spring, Florence eventually found the courage to admit to her mother of her intention to marry Wilfred.

Mother Walker did everything possible to end the romance. When nothing worked, she faked one illness after another, knowing that Florence would not leave a sick mother. Florence could not forgive her mother for interfering, and other than taking care of her basic needs, she ignored her—not what Mother Walker had expected. Florence wrote to Anna frequently, relaying her mother's antics for attention and described the latest drama of dizzy spells, sometimes resulting in her gracefully fainting, always close enough to the sofa so as not to hurt herself. Florence wrote with amusement at this latest drama, describing her mother laying prone on the sofa moaning. She assured Anna and Alex that the doctor could find nothing wrong, attesting to her being in fine health for her age, implying she had many more years to live.

Anna felt shame and disappointment at the latter and she wondered how Florence felt. If Mother Walker was strong and healthy, there should be nothing stopping them returning to Canada. Anna winced at the thought but she saw no reason why Florence and Wilfred should not marry as long as Mother Walker did not live at 72 Forest Road. Anna thought it a good idea and wrote to encourage Florence to return in the summer.

Three weeks later, Anna received a letter to say Mother Walker had misjudged the distance from the sofa when faking one of her fainting spells resulting in a bad fall and a bruised hip. Florence sounded quite defeated as she explained her mother refused to walk because of the pain and the doctor said it would be several weeks before the bruising healed.

Petunia Walker never recovered. The bruised hip was a misdiagnosed fractured hip and her inability to move caused pneumonia. She died late that summer. Neither Alex nor Jim had any desire to return for their mother's funeral. Wilfred, anxious to be with Florence for the funeral, left for New York on the night train the same day, and took the sea passage to Scotland.

Wilfred and Florence married a week after the funeral. She wrote to Anna, asking her forgiveness for marrying in such haste. She missed her family but her mother had cheated her out of a year of happiness with Wilfred and she couldn't wait. It was a small wedding in the Registrar's office in Edinburgh. Her friend Martha was maid of honour and Charlie represented the Neale family. He took the train from Rugby to be Wilfred's best man. Florence had enclosed a photograph and they looked so very happy. Anna put the letter down, remembering how thrilled she had been at her wedding when Charlie and Uncle Bertie surprised her on that happy day. She wasn't sure how happy she was eleven years later.

It occurred to her that Alex never remembered their anniversary, not even their tenth last year. In spite of her disappointment that Florence and Wilfred were not coming back to Canada, she was happy for them. She missed Wilfred at the hospital and had been looking forward to having Florence back as a friend. Anna felt a sense of abandonment. Bill had been talking about working the summer at the Banff Springs Hotel in Alberta. He wanted to experience the Rocky Mountains.

Alex had been home very little in the last month. He seemed distracted and irritable, paying little attention to her when he was home and the nightmares had returned. At times, love making was distracted and rough, lacking affection and other times he wrapped his arms around her so tight she couldn't breathe. He refused to talk about it, saying she was imagining things.

Anna could only describe her feelings as despondent. Her life had no purpose. Alex's mood swings frightened her and nothing she said made him better. Isabelle sensed the mood changes. She missed her Papa and wanted her Auntie Florence and Uncle Wilfred to come home. She expressed her displeasure by behaving like the spoiled child she was, throwing tantrums and crying, being defiant to Anna and spiteful to her friends.

The day Isabelle brought a note home from school requesting an interview with Anna and Alex concerning their daughter's behaviour, Anna began to worry. Alex, of course, could not attend. Anna, alone, met with Miss Umbridge, the headmistress, to discover Isabelle's defiance had led to her kicking a teacher. Horrified, Anna listened to Miss Umbridge drone on about class disruption, fighting with other children and more. Finally, she suggested that as Isabelle's mother, she had better discipline her daughter before there were serious consequences. She then requested to meet with Mr. Walker with a clear implication that he needed to take control of his household. Under normal circumstances this would have sent Anna into a rage but she felt only despair and it took her all of her strength not to weep. Anna's tone and demeanour was unnaturally subservient as she thanked Miss Umbridge. She left the school and walked towards Kenwood Bakery—talking to Helga might help.

As Anna stepped into the bakery and the old familiar bell jingled, her mind flooded with memories of the days she had had purpose. At

Henry's cheery greeting, she nearly broke down. Helga had gone to Ned's Warehouse, an errand Anna had enjoyed, especially bargaining with Ned. Nick offered to make her a cuppa while she waited. Anna declined, her emotions too high for small talk.

That afternoon, Anna asked Daisy to collect Isabelle from school and prepare a cold dinner for Mr. Blaine as she wasn't feeling well and needed to lie down. Anna closed the bedroom door and lay on the bed staring at the ceiling and, only then, did she allow the quiet relentless sorrow to flow until she slept. The falling summer sun woke her as it streamed orange across the bed. She squinted, opening her eyes. Her head ached and her body felt lifeless.

She heard a little voice whisper, "Mummy, are you awake? Uncle Bill says it's time for me to go to bed."

"Isabelle, come sit with me?" Isabelle climbed on the bed and cuddled up to Anna.

Her bottom lip dropped into a pout. "I'm not tired. Why do I have to go to bed?" Defiantly she turned to Anna but her expression changed to a deep frown. "Are you sick, Mummy?"

"Just a headache, but it would really help my headache if you would go to bed quietly." Isabelle kissed her, jumped off the bed and much to Anna's dismay she put herself to bed.

The evening air had cooled. Anna felt chilled and decided to get ready for bed. Hanging her blouse and skirt in the closet, she heard Bill's footsteps but before she could grab her dressing gown he had entered the room.

"Oh, Anna, I'm sorry, I should have knocked." Bill's face was scarlet, turning his back he said, "I wanted to ask how you were feeling."

"Give me a minute."

As soon as the door closed, Anna pulled her nightdress on, fluffed the pillows and pulled the covers up leaning her pounding head against the headboard.

Bill knocked before his head appeared around the door. "How are you feeling? Would you like a cup of tea and something to eat?"

"A little better. It's just a headache." Anna smiled. Even the top of Bill's balding head was still glowing a scarlet red. "I'm not hungry but tea would be lovely, thank you."

Bill returned with a pot of tea, two cups and saucers and two slices of cake. He placed the neatly set tray on the nightstand and sat on the side of the bed, waiting for an explanation. She kept her eyes down drinking her tea and began to nibble on the cake. She looked up at him. "Spice cake! You remembered."

"Of course I remembered. You have been so down lately I wanted to cheer you up. So the hotel guests had spice cake for tea this afternoon and some just happened to come home with me. And judging by that empty plate and smile, I was right. It has cheered you up." Bill put Anna's cup and plate back on the tray and moved closer.

"Anna, what is wrong? What can I do to help?"

The softness in Bill's voice triggered her despair. She tried to speak, "I don't know. I've never felt like this before. I'm lonely, I miss everyone. Alex is away..." her eyes stinging as her words petered out.

"This isn't like you. Do you think you could work again? I mean paid work, not just volunteer work?" Anna shook her head. Bill's kindness had released more tears. Gently, he touched her hand, she caught her breath, tingling flowed along her arm into her heart.

"I have given up looking for work." Anna needed to change the subject; her desire for Bill was wild. She coughed nervously as though coughing would remove the aching. "My interview at the Royal York was humiliating."

Bill moved closer, brushing a wayward curl behind her ear. "What happened?" He pulled out his handkerchief and wiped her wet cheeks.

"Mr. Engle thought me too old and too married. I didn't tell anyone." She took a deep breath and reached out to stroke the side of his face, without thought or direction her arms embraced him. It felt so good to be in his arms. She felt his chest press against hers; their hearts beat in unison and their lips met. She slid down the bed. Bill kicked off his shoes and lay beside her. Her hands cupped his face kissing him and pulling him towards her. His warm body pressed hard against hers.

"Bill," she whispered, "make love to me."

Bill began to unbutton his shirt. He paused, his fingers still on the buttons and said, "Anna…"

Her fingers pressed his lips. "Shush!" She finished unbuttoning his shirt and felt his warm flesh on her cheeks as she leaned against his chest. Caressing her shoulders, he began kissing her shoulders so tenderly she could hardly breathe. So full of desire for this wonderful man nothing else mattered.

His quickening breath on her neck sent quivers down her spine. She groaned, pulling him on top of her. He wound his legs around her, clinging to her. He whispered, sending shivers to every cell in her body. He whispered again, "The door…" and he disappeared off the bed. She lay, hot with desire, listening to her own breathing filling her ears and then she heard it. Click, from the doorknob and the door slowly opened. Fright gripped her stomach. Had Alex come home? She pulled the covers to her neck. Next she heard, "Mummy where is Uncle Bill? He promised me a story about Mogi and Boo."

Releasing a long breath, Anna coughed to stifle a gasp, praying that Bill was out of sight on the floor. She smiled at her daughter's pronunciation of, *The Jungle Book's* characters and calmly replied, "I don't know where Uncle Bill is. Why don't you go back to bed and I will find him?"

She swung her legs over the far side of the bed and she burst into laughter at the sight of Bill, half lying, half sitting on the floor, trying to tuck his shirt into his trousers, his face guilty as a schoolboy.

"Saved by Mowgli and Baloo! Kind of appropriate, don't you think? Those characters are always saving each other." Standing up, his back to the door, he said, "I had better keep my promise."

"I wish we had not been saved," Anna said, holding out her hand.

"Perhaps it is for the better. I'm sorry, Anna. This was a mistake."

"No, Bill, I need you."

"You need your husband. Anna, you must tell him how you feel. Alex rarely sees beyond his own needs but he loves you, of that, I am certain. I will always be your friend and as much as I love you, it can never be more.

What happened tonight should never have happened. I took advantage of your vulnerability, and I am deeply sorry and ashamed." Bill hurried out of the bedroom into the hall.

"There you are, Uncle Bill." Isabelle sighed, holding her storybook in one hand, the other cheekily on her hip.

A smile came from somewhere deep in Anna's motherly heart in recognition that mother and daughter shared the same tenacity. In Isabelle, it was cute, although needing discipline, but in Anna it could not happen. Whether it was naiveté or denial she couldn't be sure, but tonight they had declared their love for each other. In her heart of hearts, she knew Bill was right and it could never be anything more. But the memory she would keep in her heart for eternity. Now, it was her job to find a way to make things work with Alex.

Twenty-Six

Rocky Mountain Adventure

nna struggled with conflict. In spite of her efforts to pretend friendship, her body yearned for more. Her mind's acute melancholy had passed, leaving confusion and ambiguity and yet, strangely, knowing that Bill loved her brought her comfort.

She had three days to compose herself before Alex arrived home. She resolved to be cheerful and enjoy his stay. She planned family outings to the beach and she thought perhaps just the two of them could have dinner at the Chinese restaurant just off Lakeshore.

Alex arrived home tired so she cooked at home. Saturday, Isabelle waited impatiently for Alex to get up and have breakfast. Sitting at the kitchen table drinking coffee, Alex tousled Isabelle's curls and said, "Why so excited this morning?"

"Papa, did you forget? We are going to the beach."

Alex scowled in Anna's direction and glanced at the window. "It is cloudy. I think it might rain. Not a good day for the beach. We'll try another day."

"But Papa, Mummy promised." Isabelle stomped her feet, her bottom lip pouted and quivered.

"Isabelle, that's enough." The last thing Anna wanted was for Isabelle to have a temper tantrum and for Alex to lose his temper. Miss. Umbridge's words of discipline hung over Anna's head. However, she would rather discuss it with Alex than have an outburst from both.

"Papa is right, it would not be fun if it rained. We'll go tomorrow when Papa is feeling better."

"Do you have a headache like Mummy? Uncle Bill made Mummy's all better with tea and cake but he forgot about Moo and Bloo."

Anna froze as emotion flooded through her, not the least of which was guilt. As much as she told herself nothing really happened, she could not deny the intent and desire had most definitely been there.

"It was nothing. I had had a bad day and went to lie down after a rather unpleasant interview with Miss Umbridge."

"Who is Miss Umbridge?" Alex asked.

"She's the headmistress at Isabelle's school." Anna glanced towards Isabelle. "She asked to meet with you. I explained your work took you away. We'll talk about it later."

Alex picked up Isabelle and started tickling her. "So what has my little princess been up to at school?" Isabelle's infectious laugh had them both laughing. "How about I take you to the park and push you on the swings?" Delighted at this suggestion, she forgot to pout. Relieved and grateful, Anna let out a long sigh, realizing how easily her secret could be revealed. The rest of the day turned out to be a fun family day right up until Alex tucked Isabelle in bed.

Anna was cleaning up in the kitchen when she heard Bill arrive home from work and she could hear the two men talking. She wished she could have warned Bill about Isabelle's comment even though it was probably quite unnecessary. Bill hid his feelings well and he would not compete with Alex. Suddenly Bill's voice rose and then a fist, most likely Alex's, she thought, slammed on something. She stopped washing the dishes and listened intently, her heart pounding with fear and guilt. What was going on in there? She dared not go and find out, she just listened.

Alex yelled, "She is *my* wife. Don't you tell me what to do!"

Bill shouted back, "Well, treat her with the love and respect she deserves. Alex she misses you. She is lonely, and when you are home, you practically ignore her."

Rooted to the floor, Anna held her breath, waiting for Alex to explode.

"I do love her. I have a job that takes me away from home but that doesn't give you free range to fill her lonely nights. If I ever find out you have touched her, I will kill you."

Remarkably calm Bill said, "Alex... some advice..."

"I don't need your damned advice. Stay out of my affairs and my wife's bedroom."

Bill lowered his voice and Anna had to strain her ears to hear him. "I know you love Anna, so for God's sake show it. Time and again I have told you my relationship with Anna is friendship and when I see her crying with loneliness because her husband ignores her, I *am* going to comfort a friend."

"My daughter tells me you comfort Anna in her bedroom. I should punch you now!"

Anna heard another bang. This time it sounded like the clock on the mantelpiece bouncing. She felt cold. Had Isabelle seen more than they thought? No, she remembered seeing the door open after Bill rolled on the floor. She couldn't have seen him on the opposite side of the bed. But what had she told Alex, or was he guessing?

"Alex, you are being ridiculous. I took her tea and cake because she had a headache and hadn't eaten. She'd had a bad day and as usual you were not here."

"So you did it for me, is that it!?"

Anna heard scuffling. Were they fighting? This is a nightmare, she thought, and then Alex spoke calmly. "My job is important to me and I have to be away. I will not give up my work."

"Why not suggest Anna finds work as a receptionist? I know she has tried but with your encouragement she may try harder."

"I don't want her working. I can provide for her. The volunteer work at the hospital keeps her occupied."

Bill's voice rose with exasperation. "Alex, stop being so condescending. You have always known Anna liked to work. She needs a purpose in life."

"I am her *purpose* and so is Isabelle of course."

"That's your problem. You are so self-centered you can't see beyond your nose. If you don't want her to work, take her on a trip. She has always wanted to see the Rocky Mountains. Share with her what you can, show her you care."

Suddenly the atmosphere changed. Both men had relaxed. Alex spoke quietly. She had to go to the hallway to hear him.

"I never thought of that. Brilliant. I will make the arrangements. Anna can ask Abigail to look after Isabelle. I can't do it this trip since I leave tomorrow, but I could for the next one." Alex raised his voice again, "Bill, I am warning you, stay away from my wife."

"And as long as you love her and pay attention to her, I will stay away but if you ignore her I *will* comfort her. The choice is yours, Alex." Bill paused. "You won't have to worry about me this summer as I have been transferred to Banff Springs Hotel in Alberta until October. I leave on Wednesday."

Turmoil spun in Anna's head. How much did Alex know? Had Bill's answer quelled his paranoia? It felt good to have Bill fight for her, but she felt hurt that he hadn't told her he was going away. The thought of travelling with Alex on the train to see the Rockies and turquoise lakes thrilled her. Fear and nerves made Anna stay in the kitchen, gathering her thoughts before talking to either man. She quietly opened the back door and decided to walk over to visit Abigail. Then she could return, pretending to be unaware of the fight and innocently listen to Alex's wonderful idea of travelling to the Rockies.

Alex was assigned to shorter trips throughout the summer, allowing him to be home more often and for the past few months he had been very attentive. Anna surmised it was the row with Bill that had had a positive effect on him. She had never doubted that he loved her, but his fear of losing her had put excitement back in their marriage.

The long-awaited trip to the Rockies was arranged for September when Isabelle started school, making it easier for Abigail.

Standing on the platform of Toronto's Union Station, breathing in the smell of steam and soot, Anna was transported back thirteen years to Bexhill Station. She looked around at the 1st Class passengers, not so different to 1913. She half expected to hear Lady Thornton bark orders to the porter. The people were the same, but there were no big skirts or enormous hats—the fashions were more subdued in style. Anna had on a soft floral shift dress and a lightweight cream wool coat. The latest short, smooth, bobbed hairstyles did not suit Anna's wayward curls, but she tamed the curls by making finger-waves and placing a tight-fitting cream cloche hat on her head, keeping the waves in place at least until she removed her hat. Anna not only looked the part, but she felt the part. *Lady Thornton would be proud of me,* she thought as she joined the ranks of first class travellers. Her thoughts were interrupted by a man's voice, "Mrs. Walker, would you care to board? I'll show you to your compartment. Your luggage will be delivered shortly. Coffee is served in the lounge while you wait."

"Thank you." Anna grinned from ear to ear.

The porter knocked on the compartment door and Alex opened it. He gave the porter a tip and ushered Anna inside.

"I only have a few minutes to welcome you. What do you think?"

"It's wonderful. Thank you, Alex." They kissed.

"I have to inspect the lunch preparations. We had a complaint on the last trip. There is coffee in the lounge. Turn to your left and follow the corridor, it's not far." He kissed her again.

The lounge resembled a narrow drawing room, with small tables, comfortable chairs and heavy red and gold curtains at the windows. Anna elected to sit close to the window and a waiter brought coffee and pastries to her table. The guard's whistle blew and the train made a few hesitant starts and gradually began to chug smoothly out of Union Station. Moving slowly along Lake Ontario and Lakeshore, she recognized the beach and the street names until the train picked up speed and urban Toronto disappeared. Returning to the compartment, she unpacked and took out her book and found a comfortable chair in the lounge.

The first couple of days, Anna kept to herself, enjoying the solitude and admiring Ontario's autumn scenery. She wished she had an artist's talent to paint the vibrant gold, burgundy and red; the overall effect glowed as they travelled northwest. Alex joined her for dinner and sometimes for his breaks when his duties allowed.

Anna noticed another lady travelling alone. Rather modern, in trousers, and somewhat masculine. Her small frame and blond bob, soft around her doll-like face belied the attempted look of masculinity. Perhaps it was the delicate pink silk blouse that confused the image. She looked drawn and Anna instinctively sensed sadness, recognizing the melancholy she herself had experienced only a few months ago. When the waiter addressed her, her name sounded Italian but her accent was definitely American and she had possibly a southern drawl. She too read intently while admiring the scenery and they had exchanged smiles and nods but never actually spoke.

The prairie scenery became monotonous and Anna's current reading was not holding her attention. She decided to invite the American lady to join her for luncheon. Anna arrived in the dining room a little before one o'clock and when she saw her approach the entrance, she beckoned the maître d' and asked him to show the lady to her table.

"I wondered if you would like to join me for luncheon today." Anna stood up and offered her hand. "Anna Walker."

"Thank you, Mrs. Walker, how kind of you. Julia Castillo," the lady replied, shaking Anna's hand and taking the seat opposite.

By the end of lunch, they were on a first name basis, talking like old friends. Their interests paralleled. Both avid readers, even enjoying the same authors, both had had careers and now had husbands who prevented them from working. Both had a thirst for adventure, although Julia had travelled extensively and Anna had not. Julia's description of studying at university and working as a social worker in Chicago fascinated Anna. She suspected Julia's marriage had been disappointing. Julia expressed wonder at Anna's stories of her days as a hotel receptionist and of running a bakery in Toronto. Anna didn't quite admit that this was her first trip. The waiter hovered around their table and noticing the empty dining room, she realized he needed them to leave the dining car. They agreed to meet for afternoon tea in the lounge at four-thirty.

Anna returned to the compartment to rest and was delighted when she met Alex in the corridor.

"I have a whole hour before I meet with Chef about the cleaning regime in the kitchen."

"Oh, good, I can't wait to tell you about this lady I met today. She's from Chicago."

Alex smiled admiringly as he opened the compartment door. "Did I ever tell you how beautiful you are? Your blue eyes are brilliant today." He kissed her. "Are you enjoying the trip?"

"It is wonderful. Thank you, darling."

Alex sat down and gently pulled her on his lap. He kissed her again. "I love you, Anna Walker. Never leave me."

"Alex, I will not leave you."

She leaned against him, her head on his shoulder, feeling the old spark of love return. Alex had been so serious since the big row and she wished he would tease her just a little. She turned her head, looked up as his beguiling green eyes captured hers, taking her back in time to the first day she had met this charming man. Suddenly she craved the carefree days of her youth, and then it became clear: Alex had never grown up. Life's experiences only inflicted wounds on the boy inside, and her behavior with Bill had cut a deep wound. Anna had found her purpose. She must take care of Alex. Did Alex sense her resolve? She felt him relax as they sat in each other's arms silently rocking to the rhythm of the train.

Someone called from the corridor and tapped on the door, "Mr. Walker, sorry to disturb you but you are needed in the galley."

"I'll be right there." He gave Anna a squeeze. "Duty calls. I'll see you at dinner. Why don't you invite your new friend to join us?"

Julia ordered tea and scones as Anna approached a small round table with two tub style chairs. "I hope you like scones. It must be the British influence in Canada that allows the cooks to bake delicious scones, something the Americans cannot make. My friends Lord and Lady Thornton introduced me to scones with Devonshire cream and strawberries. Here the scones are good but I make do with butter and strawberry jam." Julia stopped talking and stared at Anna. "Anna what is it? You look as though you've seen a ghost?"

"I think I have. Did you say Lady Thornton? But she died seven years ago and Lord Thornton drowned on the Titanic. I took care of her correspondence when she stayed at The Sackville Hotel in Bexhill, where I worked as front desk clerk, during the war."

Julia shook her head in amazement. "I am talking of Lord Darcy Thornton. His wife, Belle Tully, is my closest friend. We went to university together and were practicing social workers until we both married. Darcy and Belle lived in Chicago during the war. They returned to England about two years ago."

It was Anna's turn to smile in amazement. "What a coincidence. I met Belle Tully at Lady Thornton's suite one day. I remember being in awe of this modern lady, and also embarrassed as Mr. Thornton insisted on singing her praises directly to me, a mere secretary. Lady Thornton scolded him for interrupting my work, making no secret of her disapproval of Belle Tully."

"They are a wonderful couple and they have a wonderful marriage." Julia looked away, her little finger delicately touching the corner of her eye. She curled her mouth, trying to smile towards Anna, but the pain was too much. She looked away again. Anna wondered if the pain was for her friend or for her own marriage.

"I never understood why he was not Lord Thornton after his father's death."

"He had an older brother, Felix, who refused to acknowledge the title. It wasn't until Felix died in Africa that the title came to Darcy."

"That explains many things." Thinking it best to move the conversation, Anna continued. "Alex, my husband, suggested that I invite you to join us for dinner tonight. Shall we say nine?"

"Thank you. I would like that. I didn't realize your husband was travelling with you?"

"My husband is the inspector for passenger services. He is working so I am more or less travelling alone. This is my first trip and I am excited to travel through the Rocky Mountains."

"Me too! I hear they are magnificent. If you will excuse me, I think I will rest before dinner. I'll see you at nine."

Two people dressing for dinner in the confines of the compartment caused Alex and Anna to trip over each other, laughing and Alex teasing, something he hadn't done in a long time.

"I'll never learn how to tie these things," Alex said, struggling with his bow tie. Anna finished applying a red lipstick and tied it for him. Lightly holding her chin, he kissed her. "Did I tell you how beautiful you look?" He took her hands and stepped back as far as the space would allow, the old charming Alex admiring her. He made her feel like a million dollars.

The assistant in Eaton's had told her how black suited her and the new rayon crepe, although not silk, did make fashionable dresses affordable. Self-consciously, she released Alex's hand and felt the softness of the fabric as it fell from her shoulders straight to a wide satin ribbon that surrounded the drop waist, the skirt bright with sequins. Black silk stockings, black slippers and a black beaded purse with matching headband—an accessory the shop assistant had recommended to keep Anna's finger-waved hair in place—completed the outfit.

Anna slipped her arm in his and they walked to the dining car. As they stood waiting for the maître d' to show them to their table, Anna saw heads turn, admiring this handsome, and obviously important, couple. The importance related to Alex's status on the train but Anna enjoyed it anyway. Julia arrived almost immediately and Alex stood up to greet her. The pastel green silk flapper dress flowed as she approached the table. His height dwarfed this tiny lady. Her short blond hair framed her porcelain face and a long white shawl balanced around her shoulders, falling almost to the floor. The femininity made her appear vulnerable and yet, Anna thought, she had seen a strong resilient woman earlier. Possibly the reason she favoured more masculine attire during the day.

329

Having been privy to the menu, Alex ordered white wine to match the salmon entrée that was to be served. Anna enjoyed every morsel, finding room for a second dessert of chocolate mousse while Alex indulged in the cheese tray. Julia seemed distracted and pecked at her food.

"Anna tells me you are from Chicago. It sounds like a fun, if somewhat dangerous city, or is that all journalistic hype? Is it true what they say about prohibition and gangster activity?"

Julia laughed. "Alcohol flows like water and, yes the crime and gangsters associated with prohibition are a problem, as is corruption. The wealth of some is abhorrent and contrasts with the extreme poverty in the ghettoes and slums. I wish my husband would allow me to work. At least in my profession as a social worker I could do some good." Julia took a breath. "I'm sorry, not exactly dinner conversation."

"Anna does volunteer work at the hospital and that occupies her time."

Anna glared at Alex. "I would rather work, as I did in Bexhill, managing the front desk."

"That was before we were married, my dear."

Anna didn't like the tone of the conversation, but being aware that their relationship had turned a corner, she decided not to respond and jeopardize their newfound love.

"We have a six-year-old daughter, Isabelle. The apple of her father's eye."

"My husband and I have not been blessed with children. Travelling fills my time and I can keep my brain active. I prefer to travel in Canada, enjoying the slower pace and intelligent conversation. Luigi does not travel outside America, so I travel alone."

"We have a friend, Bill Blaine, who enjoys travel. He travelled the world as a merchant sailor during the war and spent some time in America, although he rarely speaks of it. I believe he was in Chicago before he settled in Canada," Alex said.

The maître d' came over to the table and whispered something to Alex, his eyes shifting to a table at the end of the car.

Alex leaned forward. "Ladies, please excuse me. It appears we have a dissatisfied passenger. Mr. Page, would you be kind enough to escort the ladies to the lounge for coffee?"

Once settled in the more comfortable chairs in the lounge, Anna noticed that Julia had lost what little colour she had had in her cheeks.

"You look tired Julia, are you feeling ill?"

"A little tired maybe. Did you say Bill Blaine was a friend?"

"Yes. Do you know him?" Anna clapped her hands together. "Goodness it is a small world." She straightened her skirt, giving a nervous cough, realizing that she had embraced the news with rather more exuberance than she intended. However, it did not stop her telling Julia the full story of how they all met at The Sackville Hotel.

"How did you meet Bill?" Anna inquired.

Julia hesitated as though she wasn't sure how to answer. "I didn't know him well. He was a friend of Darcy Thornton's when they lived in Chicago. I told you Belle, Darcy's wife, is my friend."

Anna frowned, wondering how Bill had become a friend of Lord Darcy Thornton. Julia's demeanour changed so drastically. Anna had the unsettling feeling that she was hiding a secret of great magnitude and discovery would have dire consequences.

In spite of sensing Julia's fear, Anna pursued her inquiry, adjusting to a lighter almost whimsical tone. "You and Bill are a pair. I think there is some delightful secret in Chicago. Bill avoids my questions and brushes me off with comments like 'You are better off not knowing.' Now what kind of words are those?" Anna laughed but Julia remained serious.

Julia glanced over her shoulder and lowered her voice so much Anna had to lean into her to hear. "Anna, there is a secret, but I can't say any more. Knowing would put all of us in danger, especially Bill." She glanced over her shoulder again. "I have seen how your eyes sparkle just at the mention of his name and he used to do the same when he spoke, rarely, of old times in Bexhill, but I never knew who you were."

Anna felt uncomfortable and pretended not to understand the meaning in Julia's comment. "Why would you say such a thing? Are you in love with him?"

"No, nothing like that. But we had things in common. Anna, please do

331

not ask anymore." Julia appealed to Anna, her face taught with fear.

"No more questions. Well, not now, but we are meeting Bill in Banff. He is working at the Banff Springs Hotel and he has arranged to meet the train. I understand it stops for an hour or so in Banff."

Julia went from white to a pale shade of green. Standing up, she said, "Anna, please excuse me, I really am not feeling well." Anna watched Julia walk hurriedly out of the lounge.

Early the next morning the train pulled into Calgary. Noise and confusion littered the corridors and platform and agitated passengers yelled for porters. Anna decided to stay in bed and read. The steward had brought her coffee and toast and she enjoyed the solitude.

It didn't surprise her that Julia had not been seen all day. She assumed she had done the same as Anna. A wise choice as she had not looked well the previous night.

Anna did not feel like dressing in her evening gown, so she chose a simple shift dress and ate a light supper alone in the lounge. Alex had been called away. Concerned for Julia's health, she wrote a note and called the steward. "Would you see that this is delivered to Mrs. Castillo's compartment please?"

"I am sorry Mrs. Walker, but Mrs. Castillo left the train in Calgary this morning. She ordered her luggage to be sent on the next train to Chicago."

"Did she leave a note for me?"

The steward shook his head. "Sorry ma'am, a family emergency perhaps?"

"What a strange encounter," she whispered to herself, thinking of the bizarre coincidences and connection to Bill.

She moved closer to the window and her fingers caressed the crystal pendant, remembering Uncle Bertie as she had her first glimpse of the Rocky Mountains. The white snow caps were illuminated by moonlight. Alex touched her shoulder, "Aren't they magnificent? Wait until you see them tomorrow."

Alighting from the train in Banff, Anna was glad she had thought to put her coat on. She could see her breath in the chilly but fresh clear air. The blue of the sky was as vibrant as an artist's pallet. The energy from the enormous mountains sang, making her feet want to dance. Alex spotted Bill and they greeted each other with great enthusiasm. Anna couldn't deny she felt awkward.

Afraid to look in Bill's direction, Anna intently observed the mountains and sky. When she finally dropped her gaze to a normal level, Bill was in deep conversation with Alex as they walked Banff's only street. The train had been late into Banff, so there wasn't much time to do anything more than stretch their legs and get a brief glimpse of the turquoise water of Lake Louise. Speechless, she stared, having seen pictures and thought the artist had exaggerated the colour. It really was the richest turquoise on earth.

Walking back to the train, Anna finally decided to ask the question. "Bill, we had dinner with Mrs. Julia Castillo from Chicago the other night. She said she knew you. I enjoyed her pleasant company but she suddenly became shrouded in secrecy and ultimately disappeared. The steward said she left the train in Calgary."

Bill's fresh healthy mountain-air glow, immediately drained out of him. His voice sharp, he said, "What did she tell you?"

"Nothing. She mentioned you met at Darcy Thornton's in Chicago. Darcy's wife Belle is her best friend, but she said she didn't really know you."

"That's right."

"Why didn't you tell us? And how did you become a friend of Lord Thornton?"

"There is nothing to tell. It's a part of my life I don't wish to talk about. I am not pr...." The train's whistle blew, drowning Bill's words. Anna thought he had said 'not proud.' Disappointed at Bill's reluctance to reveal the secret, and curious at his reaction to Julia, Anna had no choice but to board the train with more questions than answers. Whatever the secret these two people coveted, it would, for the time being, remain a mystery to Anna.

The train, dwarfed by the massive mountains on each side, continued its arduous journey up steep inclines and plunging into long dark tunnels. Uncle Bertie's stories flooded her memory. She felt him at her side. Anna felt happy and loved sharing the magnificence of this journey as the train pulled into Vancouver.

Alex had work to do so Anna set out alone to explore Vancouver and the beauty of the Pacific coast. There were ancient Douglas fir trees with girths that ten people linking arms could not reach around, flowers blooming in abundance, fed by the mountain rain. The dampness reminded her of Britain, something she did not miss. A soft drizzle began to fall, prompting Anna to find shelter in a quaint café not far from the station.

A magnificent painting caught her eye as she walked into the café and sat at a table already occupied by an elderly lady. Fascinated by the painting, Anna initiated a conversation as they sipped tea and ate buttered scones. She learned from her table companion that the artist was a local named Emily Carr, a free-spirited woman of great talent and dubious temperament.

According to Anna's table companion, an artist herself, she and Emily Carr had been friends, after meeting at the prestigious Vancouver Ladies Art Club some twenty years earlier. Her face lit up with amusement as she described the lady club members' outrage at Emily's smoking habits and use of coarse language. The lady concluded that Emily was unfortunately asked to leave. Mesmerized, Anna listened intently to Emily's friend recount her travels to Europe, contrasted by her solitary trips to paint nature on the Pacific coast.

Anna felt a strong and unexplained connection to Emily Carr, and yet the only painting she had seen was the one in the café. She wanted to see more of her art and experience her free spirit but it was not possible, on this trip, to travel to Emily Carr's home on Vancouver Island. Hearing the train's whistle, she bid the lady goodbye, promising to return one day.

Anna boarded the train for the return journey, this adventure almost over. Thinking about Emily Carr made her want to explore the beautiful

Pacific coast, to feel it, touch it, breathe in the smell of the forest, listen to the sounds of nature. An adventure seen through the protection of a plate glass window from a moving train was like viewing the world through a keyhole. Happy and grateful to have had such a view, she wanted more. She wondered about her unusual encounter with Julia Castillo. Not the mystery surrounding Bill, but Julia as an independent, well-travelled woman.

Anna envied both women for their freedom, independence and fearless hunger for new places. Were they so different? She remembered the day Lady Thornton had said "You require a husband and means to travel." Lady Thornton had given her means through her legacy, but her husband did not understand her needs and had reduced rather than increased her legacy's value.

As the train laboured through the Rockies, Anna felt a powerful yearning to join Emily and Julia in the ranks of liberated women and pursue her own quest for all things new and exciting. The train entered a long, dark, deep tunnel and Anna felt her yearnings plunging into the depths of the tunnel to be locked away forever. She had married and now had a daughter. This could not be changed.

The option of independence had passed her by years ago—she had made her choice. Part of her soul needed to cling to the dream, to hope that one day she may realize at least part of her dream. Now, she wanted to return home, hoping the daily routine and her commitment to take care of Alex would ease the pain of her yearnings.

Twenty-Seven

Anna Turns Away from Canada

❧

Anna would never forget the trip to the Rocky Mountains and dreamed of taking it again but Alex considered his duty done. Another year of the hated, mundane, domestic duties ensued and as if taking care of her daughter and husband was not enough, she now had two lodgers.

Bill had returned to the Royal York and continued lodging at 72 Forest Road. Demobilized from the British military, Charlie had finally immigrated to Canada, taking a civilian position with the Royal Canadian Mounted Police. He spoke little of his work and Anna suspected his special assignment experience from the military was part of his new work, necessitating frequent travel across Canada and occasionally to Britain.

Bill and Charlie spent many evenings comparing stories of foreign ports and Anna listened intently, feeling the excitement and living vicariously through their experiences, while quelling her own desires. For as long as she didn't think of what could have been, she became content—even happy. She and Alex had settled into a comfortable life. The rivalry between him and Bill was inconspicuous, possibly because her brother Charlie acted as a buffer. Anna knew her husband well enough to sense his insecurities, knowing it would not take much to trigger his jealousy. Wisely, she never displayed any form of affection for Bill either in or out of Alex's presence.

The fall, usually Anna's favourite time of the year, had been miserable with high winds and heavy rain causing the leaves to fall early. She was attempting to rake the damp, mold-ridden oak leaves from the front lawn when Charlie jumped out of a taxi.

"Charlie! You are back early. Is everything okay?" Anna knew better than to make a direct inquiry, knowing Charlie couldn't talk about his work.

"The meeting in Ottawa finished early, a first for politicians," he said smiling. "And I caught the early train."

Anna propped the rake against the tree and took one of Charlie's bags, leaving him a free arm to give her a hug.

"I can't wait to tell you about my visit to the National Museum. I went to see an art exhibition called…" Charlie pulled a pamphlet from his jacket pocket. "*Canadian West Coast Art, Native and Modern,* by Emily Carr. The same artist you told me about from your trip to the Rockies. Sis, you must go. Absolutely the cat's meow."

Anna laughed at his choice of words. Modern slang was invading the English language and she had trouble getting used to the strange phrases.

Charlie kept the whole family amused all evening describing Emily Carr's art exhibition. Alex had been watching Anna throughout the evening, her face lit up, her eyes bright with excitement.

"Anna, would you like to see the exhibition?"

"Oh yes! Can we go?" Anna's heart jumped into her throat. She could hardly contain her excitement.

"I could arrange a weekend off in November."

"Can you make it earlier?" Charlie asked. "I believe the exhibition finishes at the end of October."

Anna's heart sank, her mind thinking of how she could get there. "I can go alone. Plenty of women travel alone today." Thoughts of Julia sprang to Anna's mind.

"No, it isn't safe," Alex retorted.

"Alex, stop being so old fashioned. What if I asked Abigail to come with me?"

Alex hesitated. "Would she be interested? Abigail is sensible."

"Are you implying I am not?" she knew raising her voice was not the answer and Anna softened her reply. "I am sure Abigail would enjoy a trip to Ottawa. I will telephone her now." Anna went into the hall and returned smiling. "It's all set. The weekend after next. Can you arrange the train, Alex?"

Anna did not wait for a reply but turned to Charlie. "Charlie, will you be in town? Can you look after Isabelle?"

Anna and Abigail walked out of Ottawa's Union Station and looked up at the imposing towers of the castle-like Chateau Laurier Hotel. Anna felt ten feet tall, striding under the portico and into the capaciousness of the hotel lobby, richly panelled in dark wood. Oak or mahogany? She wasn't sure. The lobby was furnished with huge armchairs, some leather, some floral, and an exquisite chandelier, its crystals reflecting on the marble and brass staircase that swept up to the mezzanine.

Oversized vases full of fresh flowers emitted a faint floral aroma, taking the edge off the heavy masculinity of wood and leather. Abigail shrivelled at Anna's side, leaving her to do the talking as they registered and were escorted to their accommodation.

The afternoon sun, low in the sky, streamed in through the window. Anna stood in the sunlight, absorbing its warmth on her face, staring across the Ottawa River and looking down at the locks of the Rideau Canal as it dropped into the river. On her left stood the Houses of Parliament. Hearing five booming chimes, she wanted to see as well as hear the famous clock.

"Abigail, I would like to take a walk before we change for dinner. Let's explore Ottawa."

Abigail tensed, glancing warily at Anna. "We might get lost. It will soon be dark. I would prefer to stay here."

"We'll just walk up the street and back. We'll be back before dark and we can't get lost if we stay on the one street."

The concierge directed them to turn right and over the canal bridge to Wellington Street. They peered over the bridge at the canal and the massive lock gates spilling water into the next lock. The locks looked like enormous oversized boots climbing down a flight of stairs and stepping into the Ottawa River at the bottom. They strolled along Wellington Street to the new Centre Block of Parliament, rebuilt after the 1916 fire. The Tower of Victory and Peace, now chiming the half-hour, stood majestically in the centre of the building, a memorial to all those lost in the Great War. The parliamentary seat of the Dominion of Canada stood on the cliffs above the Ottawa River.

The next morning, after a late breakfast, they ordered a taxi and spent the day at the National Gallery. This Gothic style, Victoria Memorial Building, stood at one end of Metcalfe Street and mirrored the Houses of Parliament that stood at the top of the same street.

Anna, already impressed by the architecture of the building, was in awe of its contents, not the least of which was Emily Carr's exhibition of twenty-six paintings. She learned more about the incredible woman: the impressionist style of some paintings reflected her travels to Europe and the exquisite and unusual paintings of the indigenous peoples of the west coast expressed an understanding of a way of life Anna had no idea existed. She could only admire the totem poles and sense of movement in the massive living forests and lose herself in something she desperately wanted to appreciate more.

Filled with awe and longing, Anna hardly spoke on the journey home. She smiled at Abigail's constant chatter, showing her relief to be going home. They were so different but Anna was grateful for Abigail's company. Knowing Alex would not have allowed her to come on her own, she let her chatter on.

The trip to Ottawa had incited restlessness in Anna. She developed a thirst to learn more about the world, at least the world of North America. She considered trying to find Julia Castillo and visiting Chicago. She had the money as she had quietly allowed what was left of her inheritance to gather interest in the bank. Curious about her financial worth, Anna made an appointment to meet with Mr. Peabody who had, reluctantly, learned to respect Anna's head for business and finance.

Anna was pleasantly surprised to discover that the value of her remaining inheritance plus the sale of Kenwood Bakery and interest earned over the years had boosted her worth to a tidy sum of $10,000. Mr. Peabody explained the advantages of investing her money in stocks and bonds, growing her money even faster than with regular interest rates. Mr. Peabody pleaded a tempting scenario of how, with his careful guidance, she could double her money in less than a year.

Recalling financial reports in the *Toronto Star* of how ordinary people were making large profits, Anna listened carefully. She left the Toronto Bank pleased that her money had grown considerably on interest alone. Her father had taught her all things in moderation and although Anna was guilty of excess in some things, money was not one of them. Lady Thornton's inheritance was precious and, after Alex had squandered it on Kenwood Bakery, albeit a sound investment, more by accident than good judgment, Anna had spent the money cautiously. Intuitively, this current propensity to instant profit and careless spending scared her. She thought it too good to be true. It was only a matter of time before something catastrophic happened. She decided to leave the money gathering a moderate interest.

October 25, 1929, only two years after Mr. Peabody had been less than gracious when Anna had disregarded his financial advice, *The Globe* headlines read, "Speculators Shaken in Wild Day of Panic." The financial bubble had burst and all those people, not just wealthy speculators and business giants but ordinary folks, were ruined. Anna breathed a sigh of relief that she was not one of them but she was aware of how close she had come to financial ruin and recognized the seriousness of the situation that was driving the country into a depression deeper than most parts of the industrial world.

Anna's thoughts of travel and adventure were halted once more as she turned to using her time to help in Toronto's soup kitchens. Alex feared for his job but was grateful to still have one. He came home with stories of worse poverty in the prairies. He spoke of swarms of grasshoppers devouring the meagre crops trying to grow in drought conditions, of desperate men climbing onto the roof of the train hoping to get a free ride into the city for work, only to be pushed off by authorities.

By 1933, journeys to the west coast were troubling and difficult. Alex grew thinner and more drawn looking after each trip, his mood swings more dramatic. He spoke little of the journeys until one night when he woke screaming, dripping in sweat and babbling incoherently. Terrified by her father's screaming, Isabelle woke up crying. Torn between attending to Isabelle and helping Alex, Anna called Charlie to wake Alex from his nightmare while she comforted Isabelle. Exhausted, Alex fell back to sleep, as did Isabelle. Anna and Charlie were wide awake and went downstairs.

"Charlie, I don't know what to do. Alex has had nightmares for as long as I can remember, but nothing like tonight."

"I used to have those nightmares after the war. I dreamt of the dead, friends and comrades, of limbs flying through the air, of open eyes staring, Huns stalking me. Reliving the violence and images of war, not fit for man nor beast, were real and terrifying."

"It is fourteen years since the end of the war. Surely it goes away."

"I don't think it does for some or I think it can be triggered by something else. I'm lucky. After the first couple of years the nightmares stopped but I think Alex is still living them."

"Something is going on at work. He comes home more and more depressed but he has said nothing."

The following morning Alex slumped into a chair at the kitchen table and Anna saw her opportunity to find out what terrified him.

"That was a nasty nightmare you had last night. Can you tell me about it?"

Alex grunted. "It was nothing."

"It was *not* nothing. Alex, you frightened me, woke Isabelle, and I had to call Charlie to talk you down. Please stop dismissing me. I deserve to know what is happening. Maybe I can help you." Anna waited for a response but Alex just stared at his coffee cup. Anna continued, "Is it the work, the trains? Alex? Tell me, *please*."

Alex smashed his fist on the table spilling coffee, his face red and angry. He looked at Anna and for a second she thought he might strike her but instead he took her hand. "Anna, it's terrible. Every trip some poor bastard throws himself in the path of the train. Last week we had three suicides, desperate Prairie farmers seeking an end to their misery. As inspector, I am the first to investigate. It's a war scene—I saw the same thing in Passchendaele and it brings back terrible images." Terror lingered in his eyes and face. "I am afraid to sleep on the train because the guys have to shake me so I'll stop screaming in my sleep."

Anna leaned over and took his hand. "Alex, I am sorry. I had no idea."

"Then the train has to wait for the authorities to clean up."

"It must affect everyone. How do the passengers cope?"

"We try to keep as much from the passengers as we can. Some of the lady passengers faint and become sick and others huff and puff because the train is delayed. The men have no understanding beyond the fact that their day has been disrupted. Complaints from staff and passengers are constant. I have trouble maintaining politeness as some passengers trivialize the deaths as an inconvenience. Management is indifferent, employees are cranky, and I am afraid for my job."

"Alex, you have to do something. Another job maybe?"

"I thought about asking them to put me in the office for a while but I'm afraid I'll lose my job. I would certainly lose pay."

"Why don't you talk to Mr. Dryden and see how things are? We can manage. I still have a little saved."

Alex moved his lips to a smile. A smile that did not reach his dull, almost grey eyes. The vibrant green she loved so much was gone. She had a sinking feeling in the pit of her stomach. Unemployment was high. If Mr. Dryden didn't have a position for Alex, where would he go for work? C.P. Rail, like other railways, had suffered in the crash and was barely staying afloat. She saw the misery unemployment brought to the men she served in the soup kitchens. Her family, luckier than most, had the steady rent income from Charlie and Bill who still had jobs, and Anna had her savings. Even in the worst scenario, they would not be destitute. She felt regret at the thought of her dreams coming to an end but Alex could not go on like this. Something had to be done.

Some things are all about timing and Alex had timed his talk with Mr. Dryden perfectly, although he didn't know it the day he walked into his office.

Alex glanced at the nameplate, took a deep breath to calm his apprehension, and knocked on the door.

"Come in," a voice called. "Ah, Alex, just the person I want to see," he said with his head down, scribbling on some papers.

Puzzled by this greeting, which implied Alex had been summoned, when he had requested the meeting, made Alex hesitate. Afraid he would lose his confidence, Alex spoke without preamble. "Mr. Dryden, I would like to express some concern about the safety of the passengers and staff on the western route." Alex wasn't sure where he was going with this. "It requires some form of policing by trained personnel." Undeterred by the lack of response from Mr. Dryden, Alex continued, "I am finding it difficult to do my job properly under the circumstances, and my health is suffering. Nothing serious, but I think a temporary change in position would help. Perhaps I could work in the office for a while?"

Mr. Dryden lifted his head and looked at Alex with surprise. "Alex, this is good news."

"It is?"

"This morning I was directed to eliminate all the inspector positions," he added, "cost cutting."

Alex's heart sank. He had no job. He was being fired.

Mr. Dryden stopped scribbling and stared. "Alex, what has happened to you? Are you ill?"

"No, no, just exhausted from lack of sleep. That's why I wondered if I could be transferred to the office for a while. But it appears not."

"Transfer, yes. How would you like to be my assistant manager here in passenger services? You are well qualified for the position. This cost cutting has diminished my office staff down to two people, an assistant and me. I am afraid it will be a great deal of work and a considerable drop in pay. But you'll be home with your wife most nights. If that is an advantage, to some it might not be." He chuckled. "Can you start on Monday?"

"Of course, and Anna will be happy to have me home."

Anna managed the household budget well. There was always a good meal on the table, clothes on their backs and the bills all paid. Travel and adventure were, of course, completely out of the question. Alex's new job did not allow him the family travel privileges but he was grateful to have one. The nightmares continued but they decreased both in number and intensity. He gained weight and looked like his old self, teasing and joking. Anna liked having him home every night.

The Depression had changed the industrial world and politicians had somehow disconnected from reality. The workers were threatening strikes and the talk in the soup kitchens was angry. They wanted jobs and homes, wives and children. The system had let them down.

The newspapers reported unrest and fascism in Europe. Concerned it might happen in Canada, Anna began to think about returning to England. Alex said it would blow over and as the economy moved forward, such ideas would be forgotten. Anna did not share Alex's optimism. Charlie, having more knowledge of such things, shared her concerns for the rising violence promoted by Hitler's Nazi group in Germany.

When her beloved Papa fell ill with bronchial-pneumonia, she decided to escalate her plans. Alex persuaded her to wait, mainly because Isabelle still had a year of school to complete. Charlie offered to take some extra time while in England to visit the family in Rugby and Anna relaxed knowing Charlie would take care of things.

Charlie arrived back in Canada with the sad news that their father had taken a turn for the worse and had died of pneumonia only a few days after he had arrived. On his deathbed, he had spoken of Anna and asked Charlie to deliver a message. Distraught with grief, Anna ignored the message. The pain of losing her Papa and the subsequent guilt for not being there almost destroyed her, and her zest for life had died with him. Anna needed an outlet for her guilt and in her grief she turned on Canada—hating everything Canadian.

Six months later, Anna's mother had a mild heart attack. Charlie assured her she was doing well and there was nothing to worry about. Lou was taking care of her and the doctors were not concerned. She only believed half of what they told her and continued to discuss selling up and going back to England.

Alarmed at the thought of returning to Britain, Alex argued that this was a bad time to sell the house and an even worse time to uproot Isabelle, taking her away from her life and friends. He suggested she and Isabelle plan a long holiday in the summer. Anna could not explain, even to herself, why she had to leave Canada. She had lost the will to pursue her dreams. She had given up.

It seemed that nothing she did allowed her the independence she craved. Every time she came close, it was whipped away, leaving only disappointment. Family life had changed. Alex hated his office job as much as her life was boring. She cooked and cleaned, did laundry and had tea with Abigail or sometimes visited Helga at the bakery. She hated this domestic life. The Depression had limited their resources and the general sense of despair and hopelessness was more than she could bear. She tried to think about what she wanted, but all she knew was that it wasn't what she had now. Maybe by returning to England she could start again.

In May 1935, three things happened that tipped Anna over the edge. Alex applied to go back on the trains and was refused, citing his health as an issue, and a month later he was laid off from the office job. The third incident was a letter from Lou expressing grave concern for their mother's health. The guilt of dismissing her father's illness weighed heavily, and Anna resolved to be home before her mother died. Against Alex's wishes, she made preparations for the family's return in late June when Isabelle finished high school. Alex refused to go at first, but with no job, he conceded he would come for a holiday.

The day after Isabelle finished school, the three boarded a train to Halifax, each with their own agenda.

III

August 1935 - December 1947

Rugby, Warwickshire,
England

Twenty-Eight

Three Agendas Cross the Atlantic

lex had agreed, reluctantly, to return to England, reasoning that a holiday would perhaps restore his health. Unbeknownst to Anna, Alex and Mr. Dryden had made an arrangement that as soon as CP Rail reinstated more inspectors, which was expected to happen in the fall, Alex would return to Toronto.

Anna had no intention of returning, partly because the thought of one sea crossing was quite enough and she had vowed to seek a new purpose to her life in England. She had, without explanation to Alex, made arrangements with Mr. Peabody and Charlie, acting on her behalf, to start looking for a buyer for 72 Forest Road.

Isabelle, expecting to return to her friends and look for her first job, had plans to work as a sales assistant at Eaton's. Applying for a position in the fall, prior to the Christmas season, would be excellent timing. Anna had not disillusioned her, deciding to wait until they were settled.

Each having their own agenda, they happily boarded the ship for Southampton, all enjoying Isabelle's excitement at a sea voyage, her first glimpse of England, and meeting her grandmother, aunt, uncle and three cousins.

The three stood on deck watching the white cliffs of the English coast draw closer, and gradually houses appearing as dots on the horizon turned into towns and Southampton emerged on the skyline. Much to Anna's surprise, the journey had been uneventful with not one storm. The Atlantic Ocean had been as smooth as a millpond for the entire crossing. Her stomach had felt queasy for a day, but as Alex had promised, as soon as she found her sea legs she felt quite well.

Overwhelmed by the welcome home to Rugby reception, Anna couldn't believe the amount of people who crammed into the small terraced house at 45 Oak Street—her mother's current home. Lou, Robert and their children hosted the affair. Florence and Wilfred had come down from Scotland on the train, and there were relatives and people Anna hardly remembered and some she had never met.

After the guests had gone home and the dishes were put away, Lou and family left for the farm with Florence and Wilfred, who would be their guests for a few days. Exhausted, Anna and Alex retired to the spare bedroom, which Alex thought would be their home for a few weeks, but for Anna, it was a temporary arrangement until they found permanent accommodation. Anna's mother, known as Little Gran to the grandchildren, helped Isabelle convert the parlour sofa into a bed. The parlour, only used on special occasions, would be Isabelle's temporary bedroom.

Anna woke early and descended the narrow staircase, went through the small, over-furnished sitting room and into the scullery to make coffee.

"Birds," she said aloud. "Song birds." She opened the back door to listen, having forgotten how different and wonderful the morning chorus sounded in England. It didn't matter how dull or grey the day, the birds still sang, and today it was overcast; clear blue skies were rare in Rugby.

"Good morning, Anna."

"Mother, good morning! It is good to be home. The larks are singing well this morning, something you don't hear in Canada." Anna closed the door. "I was about to make coffee."

"I only have Camp coffee." Anna pulled a face. Camp coffee was a kind of coffee syrup, which tasted nothing like coffee.

"How about tea? We can take a trip to town and buy coffee later today."

Anna sat at the small wooden table, admiring a glass vase of purple and yellow pansies, no doubt picked from the garden. Their face-like petals smiled at her. She looked around the tiny scullery, watching her mother make tea. She was surprised to see her mother had aged. Her once rich brown hair was as white as the steam coming from the whistling kettle, but fifteen years was a long time. She appeared to have shrunk and Anna, at five-foot four-inches, towered over her.

"See if the milkman has been please, Anna?" Not wanting to wake Isabelle, Anna tiptoed through the parlour to the front door and gathered two bottles of milk. She poured some into a jug and put the rest in the cool larder. In all the confusion yesterday, Anna hadn't noticed how minimal the house was; nothing like the home Anna grew up in. A terraced house, two up and two down with a back scullery for a kitchen. An indoor bathroom had been added although others on the street still had a privy at the end of their gardens. Anna was grateful her mother's house was not one of them. A covered alley, wide enough for one person to walk through, positioned in the middle of the block, gave them access to a narrow back garden.

"Mother, why did you sell the house?"

"After your father died, the house was too big for me and Lou talked me into selling. I went to live on the farm for a while, but Lou fussed all the time. I missed my friends and having my own place. This is all I could afford. I like it here. It's not too big, the garden is just enough to grow some flowers and Robert comes and plants a few vegetables. The runner beans will be ready soon and you should see the size of the tomatoes."

Anna frowned. "What does the doctor say? Should you be gardening and living alone? What if you have another heart attack?" Her voice faltered. She felt tears and bit her bottom lip trying to calm her voice. "Papa died and I wasn't here for him. I felt so guilty it tore me apart. I couldn't bear to lose you too."

"Anna, whatever is going on? My heart is fine and I am very well."

"But… but Lou wrote and said you had had a heart attack."

"Oh dear." She moved her cup and saucer and squeezed Anna's hands.

351

"My darling Anna, your Papa meant the world to you and you to him, and yes, he missed you. But he was so proud of his daughter who lived in Canada. He never stopped talking about you, much to your sister's annoyance. He lived your dreams with you and never once begrudged you being so far away. The day he died, he gave Charlie a message for you. He said to tell you how much he loved you and how sorry he was that he had not made the effort to travel to Canada and visit his adventurous princess."

Pent-up grief flowed from Anna and the memory prompted a trickle of tears from her mother. Anna hugged her tiny body and they wept together. Mother took an embroidered handkerchief from her apron pocket and dabbed Anna's cheeks, wiped her own wet eyes and poured more tea.

Anna remembered Charlie saying something to her. She was so guilt ridden that she had not heard what he was saying and she had not believed him when he'd said Mother was fine. It was Lou's letter that had frightened her.

"Please tell me, why did the doctor say you had a heart attack?"

"I was heartbroken when your father died so suddenly. We thought he was getting better and then he took a turn for the worse." She wiped her cheeks. "I started to have dizzy spells. I couldn't sleep and then my chest hurt so badly, Lou called the doctor. That was when the doctor thought it might be my heart. I had told Lou and Charlie not to worry you. I didn't know Lou had written. Lou, Robert and Charlie thought it best for me to sell the big house and move to the farm. Lou took good care of me and I soon recovered. I became stronger and the doctor said he thought it was grief that broke my heart and not a physical heart condition."

They fell silent, each immersed in their own thoughts.

Mother's brow puckered and with her head slightly to one side, she said, "Is this why you came back to England? You thought I was dying?"

Anna stood up and put the kettle back on the cooker. She slid a box of Swan matches open and the burner gave a poof as the gas caught. She stared through the scullery window.

"Partly. I needed to forgive myself for not being here for Papa, and partly because Canada has been disappointing. These last few months I have begun to despise everything Canadian. Every time I have a glimpse of my dreams coming true, people or circumstances get in the way, not the least of which is Alex. I thought I might try starting a new life here in England."

"How does Alex feel about this?"

"Alex does what is good for Alex. He only agreed to come for a holiday. Once here, I expect him to agree to stay and look for work. There is no work in Toronto, the depression is worse than here. His health is not good and he has violent outbursts, especially at night."

"Is he mistreating you?"

"No. No, nothing, like that, unless you take into account his lack of understanding. Alex made promises when I agreed to marry him. He thinks he has fulfilled his promises but truly he has never understood my need to explore beyond the limits we impose on our lives. There are so many exciting things in the world."

"Anna, you would tell me if he was mistreating you, wouldn't you?"

"Yes, I would tell you. He has provided well for us. He loves me very much and he adores our daughter. He and Isabelle remind me of Papa and me and he over indulges her as Papa did with me. As you get to know your granddaughter, you will discover how demanding she can be."

"So why are you so sad? You can't fool me, Anna. I'm your mother. Something is wrong."

"It's too late now but there are times when I wonder if I married the right person. There was a time years ago when Bill Blaine wanted to marry me. He reminds me of Uncle Bertie. Not as brash; a quiet version of Uncle Bertie with the same sense of adventure. We have much in common but I surrendered to Alex's charm and Bill ran away."

"Your place is with your family. I thought you would get over those fanciful ideas once you had settled in Canada. Uncle Bertie planted dreams of adventure in your head. You and Charlie would sit for hours, listening to his stories."

Anna suddenly felt irritated as she realized her mother did not understand her any more than Alex. Reacting without thought she said, "Why is it acceptable for Charlie to fulfill his dreams of travelling to Africa, India,

Canada and wherever his heart desires and I am expected to be a maid to my husband? You of all people must remember how I hate the domestic scene. I expected more from you. Papa always cared for me and listened to me. Domestic Lou, who became the perfect wife and mother, was always *your* favourite."

Seeing her mother's face pale with shock and hurt, Anna immediately regretted her words. "Mother, I'm sorry. I didn't mean to hurt you. I'm frustrated. I would like you to try to appreciate the passion I feel. You always supported and defended Uncle Bertie when Papa criticized his wanderlust. Is it too much to ask that you do the same for me?"

"Anna, I am old and of another generation. When Bertie and I were children, I had the same passion for adventure as Bertie. I have always seen that passion in you, but unlike you, my passion remained in my childhood memories. It never occurred to me to be anything other than a wife and mother, nor did I question the freedom that Bertie had to follow his dreams. So in a way I do understand, but at some point we have to grow up. I don't understand why you must fight against your role as a wife. You say Alex is a good husband. What more do you want?"

Her mother made it all sound so simple. Anna didn't want the life she had with Alex, but what *did* she want? Bill immediately came to mind. Could Bill give her the life she wanted? She reminded herself that Bill could never be more than a friend, and her mother was right. Perhaps it was time to accept her role in life.

"Anna, what is it? You are hiding something. Does it have something to do with Bill?"

Anna felt her cheeks flush, and hoping her mother hadn't noticed, she said, "No, of course not! There's nothing to hide."

Anna wanted to confide in her mother but decided not to. "You are right." she smiled. "I must accept my role. I am thinking that when the house sells in Toronto, I could buy a small business. Alex and I had fun running the bakery until the flour dust made it impossible for him to work or live at the bakery."

"How is Alex?"

"I am well, Mother Neale," Alex said. Neither Anna nor her mother had heard him come into the kitchen. Anna felt herself shrinking as she wondered how much of the conversation he had heard.

"Oh for goodness' sake, Alex, call me Mother. Times are changing and we don't need to be so formal anymore."

"Mother it is," Alex said, giving her a kiss on the cheek.

"What's this I hear about buying a business?"

Anna gulped, glancing towards her mother, who was busy taking eggs and a brown paper package of bacon from the larder, ignoring the onset of a strained atmosphere. Anna's thoughts flashed before her. Should she tell him of her plans, which were not really plans yet, or should she pretend he had heard incorrectly?

Alex poured a cup of tea and sat at the table, a question mark on his face, waiting for Anna's reply.

"I've been thinking." She coughed and cleared her throat. "When the house is sold in Toronto, we could use that money to buy a business here. We could work together like we did at Kenwood Bakery."

Alex's temper flared, flushing from his neck to his brow. He opened his mouth and growled, "WHEN… the house sells. Who put it up for sale?"

"Um!" Anna's heart was racing. "I spoke with Mr. Peabody before we left and suggested he start looking for a buyer. With the economy being so fragile, it will take a while to sell. Charlie is looking after things."

"What has Charlie got to do with it? Anna, I told you I am going back to Toronto. You agreed this would be an extended holiday and nothing more." Alex slammed his fist on the table. "Mr. Dryden has agreed to contact me as soon as an inspector's position becomes…" Alex stopped abruptly

"What?" Anna looked at her mother and then saw Isabelle standing in the doorway. "We will finish this conversation later."

A bleary-eyed Isabelle flipped her long red curls from her face and said, "What's all the shouting about? Papa, has Mr. Dryden got a job for you? When do we go back?"

Anna responded quickly, relieved that Isabelle had not heard all the conversation. "No, Papa was just talking about it." Anna and Alex

355

exchanged angry glances. The atmosphere relaxed as they all ate bacon and eggs. Isabelle laughed at the wire contraption that sat on the gas burner to make toast, declaring England to be quaint and old-fashioned.

Little Gran suggested to Isabelle that they catch the bus into town and do some shopping, leaving Mum and Papa to unpack and get settled. Shopping, as for any fifteen-year-old girl, was one of Isabelle's favourite pastimes and she readily agreed. Anna suggested she join them but her mother's glare told her to get things sorted out with Alex while they were gone. She was not looking forward to it.

Alex spoke first, his voice edgy but his temper subdued. "How could you consider selling the house? I told you this is a holiday. My place is with CP Rail. That is my job."

"Alex, you don't have a job and without income we will have to sell the house, whether we stay in Canada or stay in England. Thankfully, the mortgage is small and there's enough money to keep Mr. Peabody happy but that won't last forever. Instead of rent, Charlie and Bill agreed to pay the house expenses."

"It seems to me you made plans with everyone but me. Did you forget that I am your husband and this is my life too. What about our daughter?"

Anna needed time to think and went to the cooker. Shaking the empty kettle, she said, "I hope Mother remembers the coffee. Tea's okay but I miss coffee." She turned and faced Alex and blurted out, "I don't want to go back to Canada. There is nothing there for me, Alex. I want to work or run a business. We could do it together like we did before. Toronto is too depressed but England is beginning to prosper. The money for the house would set us up nicely for a café, a pub, even a small hotel or a shop. Remember when you bought the Kenwood Bakery, without my permission I may add, you said to me, 'It gives us a place to live and work.' And it did. We could do it again." She smiled and held her breath, waiting for his reaction.

"Yes and the flour dust in the bakery nearly killed me." Alex scowled. "I was glad to be rid of it. I don't want to own a business. Mr. Dryden has offered me my old job as soon as things pick up and he expects that to be in September or October. We can go home." He stretched out his arm and held Anna's hand. "That's settled. Come here and let me give you a kiss."

Anna pulled away. "No. Alex, you are not listening. I don't want to go back. I am serious. I want to start a business."

In the briefest of seconds his eyes flashed from temper to allure, his lips broke into a smile, his face warm and loving. "What if I agreed to you finding work? I'll even help you. You could take up a position at the Royal York. I promise I won't stand in your way. I'll ask Mr. Dryden to put a good word in for you, and Isabelle can work at Eaton's—she has set her heart on being a shop assistant."

Anna hesitated. Her interview experience at the Royal York flashed before her but there were other hotels. It was what she had wanted to do a couple of years ago and she did enjoy the hotel life. Perhaps she should think about it. The thought of the temper tantrums that would come from Isabelle when she learned that the family would not be returning to Canada was daunting.

"Alright. We wait until October. If Mr. Dryden offers you your job back and you promise to allow me to work as a receptionist and help me find a job, I will think about going back to Canada."

Alex pulled her playfully on his lap, wrapped his arms around her and whispered, "I promise." He hugged her tight and she felt herself being seduced by his charm. He whispered, "Make love, my darling." She shuddered as his warm breath tickled her ear. Giggling on the narrow staircase as they tried to climb the stairs side by side, Anna suddenly put her fingers to her mouth. "Shush! I heard something." They stopped mid stair as the back door slammed shut.

"Hello!" shouted Isabelle. "Where are you? We bought coffee and the bakery had fresh hot bread."

"I'm right here," Anna replied, walking into the kitchen.

"Mum, guess what? I tasted the cheese before we bought it and it's delicious."

"The smell of that bread is making me very hungry. Fresh bread and cheese and a pot of coffee for lunch, what more could we ask for?"

"Where's Alex? Is everything all right?" Mother asked, raising her eyebrows.

"Yes, everything is fine." Anna nodded slightly and smiled towards her mother. "Alex is upstairs finishing the unpacking."

The aroma of percolating coffee brought Alex downstairs. The table was now full of fresh baked bread, old cheddar cheese, piccalilli, pickled onions and homemade tomato chutney. He immediately sat down and began buttering a slice of bread.

"Papa, it is rude to start before we are all at the table," Isabelle teased.

"I am hungry and where is everyone?"

Isabelle frowned as a jumble of voices came from the scullery. "It's Aunt Lou, Auntie Florence and Uncle Wilfred." Isabelle jumped up and down as though she were five-years-old again, waiting for Wilfred to take her to the park.

Alex carried extra chairs from the parlour while Little Gran cut more bread and fetched a block of Lancashire cheese from the larder. Everyone sat round the dining room table, a cacophony of conversation all going at the same time. Anna felt warm and cozy but suddenly missed Papa's voice. Tears lurked as the memories of a loving childhood flooded her mind. Was this what was missing from her life; the warmth of her mother's house? How could that be? She had a family of her own and, for as long as she could remember, she had fought the domestic lifestyle her mother held so dear. Had she traded warmth and love for the illusive coolness of liberation that had escaped her at every turn?

"Move over, Anna," Lou's voice commanded as she placed a large, steaming rhubarb pie on the table. Anna glared at her, partly for her rudeness and partly for interrupting her thoughts.

Wilfred licked his lips. "The smell of that pie in the farmhouse all morning has had my taste buds on edge." Everyone laughed

"Fresh from the farm," Mother said, placing a large pudding bowl of whipped cream next to the pie.

"Lou, this is wonderful," Alex and Isabelle said in unison.

The conversation subsided to subtle ums and ahs as the pie was

358

consumed. Anna felt the shadow of inadequacy roll over her. Lou's ease at the domestic life had always been intimidating. An ulterior motive in mind, she suggested Lou help her clear the table and do the washing-up, giving her an opportunity to have it out with Lou about their mother's illness. Rivalry between the sisters, especially about anything to do with their parents, constantly lurked below the surface. Conflicted by her see-saw emotions, reasons for returning to England and Alex's charm, Anna needed someone to blame for her impulsive and irrational exodus from Toronto.

"Lou, why did you write and tell me mother was gravely ill?"

"Because the doctor said she had had a heart attack and I thought you should know."

"But you omitted to write that the doctor changed his diagnosis. Do you realize what I have done because of *you*?" Anna could feel her voice climbing in volume. "I uprooted my family, expecting to find mother seriously ill."

"Oh, don't be so dramatic. Father is no longer around to pamper you." Lou scrubbed at the plates, sloshing water on the floor. "Now look what you made me do. And where were you when Father was ill? Who nursed him, worried about him and all *he* could talk about was his wonderful daughter in Canada."

"Mother told me he was getting better and then it was too late and I didn't have time to come home."

"You could have come home to help mother. She was heartbroken and so ill with grief. I sent that letter because it was time you came home and did your duty. Charlie did what he could and I was left to do everything else. Robert was busy on the farm. I had three children to look after and my pampered princess sister sat there in her big house across the Atlantic Ocean, doing nothing."

"I am not a pampered princess. My life in Canada has not been as glamorous as you may think." Anna dropped her bottom lip and began to pout.

"Oh, for God's sake, Anna, you are not a child," Lou scoffed

Lou's words shocked Anna into realizing her behavior was silly and childish. Embarrassed she retorted, "You have no idea what my life was like. I worked just as hard as you." Anna's voice quivered, "The consequences of your letter may have caused me to make a big mistake." She banged the draining board smashing two plates together, one breaking. They both stopped and stared at the broken pieces of china.

"What is going on in here?" Mother's voice reprimanded them as she glanced at the broken plate. "Stop this nonsense, both of you. You are sisters. You both have difficulties in your lives. Try talking to each other instead of blaming each other. I know you both care for me and have my interests at heart but using me as an excuse to lay blame is not acceptable. I may add that I am quite capable of looking after myself." Hands on her hips, she glared determinedly from one daughter to the other and added, "Now…work it out." She turned abruptly and walked back to the sitting room. There was silence. Lou picked up the pieces of plate and threw them in the waste-bin, the clatter breaking the silence.

"Mother's right," Anna said. "Lou, I'm sorry. I do want someone to blame. My life has not turned out the way I expected."

"I'm sorry too and things didn't work out so well for me. Robert is not the greatest of husbands and farm life is not easy. I resented you being away and at times I was lonely, especially when Papa was so ill, and the thought of losing Mama too was more than I could bear."

Anna and Lou called a truce. It seemed their differences could only be put aside for short periods of time but they learned to talk and laugh like sisters. In fact, much of Anna's anger began to dispel in the warmth of her mother's home. The family found themselves in a comfortable routine.

By mid-October, Alex received the news from Mr. Dryden that he too no longer had a job with CP Rail and, as such, Alex would not be re-hired. The news for Anna was no better. Mr. Peabody could not find a buyer for 72 Forest Road. It became obvious that there would be no decision on returning to Canada, at least until after the New Year. As expected, Isabelle threw a temper tantrum when told they would be staying in Rugby for Christmas and her dream of working at Eaton's was shattered.

360

Tempered by the excitement of the family being together for Christmas, neither Alex nor Anna felt disappointed. Isabelle announced that she had been offered a job in a ladies' dress shop for the Christmas season. All three were then content to enjoy the season.

Lou and Robert hosted the largest Christmas the Neale family had seen in many years. The big rambling farmhouse could accommodate a dozen or more extra family to sleep and dine. This included Florence and Wilfred and a surprise visit from Charlie, who arrived from Canada with a delightful young lady named Beth on his arm. Anna secretly wished Bill had come. He seemed to be the missing link in her life but, deep inside, she thought it was for the best.

Twenty-Nine

The King's Head Inn

lex no longer spoke of returning to Canada but neither did he speak of staying in England. It had been pleasant not to shiver in Toronto's inhumane winter temperatures and even more so to see snowdrops bloom in February. Now in early March the daffodils were cheerfully blowing their yellow trumpets under the magnolia tree.

Anna had a sense of permanency and began to make plans. She couldn't explain why, but even with Alex's assurances that she could work, it was not enough to tempt her to return to Canada. The warmth and love of her family, something she had fought against most of her adult life, had become a sanctuary. It was more than that, she thought. Sensing a sinister dark shadow hover around her, she gave an involuntary shudder. "In the midst of this darkness I will need my family." Fear fluttered Anna's heart as the words spoke themselves. "Where did that come from?" She continued speaking aloud, shaking it off as her overzealous imagination, all the while knowing, but not able to explain, the truth of her fear.

The warm, fuzzy, household was beginning to break down. Mother wanted her parlour back. Isabelle, no longer working, slept till noon and stayed up listening to the wireless half the night. Alex seemed to be suffering uncharacteristically from inertia, moping about and doing nothing. It was a strain on everyone. Anna took it upon herself to make plans that would delay returning to Canada by at least a year or more.

Choosing her time carefully, she suggested to her mother that Isabelle accompany her to town and help with the shopping. Isabelle was roused early from her bed with the promise of a new dress for spring. Once they were alone in the house, Anna called Alex into the dining room.

"Alex, we need to talk." Anna coughed nervously. "We have to find our own place to live. We are not being fair to Mother. Isabelle needs something to do and I would like her to go to secretarial school. Mrs. Wordsworth's Secretarial School for Young Ladies, where I trained, is still open and has vacancies for the next session, starting in April. It would deplete our savings but she would have a skill to use wherever she wanted to go. I know she likes working in a shop but in this day and age she needs more."

"Why don't we go back to Toronto? We have a house waiting for us. I'll get my old job back."

"Of course we can go back to Toronto" Anna lied, hoping it didn't show. "But we don't have the resources yet. If we work, we can build some savings and secretarial school will give Isabelle a skill she can use whichever side of the Atlantic we settle on. I thought you were beginning to like being in England?"

"I do but I prefer Toronto and I really do want my job back at CP Rail. Rugby has nothing to offer me. However, I like the idea of Isabelle going to secretarial school. Working as a shop assistant will give her nothing but secretarial skills will give her opportunities."

"We have a choice," Anna said. "Spend our savings on returning to Toronto and hope you get your job back or spend the money on Isabelle's education, find work and save, perhaps returning in a year or so when the job market is better. Alex, be realistic. It is unlikely you will work at CP Rail again, especially now that Mr. Dryden has gone." Anna watched his expression. She had deliberately used Isabelle's future as leverage, knowing that spending the last of their savings on an ocean passage would not persuade Alex to stay. His impulsive nature would gamble at finding work in Toronto but he *would* give up everything for his daughter's future.

Alex stood up with one hand in his trouser pocket and strolled to the window. A stream of sunlight reflected on his reddish curls as he ran his fingers through his hair.

"Spring is beautiful here and no doubt it is still snowing in Toronto. I don't miss the winter, trying to breathe through that cold, shovelling snow or calming pampered passengers as the train stalled in yet another snowdrift." He stood, pensively staring at the magnolia tree now in full bloom. Anna held her breath, willing herself to stay silent, waiting for his answer.

"I want the best for Isabelle. We stay until she has finished her education. Tom Mulligan at the King's Head has offered me a job as a barman. I turned him down in the hopes that CP Rail would hire me. You are right. That is not going to happen. I will go and have a pint when they open at lunchtime and see if the offer still stands. Why don't you register Isabelle at secretarial school and we'll tell her and Mother of our plans at dinner tonight?" He looked at his watch and said. "I'm off. See you tonight."

She could hardly believe how easy it had been to convince Alex to stay. She wondered why he hadn't told her about Tom Mulligan's offer but he had changed his mind and that was what mattered. She had reservations. A barman's wage was hardly enough to live on but, not wanting to discourage him, she stayed silent. To make ends meet, she too would have to find work. The notion of having a legitimate reason for working would normally make her happy. Why did she feel it a burden? There were many things about how she felt these days that she could not explain. Twenty-three years ago, she couldn't wait to escape dreary grey Rugby to seek her dreams of adventure and independence and yet here she was, forty-two years old, back in Rugby trying to escape a life that had brought her as close as she would ever come to her dreams. Close was not enough. Close meant disappointment and she couldn't take anymore.

I have given up, she thought. *Is that why I am clinging to home?* Suddenly, a clear vision of Bill appeared at her side, his smiling eyes, his gentle arms comforting her. She remembered the spark inside her that fired her with excitement when they read and talked of Rudyard Kipling's travels to India or his intent interest as she retold Uncle Bertie's stories. An unbidden tear trickled quietly down her cheek, one lonely tear overflowing with grief for lost dreams and deep sadness for a lost love.

Dinner did not go as expected. Firstly, Mother tried to say they could stay as long as they wanted but it wasn't hard to see that she really wanted her place back. Alex's surprise proposal was promising and she brightened somewhat as she listened. Tom Mulligan at the King's Head was considering retiring to the seaside and, if that happened, Alex would take over the pub and they could live in the flat upstairs. As the latter had not been mentioned in their earlier discussion, Anna raised her eyebrow questioningly at Alex as she was not sure if this was 'Alex talk' or fact.

Isabelle burst into an indecipherable tirade of reasons why she could not live in a public house, finally declaring that she would lose all her friends and never again would she be able to show her face at the Palais de Danse. No one would hire a shop assistant who lived at a pub, miles from anywhere. Anna and Alex were stunned at her reaction. Anna was surprised that Isabelle had said nothing about going back to Canada. She thought this might be a good sign, although that would be short lived.

She calmed Isabelle by convincing her that the decision about where they would live had not yet been made. But Papa had to work as they were running out of money. Isabelle calmed down and Anna decided to pass on the good news.

"Isabelle, Papa and I have a surprise for you. We have been talking about your future. How would you like to go to secretarial school? I registered you today at the same school I went too. You start in April." Anna felt smug and smiled across at Alex and they both smiled at Isabelle, waiting for her excitement and gratitude.

Isabelle stood up and stared at her parents and calmly said, "I do *not* want to be a secretary and I will *not* go to secretarial school."

"Isabelle, it is a wonderful opportunity. Your mother has spent the last of our savings to give you a better chance in life. I have taken a job at the pub to support you." Alex's voice was almost a whine—clearly he was hurt.

Suddenly, this beautiful sixteen-year-old turned into a spoiled six-year-old, throwing an enormous temper tantrum, crying, and between sobs yelling. "You said this was a holiday…. When are we going back to Canada? You told me October, in time for Christmas and then you said in the New Year. I want… my friends and I want to work at Eaton's. I want my old room back. I hate it here. I hate all of you." Stamping her feet, she ran into the parlour, shouting, "I hate sleeping in the parlour." Gasping through sobs she slammed the door.

"I'll speak to her," Anna said, seeing the hurt and disbelief on Alex's face.

"No," Mother said, gently tapping Anna's arm. "Leave her for a while and I'll go and talk to her. She is very angry with both of you. You didn't tell her you planned to stay in England?"

Anna looked at her mother sheepishly, but it was Alex who spoke. "I cannot get my old job back, Mother, so we decided to stay another year. But I think we need to re-think this. I can't bear to see Isabelle so upset. We *have* to return to Canada, and soon."

Anna's heart sank. Her plan had backfired. Alex would do anything for his daughter, including going back to Canada.

"Alex, you can't keep giving into her. She is spoiled and demanding. She needs to learn that things *do not* always work out the way we want them too. But you do need to include her in your plans." Mother turned to Anna, "And that goes for you too, Anna. I remember how you rebelled against the choices your father and I made for you instead of with you, and the world is a different place today." Anna felt reprimanded and ashamed that she had not considered Isabelle in these decisions. Her mother continued, "Uprooting a girl from all she loves and knows is bound to have consequences. As spoiled as she is, you are not being fair to her."

Drained of energy, Anna needed some air. She needed to digest the truth of her mother's wise words. Blinded by her own obsessions, she had not seen the resulting effect on her daughter. Picking up her mother's shawl by the door, she flipped it around her shoulders. The air damp and grey, she began walking. A light drizzly rain had started. A red brick wall of homes stretched as far as she could see along Oak Street. Warm yellow light escaped from front parlour windows and front doors that opened onto a flagstone pavement were all that distinguished the individual homes.

She thought of the crisp, clear air of Toronto, the lush front yard and the oak tree at Forest Road, with the wide-open spaces of the green park just a short walk away. Had her personal obsession drawn them away? She thought not but she did question her motives, reminding herself that the green open space would currently be covered in snow and ice. Whether it was the reality of cold Canadian winters or something else, Anna didn't know. She shuddered as the sense of darkness hovered over her again, pulling her to the warmth and security of the lit parlour windows. She turned around, hurrying through the dark passageway to her mother's back door. Confused and uncertain of what she wanted or where she wanted to be, her mother's words had brought a sense of shame. Anna crawled into bed and wrapped her arms around Alex.

Little Gran worked miracles with Isabelle who apologized to her parents and seemed to forgive Alex. There was no forgiveness coming Anna's way. She barely spoke to her mother but, on Little Gran's advice, she agreed to give secretarial school a try.

At first she was happy and enjoyed the camaraderie of the other girls, making many friends—she was her father's daughter, a charming social butterfly. The academic side of school was a different story and she was failing both typewriting and shorthand. By October, she quit before the school failed her. Almost immediately, she was hired as a shop assistant at Draper's Department Store in town, a far cry from Eaton's in physical size, but the upper class clientele, including lords and ladies and dukes and duchesses, suited Isabelle's ideals of grandeur. One of Rugby's claims to fame was the Rugby School for Boys, which housed and educated the privileged youth of the British elite. Pre- and post-school terms the families would shop for school uniforms, gifts and personal items for students and family at Draper's Department Store. The prestige far outweighed the mass-market Eaton's, and Isabelle's desire to return to Canada vanished.

At the same time, Tom Mulligan retired to the warmer climes of Devon, leaving Alex in charge and vacating the living quarters for Alex and family. Isabelle reiterated her disdain and refused to live in a pub. Little Gran offered her the spare bedroom at Oak Street. The arrangement worked well. Isabelle loved and respected Little Gran. Anna stopped worrying, knowing they would look out for each other. Isabelle blossomed into a beautiful, if snobbish, young woman.

The King's Head, an old Tudor-style inn dating back to the nineteenth century, sat at the edge of town on the old stagecoach route to Coventry. It looked out of place sitting rather grandly in a recent suburban neighbourhood, defying the newness of its surroundings.

Inside, the heavy-beamed ceilings, stone floor and massive open fireplace warped its contemporary patrons into a different time zone. The original wooden bar had dark patches of smooth-worn indents from centuries of elbows and tankards of ale. The saloon, or lounge bar as it was now called, spread endlessly. There were no internal walls, just thick, heavy oak beam supports throughout the space.

At intervals around the thick stone outside wall, there were small leaded windows that served well for heat or cold but let little or no light in. The little table lamps with their warm red shades gave this enormous room a cozy feeling, enhanced by the glow from the fireplace reflecting on the old polished brass and shiny copper ornaments. Once useful tools were now part of the décor that hung on the whitewashed walls between the dark beams.

Anna wasn't sure she would ever get used to the pub smell: a mixture of fresh and stale beer, sweaty men, and cigarette smoke with a hint of sweet pipe tobacco and cigars. Everyone smoked these days, except Alex and Anna. The smoke made Anna sick and Alex's weak chest made him cough. Upstairs, there were six unused bedrooms that once accommodated travelers needing rest from their arduous stagecoach journey. Anna thought she might open them up as guest rooms.

The publican's accommodation was a flat located on the ground floor behind the bar area, consisting of a large old-fashioned kitchen and scullery, a sitting room and small, damp, dark bedroom that was probably the old pantry. Anna decided to use that as an office and they would use one of the bedrooms on the second floor close to the back stairs.

The kitchen door opened onto a large courtyard surrounded by out-buildings, once stables and tackle rooms with spacious lofts above. The carriage house now housed an old Ford that had once belonged to Anna's father. Alex had found it in Lou's barn and resurrected it to run errands into town.

Creeping suburbia fringed the back of the inn, leaving a view of open meadows, hedgerows and the meandering Avon River. Anna could see sheep grazing and a farmhouse in the distance. The view gave her hope. Perhaps The King's Head would bring a new and satisfying focus to her life. It certainly had for Alex. The old charming Alex she had known at The Sackville had reappeared and talk of returning to Canada had ceased.

It felt good to be near green spaces and out of the greyness of industry and the noise of whistling trains. Rugby had blossomed from a small market town as the railways expanded into a major rail junction, bringing industry and rich school boys and their families to town. The latter prompted Anna's business mind into visualizing the refurbishing and expansion of the King's Head pub into a small hotel. Could this be her dream materializing? She smiled as she felt the long-forgotten butterflies of excitement inside. But, she thought, it would take money and her only asset was an unsold house in Toronto. Even that would not be enough to buy the property and renovate.

On Christmas Eve 1936, Anna received an unexpected gift. The pub crammed with merry makers, Anna was helping Alex behind the bar pulling pints and mixing cocktails. Concentrating on a pewter tankard as it filled with beer, she eased the brass handle, judging just the right amount of foam, when a familiar voice said, "I never thought I would see Papa's little girl pulling pints." She looked up, spilling the beer, to see Bill Blaine grinning from ear to ear. She pushed the beer to the customer and said,

"On the house," before the customer complained of a short pint.

Standing next to Bill, Charlie said, "It looks as if you could do with some help, Sis."

Anna screamed with delight. "Alex, look who's here." She ran from behind the bar and wrapped her arms around Bill and then Charlie with hoots and whistles coming from the customers. "Hey!" Anna yelled across the room. "Everyone, I would like you to meet two very special people: my brother, Charlie, and our long-time friend, Bill, from Canada."

Bill and Charlie rolled up their sleeves and began serving drinks. By the ten o'clock last call, the crowd had thinned as people went home to be with their families, shouting a bluster of Merry Christmases. Finally, the pub cleaned up, Alex stoked the sitting room fire and Anna put out a plate of ham and pork pie with pickled onions, thick chunks of bread and a plate of her mother's home made mince pies. Alex poured a jug of beer from the bar.

"What in the world are you two doing here?"

"Sis, I have good news. I gave Beth an engagement ring last week and we plan to marry in the spring."

"That is wonderful news but where is Beth?"

"She went to visit her parents in Vancouver for Christmas. Her Grandfather is not well. I wanted to bring the news to my family and, as I had to be in London for work, I combined the two. But that is not all. We would like to buy 72 Forest Road. Unless you have decided to come back."

Anna raised an eyebrow and looked at Alex. He smiled. "This means we can buy the pub off Tom Mulligan." He had answered her question. They would be settling in England.

"Charlie, are you sure?"

"It was Beth's idea. She loves the house. We can work out the details while I am here and make the transaction with the bank."

"Charlie, this is the best Christmas present I have ever had. I have dreamed of turning this lovely old inn into a hotel and fancy restaurant."

"Does that mean you will need a chef?" Bill asked. "I intend to come back to England and give the lovebirds some privacy."

Tom Mulligan wanted the pub sold. He needed the money and willingly sold it far below market value and took back a mortgage. He liked Anna and Alex and wanted to see them do well. The generous negotiation meant they had enough money to start the expansion and refurbishing. Bill converted the loft above the carriage house for his own accommodation and the carriage house was permanently attached to the main building to extend Anna and Alex's living quarters, freeing space for the commercial kitchen.

Anna had successfully transformed the inside of a rambling working-man's pub into a comfortable but elegant hotel. Etched glass and oak snobbery screens divided the room into three. The carpeted Avon Lounge they named after the local river was furnished with comfortable chairs and small tables arranged in conversation groups around the fireplace. An elegant dining room with crisp white table cloths she called the Emily Carr Room, decorated with a collection of Emily Carr's paintings—Anna's pride and joy. The unusual art stimulated customer conversation and created a local landmark. In contrast, the bar area remained unchanged, with a stone floor, wooden stools, a few small round tables with the same lamps and red shades, and plenty of room to stand with elbows on the bar. A smart move on Anna's part. The locals didn't want fancy stuff; they wanted to drink good beer with good company.

For two years, the King's Head Inn flourished, as did Anna's pride. Pre- and post-Rugby School terms, the guest rooms were booked full and well in advance. Most nights the restaurant overflowed into the lounge area. Bill's exquisite cuisine, Alex's uncanny ability to charm the guests and Anna's head for business made for a thriving hotel with a reputation that spread throughout the Midlands. The happy trio worked in harmony, totally focused on the success of the King's Head Inn, letting go of any old personal feelings.

Anna desperately wanted to hold on to the euphoric experience, ignoring the wireless news reports of impending war with Germany and laughing at the government for prematurely distributing gas masks and ration books. She brushed it off as over cautious. Even after listening to Neville

Chamberlain, the Prime Minister, announce Germany's invasion of Poland and the subsequent declaration of war on September 3, 1939, Anna remained in denial. Perhaps it was reinforced by what the newspapers called, the 'phony war' because nothing much seemed to happen. Adamant in her denial of war, she could not deny the heavy black cloud that once again hovered over her. She blamed the government's fear mongering for the negative thoughts that a war might ruin them. Anna's fear was compounded by the long forgotten memory of how both Alex and Bill had brushed with death in the Great War. Was the tightness in her throat due to her self-imposed conflict or something more sinister?

Thirty

Blessed Wartime Wedding

⁓❦⁓

"T his is ridiculous!" Anna said, waving a khaki ration in the air. "In January it was bacon, butter and sugar measured out as though we were children. Today, the grocer refused to sell me strawberry jam. Every week something else is added. Soon everything will be rationed and then the government will have to reverse everything when the war doesn't materialize."

Alex glanced at Bill across the kitchen table and patted Anna's shoulder. "Anna, we are at war. Most of the fighting is in Europe but Hitler will invade Britain. It is only a matter of time."

She put her hand up to her shoulder and squeezed his fingers. "I know." She sniffed back tears. "It seems so unfair. We already went through one war. I can't go through all that worrying, wondering if you are safe, and what about the King's Head?" she sighed. "I was so happy. We worked hard and now we have our own successful little hotel. I am afraid with rationing and war we will be ruined."

"It is unlikely that either Bill or I will see active service," Alex laughed. "We are too old. An army going into battle needs young men unless you're a colonel whose wisdom from the mistakes of the Great War should make for better leadership." Alex sighed, raising a skeptical eyebrow.

Bill laughed and said, "I have no intention of going back to sea. One war with German U-boats is quite enough for me. So far I haven't seen any change in the restaurant. Maybe an increase as people try to supplement their food rations, since restaurants are exempt. Shortages might be a problem and I will have to be creative with recipes. Anna, you have nothing to worry about."

The warmth in Bill's voice gave her heart an unexpected jolt. She quickly looked away. "You are both right, and I doubt the war will stop boys attending Rugby School. Parents will still need to eat and have somewhere to stay."

"Should we try growing our own vegetables? We have plenty of land at the back. I like the idea of gardening. I never got around to it at Forest Road but here I have the time," Alex said.

"Ah, fresh vegetables from garden to table. I like that idea and we would be contributing to the war effort, what's the saying—digging for victory? What do you think, Anna?"

The conversation had reassured her they would survive even if the war escalated, which she stubbornly tried to deny. A quick resolution would be the only thing that would release this darkness that persisted in hovering around her.

Although she and Lou had patched their differences, they had never been close sisters. Lou arrived at the King's Head Inn driving Robert's van—the government allowed farmers extra petrol. She often helped Robert by delivering the eggs and milk while he and Simon worked the land. The King's Head Inn was on the regular route and that day Lou used it as an excuse to visit Anna.

"Lou, this is a nice surprise. Have you time to stay for lunch?"

"Thank you. I need to talk to you, Anna."

Anna frowned. Her sister was pale and she had noticed how much she had aged in the last little while. Farm life was hard work and Anna had no doubt that Robert was hard to live with. "Is something wrong?"

Lou nodded. Anna led her into a quiet corner of the Emily Carr dining room. "Did you hear the news today?" Lou looked down at the table, her finger worrying an imagined crumb.

"No, I haven't had the wireless on."

"Germany has taken Paris. Hitler has conquered France and we are next." Lou's voice trembled, catching rasps of breath. She blurted in a barrage of tears, "Robbie has enlisted in the RAF…" Anna put her arm around her sister but said nothing. "Anna, I am so afraid for him. I should be proud, and I am, and so is Robert, but what if he gets ki…" She stopped, unable to utter the word.

"You mustn't think that way." Anna remembered how she'd worried about Alex. Lou hadn't experienced a loved one going to war. In the last war, farming, an essential occupation, exempted Robert from service. But now she had three boys: nineteen-year-old Robbie, the eldest, Simon, eighteen, who worked on the farm and Peter, sixteen, in his last year at school.

Lou verbalized what Anna was thinking. "I could lose all three of my sons in this horrible war. Robbie reported for duty this morning. Peter's school sponsors senior boys to dig air raid shelters a couple of mornings a week, filling his head with propaganda, and now, full of pride for his brother, he can't wait to enlist. Simon, not so much. I think he is relieved that farmers are exempt at the moment and Robert needs him on the farm."

"Perhaps our new Prime Minister, Winston Churchill, will change things. Britain is strong, and young men like Robbie will fight off the Germans before they even get to Britain. You have to believe Robbie will come home." Anna smiled, knowing her words sounded empty, not comforting as she'd intended.

Lou's drawn face spoke of her misery and her half-smile thanked Anna for the attempt at comfort. Anna felt ashamed of how stubbornly and selfishly she had tried to deny this war. Lou's tear-stained face was proof enough that consequences of war were on their doorstep. She embraced her sister, hugging her tightly until her sobs subsided. Anna waved at the van as Lou drove back to the farm.

Although it was only eight in the morning, Lou squinted at the warm July sun reflecting off the windshield as she stepped out of the van. "Good morning, Anna!"

Anna turned, a clothespin protruding from her mouth and mumbled, "Good morning," as she stuck the clothespin into the corner of a sheet, attaching it to the clothesline.

"Washing? Not something I expect to see you doing," Lou said, jumping out of the van and holding up three dead rabbits. "Robert has sent these for Bill, shot this morning."

"Yuck! Get them away from my white sheets. Bill's in the kitchen." Anna pulled a face at the dead animals and tried to ignore the old hurt from Lou's comment. Aware of how hard Lou worked in a practical sense, she easily took offence when Lou insinuated that she did not, which of course she did, but not usually doing domestic chores.

"Nice day for drying washing," Lou said, looking puzzled. "Where are the maids?"

"Both quit for better wages at the munitions factory, more than I can afford to pay. Do you know of anyone looking for domestic work? We are fully booked this week and next. Being the end of the school year, all the Rugby boys' parents are coming into town."

Lou shook her head. "Can't Isabelle give you a hand?"

"She still has not forgiven me. We hardly see her." Anna felt sadness as she spoke. "Mother tells me she has a boyfriend. I wish I could meet him." She stared across the garden, deliberately avoiding Lou and waiting for a sarcastic remark from the perfect mother but Lou said nothing, giving her an empathetic smile.

Anna changed the subject. "Bill will be happy with the rabbits. He'll make his famous rabbit fricassee. Meat is in such short supply. Do you have time for coffee? I have some real coffee that Charlie sent from Canada."

Anna and Lou sat on a bench, soaking up the sun and sipping coffee when they heard a droning noise, first in the distance and then louder as several planes soared so low above their heads they could see the pilots. The sisters grabbed each other's hands, relaxing only after recognizing the circular RAF markings.

Alex ran to Anna, his face parchment. "What was that all about?"

Lou spoke first, "I think Britain is preparing for something big. I had a letter from Robbie telling me not worry. He couldn't explain, but his squadron was on high alert."

That night, Anna woke to a loud BOOM and the bed shaking from what felt like an earthquake—the first bomb had dropped on Rugby. Alex screamed, his hands over his face and ears. She pulled him into her arms and they clung to each other, listening for planes. Relieved at the silence, they peered through a corner of the blackout curtains, a few miles away the sky glowed with fire. Anna's heart sank so low she felt it beating in the earth below her feet. Alex's eyes were fixed with fear, his breathing fast, and his skin damp and pasty. He didn't need to tell her that the ghosts from his past had escaped his careful cloistering, invading his mind as he lived the Great War all over again.

Reality had hit home and they needed to be prepared. The next day, Alex cleared out one of the deepest cellars. He moved the wine to the beer cellar. Anna furnished it with cots, blankets, pillows, chairs, water and emergency food supplies. It was big enough to accommodate about fifteen people, which would include the hotel guests. The bar and restaurant patrons would be directed by the warden to the public shelter.

The air raid warnings wailed almost every night through the summer but there were no more bombs on Rugby. The days were normal except for squadrons of Hawker Hurricanes and Spitfires flying to and from the airfields. Sometimes the sheer numbers blocked the sun but Anna felt only comfort and pride. Lou was convinced that Robbie was one of the pilots. The Battle of Britain, the first airborne battle, was won in September. The Luftwaffe was crippled by the loss of planes and pilots and limped back to Germany.

The skies would be quiet for a while which was more than Anna could say for the King's Head Inn. The autumn term parents had departed and Anna was struggling down the stairs with a basket of laundry when Isabelle's voice came from the back door, "Mum, it's me, Isabelle!"

Anna ran down the stairs, laundry spilling from the basket. "Isabelle, how wonderful to see you." She stood in front of her daughter, half-gesturing for a hug, feeling awkward and actually grateful the laundry basket was between them, afraid of rejection. They had not spoken more than perfunctory greetings for a long time—was Isabelle ever going to forgive her, she wondered?

Isabelle looked anxious. "Is something wrong?" Anna asked. "Is it Little Gran?"

"No, Mum, nothing is wrong. I want to talk to you and Papa." Isabelle looked sheepish and happy at the same time.

Anna decided to confront her daughter. "Isabelle, will you ever forgive me for tearing you away from your life in Canada? I am sorry."

"It was cruel what you did and forgiveness, I am not sure about, but as things turned out, I am happy. I have done well at Draper's. I am now the manager of ladies' fashions, and although I never expected to say this, what I learned at secretarial school has been useful and perhaps even had an influence on my promotions." She smiled and Anna thought she caught a glimpse of forgiveness. Still holding the basket, Anna smiled, thinking how much she loved this young woman.

"Mum, if you put the wretched laundry basket down, I'll give you a hug… and why are you doing laundry? I thought you hated domestic stuff."

Anna dropped the basket. "I do but no one wants to be a maid when the factories pay more." She squeezed her daughter so tight she thought she might burst.

"Well, this is a surprise," Alex said, wrapping his arms around both women.

Next it was Bill's turn, "Do I get a hug too?"

"Uncle Bill, I am so glad you are here. I have something to tell you all." Isabelle's cheeks were quite pink. She cleared her throat the same way Anna did when she was nervous. "I have been courting a young man. His name is Alexander Wexford. Would you believe the same name as you Papa, except he prefers Sandy to Alex? He has asked me to marry him, with your permission of course." Isabelle glowed.

On this occasion, Anna left Alex to do the talking. "That sounds wonderful but I think your mother and I would like to know more about him and meet him. Has Gran met him?"

"Yes, lots of times. He likes Little Gran's cooking and she likes his jokes. He has a wonderful sense of humour."

"Where does he work or has he signed up? Is he a local boy? Do we know his family?"

"Why all the questions, Papa?"

"I need to know everything about a man who wants to marry my daughter."

"He works in the office at Draper's during the day and as a fireman, Auxiliary Fire Service, at night. They need him in the AFS, so he hasn't been called up yet. I think he was born in Guildford, but they live in Coventry and he cycles every day to Rugby. His father was a military man but has retired and owns a hardware store." Isabelle took a breath and giggled. "And I love him very much, and he is handsome, kind, loving and just wonderful." Isabelle scrunched her shoulders to her ears and closed her eyes as though she was embracing him. "Can I bring him for dinner tonight? Uncle Bill, would you make something special?"

"He sounds like a great person. I can't wait to meet him." Alex kissed Isabelle on the cheek. "I can't believe you are old enough to marry."

Anna added her seal of approval. "How does seven o'clock sound? Why don't you bring Little Gran too?"

At ten minutes before seven, a small van with Wexford Hardware written on the side pulled in front of the King's Head Inn. A tall, good-looking young man with thick, short brown hair held the door open for Little Gran and Isabelle. Anna was impressed. At least he had good manners.

It was a splendid evening, not just for the company and celebration, but Anna felt that her daughter's affections had returned. Watching Isabelle and Little Gran share something she had never been a part of irked her a little, but as Anna aged, she realized that motherhood had always been a struggle.

Sandy did have a great sense of humour; his cute one-liners and teasing kept the group laughing all evening. He reminded Anna of Alex in his twenties, and she hoped he had a serious side.

The wedding day was set for November 14th, a Thursday, so they could honeymoon over the weekend. A wedding breakfast would follow at the King's Head Inn. They had six weeks to plan the wedding, and Anna was in her element organizing everything and everyone, except Isabelle, who had her own ideas—mother and daughter clashed on several occasions.

The next day Isabelle arrived at the King's Head and joined her mother and aunt for more wedding planning. She came to an abrupt halt as she entered the room and stared at a white satin gown hanging from the picture rail.

Lou smiled. "Isabelle, I would like you to have my wedding gown." There was silence and Isabelle's face looked like thunder as she glared at Anna.

"Is this your doing? Papa said I could have the new dress from Draper's, if they agreed to give me a discount."

"Isabelle, please! We don't have enough money. Papa wants the best for you, we all do, but even he thinks the dress is too extravagant." Anna couldn't help remembering how she had pleaded with her father for the big blue hat. Her heart went out to her daughter, knowing what it felt like to want something so badly.

"It's not fair." Isabelle stamped her feet shouting, "You always make Papa do what you want to do. You don't care about me. I'm going home to Little Gran."

Anna jumped in her chair as the door slammed. Feeling the warm tears prickling her eyes, she looked at Lou, expecting a lecture but Lou's expression was kind and sympathetic.

"Anna, I'm sorry. She'll come 'round. Wedding nerves, I expect. Mum will talk to her. I can see how Alex has spoiled her. I am glad I have boys. I think girls are too emotional."

Rubbing her face with the back of her hand, Anna gave a brief laugh and said, "I think you're right about that. Thank you, Lou. Sometimes I feel like a failure where Isabelle is concerned. Let's talk about the wedding. Bill already has the meal planned and Florence and Wilfred are going to try to get travel coupons. Charlie wrote that it is too dangerous crossing the Atlantic so he and Beth won't make it. The Wexfords are coming with Sandy's brother, the best man. The rest of their family is scattered and travelling is so difficult that I don't think anyone else can make it. I think with the bridesmaid and a couple of friends that makes fifteen of us. The church is booked for eleven o'clock."

Grateful for the rain, which meant low cloud cover, reducing the risk of daytime air raids, the wedding went off without a hitch. Little Gran had altered Lou's wedding dress and added lace and pearls. The girls at Draper's had given Isabelle a veil and Bill managed to talk his greengrocer into finding flowers for a bouquet. Isabelle looked radiant walking down the aisle. Anna and Alex held hands, looking almost as radiant. The wedding breakfast was a feast, thanks to Bill's culinary skills: a roasted capon with all the trimmings, a gift from Robert and Lou's farm and a wedding cake made by Little Gran from ingredients her friends and neighbours had generously contributed from their meagre rations. Alex had acquired champagne for the toast, and even the rain stopped while they took pictures before the bride and groom changed for the train journey to the Lake District.

The wedding guests had all gone except for the Wexfords, who were staying overnight on Anna's invitation to give them an opportunity to get to know their daughter's in-laws.

Alex opened the pub at five o'clock and treated the locals to a round on the house to celebrate Isabelle's wedding. The Wexfords went to their room to rest and Anna joined Alex in the bar—the offer of a free drink filled the bar quickly. Once everyone was served, Anna went to the dining room to thank Bill, a valid reason to see him, but not the only reason.

As wonderful as the day had been, Anna's emotions stirred as she looked into the past and thought of her own choices. It had nothing to do with happiness. She was not unhappy. Watching Isabelle and Sandy walk out of the church, she saw a woman in love. Happy and content, Isabelle had completely surrendered her love to Sandy. Anna loved Alex, but she had never been able to surrender so completely to him. She knew Bill would understand.

The restaurant was empty of diners, who were all currently drinking their celebratory drink in the bar. Bill poured two glasses of champagne. "Congratulations to the beautiful mother of the bride."

"Thank you, and thank you for making the day so special. The food was delicious. I don't know how you do it with all the shortages." They clinked glasses. Neither moved nor spoke. Anna felt quite giddy. She wanted the moment to go on forever.

Bill broke the gaze. "I had help from many generous people."

"Bill...do you ever have regrets about choices you made in the past?"

"I think everyone does, but yes, if I had my time over again there are some things I would do differently. But I am grateful for the life I have. Regrets can be dangerous, Anna."

"At times today," she said, giving a little cough before continuing, "Isabelle's wedding took me back to events surrounding my own wedding and I realized I do have regrets."

"Don't, Anna. There are things you don't know about me and what we—you, Alex and me—have now is as good as it will ever get."

Anna raised her glass. "To sagacious Bill and the best chef in England!" She kissed him on the cheek knowing that the unspoken words had said more than those spoken. The familiar wail of the air raid sirens ended her thoughts as she went to find the Wexfords.

The warden appeared at the doorway. "It looks real bad, take shelter now," he shouted. "Alex 'ow many can y'ur take in y'ur cellars?"

"About fifteen,"

"Ok, the rest of y'ur come with me."

The cellar trembled but there was only one notable explosion. The rest of the time they felt a continual rumble through the earth, with an eerie quietness above. Fear and anticipation hung in the air. Faces that had been laughing only a while ago were grave and puzzled. Anna watched Alex carefully, knowing that the memories from the previous war sometimes caused an extreme reaction in air raids. But looking after his guests tonight he seemed to be coping. She made tea, knowing a good cuppa helped to calm the nerves. The all-clear sounded as dawn broke. Alex emerged into the bar and opened the front door. Everything looked fine until he saw bright orange light on the horizon stretching in both directions.

"Oh my God! Coventry is on fire."

That night the Luftwaffe had blitzed many cities, the worst being Coventry. The Wexford's store and flat were badly damaged and had they been home they would surely have been killed. Because the bombing had been relentless, many of the AFS firemen were wiped out. Sandy might not have survived had he been on duty. Anna wondered what divine intervention had selected November 14th for the wedding, which had undoubtedly saved lives in her extended family. Residents of Coventry had not been so lucky.

Hitler continued to bomb the cities. London worse than anywhere, but the industrial Midlands had its share. After Coventry was flattened, there were fewer air raids and Rugby was lulled into an uneasy calmness. This strange calmness induced Anna into a familiar, sinister darkness, a premonition she could not shake off. Repercussions of war would take their toll.

Thirty-One

Christmas 1944 and Heartbreak

◈◈◈

Scrubbing the bathrooms, a chore Anna hated, was cathartic; it allowed her to scrub at her internal thoughts. Thoughts she could not verbalize as she worried, watching Alex constantly cover-up an illness that was considerably more than a cough. She scrubbed the last washbasin, cursing at the mess to distract her thoughts, wondering why people forgot their manners when they were away from home. But as she stood back and admired the last sparkling clean bathroom, she had a surprising sense of satisfaction.

Grabbing the Hoover, she mindlessly moved it to and fro on the hallway carpet. Numbness filtered through her mind and body, a kind of protection. She feared the feelings of failure and disappointment as her life and Alex's life slipped further apart.

A constant state of inertia allowed her to manage day to day living. Everyone was tired. Tired of the war, which seemed to be endless, in spite of the recent Allied success in France. Anna was tired of worrying and not knowing.

Alex's tall frame looked like a beanpole. His skin was grey and even his red curls were lank and dull. His cough and nightmares kept them up most nights. The King's Head, thankfully, continued to provide a living for them. The locals drank beer and the Rugby School parents still booked rooms.

Bill worked miracles with the rationing and shortages, upholding the Emily Carr's reputation for excellent cuisine. How he managed to produce a decent meal for five shillings (the forced government price), and make a small profit, was a miracle to Anna. At least she didn't have to cook. But, she pondered, cooking was perhaps the one domestic chore she did enjoy. She sighed, content that the guest rooms were ready for the Michaelmas term of visiting parents. She tried to be grateful that they still had a roof over their heads.

As she approached the bottom of the stairs, she heard a little voice, "Nana." One wartime blessing was the birth of her granddaughter, Sarah Anne, who was now two-years-old—the one joy in her life that brought smiles and sometimes a tear, but always of happiness.

"Sarah, come give Nana a kiss." Sarah's chubby little legs ran to Anna, her white strap shoes clicking on the stone floor and her white socks bobbing up and down. White, always white. Anna never understood why Isabelle insisted on dressing her from top to toe in white. Anna lifted Sarah in her arms and hugged her, smothering her with kisses.

"Nana, too tight," Sarah pushed away and slid to the floor.

Alex appeared from the bar. "I thought I heard my baby princess." Sarah immediately jumped into Alex's arms and began chatting in her two-year-old language. Alex listened intently, with great interest but little understanding.

Isabelle huffed, glancing first at Anna and then Alex as he hugged Sarah. "I guess I don't count these days."

"Of course you do," Anna said giving her daughter a hug. She moved away before she could kiss her.

"Papa, how are you? You look pale."

Bouncing Sarah in his arms until she started giggling, Alex replied, "I am fine. The doc gave me some medicine for the cough. How is my other princess?" He spoke without even glancing at Isabelle.

"I am fine but it seems I have been replaced." Isabelle laughed a cold, joyless laugh.

Anna frowned. There it was again. She couldn't put her finger on it but there was an edge to Isabelle's voice. If she didn't know better, she would say that she sounded jealous of Sarah. She'd heard it before and it worried Anna. Isabelle had always been the centre of Alex's universe and now all his attention revolved around little Sarah. Anna had mentioned it to Alex but he was oblivious, saying Isabelle was an adult, and accusing Anna of imagining things.

Bill quietly sidled up to Isabelle. Squeezing her shoulders and kissing her cheek, he said, "Good morning, honey. I hope you are staying for lunch."

Anna glanced at Bill and realized that he had also seen what she had.

Isabelle swung around, all smiles. "Good morning, Uncle Bill. Yes, we'd love to stay for lunch."

"I want your opinion on my new pie. It's an adaptation of the Woolton Pie."

"Oh, isn't that the all-vegetable pie made at the Savoy Hotel in London? Vegetables!" Isabelle screwed up her nose. "Not my favourite food, Uncle Bill."

"I have changed the recipe. It's good. I promise even Sarah will like it." Turning to Anna, he added, "I made a spice cake pudding to follow."

Bill had changed Isabelle's mood, in spite of vegetable pie. Although it was delicious, vegetables were not in Isabelle's diet. Perhaps he caught her sweet tooth with the pudding.

Alex had excused himself from lunch, saying he wasn't hungry and he was needed in the bar. No one except Anna had noticed his grey complexion taking on a yellow tone and his cheeks flushed as he tried to eat. Anna was filled with dread as she heard him almost choking in the background, either from the food that wouldn't go down or his attempts to stifle his cough.

That afternoon, he lay on the bed feverish, his voice croaking or disappearing altogether. She thought he might have flu or laryngitis and called the doctor.

Anna analyzed every frown and expression on the doctor's face while he examined Alex. Dread almost overcame her as she waited for his response.

"Mr. Walker, I will give you a stronger cough medicine so you can get some rest, but I am concerned and would like another professional opinion." He glanced at Anna's worried face and smiled. "I'm sure it's nothing, but I would like you to go to the hospital tomorrow morning for tests."

A dark shadow engulfed Anna as she walked the doctor to the door and asked, "It's serious isn't it?"

"I won't know until after the tests but I suspect there is something more serious than a cough. Once we know, we can treat it accordingly." He smiled and touched her arm. "Try not to worry."

The new medicine soothed Alex's throat and eased his cough, subsequently giving them both a few good nights' sleep. A week later, Alex was feeling much better and in good spirits. He went to see the doctor for his test results. Anna tried to be optimistic but the black shadow persisted. She pleaded with Alex to let her go to the hospital with him but full of his usual bravado, Alex had insisted on going alone.

Anna often had strange premonitions. She rarely spoke of them and they scared her when they materialized. This premonition had been hovering on and off for years. She remembered the same sense of foreboding during the Great War and again when they lived in Canada. It never materialized into anything but neither did it go away. Whatever it was, it was big and would change their lives forever. Until today, she had brushed it aside as part of her own melancholy. Today, she thought differently.

When she saw Alex's waxen face strained with grief as he walked towards the pub door, her instinct told the premonition had materialized—Alex was dying. It took all of her strength not to scream at the top of her lungs... NO!

Pushing her grief deep inside her, she greeted him at the door and wrapped her arms around him, leading him to his comfortable chair in their private sitting room. She poured them both a brandy. Sipping brandy, they linked their free hands. Pain and fear emanated from Alex's dull green eyes and an animal-like sob caught in his throat.

"Anna... my darling, Anna...," he stopped, allowing the sorrow to trickle down his face. "I have cancer. I am dying."

Sitting on the arm of the chair, she gently moved his head and rested it against her heart, lightly kissing his hair. The soft curls brushed her cheek as she laid her head on his. She gulped to hold back her own hot, stinging tears.

"I know, my darling," she whispered, and together they wept.

Anna and Alex had not told a soul of the throat cancer diagnosis; it was something they needed to get used to before they could share. Anna surmised they were hoping for a miracle, some innovative treatment or even a misdiagnosis, enabling them to give some good news to the family before the bad, but there was no good news to give. Telling the family would be hard enough. Letters would be sent to Florence in Scotland and Jimmy in Canada. Anna would go visit Lou and Little Gran, who now lived with Lou and Robert. But how would they break the news to Isabelle? Astute and calm, Bill had guessed something was seriously wrong, so he was the first to be told and he quickly reached out to Alex, making it easy for him to confide in his best friend. He leaned on Bill for support, taking some of the pressure off Anna.

In most households, Sunday dinner was eaten at two in the afternoon after the pub closed. Before the war it would always be a roast of beef, pork, lamb or on special occasions a chicken, but since the war, Sunday dinner was whatever rations allowed, and it was rarely a roast.

Anna and Alex decided that a family dinner would be an appropriate time to break the news to Isabelle. Anna, with Bill's help, would cook and Isabelle, Sandy and little Sarah were invited for Sunday dinner. Bill scrounged a small roast of pork from the restaurant. Anna picked apples from the garden for applesauce and apple crumble, and she even saved crusts of bread all week to make sage and onion stuffing. They set the rarely used dining room table in their flat. They usually ate in the restaurant but today they needed privacy as they delivered the bad news.

At first the dinner had an almost festive feel to it, just the immediate family, lots of good food and much laughter. Suddenly, Isabelle looked at her father, frowned, and said, "Papa, you are not eating." She stopped and stared more intently. "Are you well, Papa? You look pale and tired?"

The chatter ceased and the table went into a time warp. Anna glanced at Alex whose complexion now matched the white table linen. He cleared his throat, which made him cough. Anna poured him a glass of water and sat beside him placing her hand on his.

"I have some bad news I am afraid." Anna squeezed his hand, smiled and nodded for him to continue. "It appears that my recurring sore throats and cough are not just the result of bronchitis. The doctor sent me for tests at the hospital and the results show that I have a cancerous growth somewhere in my throat. There's a fancy name for it, but I don't remember." Alex's voice began to fade; he gave a half smile and said, "The doctor said to expect more of this fading, raspy voice."

Isabelle had turned white and Anna was afraid she might faint. Sandy put his arm around her shoulder and Sarah, sensing something was wrong, tried to climb on her mother's knee, but Isabelle pushed her away. Sarah ran to Anna, her bottom lip quivering. She lifted her onto her knee without making a sound.

"Papa, what kind of treatment are you having? You are going to get better—right?"

"I don't know, Isabelle. There isn't much they can do to cure cancer. The doctor says there is an operation that cuts away the tumour, but it has lots of side effects and doesn't always work."

"You're going to have the operation, right Papa?" Isabelle stared at him. "And then you'll be better."

"I can't promise. The operation is very dangerous and even if I came through, I will never be able to speak again. Isabelle, this is one thing I can't make better. I can't fix this..." Alex's expression said the rest, pleading with his daughter to understand. His voice had gone. He whispered, "I'm sorry, Princess."

Sarah had buried her head in Anna's chest. She could feel the tiny body quietly sobbing. Anna shushed and tenderly stroked her back, her own throat tight, rocking her granddaughter as she watched her husband and daughter dissolve into uninhibited grief. Bill walked over to her and put his hand on Anna's shoulder. The kindness almost prompted her to lose control.

Alex stood up. Swaying slightly, he grasped the chair backs as he moved round the table to Isabelle. Smiling, he pulled his handkerchief from his pocket and dabbed her tears. "I haven't done that for a very long time," he said and sat down in the leather chair, and patted the arm for Isabelle to join him. Tears quietly ran down her cheeks. Anna handed Sarah over to Sandy and she and Bill cleared the table and began the kitchen clean up.

It was a sad little group that hugged and said goodbye late Sunday afternoon—it was the beginning of the end.

Anna's worst nightmare was unfolding before her. The darkness she had dismissed for all those years had materialized. At first it was a relief, then guilt. Was she wishing Alex harm or was it the relief of knowing at last? She searched for another premonition to tell her all would be well. He would have the operation. It would be successful and Alex would be cured or at the very least, it would buy him some time. She searched every corner of her intuition to confirm that Alex would be cured but all she found was a deep sense of loss and a chapter of her life closing.

Anna pleaded with him to have the operation to get rid of the tumour. She threw her intuition to the side—she wanted to believe Alex would get better. The doctors were skeptical. The surgeon had concerns that Alex was not strong enough to endure the operation. Complications were normal and if Alex survived the surgery, it was a certainty that he would never speak again. Alex refused to discuss his illness but he did make it quite clear that he could not live without his voice. He would not consent to the operation.

The stronger medicines eased his pain and almost eased his cough and Alex went into remission. His raspy voice became his signature. He worked the bar every day, joking and teasing with the locals. Convinced that her father had turned a corner and was getting better, Isabelle didn't see what

Anna saw. His clothes hung over a skeleton of a man. His grey pallor had become translucent and, by Christmas, it was obvious his energy was all but depleted. At ten o'clock he called "last call" and crawled out of the bar, barely managing to get to his bed, leaving Anna and Bill to close up.

Lou had planned a family Christmas. Nobody wanted to say it outright, but all knew it would be Alex's last. Robbie had been granted leave and was expected Christmas Eve, but Peter, now an army officer in the Middle East, had no chance of coming home. Anna hired a couple from Rugby to serve in the pub over Christmas. Alex did not have the strength to both work and enjoy celebrating Christmas at Lou's.

Lou, still responsible for the farm deliveries, finished her route as usual at The King's Head on Christmas Eve. Anna, offering to help with the festive preparations, hitched a ride with Lou to the farm. As Lou drove the van into the farmyard, Robert rushed out of the house and stopped, staring at Lou as though his feet were stuck to the ground.

"Robert!" Lou called. "What's wrong?"

He held his hand out, a small buff envelope clutched between his forefinger and thumb. The colour drained from Lou's face and Anna grabbed her arm to steady her.

"NO! Not a telegram."

"Robbie is missing in action!" Sensitivity was not one of Robert's strong points.

Lou crumpled into Anna's arms. Simon came out of the barn and guided his mother into the house. Anna made some strong, sweet tea. Robert poured brandy into his and gulped it down without saying a word and went out to the barn. Simon sat with his mother on the sofa, staring into nothing. Not a word was spoken. Anna felt as if she'd been punched in the stomach. She wasn't sure how much more grief she could take. Without warning, Lou leapt off the sofa, wiped her eyes and blew her nose.

"Missing. That's what it said, missing. Anna, they told you Alex was missing but he came home. I know Robbie is still alive. Mothers know these things."

Lou went into the kitchen and began scrubbing potatoes as though her life depended on it, and at that moment, Anna thought, it probably did.

"Lou, what are you doing?"

"Getting dinner ready, we've a lot of people coming tonight and tomorrow."

"Are you sure you want to go ahead? Everyone would understand if you cancelled." Anna put her arms around Lou. "I did the same, keeping busy seemed to help. Robbie will be home, just like Alex."

In a few short hours, Lou's face had withered into an old crone's. Her brow creased into deep furrows and her eyes were cold and lifeless. She clung to Anna, the only person who understood.

"I have to keep going, Anna. I have to believe he's going to come through that door any minute." She yanked an apron off the back of the door and threw it to Anna, only just missing Little Gran who had quietly entered the kitchen. Ignoring her mother, she continued, "We have a meal to get ready."

"Hello, Mother," Anna's heart missed a beat upon seeing her mother's flushed face. Her blood pressure had spiked.

"Mother, I am sorry. Such worries you should not have to bear at your age." Holding her hands, she pulled her towards her and gave her a kiss.

"I'll be fine. I'm here for you both. It's all so sad. How is Alex?"

"He's doing well, still working in the bar. He's a fighter. It's important that he keeps busy, too busy."

Still sitting on the sofa, bewildered and obviously upset, Simon appealed to Anna. "Aunt Anna, what shall I do?"

"Go help your father," Lou shouted from the kitchen. "We need to get the animals settled early today. No point moping around. There's work to be done."

Simon hesitated and Anna caught him wiping his wet face. She felt sorry for him. All he wanted to do was weep for his brother. She went over to him and gently brushed her hand across his cheek and squeezed his shoulders. "It's going to be okay, Simon. Best do as your mum says."

Lou talked with a cheery voice all through dinner, laughing a harsh, haunting laugh at jokes that were not really jokes. Robert grunted and told Lou to shut up on several occasions. Little Gran took deep breaths, placing her hand over her heart. Anna wasn't sure if it was an emotional reflex or she had angina. Isabelle came to her rescue and calmed Little Gran.

Alex, Bill and Sandy rallied round Robert, and after dinner the men went into the sitting room to smoke cigars and talk man talk while the women cleaned up in the kitchen. Less than festive, the evening finished early. Isabelle and Sandy departed first with an excited Sarah, not understanding the prevailing sadness. Sarah's only interest was in Santa Claus and the promise of a doll that could walk.

Anna once again suggested that they cancel until they had good news of Robbie's whereabouts. Lou screamed at Anna, "Christmas will go ahead as planned! The opening of the presents will be at nine in the morning." Without another word, Lou ascended the stairs and retired for the night.

Christmas morning was not much better. Coffee and brandy was served as they opened boxes, pulled ribbons from presents with subdued 'thank yous' and forced smiles. No one was comfortable being joyous under such a dark cloud, knowing it might get darker at any moment. The brandy played its part and relaxed the tension somewhat until it became obvious that Robert had drunk more brandy than coffee. Lou's anxiety level heightened as she watched her husband become more aggressive and throw insults in the guise of teasing.

"Robert, dear, I think you should ease off the brandy. It's only eleven in the morning and we have a long..." Lou stopped as Robert's hand flew towards her face, missing her by a fraction.

"Shut up, woman!"

Lou tried to laugh. Simon stood by her side, protecting her, as Anna suspected he had done many times before. The room fell into silence. It was then that Anna saw the pain, not only of her fear for Robbie's mortality but fear of an abusive, drunken husband. She had glimpsed it before but Lou covered it well and Anna hadn't taken it seriously.

Anna caught Alex's attention. He looked exhausted, his pallor an unhealthy greyish yellow. He took her hand and squeezed it, taking a raspy guttural breath he said, "Robert is breaking down. I'll get Bill to help me take him for a walk. The cool air might sober him up." Anna smiled her thanks, knowing that if she spoke she would lose control, and both Alex and Lou needed her to stay strong. At the first signs of Robert's aggression, Isabelle had sensibly taken Sarah for a nap, as though she knew what was coming.

Alex tried to talk sense into Robert's drunken head while Sandy and Bill coaxed him towards the door without success, and finally with great difficulty, they carried this big hulk of a man into the farmyard. If the situation had not been so serious, Anna would have found the scene quite comical.

"Mum, did you know about this?" Anna asked.

Lou glanced at her mother and then Anna. "I told Mum not to say anything. It doesn't happen often. Only when he's upset. And he's worried about Robbie." At the sound of Robbie's name, the floodgates opened and Lou cried and cried. Anna tried to comfort her but it was no use.

"Let her cry. She needs to cry," Little Gran said. "Anna, help me get her on the sofa." Anna covered her with a blanket. Little Gran sat next to her until her sobbing exhausted her and she fell asleep, leaving Anna and Little Gran to prepare what would be the most joyless Christmas dinner she had ever experienced.

Anna's heart was heavy with guilt when she refused to join the family for New Year. She had been cheated out of a memorable Christmas with Alex and desperately wanted a pleasant memory of the season. She couldn't face Lou and Robert's sadness as they worried about their son. The King's Head Inn would be busy, but Sandy and Isabelle offered to serve in the bar. Sarah would stay overnight, with the added bonus of giving Sandy and Isabelle a night and morning to themselves. Anna planned a Hogmanay dinner with haggis, Alex's favourite meal, prepared by Bill. She set the dining room table for two with candles and the best glass and china.

Alex sat down with a twinkle in his eye. He said, "This is so romantic. I do love you, Anna." He began to serve the haggis. "Not your favourite?"

"No, but it is yours. Can you manage to eat?"

Alex cut it into tiny pieces. "I am savouring every morsel and it tastes wonderful. Thank you."

She watched him swallow with care, eating more than she had seen in a long time. After dinner they moved to the sofa. Alex poked the fire into action and they curled up together, sipping Scotch and waiting for the countdown. Anna rested her head on his chest, listening to his laboured breaths.

"Alex, are you feeling all right? Your chest sounds worse."

"I know. It is getting harder to breathe. Anna, I don't think I have too much longer."

"Alex, please don't say that. Not tonight."

"There is something I have to say to you while I still have some voice." He brushed a curl from her forehead. "I always loved your curls." He kissed her forehead. "And the way you frown when you're mad with me. I fell in love with you that very first day Bill introduced me to you as 'his girl' at The Sackville. I tried hard not to love you. I'm sorry I tricked you on the beach that day but I was afraid you would marry Bill."

"You were right to be afraid because I almost did marry Bill."

"You are in love with Bill. I know. In fact, I've always known."

Anna's cheeks flushed with so much heat she felt moisture trickle down her back. Alex continued, "It's okay." He pulled her towards him. "It's a good thing. I also know that Bill loves you even more than I do if that's possible. Bill never married because he only ever loved one woman, and that woman is you. And if I am honest, he would have made a much better husband than I did."

"Alex, don't talk like that. We have loved each other for thirty years and we have a daughter, the apple of your eye, and the source of some jealousy on my part," she teased.

"We've had a good life together. I'm sorry for some of the things I've done or didn't do, but now I am moving on and so must you."

Anna opened her mouth to object but Alex clasped his hands around her head and kissed her with a passion she had not felt in years. He broke away, gasping, and took a sip of brandy, gulping air so he could continue.

Anna could barely make out his raspy words. "Anna, I want you to marry Bill. I don't want you to be an unhappy widow. Bill will treat you well. He'll provide for you. You can read books together. I never was a reader." He laughed and winced in pain.

"Alex, I don't know if I want to marry again and Bill might not want to marry me. This is so strange and I can't believe what we're saying." She felt so sad but she didn't want to cry for Alex's sake.

"Believe me, Anna, Bill has waited thirty years. He wants you."

They stayed in each other's arms, content and still until Alex's breath became steady. The clock on the mantelpiece ticked rhythmically as they counted down to midnight. They clinked glasses, toasting 1945 with fine Scotch whiskey. Toasting a New Year when she knew Alex would be gone before the year was out.

"Remember me on New Year's Eve and toast me with a fine Scotch whiskey. The rest of the year, have fun and forget me."

The mood was suddenly broken by a raucousness coming from the Maple Bar, and the sitting room door flung open and Lou burst in.

"Lou, what is going on? What are you doing here?"

"It's Robbie."

Anna's heart sank. *Oh no,* she thought, *is Robbie truly dead?* It must have shown on her face.

"No Sis, he's not dead. He's come home!"

Thirty-Two

Life and Death

"Aunt Anna, Uncle Alex, it's good to see you." Robbie stood behind Lou in the sitting room doorway.

"Not nearly as good as it is to see you, lad." Alex stood up and shook Robbie's hand and patted him on the back. Robbie winced.

"Are you hurt?" Anna looked at Lou.

"It's nothing. Shot down over the English Channel, only ten miles off the Sussex coast. A couple of Jerries caught us by surprise." He lifted his cane, pointed to his leg. "A bad parachute landing, banged up my ankle and broke some ribs. I made it, the others didn't... I lost a couple of... crr... um, good mates in the English Channel. That's why I was reported missing. Nobody realized that my plane had reached land. It took a few days to get help and then word to the squadron. Sorry, it must have given everyone a terrible fright, over Christmas and all that."

"No need to apologize. We are happy you're safe," Anna said, feeling one burden lift from her shoulders. Suddenly the tension of the last week drained out of her, leaving her exhausted. She and Alex excused themselves and retired to their room, leaving the family to celebrate.

Robbie recovered from his injuries and returned to his squadron at the beginning of March. Lou worried about him constantly, and the fuse leading to Robert's temper and outbursts was getting shorter. Anna couldn't help Lou. She had her hands full and Lou would have to cope on her own.

As weak as Alex was, he insisted on serving in the bar. His voice barely a whisper, he still laughed and joked with the locals. Bill picked up the slack where needed—best friends once again. Isabelle, still in denial, talked about the things they would do when Alex got better. It was her way of coping. It pleased Anna to see how Bill gave Isabelle strength and comfort. Deep down, Anna knew that Isabelle was only trying to delay the inevitable.

By the middle of March, Alex could no longer get out of bed. He had wasted away to a mere shadow. The doctor visited twice a day to give him a shot of morphine. He could no longer speak or eat and Anna found herself wishing the Lord would take him. His suffering was too much. She and Isabelle kept vigil at his side day and night. One morning Anna woke with the sun in her eyes. She had fallen asleep in the chair at his bedside and he was talking to her.

"Anna," he whispered. "Bill. Fetch Bill." Anna frowned. He hadn't spoken in weeks and, although his voice was weak and raspy, she could hear him. Her heart skipped a beat and for a brief second her foggy mind wanted to believe there had been a miracle. She ran to find Bill.

Bill sat on the side of the bed and Alex slowly moved his arm to hold Bill's hand and gestured to Anna to move closer and place her hand on theirs.

"Bill… I have always known… how much… you love Anna…" Alex gasped, tears on his cheeks. "Please take care of her… I want you to marry…." His mouth slowly curved into a smile. "And read to her… books…" He gasped and a sinister rattle came from his chest. "Isabelle."

Bill nodded and squeezed Alex's hand. "Shush, you must rest. I promise I will take care of Anna. Isabelle is sleeping. I'll fetch her."

Anna bent over Alex and kissed him for the last time. "I love you." Their tears, no longer restrained, spilled silently.

Isabelle came running into the room. "Papa! I love you. Please don't leave me." She lay on the bed next to him, sobbing, her arms clinging to him.

"Princess... love you... Isabelle..." His energy spent, he closed his eyes, drifting into sleep.

Alex never woke up.

The funeral was intended to be a quiet family affair. Florence and Wilfred arrived from Scotland. Florence had picked a bunch of purple heather off the moors and asked Anna if she would mind if they put the heather on his coffin. Delighted, Anna couldn't think of anything Alex would like more than heather from his beloved Scottish moorlands. Jim and Abigail couldn't get a passage in time. Beth wrote to say Charlie was on a mission and couldn't be reached.

Anna couldn't believe how many people attended the church service, standing room only at the back and sides of the church and mourners overflowed outside. The vicar left the doors open so they could hear the service. The cards and letters kept coming from all over Scotland, England and Canada. Mrs. Banks, now retired and living in Hastings, sent a lovely letter that flooded Anna with memories. James Lytton sent his condolences from The Sackville.

The biggest surprise, a wreath, made up of rare and practically unobtainable calla lilies, arrived on the morning of the funeral from Lord and Lady Thornton. Anna struggled with emotion as her fingers traced the familiar crest on the card, remembering the many such cards she had typed for old Lady Thornton. She read, *Our deepest sympathies. My mother would have wanted to remember you at this sad time. Darcy and Belle Thornton.* How she would have liked to have Lady Thornton's advice at this crossroads in her life. She remembered her dream of Lady Thornton embracing her baby son as he entered heaven. Anna prayed that Alex would be united with Baby John.

Bill took over running the King's Head Inn, which he had been doing for the last few months with Anna, but now she allowed him to take over completely. She had no heart for the pub. Every time she walked into the bar she expected to see Alex pulling pints.

Devastated by her father's death, Isabelle could barely function and fate was about to hand her yet another blow. Less than a week after her father's funeral, Sandy received the letter 'On His Majesty's Service.' He had been called up for military service and was to report for army officers training in Aldershot. So distraught by this news, Isabelle fell apart; crying, screaming and throwing things in a child-like temper tantrum.

Shocked, Anna watched her pick up a china vase and throw it to the floor. It shattered into tiny pieces. Afraid her daughter was losing her mind and terrified for Sarah's safety, Anna called the doctor. Isabelle had to be sedated but the doctor assured Anna she would be fine in a few days. Anna stayed with her and looked after a frightened little Sarah who couldn't understand what had happened to Mummy or where Grandpa had gone. Confused and tearful, she watched Daddy pack a bag and, in his captain's uniform, get into a taxi and drive away. Although she would never wish such tragic circumstances on anyone, in some ways it was a blessing for Anna to have something to occupy her mind while she mourned Alex. *But, she wondered, when does it all end?*

Florence and Wilfred had stayed on at the King's Head Inn after the funeral, offering whatever help they could give. Isabelle and Uncle Wilfred had been close back in Canada when she was a little girl. The magic rekindled and Uncle Wilfred sat with her and talked to her until her grief tumbled out in floods of tears. He comforted her until she became calm and rational, discarding the sedatives. Still sad and grieving, Isabelle began to live her life again.

Bill had quietly faded into the background. The people he loved the most, Anna and Isabelle, were so caught up in their own grief they had abandoned him, leaving him to pick up the pieces and mourn alone. Florence, concerned for Bill, suggested Anna return home to the King's Head. Bill needed her, not just to help with the guests but he needed to mourn his friend. Anna insisted she could not leave Isabelle and Sarah.

Knowing her words had fallen on deaf ears, Florence asked Wilfred to talk to Anna.

After a month of April showers, spring had burst forth with flowers and singing birds and today the sun felt warm. Wilfred knocked on Isabelle's front door.

Anna opened the door. "Wilfred, what a pleasant surprise. Come in. Isabelle has gone shopping with a friend. Thanks to you, she is venturing out."

"Actually, I came to talk to you, Anna."

"Oh, why me?" Anna knew the answer and was grateful when she heard Sarah running down the hallway.

"Uncle, pick up." Wilfred picked her up and hugged her but he was not going to be dismissed that easily.

"It is a beautiful day. Let's take Sarah for a walk in the park."

Sarah wriggled out of his arms and sat in her pushchair. With a determined look on her face, she bent her head cutely to one side and said, "Go, push."

Wilfred laughed and looked at Anna. "How can you resist those pretty hazel eyes?"

"All right, I'll fetch her coat."

Anna took a deep breath of fresh air and for the first time in a while she smiled. "I love spring, the fresh air, the song birds busy with their nests, and flowers. When did that happen? Daffodils and jonquils are in full bloom and the primroses sprouted overnight."

Wilfred smiled. "You've had other things on your mind and that is what I want to talk to you about."

"I know. Florence has talked to me, but I can't leave Isabelle. I'm not ready to go home." They walked in silence until they reached the park. Sarah had fallen asleep so they walked past the swings and sat on a bench under a lilac tree, surrounded by its sweet fragrance.

Anna stared at the lilac. "Purple. Alex's favourite colour. The colour of the moorland heather. Alex loved the Scottish moors."

"Florence and I walk along the moors almost every day." Wilfred placed his hand on her arm. "Anna, you'll always have fond memories of Alex, whether it's moorland heather or pulling pints in the bar. Some of those memories are raw at the moment, but running away won't take the pain away. I thought my life was over when my Lilly died. I loved her so much I thought the pain would never go away. I remember the day I saw you staring at our house on Forest Road. I had no hope. I thought my life was over. I planned to move into a small apartment and wait to die so I could join my Lilly. How things changed."

"I remember a sad, lonely old man standing on the doorstep, your cardigan buttoned up askew, apologizing to Lilly for showing me a messy house."

"Look at me now. Happily married to Florence in another country with a whole new family. My memories of Lilly are all there and I cherish them. I was lucky. I found love again with Florence and I am a happy man. Had you told me that the first day we met, I would have said you were crazy. Life goes on, Anna. Isabelle is well now. It is time for you to go home. Bill needs a friend and, in a practical sense, he needs your help in the pub. You have a business to run."

"There are things you don't understand. Promises were made and I don't know if they can be kept. I am afraid of finding out the truth. I am scared and confused."

Wilfred frowned. "What promises?"

Anna felt as though she had opened Pandora's box as the words poured out, describing to Wilfred Alex's deathbed wishes. She couldn't stop and surprised herself by telling him how it all started in Bexhill-on-Sea at The Sackville Hotel.

Wilfred listened intently. "I never quite believed the three of you were just friends, but you gave me no reason to think otherwise. Now I understand your dilemma but staying away from the King's Head will not solve the problem. Bill needs you, if as nothing more than a friend. Can you be his friend?"

"That's the problem. I don't know."

"Anna, for both your sakes, you have to try. Go home, face Alex's ghost and trust in Bill's friendship. Florence and I will stay with Isabelle and Sarah until we are sure she is well enough to cope on her own. Sandy will be home soon. Now that Hitler is dead, it is only a matter of time before this terrible war will be over."

Anna nodded in agreement but not quite ready to commit. "I'll think about it."

"That's all I ask." Wilfred pecked her on the cheek. "I know you can do it."

Two days later, Anna switched places with Wilfred and Florence, and the next day, May 7th, 1945, Germany surrendered unconditionally. The war was over, at least in Europe, and the following day was celebrated as VE Day.

The King's Head Inn exploded into massive celebrations, keeping Anna and Bill too busy to feel awkward. Needing help in both the Emily Carr Dining Room and the bars, they called in Isabelle, Florence and Wilfred to help. Anna relaxed as she saw her family pull together. They were going to be okay. The final piece of good news was that Sandy's extensive service in the civil defense meant his experience was needed to clean up and rebuild at home—he would not be sent to fight in the Pacific—much to Isabelle's relief.

Wilfred, knowing Anna and Bill's secret, wanted to give them time alone, to adjust to their new lives and consider their future. He invited Isabelle and Sarah to return to Scotland with them for a holiday. Florence thought it a wonderful idea, giving Isabelle a chance to experience her father's love of the Scottish moorlands. Isabelle declined at first, afraid that Sandy would come home to an empty house. Sandy wrote to say leave was unlikely and a holiday would do her good. He promised to write, explaining that he could just as easily post his letters to Edinburgh as to Rugby. Sandy's letter and Florence's description of walking on the Scottish moors in her father's footsteps was enough to persuade her that she was doing the right thing.

Sarah bounced up and down with excitement as they stood on the platform waiting for their luggage to be loaded on the train. Wilfred herded his little extended family into the compartment. Anna saw delight in his face. His own children were in Canada and Anna realized how much he missed them.

The guard blew his whistle, the train let out a blast of steam and slowly pulled out of the station. Anna and Bill stood together waving goodbye until the caboose was a tiny black dot. They drove home in silence.

Anna wondered what Bill was thinking. He had not mentioned Alex's death or his promise. In fact, she thought, he had grown distant, retreating into himself. Perhaps he regretted his promise. She brushed that thought out of her mind. He was still in mourning as was she. It had only been two months since Alex had died. Anna could not deny there were days when butterflies fluttered in her stomach thinking of a future with Bill, but the feeling was tempered with guilt and disloyalty to Alex. They both needed time. Wilfred was right; friendship was a good place to start.

The revelry went on through most of the summer with an enormous boost in August when Japan, finally brought to its knees by the atomic bomb, surrendered. The world had never seen such devastation before.

The King's Head Inn grew in popularity under Anna and Bill's synchronous partnership, in spite of the even tighter rationing and shortages in post-war Britain. The munitions factories closed, the soldiers returned home and people started to look for civilian work. Anna had a queue of anxious women looking for a job at the King's Head and she immediately hired two maids. Bill hired a barman and a gardener to replace Alex's duties and an assistant chef to lighten his load. Their futures should have been promising, and it seemed to be for Bill, but not for Anna.

Bill had shown not the slightest interest in her, other than business. He seemed afraid to touch her or show any affection and he constantly appeared troubled; the deep furrows in his forehead had aged him ten years. And yet, occasionally, when he thought she was not paying attention, his face would soften and for a brief second she would see gentleness and love, but it was gone before she could turn her head.

It had been seven months since Alex's death. She didn't expect an immediate proposal. All she wanted was a sign that he still loved her, an acknowledgement of his intentions. Except for the times they discussed business, there was nothing. Nothing of the warm, caring Bill she once knew. She tried to get him to talk about the many books they had once enjoyed together. He brushed her off, sarcasm in his voice, saying he had no time to read. He appeared cold, unfeeling and a stranger. Who was this Bill Blaine?

Isabelle and Sarah returned from Scotland in October. Anna was delighted to have her granddaughter close by again. It helped to keep her mind off Bill. Isabelle had acquired a green thumb during the summer and, seeing her father's garden neglected, she worked with the gardener, digging and preparing the soil for the next growing season. Sarah wanted to help but Isabelle couldn't stand to see her daughter get dirty in the mud. Anna harnessed the opportunity to spend time with Sarah.

Anna's life gradually progressed into a normal, if different, one without Alex. The dramas had settled. It was nine months since Alex had died and Christmas was upon them. Anna expected painful memories to resurface but she found herself cosseting the happy memories. She was looking forward to the first toast to the 1946 New Year—a toast to Alex's memory. At ten minutes to midnight, Bill called, "drinks on the house" as he pulled pints, readying for the countdown.

Anna raised her glass, waiting for the stroke of midnight. "To Alex!"

"To Alex," the patrons roared in unison.

Smiling, Anna looked upwards and quietly said, "To Alex, I miss you. I'm okay. Bill is taking good care of me but I think we were mistaken about his feelings for me." Anna dropped her gaze. Feeling guilty, even with Alex's permission, for her thoughts of love, she quickly glanced towards Bill, hoping he had not overheard. Busy wishing everyone a Happy New Year while persuading the drunks there were no more free drinks, Bill had not heard a word.

Immersed in her own world of thought as she cleared the tables, Anna was startled when Bill suddenly started talking. "Anna, I think we should be taking advantage of the festive mood."

Wondering if Alex had spoken from on high, Anna took a moment to reply. "Um...festive mood? Sorry, I was miles away."

"Hey, what's going on? You look sad." Bill picked up the clean beer tankards and hung them over the bar.

Anna wiped down the already clean tables. "Oh, nothing. Just tired. Tell me more."

"What do you think about making a small dance floor in the dining room? Have you heard of the new Jitterbug dance from America?" Bill started hopping around the bar, gyrating in the strangest movements and grabbed Anna to join him. Anna laughed so hard her sides hurt. Neither she nor Bill had laughed like that since Alex's death.

"Where did you learn to dance like that?"

"Chicago clubs. Dances similar to the Jitterbug were all the rage twenty years ago. Chicago was a fun city without a conscience." He stopped talking. So many emotions flashed through his face, Anna couldn't make out any one in particular.

"You never talk about your time in Chicago."

Bill's expression had turned to ice. "No, some things are better left alone. I have some unfinished business in Chicago but it's too dangerous to return." He looked at Anna and there was no mistaking the intense emotion. Was it fear or maybe regret? It was something she could not quite put her finger on it.

Seeing Anna's concern, he responded immediately. "Nothing. It has nothing to do with you—it's my past."

Anna's intuition had kicked in and she was in no doubt that it had everything to do with her. Bill's past was affecting her future. She had opened a door and a tiny chink of Bill's past had squeezed through. But what was it?

"The Jitterbug would be fun. We could have Saturday night dances and maybe tea dances in the afternoon. I like the idea."

Bill yawned and checked the clock over the bar. "Two-thirty! Anna, it's time to call it a night."

"The fire is still going in the sitting room. Come join me in a nightcap." Desperate to know more, she wanted to keep him talking.

"I am beat. We can talk tomorrow." He switched the lights off in the bar, said, "Good night," and walked to his loft.

Anna poured herself a brandy and sat by the dwindling fire, missing Alex and reflecting on his courage and generosity for acknowledging her love for his best friend. Speaking aloud she said, "I think, at times, I judged you too harshly, Alex Walker. Underneath all that bravado was a kind man I didn't really get to know." A tear meandered down her cheek. "And now, it looks as though I have misjudged Bill. We both did." She pulled her cardigan around her tightly and stared at the dying embers, feeling the warmth of the brandy inside her. She should go to bed but she wouldn't sleep. Bill's words kept repeating in her head, 'I have some unfinished business in Chicago but it's too dangerous to return.' She recalled his odd behaviour the day she visited the Front Street Café and that same look of mixed emotions at the mention of Mrs. Castillo. The predominate emotion—fear. What frightened Bill so much?

The crackling of the fire woke her. She woke up shivering and realized it was morning and Bill was up and dressed. "It's cold."

"I just lit the fire. Drink this." Bill handed her a cup of steaming coffee. "Did you go to bed at all?"

"No, I must have fallen asleep here." Anna stretched. "I stayed up as I had too many things to think about." She stared at Bill, hoping for a reaction.

He avoided her stare. "A busy day ahead. How many guests do we have staying? Although I don't think they will be too early for breakfast today. However, we are fully booked for New Year's Day lunch."

Anna never found another opportunity to speak openly with Bill. He became a master at avoiding her for any conversation other than business. They built a dance floor and hired a trio for the Saturday night dance which became a popular local event. The word spread beyond Rugby, bringing people from Coventry, Warwick and as far away as Nottingham

407

and Derby, filling the inn's guest rooms. The Afternoon Tea Dances were a hit for local families on Sundays, and the local shop girls on Wednesday afternoons, their half-day.

Another year passed and Christmas brought snow and freezing temperature. As the winter dragged on and more snow came down, business began to flag as people stayed at home. The worst winter in decades caused power outages and brown outs and a severe coal shortage, keeping Britain shivering in the dark. Reminded of Canadian winters, Isabelle convinced Bill to build a skating rink on the snow-covered beer garden. Sarah learned to skate and other neighbourhood children joined her. Anna encouraged them to build igloos, snowmen and snow forts and the King's Head Inn became a winter playground.

Families came out in droves on the weekend. Bill made a hot, creamy cocoa drink, similar to the Canadian hot chocolate. The King's Head Inn, now famous for dancing, added Canadian Winter fun to its reputation.

By early March, the igloos melted to a few lumps of ice and the skating rink became a puddle of water. Exhausted after a long and successful winter, both Anna and Bill were happy to relax as the snow melted and their visitors departed. Rugby School had broken up for the Easter holiday and it would be two more weeks before the boys would start their summer term.

With more time on her hands, Anna agonized over whether or not to talk to Bill. She had spent the last two months trying to convince herself that she did not love him, but the more she tried the more she loved him. Although his behaviour of late indicated otherwise, she did believe he loved her and she was convinced the only explanation for his coldness had something to do with Chicago.

Thirty-Three

Broken Hearts

I t was time. Anna decided she would live with the consequences and confront Bill. The opportunity arose the next evening when Bill tapped on the sitting room door.

"Have you got a minute?" Bill asked Anna.

"Yes, come on in, take a seat." Anna gave him a quizzical look but seized the opportunity. "As a matter of fact, I wanted to talk to you." Anna's heart raced in her chest—this was the point of no return. Questions she had kept guarded for so long would be answered.

"Oh, what about?"

Taking a deep breath to buy some time Anna hesitated, not knowing where to start. She let the words tumble out. "Bill, it is two years since Alex died. We loved each other when he was alive and you made a promise to Alex and yet you keep me at arm's length. Now that we are free to show our love, you push me aside. The Bill who sits before me today is cold, unfeeling, someone I don't know anymore. If you don't love me, I need to hear you say it. Please let me get on with my life." She wondered where those last words had come from and if she truly meant what she was saying. How would she get on with her life without Bill?

Anna panicked when Bill did not respond. "Stay focused," she said under

409

her breath, giving a nervous cough she continued, "I'm tired of the secrecy. Something happened in Chicago that changed you and yet you refuse to talk about it. Be a mature adult, like the man I once knew, and face whatever it is you have to face." Anna heard the volume rising in her voice as anger began to surface.

Bill stared at her but didn't say a word. Angered by his silence she kept talking, "Can you not see how you are hurting me? I may not be young anymore but love and affection doesn't die with youth. It grows and matures but maturity seems to have escaped you. You never embrace me or even touch me. Your words are cold, static and all business, business, business. It's as though the personal connection was never there. You loved me once. I don't understand or know you anymore." Anna's words caught in her throat. Bill said nothing. "I can't believe I loved you all those years. Are you punishing me for making a mistake and marrying Alex instead of you?" She shook her head, raising her eyebrows in a sarcastic move, almost a smile but not quite. "Hah, now I see it. You couldn't say it back then. You gave up. You let Alex marry me because you couldn't bring yourself to fight for me. All you had to do was show me you cared and wanted to marry me. That was thirty years ago, so tell me, what is your excuse now?"

Bill remained silent. Anna sprang from her chair knocking over the footstool. She felt her cheeks flushing as she stomped towards the door, hoping the sharp movement would quell her quivering lips.

Bill grabbed her arm and stopped her. "I'm sorry, Anna. I'm sorry I didn't insist that you marry me all those years ago. I have lived with that regret for thirty years. I love you and always have loved you and I always will."

Hearing the words that she had longed to hear pushed her over the edge. The pent up sadness and anger cracked open and tears flowed silently from her heart. She calmed as Bill wrapped his arms around her. She felt safe and loved at last. He lifted her chin and kissed her.

"I have to go to London for a few days. Arthur will take care of the dining room. He's good. I trained him well so you don't need to worry about that."

Composing herself, Anna spoke carefully, "Why London?"

"I have business to attend to that requires I consult a particular London solicitor, and while I am there I am meeting an old friend. I'll be away for two or three days. If things take longer, it may be a week or more."

"Can I come with you? I would enjoy a break."

Bill's eyes darkened and his body stiffened. The tenderness was gone in a flash and he yelled, "No! I have some unfinished business to deal with. Stop asking questions." Seeing Anna's hurt face, he quickly said, "I'm sorry, Anna. I didn't mean to shout. Please understand this is something I have to deal with alone."

Never in the thirty years Anna had known Bill had she heard him speak that way. Too shocked to respond, she quietly said, "I'm going to bed," and left the room.

A car engine idling in front of the pub woke Anna before dawn the next morning. Her eyes stinging and swollen from crying, she stepped over to the window. A dark figure, Bill, looked up at her window, blew her a kiss and got into a taxi. Throwing herself back on the bed, she guessed he was heading to the station for the morning train to London.

She wished she had gone downstairs and kissed him goodbye or even gone to the window and waved goodbye. Was it a last goodbye? The words she had longed to hear were finally said last night, 'I love you.' So why the doubts? She believed him, and yet as he stood under her window, in the shadow of a breaking dawn, she had felt a persistent darkness—danger. Her questions were unanswered and the truth still a mystery. Her only hope was that his trip to London would resolve whatever needed to be.

Anna wasn't sure if Isabelle really enjoyed gardening or if it was something that reminded her of Alex, but there she was almost every day, poking around in the dirt. The work was hard after such a harsh winter. Planting had been late, but the warm May sunshine had dried the soil, encouraging the vegetables to grow. Anna kept Sarah out of the dirt

411

although, in her opinion, it would be good for the little girl to dig in the soil. But Isabelle would not allow her to get her clothes dirty.

"Uncle Bill should have a good selection of vegetables for the dining room this year." Isabelle frowned. "Where is Uncle Bill? I thought you said he would be gone a few days."

"He went to London to tend to some business. I thought he would be back by now. It must have taken longer than expected."

"Mum, what is it? You look worried." Isabelle didn't wait for an answer. "You know, I thought you and Uncle Bill would be married by now. Just in case you were wondering, you do have my blessing."

"That's nice of you but I don't think that will happen. Uncle Bill has changed. He said he'd be away a few days and it is over two weeks and not even a postcard."

Isabelle picked some primroses from the corner where she grew a few flowers. "I think I'll take some to Little Gran. She isn't feeling well. I'm heading up to the farm when I've finished this."

"What's wrong? Lou didn't say anything when she delivered the milk this morning."

"Oh, Mum, it's nothing. She has a bit of a cold."

"I'll come with you. I think we have enough petrol and it will save you and Sarah getting the bus."

The chickens scattered and Prince, the sheep dog, barked as Anna pulled the old Ford into the farmyard. Robert jumped down from the tractor, a cigarette hanging from his bottom lip. He yelled at Prince, "Shut-up, you mutt." Then he shouted towards the car. "Lou's finishing off the chickens."

"Hello Robert, can you tell Lou we're here?"

"Got too much work to do. She'll come when she's finished. Little Gran's in the kitchen."

Anna stepped out of the car and opened the rear door for Sarah, looking at Isabelle. "Charming as ever. He doesn't look well. His face is puffy and his eyes are bloodshot."

"He's been drinking, Mum. He keeps a flask in his overalls. Auntie Lou won't talk about it. She pretends it's not happening."

"I have suspected for a long time that things were not okay here, but Lou tells me everything is fine."

Isabelle shrugged her shoulders and shook her head. Obviously it wasn't fine, Anna thought, feeling ashamed. She had been so wrapped up in her own problems that she hadn't tried to reach out to Lou.

Sarah squealed as Little Gran opened the door. "Li'l Gran, do you have any sweets?"

Little Gran nodded. "You know where the tin is, by my chair. You can have two." She smiled. "Come in, what a lovely surprise. I'll put the kettle on."

"I'll do that Gran. You sit and talk to Mum."

Anna hugged her mother and they sat down. "Isabelle tells me you have a cold. How are you feeling?"

"I'm fine. Just a bit of a cough. I'm getting old, Anna." As though on cue she started coughing and Anna didn't like the sound of her rattling chest and her cheeks flushed brightly against her pasty skin.

"Mum, you need to see the doctor."

"I've been telling her that," Lou's voice answered. "Good to see you, Sis. What brings you to the farm?"

"Isabelle said she was coming to visit and I came for the ride." Anna lowered her voice. "Why won't Mum see the doctor?"

"I can hear you. There is nothing wrong with my hearing," Little Gran shouted over the shriek of the kettle whistling. "I don't want those doctors poking around me. But if the cough has not gone by the end of the week, Lou can telephone him. Will that satisfy you?"

"Yes Mum, but we will keep you to that promise. Now, let's have some tea."

Anna took Isabelle and Sarah home in time to make Sandy his dinner. Sandy had finished his National Service and had returned to working as an engineer. Isabelle had her family back. It was important that everything was just so and Isabelle's controlling ways sometimes worried Anna, especially for Sarah's sake. But this was yet another thing she could do nothing about. Driving back to The King's Head Inn, she couldn't help wondering what had happened to Bill. Why hadn't he telephoned or sent a letter? It annoyed her that he would be so insensitive but then she didn't expect much from Bill these days.

It would be another week before she received a letter from Bill and the contents did little to ease her worries, either for Bill or his return. If anything, it made matters worse.

Dearest Anna,

I am still in London. My business here is not settled. Please do not worry. It is taking longer than expected. I wish I could tell you how much longer. My friend Darcy Thornton has been of great assistance but so far the issue has not been resolved. It appears that I will be forced to take a journey overseas. I do not know if it can be resolved but I have to try. I will do everything I can to return in one piece.

If I have not returned by August 1st, please contact Darcy Thornton and he will direct you to my solicitor in London. I have entrusted the solicitor with some documents that will bring to light my strange behaviour and I hope you can forgive me. The documents also include my last will and testimony. I cannot say more for fear that I may put you in danger. The less you know, the safer you will be.

I have been staying at Darcy's London flat and he has a wonderful library, including our favourite author, Rudyard Kipling. I thought you might enjoy this poem from his poetry collection. We may be getting older but when I think of you I feel young again. Keep these words of Rudyard Kipling in your heart until I return.

Cross that rules the Southern Sky!
Stars that sweep, and wheel, and fly
Hear the Lovers' Litany:
"Love like ours can never die!"
Love always, Bill

Anna thought she would burst as the sensation of young love burned inside her. The poem took her back to the staff dining hall; sitting by the fire, gently moving in the rocking chair, Bill sitting next to her as they read. The old Bill was back and he loved her. She wanted to weep, or giggle like a schoolgirl.

Reading the letter a second time quickly changed the euphoria to fear as the magnitude and finality of his words registered. Now she wanted to scream. Questions, more questions; enigmatic questions and no answers, except his words told her that his life was in danger.

Her heart filled with dread. Could she lose him after waiting all these years? Could he die too like Alex, leaving her alone? Closing her eyes, she could see and feel the shards of shattering dreams, tiny jagged pieces of once brilliant crystal dreams scattered into oblivion. In that moment she realized that Bill was her dream, her dream of love, of adventure and success and, without him, she had nothing.

The familiar sense of foreboding once again nestled in the pit of her stomach. She jumped when the telephone rang. She greeted the postman every day with a mixture of hope and dread, followed by disappointment. She had to do something.

Curious about the connection with Darcy Thornton and Bill's reference to him as the friend who was helping him, Anna decided to contact Lord Thornton for some answers. She had written to him thanking him for the flowers at Alex's funeral and had kept the Hillcrest Estate address. She assumed letters would be forwarded to London. When no reply arrived, Anna telephoned.

A rather old and proper voice answered the phone, "Hillcrest Estate, Gordon the butler speaking."

Anna was informed that Lord Thornton was not in residence. He and Lady Thornton were travelling. The letter had been received at Hillcrest but Lord Thornton had not received it and was not likely to until his return in September. Anna left a message with her telephone number, with little hope of hearing back.

Frantic to find Bill, Anna started sending letters and telephoning London solicitors, none of whom would admit to knowing either Bill or Lord Thornton, citing confidentiality. Every unproductive call took Anna one step further into despair, losing sight of all else. She had taken her mind off the business, assuming the King's Head Inn could take care of itself.

The first sign of trouble came when Miss Mosedale, the local gossip, told Anna that her chef, Arthur, had been seen delivering packages in the neighbourhood. Giving Anna a you-know-what-I-mean look, tapping the side of her nose.

Anna didn't know what she meant but spoke to Arthur who explained that he picked up groceries for his sick aunt. Anna dismissed the incident as gossip. That same day Isabelle called her to say that the doctor had been to see Little Gran and she had a lung infection. Anna looked at the petrol gauge on the car and hoped she had enough to get to the farm and back. Rationing was getting to her with all the other things she had to deal with.

An anxious Isabelle greeted Anna. Little Gran lay in bed, pale and still. She had trouble breathing. The sound brought memories of Alex flooding back.

Anna held her mother's hand. "How are you feeling?"

"You worry too much, Lou."

Anna frowned. "Mum, it's Anna. Lou is on her milk round."

"What's she doing on a milk round? And where is Charlie?" The glassiness in her mother's eyes told Anna she was in another place and time. *Fever,* Anna thought.

Relieved to hear the van pull into the yard, Anna said, "Here's Lou now. I'll send her up in a minute. I want to talk to her. Isabelle will sit with you."

Lou's first words were, "What did the doctor say?"

"She has an infection. Lou, she didn't recognize me and she was asking for Charlie."

"I mentioned she seemed confused when I called the doctor's surgery. The nurse said it would be the fever."

Lou put her arms around Anna. "I knew I should have called the doctor earlier but you know what she is like."

Lou sat at the kitchen table. "This may not be the right time, but there is something I have to tell you. There is gossip going around that Arthur is selling on the black market."

"Black market?" Anna sighed. "Miss Mosedale and her wagging tongue. Arthur is helping his sick aunt."

"Arthur doesn't have a sick aunt. While I was collecting the week's milk money, Mrs. Jones and Mrs. Cotter told me Arthur tried to sell them beef and butter. Anna, I think he's stealing from you. Have you noticed anything odd in your invoices or the meals he's cooking? I didn't want to say anything but word has it that since Bill went away the food has gone downhill at the King's Head. I didn't take much notice, thinking Bill would put it right when he returned but he's been away a long time."

"What should I do? I need Arthur and I'm not sure Bill is coming back. I think he's in some kind of trouble, something to do with his past." Anna told Lou about the letter and how she was trying to find him.

"Why didn't you tell me before? He'll be back. Good old solid Bill. He wouldn't do anything to hurt you. I wouldn't worry about Bill but you do need to worry about the pub."

"I'll go and talk to Arthur now, while he is preparing lunch. Let me know how Mother is doing?"

Driving home, constantly glancing at the petrol gauge, she practiced what she would say to Arthur. *I can't fire him. I need him. I know, I will threaten to report him to the authorities. The penalties for selling on the black market are severe. That should stop him and buy me time to find another chef.*

Arthur denied everything but, although it would be difficult to prove, the invoices did show discrepancies. Knowing he was being watched curtailed his activities, but the cooking didn't improve. His explanation was that the work was too much. Anna started helping with the dinner and soon realized the food had declined to the level of a bad greasy spoon.

Discussing the menu with Arthur, they decided to simplify the dishes, and although the food was not at Bill's standard, the meals were wholesome and tasty and, with Anna's touch, the presentation made it look appetizing. She decided to suspend the afternoon tea dances and limit the menu for the Saturday night dances until Bill returned. She sighed with relief, content that she had things under control.

The Rugby parents arrived to pick up their sons for the summer holidays and, without notice, the housekeeper quit, leaving Anna to clean the guest rooms in the mornings and work in the kitchen afternoons and evenings. Isabelle's time was taken up looking after Little Gran. Anna was alone again. Desperate, she tried to find Bill, but nothing. It was as though he had never existed. It was over. A powerful sense of dread occupied Anna's thoughts day and night.

In the middle of the busiest week of the year, Little Gran took a turn for the worse. Lou, Isabelle and Anna sat by her bedside. She managed to hold on until Charlie arrived from Canada and she died in peace. When Anna returned to the King's Head Inn, she was greeted with a litany of complaints about dirty rooms and bad food. She fired Arthur, let everyone go except the bar staff and closed the Emily Carr Dining Room until further notice.

The only bright spot in Anna's life was having Charlie's company. She envied him. He had achieved his goals of travel through his career in the military. He had married late in life but was blessed with a daughter. Looking at his too-wrinkled face, she wondered if the secret missions had not taken their toll on him. He didn't laugh as much, but that seemed to happen with most people as they aged.

Anna had a decision to make, and Charlie's company eased the anxiety. Whitbread Brewery had been making overtures for some time about buying the King's Head Inn. Most pubs were brewery owned but Anna's was a free house. She thought it was time to negotiate but wanted Charlie's advice.

The bees buzzed around the sweet beer stains on the wooden table in the beer garden. Anna sat, sipping a gin and tonic, the late summer sun hot on her arms. She felt nothing. Charlie, enjoying a pint, sat beside her and rubbed her tense neck.

"Things will work out."

"I don't think so, Charlie. Bill's not coming back." Charlie didn't answer, which told Anna that from a man's perspective he thought Bill was gone too, and it made it final.

"I've had an offer from Whitbread's brewery. They want to buy the pub.

I think I'm going to accept their offer."

"I think that would be a wise move, Anna. Why don't you come back to Canada with me? Beth would love to have you. Charlotte has never met her Aunt Anna." He laughed, "Move into your old house. As you know, we have lots of room, unless that would be too difficult?"

"No, it wouldn't be difficult. I would like to live with memories of Alex. But I couldn't leave Sarah and Isabelle, and what if the pub doesn't sell?" She also thought about Bill's letter. August first had passed two days ago, and all attempts to contact Lord Thornton had failed.

"Sis, there is something you don't know. Isabelle was afraid to tell you with everything that has been going on. Sandy was offered a job in Edinburgh, back in June. Isabelle wouldn't move and leave Little Gran while she was ill. You know she fell in love with Scotland, and Florence and Wilfred mean the world to her. She says she feels close to Alex on the moors."

A wave of sadness came over Anna. She had always known Isabelle cared more for her Papa than Anna but now she realized that her daughter cared more for Little Gran, Florence and Wilfred than she did for her, and she feared it was her own fault. She wondered if her guilt over not wanting to be a mother had somehow filtered through to Isabelle even though she loved her and blessed the day she was born.

"I know where Isabelle's heart lies and losing her father and then Little Gran is hard for her to bear. The move will be good for her. I shall miss Sarah so much."

Charlie used his influence to reschedule his return and find a ship to take them across the Atlantic. Postwar travel was not easy. The foreign travel restrictions had been lifted but the ocean liners were not yet back in full service. Charlie booked two first class passages on the R.M.S Aquitania. Second class, or tourist class as it was now called, was booked with war brides heading to a new life in Canada and America.

Whitbread Brewery bought The King's Head Inn complete with furnishings, including most of Anna's furniture in the publican's flat, for a handsome sum. Anna stored the remains of her belongings in the barn at Lou's farm. She was sorry to leave Lou. After many years of rivalry, maturity had brought them as close as sisters should be. She worried about the way Robert treated her but Lou refused to admit there was a problem. All three boys were home, curtailing Robert's drinking and temper. Robbie was to be married soon and Lou talked about having grandchildren.

Saying goodbye to Isabelle and Sarah tore her apart. She helped Isabelle clean up the house and pack up the car for their long trip to Edinburgh. Sandy pulled the front door closed and waited in the car. A tearful Isabelle and Anna hugged, no words needed.

Sarah jumped up and down at Anna's feet. "Nana, can you come and take me to my first day at school." Stunned by Sarah's innocent comment, Anna almost changed her mind about going to Canada.

"Nana and Uncle Charlie are going away on a big ship. Remember I told you that you have to cross a big ocean before you reach Canada. It is too far to come back for when you start school but I will come and visit soon and you can send me pictures and one day you can come visit me."

Sarah thought about this for a minute. "Promise you'll come back." She flung her arms around Anna; Anna squeezed her tight and kissed her head.

Anna's heart was breaking. "I'll miss you so much I'll have to come back for a big hug."

Satisfied with Anna's reply, Sarah hopped in the car. "Nana, one day I will live in Canada." Everyone laughed and Anna waved goodbye until the car was out of sight. She smiled. Something inside her told her that one day Sarah would become a Canadian.

The R.M.S Aquitania was a far cry from Anna's other transatlantic crossings. She was still painted battleship grey from her work of transporting troops during the war. Grateful for first class accommodation, she was able to avoid the cackle of excited women. In spite of her irritation, Anna found herself smiling at such youthful excitement.

The journey was long. The captain kept a slow, steady pace to conserve fuel, the vessel was not as steady as other ships, and Anna's tendency to seasickness kept her in her cabin several days at a time, giving her time to reflect.

The more she thought about her past, the more she fell into a pool of failure. She had failed Lady Thornton who gave her an opportunity to travel and be a woman of substance. She had failed miserably as a business owner. She questioned whether or not she had been a good wife to Alex, and Isabelle had made it clear that she had failed as a mother. Most of all, she regretted forcing Alex and Isabelle back to England. Her unhappiness was her own doing. One thing she didn't understand was how she could have lost Bill. She wondered if perhaps that was her punishment.

The closer the ship sailed towards New York, the more Anna had doubts about returning to Toronto. It had seemed like a good idea but now she wasn't so sure. What if Bill tried to reach her? She had given up trying to reach Lord Thornton, and she never found the solicitor. She kept wondering if she had made a mistake.

Finally, nine days later, they docked in New York and Anna braced herself for the long train journey to Toronto. Standing at Charlie's side, they watched as the ship glided up the Hudson River into New York Harbor. Waiting for the signal to disembark, they heard police sirens, shouting and the pop, pop of gunshots.

Charlie took Anna's arm. "We need to go inside." A steward appeared on deck and ushered the passengers into the lounges. Feeling lightheaded from an intense sense of great danger, Anna fainted. A vision of Bill running through city streets being chased by gunmen flashed in front of her. She heard his voice, "Anna wait, please wait. Remember Kipling, 'Love like ours can never die.'" Then a ghastly smell hit her nostrils as someone waved smelling salts in front of her. Confused, she looked around, expecting to see Bill, but he was not there. Charlie held her hand.

"Anna, you fainted. How do you feel?"

"I don't know. I was overcome with such danger. Charlie, I've made a mistake. I want to go back to England."

"Anna, it's all right. Some disgruntled stevedores caused a fight on the dockside. The police are dealing with it and we'll be disembarking shortly."

Seeing Charlie's worried face, Anna smiled to reassure him. "I'm a little shaken." The steward handed her a brandy.

The train journey to Toronto was a blur. All Anna could think of was the vision of Bill. She couldn't stay, but how to tell Charlie? Obviously happy to see each other, Beth and Charlie hugged, a shy ten-year-old who stood in the background waiting to hug her daddy. Anna had never met her niece, Charlotte.

It felt strange walking into 72 Forest Road. Beth showed her into what had been Bill's bedroom but she didn't feel him. She felt the negativity of Mother Walker. She tried to remember the happy times, but all she felt was Alex's selfishness and his mother's hatred and she could feel nothing of Bill. Her desire to find Bill overwhelmed her—she had to leave.

Charlie tempted her to stay with the promise of a visit to Vancouver to see Emily Carr's paintings and a trip to Vancouver Island to explore the coast that had inspired her art. Sadly for Anna, Emily Carr had died in 1945. The thought of visiting the great paintings did tempt Anna to stay and, had she been able to meet Emily Carr, she might have, but the urge she felt to find Bill was too strong and the paintings alone were not enough to keep her in Canada.

It took a few days of persuasion, but Charlie finally understood and booked her return passage to England. September 7th, 1947, yet another sea crossing but, this time, there was no mistake, she was following her heart.

Gazing forward into the horizon as the shores of England slowly appeared, she had no doubt she had done the right thing by returning to England.

Thirty-Four

Love Like Ours Can Never Die

Rugby, May 1947. Bill felt relief that he had finally declared his love for Anna but was angry with himself and regretted his harsh words. He hadn't meant to hurt her but he was afraid, afraid to tell Anna he had married a mobster's daughter, and afraid that his death might be the consequence of that union. He was not proud of how he had deceived Anna but he was determined to put it right.

Stepping out of the front door, he looked up past the squeaky King's Head sign that moved gently in the morning breeze. It was still dark but he could see Anna's shadow in the bedroom window. He wished he had woken her to kiss her goodbye and tell her he was sorry. Now it was too late to stop. He would miss his train to London. He blew her a kiss saying, "God willing, darling Anna, I'll be back soon and free to marry."

It had never occurred to him that his silence had hurt Anna. The argument the evening before had shocked him. In his naiveté, he had thought Anna would be content with friendship and a business partner. After Alex died, he had built a wall between them thick enough to hold all his secrets and, in his misguided judgment, he thought he was protecting Anna.

So intent on keeping his own secrets and hiding his deepest fear that the mobster's intelligence would find him, he regretted deeply that he had failed to notice how it had affected Anna. Regrets, he thought. How he regretted so many actions he had or hadn't taken with Anna. She was right. He needed to grow up and be a man.

Bill strode out of St. Pancras Station, looking for the taxi stand. A tall man in a chauffeur uniform stepped in front of him. "Mr. Blaine?"

Bill jumped. *It's over,* he thought. Waiting for a gun to poke his ribs, he took in a gulp of air. "Yes."

"Lord Thornton sends his regards. My name is Howard. His Lordship is waiting for you at his club." Howard opened the door of a shiny black Rolls Royce.

His heart racing, Bill took a breath of relief as he sat back on the leather seat. The car glided up to an impressive building. Feeling uncomfortable and underdressed, although he had put on his best suit, Bill climbed the steps to the double doors of the club. The doorman raised an eyebrow, scanning Bill from top to toe. He gave a glance towards Howard and the Rolls Royce, prompting Howard to say, "Lord Thornton is expecting you." Without moving a muscle, the doorman made his disdain quite clear.

"Bill! How marvellous to see you. How are you, old boy?" Darcy snapped his fingers and ordered two Scotch whiskeys. "I thought we'd luncheon here as Belle is entertaining a ladies' charity group. She is always working for a cause."

Bill sipped his Scotch. It was early to be drinking. The burn helped to ease his anxiety. Already he was regretting his decision to meet Darcy. He took a gulp, acknowledging his use of the word 'regret' yet again. He needed some Dutch courage to embark on this journey and Darcy was the first step.

"I can't tell you how delighted I was to receive your letter. It has been such a long time. It must be twenty years." Darcy hesitated for a second, but before Bill could comment he continued talking. Bill sat back and listened. It was important that Bill discover Darcy's awareness of the events in Chicago.

"Hillcrest Estate was a disaster by the time I returned from Chicago.

The estate manager had been robbing me blind and what was left, Inland Revenue had seized for death duties. I tell you, Bill, it was a shock. The thought of losing my boyhood dream brought me to my senses. I could no longer be a rebellious, irresponsible playboy. It was time to grow up and take my place as Lord Thornton. I made some drastic and somewhat innovative changes, sold some land, and I am proud to say Hillcrest will be in good shape to pass on to my son. Ah, I almost forgot. Belle and I have a son, Felix, named after my brother. He's working on a law degree at Oxford. And you, what happened to you Bill?"

"Well, my wake up call to grow up, didn't come until recently. After you returned to England, I did some damage in Chicago and then ran away. I am not sure I can fix it. I wrote to you in the hopes that you could help me. I need a really good solicitor, preferably someone in London. If I can, I would like to avoid a trip to Chicago. A trip that would undoubtedly put my life, and possibly others', in danger." Bill looked over his shoulder, observing the club members as they read the newspapers and spoke in muted tones. "I would prefer to talk somewhere more private."

"Good idea. I can't say I am too proud of my activities in Chicago. Let's have an early luncheon here and then go to the flat and talk in the privacy of my study."

Gordon, the butler, opened the front door, much to Bill's surprise. He must be in his late sixties by now, Bill thought. "Gordon, how nice to see you." Bill smiled, noticing Gordon was far more comfortable in the London environment than in Chicago.

Gordon bowed slightly. "Mr. Blaine."

Darcy melded with the masculine wood and leather in his study. They sat, one on each side of the empty fireplace.

"How can I help? First, I should tell you that I have not had any contact with anyone in Chicago since I returned to England. To be frank, I had become perturbed by the corruption and violence. I was drinking too much and losing too much money at the poker table. I didn't want any of it following me to England. I think Belle kept in touch with Julia Castillo for a while."

425

Bill interrupted, "Julia. How is she?" His mind began to race, maybe he could get a message to Julia through Belle.

"The letters stopped many years ago. I was relieved. All I needed was for the press to discover my gangster connection and I'd be plastered all over the *Daily Mirror*. Belle surprised me. I thought she would try to keep the correspondence going. She just said it was for the better. I have never really thought about it until now."

Bill thought, *Darcy doesn't know anything.* Bill suspected that Julia had written to Belle, ending the correspondence around the time of his marriage to Claudia. He was also fairly sure the details, if any, would have been vague and final. The only way Darcy could help was with a reference to a good solicitor. Bill decided it would be prudent to tell Darcy about his marriage.

"I need a divorce. I married Claudia or, I should say, she trapped me into proposing. By the time I realized what was happening, we were engaged and breaking off the engagement would have been a death sentence. I escaped to Canada on our wedding night. By coincidence, I met up with Anna and Alex living in Toronto."

Darcy frowned, "Bill, why now? Wouldn't it be better to leave it alone? Have you considered the marriage may have been annulled? Tony-the-Boss, for all his racketeering, was a family man and a Roman Catholic. He'd have his hoods searching for you and they probably still are. But when you didn't turn up, he would want his daughter to be free of you, and Claudia would soon get her claws into another unsuspecting man."

"I hadn't thought of that. How do I find out? I must be certain because I want to marry Anna, Alex's widow. By the way, how did you know about Alex's death? Anna was quite touched with the lilies."

"It was Belle. She saw the announcement in *The Telegraph* obituaries and recognized Anna Walker nee Neale. Anna had made an impression on Belle when she worked with my mother. So Anna was your secret love. You never mentioned her name, but you sure pined for her. I am curious. How did you all finish up back in England?"

Over dinner that night, Bill told Darcy and Belle about The King's Head

Inn and their lives in England.

Darcy introduced Bill to Mr. Frothington-Smith, a prominent solicitor at a large firm whose double-barrelled names were unpronounceable in one mouthful. Mr. Frothington-Smith's expertise in divorce and North American affairs made him the perfect solicitor for the job. At some great expense, he agreed to investigate, with less than satisfactory results. After two weeks of investigation, he informed Bill that Claudia could not be found and he cautioned him that he suspected the family to be connected to the Chicago mob. He wanted nothing more to do with the case.

Bill was undecided whether his tone was pompous or righteous, maybe both as he said, "Mr. Blaine, I value my reputation above all else, and my advice to you is to stay away from Chicago. But if you insist on pursuing a divorce, it will have to be done in Chicago. I suggest you contact this man. He is a reputable private detective." He wrote on his notepad. "And this man was an American colleague of mine at Oxford, but I haven't spoken to him in some years. He had a law practice in Chicago. I'm not sure he's still there, but it's worth a try."

Bill didn't want to return to Chicago. In fact, the idea terrified him and it must have shown on his face because the pompous Mr. Frothington-Smith softened his tone. "Mr. Blaine, you seem troubled. Is there anything else I can help you with?"

"Thank you. I made a mistake many years ago and I may pay for it with my life. Before I leave for Chicago, I would ask that you draw up my last will and testament and I would like pen and paper to write a letter, which I will leave in your care to be given to Lord Thornton in the event of my death."

It took Bill another week to find a passage to New York. A chance meeting in a London pub landed him a job as a cook on a beat up old freighter. Bill questioned the seaworthiness of the vessel but took the risk. He wrote to Anna, knowing she would be frantic. He explained that he had been delayed, adding the information regarding the solicitor. It never occurred to him that this might frighten her, although if he was honest, deep down the reality was that he did not expect to make it back to England.

Chicago seemed to have grown taller, the people more sophisticated, the glitz more stylish. Every building was adorned with brazen flashing lights and music blared shamelessly from bars and clubs. It seemed bigger than twenty years ago. Bill checked into a small hotel near Union Station. He had allowed his beard to grow while onboard the ship and, with less hair on his head and more pounds round his middle, he doubted anyone would recognize him.

As the solicitor had not been able to locate Claudia, he decided there was no other option but to break his promise and try to find Julia. But how? Did she live at the same address? Writing or going to the house was too dangerous. He decided to walk the streets, trying to recognize some of the old haunts, but things had changed.

Checking out the restaurants once owned by Tony-the-Boss, he discovered some were no longer there and others were run down, sleazy-looking establishments. He hadn't had the courage to walk Madison Avenue. He didn't want to see Café Lune closed or run down. Having not seen anyone he recognized and curious about the status of Café Lune, he added sunglasses to his disguise and made the effort to walk down Madison Avenue.

The sign shone with a bright moon and the words Café Lune flashed beneath it. The tables were set for dinner with white tablecloths. It looked bigger. He walked by a second time, slowly, looking directly inside. He realized they had pulled down the wall of the speakeasy at the back. Since prohibition had been lifted, obviously there would be no need to hide the drinking and partying. The bandstand and dance floor looked quite splendid. He tried to imagine it full of people and wondered who was preparing the food. He had lingered too long. Suddenly he felt piercing eyes from inside. The presence, although older and larger, was unmistakably Luigi. Bill thought his heart would stop as he casually walked out of sight towards the alley, leaning on the wall for support he noticed the door to the gambling den was still there. He quickly hailed a passing cab.

Pacing up and down his tiny hotel room, Bill tried to figure out what to do next. He doubted Luigi had recognized him, although he shuddered, remembering the sensation of his piercing eyes and reprimanded himself for being careless. It was time to find the PI, and that same afternoon he took the tramcar to the address Mr. Frothington-Smith had given him.

The red brick building housed several offices. The occupants' names were etched in the glass set in the wood panelled door. *This could be a Sam Spade movie,* Bill thought. The only light in the corridor came from a single bulb hanging from the ceiling. It smelled of stale smoke and bad cigars, with a hint of what Bill thought might be urine. He hesitated in front of the door marked *Patrick (Paddy) Flanagan, Private Investigator Confidential and Dis retion Guarante.* The spelling mistakes and missing letters did not fill Bill with confidence. He knocked and the door squeaked open. An empty desk sat in a waiting room and he could hear someone talking on the telephone in the next room.

"Hello!" Bill called.

A hoarse smoker's voice called out. "Take a seat. I'll be out in a minute. My secretary has gone to lunch."

Bill raised an eyebrow, glancing at his watch. It was three in the afternoon and the reception desk, adorned by nothing more than a thick layer of dust, indicated it had not been occupied for some months.

A cloud of white smoke preceded Patrick Flanagan as he walked into the waiting room. Several inches taller than Bill and thin to the point of being gaunt, he leaned down and pumped Bill's arm. "Paddy Flanagan at y'ur service." The cigarette bounced at the corner of his mouth, one eye shut tight to let the smoke drift past his bushy eyebrows into a mass of brown curls.

"Bill Blaine. Mr. Frothington-Smith gave me your name."

"Oh, y'u's from London. I've done a fair bit of work for him. So what you doing in Chicago?"

"Mr. Flanagan, I need to find someone, but if it is known that I am looking for this person, I will put their life and my own at risk."

"Call me Paddy. Come into the office tell me your story."

Paddy grabbed a pile of papers from the chair and motioned to Bill to sit. The piles of papers and files on Paddy's desk dwarfed Bill, but Paddy was tall enough to sit above the chaos. The yellowness of some pages suggested years without a secretary—not exactly a thriving business. But there was something about this Irishman that Bill liked and the next thing he knew he was asking Paddy to find Julia Castillo without her husband finding out.

Paddy laughed. "Well, you're a dark horse."

Bill quickly dispelled any suggestion of romance, explaining Julia was a friend and had information he needed. Tempted to mention his intention to divorce Claudia, he thought better of it. First, he wanted to meet with Julia.

Paddy sent Bill away, telling him to sit tight and he would contact him in a couple of days. Having not eaten all day, Bill stopped at a café advertising the best steaks in Chicago. He bought himself a *Chicago Tribune* to read while he ate a remarkably good dinner. Back in his hotel room, he started pacing again, worried that Luigi had recognized him. If Paddy started nosing around, he might jump to conclusions.

The intellectual part of Bill knew Luigi could not possibly have known who was staring through the window at Café Lune. In fact, now that he thought about it Chicago seemed a much more civilized city. Even the Tribune had not reported any gangster shootings. Bored but afraid to go too far, Bill walked to the Union Station newsstand and bought a copy of George Orwell's *Animal Farm*, and an Agatha Christie mystery. Satisfied the reading would keep his mind off Julia, and Paddy's progress, he read for the next three days. Walking back to the hotel after breakfast, contemplating what to do next, he walked right into Paddy.

"Top of the mor'in' to yur, Bill. I have some news. Let's take a walk down to the lakeshore." It was a cool September morning and they had the boardwalk to themselves.

"Mrs. Castillo still lives at the address you gave me. However she is

430

rarely alone. If her husband isn't with her, there's a body guard not far away. Did you know Luigi Castillo is a small time gangster?" Paddy's stern expression challenged Bill, but he didn't wait for an answer. "It's important you tell me everything. Investigating anyone associated with the mob is dangerous. I may not look slick and smart but that is part of my image and I am damn good at what I do. If we are going to work together, you have to be honest. Do you understand?" Bill nodded and Paddy continued. "Luigi is small time, sadistic and from the old school. He has too much muscle and no brain. He enjoys torturing and/or shooting his way out of anything that doesn't suit him. The cops have been after him for murder but he has a good lawyer and nothing sticks. His old man, Tony-the-Boss, was killed in a mob shooting before my time in the business. My sources tell me Luigi has no connection to the Chicago Outfit, which is good. Antonio Accardo, the Big Tuna," Paddy laughed. "The names these guys use." He shook his head. "He was one of Capone's cronies and runs 'The Outfit' like a business, preferring to keep a low profile. I would expect him to avoid a loose cannon like Luigi."

In spite of the lecture, Bill was not comfortable saying any more to Paddy. The news of Tony-the-Boss's death was good, but Luigi's rise to power had made him even more dangerous.

"Paddy, sorry, I should have told you about the mob connection, but even Tony-the-Boss was small time back twenty-five-year ago. I only want to find and talk to Julia Castillo."

"I need a couple more days to establish Mrs. Castillo's routine. The one time the bodyguard can't be with her is at the university. I'm still piecing it together but it looks as though she teaches a group of women. The bodyguard is not allowed in the department. He drives her there and then disappears."

Bill felt the excitement. "That's it. I can go to the university and blend with the crowd. Can you find out which room she's in?"

"Just a minute. I have to think this through. First of all, no men allowed includes you. Secondly we don't know if Luigi has planted a female guard in the group. And thirdly, we need a place and time for you to meet that won't arouse suspicion. If you go dancing in there like a lovesick leprechaun, you'll get both of you killed."

Bill laughed at his colourful Irish description. He obviously hadn't convinced Paddy that this was not a romance, at least not with Julia, but he decided it didn't matter as long as he could meet her.

Bill and Paddy parted ways, Bill promising to be patient and stay out of sight until he heard from Paddy in a couple more days. He picked up a couple more Agatha Christie books on his way back to the hotel and stopped at the front desk to pay for two more nights.

The cheerful clerk pointed to the books. "A mystery fan, are you?"

Bill nodded. "Yes, it passes the time."

"Waiting for someone are you? Most people only stay a night or two."

Suddenly Bill felt nervous. He was asking too many questions. This man would remember him. He should have moved out.

"I'm looking for work. Waiting for a good job to come up. I'll know in a couple of days." The explanation sounded hollow to Bill. He must talk to Paddy and find new accommodation. He headed for Union Station to find a public telephone. He reached Paddy in his office and was told to stay put, and curb his paranoia. The clerk was just being friendly.

Two mornings later, Paddy bumped into Bill returning from breakfast. "We meet again. I'd say this was planned."

Paddy actually looked like a leprechaun as he gave a cheeky grin and his bushy eyebrow popped up to his hairline. "It's my job to know where you are. My car is round the corner. We'll drive to my office."

Paddy handed Bill a small sheet of writing paper and envelope decorated with roses and slightly scented. "Is there a nickname that Mrs. Castillo would know?"

Bill shook his head. "No, you can't get much shorter than Bill." Bill thought for a minute. "Yes, there is. When I left Chicago, I travelled under the name of Thomas Jones and no one but Julia knows that."

"Good, I want you to write a note to Mrs. Castillo, not too familiar as though you are a colleague from the University. Ask her to meet with you at three in the ladies' lounge, give her a vague hint and sign it *Mrs.* Thomas

Jones.

Bill started writing. "I can't meet her in the ladies lounge—women only, remember?"

"Just do it." Paddy sounded irritated.

Dear Mrs. Castillo

We met many years ago at a mutual friend's wedding that you will remember well. At the time, you were kind enough to help me. I am visiting Chicago for a brief time and have heard about your work at the University. I believe my friend, who you may be acquainted with, would benefit from your program.

I would be most grateful if I could meet with you tomorrow at three o'clock in the ladies' lounge.

Respectfully,

Mrs. Thomas Jones.

"Assuming Mrs. Castillo realizes the note is from you, she will be in the lounge at three. I have arranged for a lady colleague to meet her as Mrs. Jones and suggest they move to a quieter location, where you will be waiting for her, in room A12. Listen carefully. The bodyguard walks her to the north door at two o'clock. He drives off, returning at four-fifteen. If she is late, he waits less than five minutes before he starts walking the halls looking for her. You have one hour. Mrs. Jones will be sitting on the bench in the hall keeping watch. At four o'clock, or if the bodyguard returns early, she will knock on the door and say, 'Julia do you have time for tea?' Mrs. Jones and Mrs. Castillo will walk together to the north door. Still in room A12, you will wait until the coast is clear and leave by the south door, the same door you entered, and look for my car. I'll be waiting." It was rare to see Paddy without a smile and right now he was deadly serious. "No heroics. Stick to my plan. Is that understood?"

"Yes." Bill's voice cracked.

Sleep eluded him that night. He thought about meeting Julia, how wonderful it would be to see her again. His hand rubbed his beard. *She*

433

probably won't recognize me. Finally, he would find out what happened to Claudia. If the marriage had been annulled, he could go back to England a free man. If not, he would have to find a way to divorce her. That would be a problem. He rifled through his bag and found the lawyer's name, Jake Dallas, but no number. He'd call the operator in the morning and make an appointment for late in the afternoon. Annulment or divorce, he needed to be sure he could marry Anna. He said aloud, "Anna, my darling Anna, at long last we can grow old together."

Visions of Luigi beating him to a pulp kept him from another night's sleep. He left the hotel early before the desk clerk came on duty. His room paid up, he decided to leave his bag in a locker at Union Station. He didn't want to admit it, but he was planning a quick getaway. So many things could go wrong.

Bill's nerves were getting the better of him. His neck felt sore from looking over his shoulder. His stomach rumbled from lack of food. He must eat. He stopped for breakfast and at nine o'clock he phoned the operator for Mr. Dallas' number. The receptionist said Mr. Dallas was in court all day. Bill persisted, saying he was leaving for New York that night and she finally gave him an appointment. He read the newspaper and checked the timetable for trains to New York. He stared at the station clock. If he stared hard enough, he could see Julia waving good-bye all those years ago.

Thirty-Five

Narrow Escapes

❧❧❧

At ten minutes to three, Bill stepped through the south door of the University of Chicago, and walked into Room A12. The room was an office with a desk with a leather chair behind it and a little sitting area with two velvet armchairs, the arms quite threadbare, separated by a small table. The lack of photographs or personal items indicated it did not have a permanent occupant. *She's late,* he thought, but looking at his watch he discovered it was three minutes before three. Each minute seemed like an hour, and then his heart jumped to his throat as the door opened. Julia walked in. Stylish as he remembered, the only sign of age was that her short blonde hair had darkened and was flecked with grey. Julia had not aged.

"Julia, I would have known you anywhere. It's good to see you."

"That's more than I can say for you, Bill." She laughed as she touched his beard. "It disguises you well, as did the letter. It seemed impossible that you would be contacting me. I spent hours trying to remember where I had met a Mrs. Thomas Jones. Finally, I saw the clue regarding the wedding. Very clever. At first I thought it might be a hoax but soon realized you and I were the only people who knew Thomas Jones and Mrs. Thomas Jones could not be a coincidence. Meeting here is the only place Luigi doesn't

435

follow me. You did your homework well. How are you? Whatever brings you here must be important." Bill saw the fear as her face tightened. "Luigi has not forgiven you."

"Julia we don't have a lot of time, so I'll get to the point. I want to marry again but I need to know if I am still married to Claudia. The solicitor suggested she probably annulled the marriage but, if not, I need a divorce."

Julia stared at him. "You don't know?"

Bill frowned. "Know what?"

"Tony was killed in a drive-by shooting, outside Café Lune in 1936. Claudia was waiting for him in the car and a stray bullet went through the car window and hit her in the heart. She died instantly."

Stunned, Bill felt sad. "I'm sorry, very sorry. Claudia didn't deserve to die like that. She was always so vibrant and full of life. Paddy, the PI who organized this meeting, told me Tony had been killed. He didn't mention Claudia but I didn't tell him the whole story."

"You are free to marry the lucky lady. No divorce necessary." Julia hesitated. "I was wrong about Claudia. She loved you very much and was heartbroken when she discovered you had gone. Tony wanted her to get the marriage annulled and she refused. The dreamy girl that she was, she expected you would come back one day. Tony and Luigi never stopped looking for you, even though our plan worked. The assumption that you had escaped to England was so strong they didn't look anywhere past New York. After six months, they stopped looking because they couldn't touch you on English soil."

"It's hard to believe I am free. All those years, I worried. The only person I could contact was you, and I couldn't do that."

"I am sorry you didn't know about Claudia but I had no way of reaching you. Luigi went to pieces after Claudia died. He's not a nice man but he loved his sister more than I would have expected he was capable of. He wanted revenge. He hated you for breaking her heart and he was obsessed with finding her assassin. He rejoiced when Tony was killed. He took over as boss of Tony's little empire and became a rich man. The hatred burned inside him and ignited his violence. He was so out of control his own men walked away. The restaurants went into disarray and his racketeering became brutal. The only thing he ever did well was Café Lune. He renovated it after prohibition and kept it as a shrine to Claudia."

"What about you, Julia? Why don't you leave him?"

"Bill, you know as well as I do, he would kill me if I tried to leave. His jealousy is as obsessive as his hatred. The last time he let me go anywhere alone was a trip to the Canadian Rockies where I met Anna and Alex on the train. I'm sure they told you. Of course I didn't know who they were until Anna mentioned they were meeting you in Banff. I panicked. I had known from the first day on the train that I was under surveillance from at least one, if not two, of his thugs. Had my uninvited escort realized Anna and Alex were acquainted with you, we would all be dead. Fortunately, Luigi doesn't hire these guys for their brains. My reasons for the sudden departure from the itinerary went right over their heads but it didn't escape Luigi. He seemed to sense something had happened on that trip. He didn't believe me when I said I just decided to come home early, he went into a jealous rage, almost killed the bodyguard and beat me so badly I ended up in hospital."

"My God, Julia, you have to leave."

"Actually, he was remorseful. Probably because the hospital involved the police, which he tried at all costs to avoid. I didn't press charges on the condition he made concessions. It was after that trip that he allowed me to work at the university. It has become a big part of my life and I enjoy mentoring young women. It helps fill the void of not having friends. Luigi is rarely home. We have separate bedrooms but I don't want for anything. Your turn, tell me about Anna and Alex, your life in Canada."

"Well, I no longer live in Canada. We, Anna, Alex and their daughter Isabelle, moved to England just before the war. Anna and Alex bought an old English inn and the three of us ran it until Alex died two years ago. Now I want to marry Anna."

"I liked Anna. We had a lovely encounter on the train. I am pleased for you."

"I met one of your old friends in London recently. I visited Darcy and

Belle Thornton at their London flat. Belle told me your letters stopped abruptly."

"I miss Belle, my closest friend. Luigi reads my mail, gets jealous and… I stopped writing. Give her my love. It's nearly time, Bill. I have to meet Bumper." They both laughed. "Yes, that is his name."

Bill took Julia in his arms. "Thank you for all you've done and take care. I hope we meet again."

"Maybe someday. But, Bill, never let your guard down. Stay away from Chicago."

There was a soft tap on the door. "Julia, do you have time for tea?"

"Bill, I almost forgot." she handed him a small envelope. "This is your bank account. Wait until you get back to England and then have your bank manager transfer the funds. Don't do it here." She handed him another larger envelope with a great deal of cash in it. This is yours. Money that was owed to you but I dare not put it in the bank. It is hard to explain why I saved it for you but I think I always hoped I would see you again."

Bill opened his mouth but she pressed her fingers on his lips. "Shush! No time to explain."

Julia kissed Bill on the cheek and opened the door. "Mrs. Jones, I would love to have tea but my driver is picking me up at four-fifteen. Walk with me to the north door. We can talk on the way."

Bill sat down, waiting for Julia and Bumper to leave. He shook his head, laughing at the name. The laughter released the tension—he was free at last. A cocktail of emotion swirled inside him. He thought he might burst with happiness, except for the sadness he felt for hurting Claudia and the violence of her death and that Julia lived with every day. Neither of these women deserved such ferocity. He questioned if his life would have been so awful if he had stayed with Claudia. Could it have been any worse than the guilty, deceitful, even fearful life he had led? The image faded, replaced with Anna brushing away a wayward curl, and the happiness returned.

Bill left the university and jumped into Paddy's car. "I'm a free man. Take me to Union Station." Bill handed Paddy a roll of bills. "This should cover your fee and any expenses. I can't tell you how grateful I am. Because of you, I can return to England and marry the woman I have loved for more than thirty years. One last thing, can you telephone Jake Dallas and cancel my five o'clock appointment? I don't need a divorce."

"Did you say Jake Dallas?" Paddy had gone quite pale. "Jake Dallas is one of the biggest mobster lawyers in Chicago. He's the lawyer that has kept Luigi Castillo out of prison. Why did you call him? It doesn't matter."

Staring at Paddy Bill said, "I'm a dead man."

Paddy pulled the car to the side of the road, carefully examined his mirrors, did a shoulder check and drove the car back into traffic.

"Let me think. Did you speak to him when you called?"

"No, a receptionist. She said he was in court all day. I told her it was urgent and she said to come at five, but I might have to wait." Bill pressed both hands to his face, feeling the physical terror spread through every cell of his body. "Julia. If he knows I met Julia…"

Paddy interrupted. "He knows nothing of your meeting. Believe me, I do my job well. Just as a precaution, I checked that nothing unusual happened when Julia and the bodyguard drove away." Checking his mirrors, Paddy continued, "and we are not being followed. Bill, I'm baffled. Why would you contact Jake Dallas for a divorce?"

"The same solicitor who recommended you, gave me his name." Sheepishly, Bill finally told Paddy the whole story about having once been married to Claudia, Luigi's sister.

"Here's the situation. If Jake Dallas recognized your name, and he may not have done, but if he did, Luigi will be waiting to ambush or follow you. I doubt he will ambush you at Dallas's office so he will be waiting to follow you. When you don't turn up at five, he will head for Union Station, he may have some hoods already watching the trains.

"Listen carefully. Use an alias, and not Thomas Jones. Buy a coach ticket but once on board the train, explain to the steward you are not feeling well. You would like a private compartment so you can sleep throughout the journey. It will cost you. Do you have enough money?" Bill nodded. "The steward will leave you alone. Stay in your compartment and keep the blinds down at all times. When you get to New York, stay out of sight and get to the ship as fast as you can."

Paddy pulled up on a side street beside the train station. "Walk through that alley and it will bring you to the back of the ticket office, buy your ticket and hide behind a newspaper until the train arrives. Good luck to y'u, Bill. It's been a pleasure."

Bill followed Paddy's instructions and picked up a Cola and a couple of sandwiches with the newspaper. Hearing the hissing and clanging as the train arrived, he melded with the crowd until he could board. The steward quickly found him a private compartment. He ate one sandwich, settling in for a long night. It was déjà vu as he felt the train leave Chicago. But this time he was heading to New York for real.

"New York, end of the line, New York!" The steward called, waking Bill from a deep sleep. He had a sickening feeling in the pit of his belly. Opening the door of the compartment he peered along the corridor, the travellers all appeared normal, at least none looked like Luigi or one of his hoods.

Trying to be positive, Bill convinced himself that the lawyer would not have connected his name. He stepped onto the platform and walked to the taxi stand. One hand on the door handle, he froze as he felt a tap on his shoulder. A deep, rough voice said, "Luigi is looking for you, Mr. Blaine. Let's take a drive." Without turning to look, Bill jumped into the cab, slammed and locked the door telling the driver to drive and fast. The startled cab driver drove off, Bill looked through the back window as two burley guys in black coats and grey trilby hats climbed into a large black car.

Bill took out his wallet. "I'll give you $40 on top of your fare if you can lose the black car that's following us and get me to the passenger dock at the harbour."

"Make it $50 and I'll take you right to the ship. Which ship are you looking for?"

"Done. What ships are sailing to Britain today?"

"The Aquitania leaves tonight. She's due to dock in half an hour."

"Good. Those men that are following us are gangsters from Chicago, armed and dangerous. Losing them will buy us some time."

The cab driver gave Bill a quizzical glance through his rear-view mirror. Bill felt the cab slow down. For a second, he thought the cab was going to stop.

"Please, this is not a hoax. These men want to kill me."

"Are you a gangster?"

"No, I'm an ordinary guy. Many years ago I made some bad choices and mobsters don't forget."

"Ah, you don't look like a gangster."

The cab lurched forward, screeching around corners, up and down side streets and finally slowing down as the dockyard came into view. Bill turned to look out of the rear window, no black sedan in sight.

The cabbie smiled in his mirror. "We lost 'em."

"Thanks. Can you call the police and tell them Luigi Castillo from Chicago is in New York? He's a wanted murderer. Suggest they start searching the passenger terminal and, for your own safety, leave the docks as fast as you can."

Bill hardly knew what he was saying and he couldn't be sure the cabbie believed him or that the police would respond. They probably wouldn't even know Luigi Castillo, a gangster from Chicago, somewhat out of their jurisdiction. He smiled at the cabbie, gave him the money and went into the booking office, praying he could get a passage.

"I need to get to England as quickly as possible. Do you have any bookings open for today's sailing?"

"Yes, sir. R.M.S. Aquitania leaves this evening. Only tourist class and forward cabins available, but if you have a strong stomach, it will get you there."

"Thank you, forward cabin is fine. I'll take whatever you have. What time can I board?"

"Come back about three this afternoon. Enjoy your voyage, Sir."

Bill looked around. He needed to get out of sight. He had three hours before he could board the ship. He spotted some timber stacked in piles near a cargo ship outside a warehouse. He sensed he was being followed but every time he did a shoulder check he saw no one other than dockworkers. Then he spotted a man in a dark suit and trilby hat. Without waiting to see where he was going, Bill started running. His heart pounded in his ears and throat. He took a quick glance over his shoulder to see the man walk into an office building.

He stooped with his hands on his knees, catching his breath and shaking his head, while convincing himself not to be so paranoid. He scanned in front and behind trying to decide if he should risk the café or hide in the dockyard. He decided on the café. There was a vacant table close to the door. If necessary, he could make a quick exit.

He ordered the all-day breakfast with coffee and opened the newspaper, his hands shaking so the paper rustled and his heart pounded loudly. He checked around the café but nobody was paying attention to him. He sighed with relief as the waitress poured the coffee and went to get his breakfast when the glass window exploded.

Bill ran into the street stopping mid-stride as a bullet whistled past his ear. He bolted into the dockyard towards the cargo ship, looking for cover; another two shots: *POP, POP*. They were wild and hit the warehouse. He dared not turn to look for the shooter, but he could hear the chaos, screams and sirens as he zigzagged between the piles of cargo and, too out-of-breath to run, he squatted behind a pile of timber.

Peering through a gap in the planks, he saw Luigi and the two hoods in black coats each had a gun pointing in his direction. His fear was greater than rounding the Cape in the greatest typhoon he had ever witnessed. He hadn't expected to live through it, but this was worse.

His life flashed before him—so close to Anna and so close to home. Another shot hit the pile of timber. He had to move. Throwing a rock, he ran in the opposite direction but Luigi spotted him. Three shots whizzed by his head. Luigi knew where he was hiding. It was over. He sat on the ground leaning against sweet smelling pine logs, clutching his legs. His head buried in his knees, he waited for the pop and the pain that would follow. Afraid to move, he thought of Anna. She was so close, he saw her face tense with fear. He wanted to hold her, kiss her. He shook his head, stretched his arm out expecting to touch her right next to him. "Anna, lovely Anna, I tried." Three shots POP, POP, POP a break and then a fourth POP. *I'm dead,* he thought, capturing the vision of Anna, his final dream.

Muffled voices came closer and someone tapped him on the shoulder. Slowly, he looked up.

"Are you all right, sir?"

Staring into the face of a NYPD cop, Bill answered, "Yes, I think so. What happened?" Afraid to move, he hesitated before slowly walking out from behind the timber, his eyes fixed on three bodies on the ground.

"Gangsters! We had a tip that one of the Chicago mob was trying to infiltrate New York and then, out of the blue, a Yellow cab driver called in, babbling about shots at the Ocean Liner Passenger Terminal and Luigi somebody was responsible. He's the Chicago guy." The policeman gestured towards Luigi's body. "That's him."

"Just for the record, sir, what were you doing here?"

"I am waiting to board the Aquitania." Bill pulled his ticket out of his jacket." I was just walking around passing the time when I heard shots and ran for cover."

As the police were not aware of any connection between him and Luigi, Bill chose to keep it that way. "Do you need me for anything, officer?"

"No, just tell the constable what you saw. Leave your name and where we can reach you, and you are free to go."

Walking back towards the terminal, the shock began to set in and Bill's knees started to wobble. He felt lightheaded as a vision of Anna appeared. "I'm hallucinating," He said aloud, "I need to sit down and get some food." His breakfast was across the street covered in bullets and glass. He walked back towards the passenger terminal and bought a coffee and a bun. He found a barber for a wash and a shave. He smiled. The beard could go.

The ship was late boarding the passengers because of the shooting incident. The disembarking passengers were delayed for over an hour. Bill waited patiently, the happiest man in the world.

Bill's heart was full of hope as the ship docked and he took the train to Rugby, but as he stepped out of the taxi in front of the King's Head Inn, he knew something was wrong. The sign on the door read, *Closed for renovations*. Bill looked up: the pub sign no longer squeaked, it was new. He read the words twice, not believing what he saw: Whitbread King's Head Inn. He knocked but nobody came. He walked to the back but everything was locked. "I waited too long." He kicked the door, angry. Angry with himself for being so foolish, disappointed she hadn't waited and an ache in his heart so big he could feel it breaking. He walked to the bus stop. Isabelle was closest. A stranger answered Isabelle's door. The family had moved to Scotland. How could so much have happened? He'd only been away…three months was a long time. He would go to the farm, Robert and Lou would never move. He held his breath as he pushed the gate open and walked down the gravel drive. The house looked the same. Someone, and he thought it might be Simon, was on the tractor harvesting. Lou came out of the front door.

"Bill. My goodness you are a sight for sore eyes." Lou hugged him. "Come in."

"Lou, where's Anna? I went to the King's Head." Bill's words halted. He was afraid to find out. Had something happened to Anna? Panic wavered in his voice, "And Isabelle has moved to Scotland."

Lou put her hand on his shoulder. "A lot has happened since you left. Anna became quite despondent when you didn't come home in August. She thought you were either dead or not coming home. After Gran died and Isabelle, Sandy and Sarah moved, Anna lost her will to live. Charlie talked her into going back to Canada with him."

Bill's heart sank. He had done it again. He was repeating the biggest regret of his life—letting Anna slip through his fingers. He wanted to cry like a baby, scream and carry on. He put his face in his hands.

"Hey, there! It's okay," Lou put her arm on his shoulder. "There's some good news, too." Lou opened the Welsh dresser draw and handed him a letter. "Read this."

Dearest Lou,

By the time this reaches you, I will be on my way back to England. I made a terrible mistake coming here. Although Charlie and Beth are wonderful, the memories are disturbing. I miss Bill more than I can say and I am determined to find him.

Charlie is booking my passage as I write this, and all being well, I will arrive in Southampton on September 30th. I will telephone when I am coming back to Rugby as I may stop in London and try to contact Lord Thornton again. I think he is the key to Bill's whereabouts.

The letter continued but Bill had read all he needed to read. He laughed aloud. He hugged Lou and ran around the kitchen like a kitten chasing a ball of wool. Robert came in and slapped Bill on the back. "I think we need to celebrate with a drink."

The next day, Bill left for London. Darcy and Beth had returned from the Continent. He needed Darcy's help with his plans. Two days later, he stood on the pier in Southampton, waiting for the passengers to disembark.

He thought he would pass out with joy as stylish Anna appeared on the gangway. The jacket of her dark green suit nipped her still tiny waist. For the first time, he noticed the escaping curls were now streaked with white, her matching hat set coyly to one side. She had never looked more beautiful.

Thirty-Six

Follow Your Dreams

A fter her first disastrous sea crossing in 1919, Anna had learned to endure the journey. At least her stomach tolerated the ship's constant motion. The sight of the English coast always filled her with joy, even more so that day. As Southampton came into view, she thought of no one but Bill. She imagined the impossible, that he greeted her on the dock. She brushed such fantasies aside, forcing herself to be practical.

First, she would telephone Lord Thornton, or better still, she would go directly to his London flat and, if necessary, she would wait until he returned home. There was no doubt in her mind that Darcy Thornton had the key to Bill's whereabouts.

The ship slid into its berth and Anna watched from the deck before gathering her things and waiting for the all-clear to disembark. She had arranged for her trunks to be sent directly to Lou's house in Rugby. She headed for the gangway. The steward had taken her one suitcase, all she would need while in London.

The excited passengers pushed and shoved. She wished she had waited a little longer for the crowds to disperse. Her heart gave a jolt when she imagined she had seen Bill in the waiting crowd. When she looked again, it was a sailor helping passengers off the gangway. Wishful thinking, she thought as she walked down the gangway. A sailor took her hand to steady her and smiling he stood to one side.

Anna shook her head. *I'm going crazy. It can't be, or can it?* she thought as a familiar voice boomed over the crowd, "Anna, will you marry me?" The whole dock and ship went silent. Stunned, Anna stood still. She looked down, not believing what she saw. There was Bill on his knees, holding a ring. He repeated, "Anna, will you marry me?"

"Yes, I'll marry you." A Cheshire cat grin spread from ear to ear and she literally fell into Bill's arms. "It only took you thirty years." The crowd laughed as Bill placed the diamond and opal ring on her finger. Cheers any football match would be proud of roared and the crowd started clapping.

Bill collected Anna's suitcase and the porter hailed a taxi to take them to the station. Once in the taxi, Bill said, "I have a surprise for you."

"More surprises! Bill, am I dreaming?"

"I have train tickets to Bexhill. I thought we might go back to where it all started." He quickly added, "If that is all right with you?"

"Is this really happening? Bexhill sounds wonderful."

Arriving under the portico of The Sackville Hotel was disappointing. The paint was peeling off, the garden was full of weeds, the long windows of the lobby were cracked and one was boarded up. It looked tired and uncared for. The chandelier, the only sign of grandeur, still hung in the worn out lobby, not even the tiniest of sparkles could penetrate the many years of dust that had coated the crystals. The once-plush Axminster carpet was clean but threadbare. An older, tired-looking James Lytton, his hair thin and grey, stood behind the mahogany counter. The cubbyholes mostly vacant of letters told the story. James' face lit up when he saw who was walking through the door, and he limped over to greet them; his war wound worsened by time.

"What a welcome sight you two are!"

"Good to see you, James." The men shook hands heartily and James gave

Anna a warm hug.

"Book us in for two nights, separate rooms with an adjoining door." Bill winked at Anna. She felt a rush of affection at the familiar endearment. "Anna and I... are officially engaged to be married."

"Congratulations. I don't mind telling you the staff here always thought you and Anna were meant for each other. I am pleased for you both. I'll give you Suite 305, it is rarely used and it has two bedrooms. I'll check with Mrs. Peterson to make sure it is ready. Mrs. Banks retired, Amy is now head housekeeper."

"Lady Thornton's suite." Anna said. "Amy is head housekeeper. I didn't realize she had stayed."

"Yes, she stayed all through the war. The army took over the hotel to house injured soldiers, often their first stop after fighting in France. Since the war, she has worked with me to try to get the hotel running again. But we are so short-staffed, it is hard." James looked ashamed. "We try our best but it's not what it used to be. Mr. Kendrick is old and no longer able to maintain the hotel. I don't know how much longer he can hang on. It has been for sale for nearly a year now."

"Poor Mr. Kendrick. This hotel was his pride and joy. I am glad you and Amy are still here, doing your best. He must appreciate your loyalty."

"He does, but I fear it is not enough. The old place needs funds for renovations and Mr. Kendrick has none. I think his kindness during the war depleted his resources."

"What happened to Chef Louis?" Bill asked. "Is the dining room open? I am hungry."

"Chef Louis retired. I don't know where he went and his successor left during the war. Chef Mike, the guy we have now, Mr. Kendrick sent from another hotel. The food is quite good. Perhaps not as good as yours, Bill, but times have changed."

Bill clanged the big brass lift gate and operated the lever that took them to the third floor. Anna felt strange standing at the door of Suite 305 as a guest. She half-expected Miss Barclay to open the door and to hear Princess yapping at her feet. Instead, Amy opened the door.

"Amy, how wonderful to see you."

Amy's face looked shocked. "Anna and Mr. Blaine. Mr. Lytton didn't tell me the suite was for you. I am so glad to see you."

"Do you have a minute, Amy? I would like to talk to you." Anna guided her into the living room.

"Amy, I wanted to thank you for what you did to put old Pickles behind bars. I am so sorry he attacked you. Mrs. Banks and I tried so hard to protect you. I didn't hear about it until my brother brought a newspaper report. We were living in Canada at the time. I always meant to write but never got around to it."

"That is all in the past now. I always appreciated how you looked out for me, but after you left, the bastard went wild. I was so glad when the police arrested him. Dr. Gregory was very kind and helped me through the worst and supported me through the trial. I did okay. I'm married now and I have two children. I chose to keep my name and not use my married name in the hotel. I am Mrs. Fulham outside the hotel. It was easier that way. I don't live in any more. Things are different from when you were here." Amy looked at Anna sadly. "I am sorry to hear about Mr. Walker passing."

"Thank you. What happened to Dr. Gregory?"

"He died about a year ago. He retired after the trial. Anna, I have to go. We are short-staffed and I have work to do."

Having not eaten in many hours, Anna and Bill went to the dining room for an early dinner. Dinner was a set menu: cream of asparagus soup, roast beef and Yorkshire pudding, followed by sherry trifle. The food was wholesome and tasty. Perhaps not Bill's standard but it didn't matter. They hardly noticed the food as they didn't stop talking.

Bill told Anna about his life in Chicago, his marriage to Claudia and his life as a mobster's chef. The pieces of the puzzle started to fit together as Bill's story unravelled. All her questions answered, even the connection with Julia Castillo and the gun chase through Manhattan, New York.

Departing The Sackville, Anna wished she had enough money to buy it. The sale of the King's Head Inn had brought her a handsome sum but it would not be enough to buy the building and meet the cost of renovations, let alone find enough money for operating costs.

Darcy and Belle gave them a great welcome in London. Thrilled to see that Anna had accepted Bill's proposal, they popped a bottle of champagne to celebrate. The wedding plans were discussed and Darcy accepted Bill's invitation to be best man, suggesting they get married at Hillcrest. Anna declined. She wanted a small wedding in Rugby with her family at Christmas.

Having sold the King's Head Inn, Bill and Anna had nowhere to live. Darcy suggested they stay at the flat. He and Belle had to return to Hillcrest. The place was theirs for as long as they liked.

Anna arranged to visit Mr. Kendrick while they were in London so she could thank him for his part in exposing Mr. Pickles. She was shocked to see Mr. Kendrick looking so old and frail but she thought that, for a man of eighty-nine, he did well. Anna kissed him and thanked him for all he had done for her.

Bill pulled a rabbit out of the hat. Unbeknownst to Anna, he had struck a deal with Mr. Kendrick. He placed a legal document on the table and asked Anna to look it over and, if it met with her approval, sign on the dotted line, just under Bill's signature.

Anna scanned the document and realized it was an agreement to purchase The Sackville Hotel. She sat at the table, reading every word. Her eyes widened and flashed from the document to Bill to Mr. Kendrick.

"Mr. Kendrick, this is very generous. I know it is worth much more than this."

"Mrs. Walker, Anna, it was always my intention for you to take over The Sackville. But when you ran away with Mr. Walker, I handed the management over to Mr. Lytton who has done well, but not as well as you would have. I am so happy to have a second chance to pass this along to you. The proceeds will keep me comfortable for my last few years and you and Mr. Blaine will revive the old Sackville. Please sign and make an old man happy."

Anna signed her name, thinking that at any minute she would wake from a dream. She wondered how Bill could afford it. She had so many questions but signing was for Mr. Kendrick.

"We are now the new owners of The Sackville Hotel." Seeing Anna's frown and bewilderment, Bill quickly added, "I had left a considerable amount of money in a Chicago bank in 1921 and, for reasons you will understand, I couldn't go back for it. Julia had kept all the bank information and I had the money transferred last week, enough to buy the hotel. The renovations we can do together."

Anna was speechless. She hugged Mr. Kendrick. "We'll take good care of her and make her grand again."

The old man smiled. "I am so proud of you, Anna. I couldn't be prouder if you were my own daughter."

On the way back to the flat, Anna held Bill's hand and said, "Pinch me. Am I dreaming? I have waited so long for this. I think I love you more now than I did in 1913, the day you called me 'papa's little girl.'" They both laughed.

It was unusual, but the vicar had agreed to marry them on Christmas Day, after the Christmas Morning service. Anna wanted to share her day and invited the Christmas worshippers to join them if they wished.

Anna, in a midnight blue taffeta suit, with matching hat and a bouquet of white roses, walked down the aisle on Charlie's arm. Lou, maid of honour, and bridesmaid Sarah, dressed in pale blue walked behind. Bill, with best man Darcy, in smart black suits, white roses in their lapels, stood in front of the vicar. Bill took Anna's hand as she approached the altar, ready to take their vows.

Anna and Bill walked slowly up the aisle as husband and wife. Smiling from ear to ear, her Cheshire cat smile, she nodded to her family: Isabelle and Sandy, Robert and the boys, including Robbie's new bride, Beth and Charlotte from Canada. The only family missing were Florence and Wilfred, who were spending Christmas with Wilfred's family in Canada. Julia Castillo had finally escaped her captive life in Chicago and had reunited with her friend Belle Thornton, joining Belle and her son Felix for Anna and Bill's wedding celebration.

Squeezing Bill's arm, Anna whispered, "You have made me the happiest woman on earth. It can't get any better."

Bill gave her a cheeky grin. "There is more to come. I have one more surprise for you." Before she could speak, he kissed her as they stood in the sunlight outside the church. The crowd cheered, the church bells rang and confetti rained around them. Bill put his hand in his inside pocket and handed Anna an envelope.

"My wedding gift to you. Two tickets to India. Adventures to be explored as we walk in Uncle Bertie's footsteps. Together, we will explore Rudyard Kipling's India."

Speechless, Anna smiled and twisted the black velvet ribbon at her neck. She could have sworn she heard the blue pendant whisper, "Follow your dreams and never let anyone destroy them."

Read on... Anna'a Legacy - Book 2.
Just one easy click and start reading today!
https://geni.us/VNlg
Anna and Bill, breath life into the hotel. Follow their journey of
adventures, hardships and successes at The New Sackville Hotel.

Epilogue

What happened next ....

Bill and Anna hired a designer to draw up plans to renovate The Sackville Hotel in the autumn of 1947. After the Christmas wedding, they closed the hotel to begin refurbishing. Post-war shortages of building materials and furnishings, and limited finances curtailed their original, and somewhat lavish, plans, but with imagination and creativity, refurbishing began in early January 1948. Leaving James Lytton in charge, Bill and Anna sailed to India for their honeymoon.

The New Sackville Hotel opened with great pomp and ceremony on a very special day, May 18th, 1948. Mr. Kendrick was invited to cut the ribbon the same day he celebrated his ninetieth birthday. The guest list included several local dignitaries, Lord and Lady Thornton, Julia Castillo, Lou and family from Rugby, although Robert did not attend. Sandy Wexford drove the Scottish contingent, Florence, Wilfred, Isabelle and of course little Sarah, down from Edinburgh. In total, a hundred and fifty guests joined in the celebration, much to Anna and Bill's delight.

Isabelle fell in love with hotel life, perhaps somewhat upscale from the pub she had rebuffed in her youth. She made overtures to her mother and Bill about using her retail skills to promote The New Sackville Hotel as a holiday destination for the rich and privileged. Little Sarah danced around the open spaces, with a devoted Nana at her heels. Anna noticed

Sarah clung to her and she thought she detected hurt and sadness. She asked about Grandpa and Anna thought she meant Bill, but realized she remembered Alex.

Anna talked about Grandpa being in heaven and how she now had a new grandpa, Uncle Bill. Perhaps missing her grandpa was the reason for the sadness, but Anna didn't think that was the whole answer. Sarah's next comment surprised her even more. "Nana, I think Grandpa went back to Canada because he liked the heaven there better than here. One day I will visit him in Canada and I think I will live in such a nice place."

Anna had no answer for Sarah. She wondered how Sarah knew that Alex had never wanted to leave Canada. Whatever the reasons, Anna knew intuitively that Sarah would travel to Canada one day. Whether to live or visit she would honour her grandfather's wishes.

Afterword

What is fact and what is fiction and other story tidbits.

Anne Neal, known to friends and family as Nancy Neal and to readers of this novel as Anna Neale, was a real person, my grandmother. Alex Walker was my grandfather and Bill Blaine became my step-grandfather. The kernel of the idea for this book is in part, Anne Neal's true story of her love for two beaus. The three worked at a hotel in Sussex, England and it may have been Bexhill-on-Sea and possibly The Sackville Hotel, which was listed on their marriage certificate, but I wasn't able to confirm it with employment records.

Built in 1890, The Sackville operated as a prestigious hotel until 1956. The Sackville today has been converted into 100 luxury apartments for the mature and senior adults.

The triangle of love, according to my family history is accurate. The amazing story of Alex walking into the sea until Anna accepted his proposal of marriage and of Bill running off to America is also true; although I have no idea what Bill did in America, so the stories of Chicago, mobsters and marriage are purely fictional.

Genealogical records revealed Alex's war record, some of the details I included. Alex was known in the family to have an impulsive nature and his sudden decision to emigrate to Canada after being unable to get a passage to Australia is also true. Anna and Alex did sail on the R.M.S. Adriatic to Halifax and settled, working and living in a bakery in Toronto.

At some point Alex took up a job on CP Rail similar to the one described in the story.

In 1935, the three abruptly returned to England. Bill had always been part of their lives as a friend and he remained a part of their lives in Canada and upon their return to England. There is no evidence of any hanky-panky as described in the novel. It is just my over-zealous imagination. Alex did die of cancer, although the dates are not accurate for the sake of the story. Bill had never been married in the past but he did quietly marry Anna, shortly after Alex's death. The drama of mobsters and shootouts in New York City are also purely fictional.

When I first sat down to write this story, I thought it would be a novel based on a true story, but I soon realized I did not have enough detail of either events or characters to expand into a whole book. The majority of the resulting story has been fictionalized. Characters, events and places, are unequivocally from my overactive imagination.

I only knew Anna as my grandmother, and I had no idea what kind of a person she would have been as a young woman, and the same for Alex and Bill. Alex, I barely remember as I was very young when he died. So, when I say the characters are fictional, they truly are a figment of my imagination. The stories, events and activities, barring the core of realism mentioned above, are also entirely from my imagination.

To the best of my knowledge, I have adhered to the historical facts regarding the Great War and World War II and other events that took place during the time period, and I believe the historical references, dates, places and times are accurate.

The Blue Pendant intertwined true events in my grandparents' and mother's lives, enhanced with a fictitious story, which grew into something far bigger than I ever expected. One novel spilled into the sequel, *Anna's Legacy*, a completely fictitious story. However, I still had more story to write, and one book turned into two and a third as I wrote *Sarah's Choice* and *The Sackville Hotel Trilogy* was born.

If you enjoyed The Blue Pendant read on: be transported to Bexhill, to

London, to Toronto and to British Columbia. Join me as I live the lives of the characters. I cry with them and feel their pain, I laugh with them and feel their happiness, I love them and feel their love. Anna's journey of love, loss, happiness, hope and destiny keeps going from 1913 through to 1964.

There is one fact that I can declare as true, which is mentioned above The Sackville Hotel was eventually bought by developers and converted into retirement apartments. While I was writing this book, I was contacted by Duncan Humber, the building manager and Roy Haynes a retired BBC journalist, both residents of The Sackville Apartments and intrigued by my association with Bexhill. Concierge, Val Crowson, came across *The Blue Pendant Book I of The Sackville Hotel Trilogy* during an online search for books for the Sackville reading group. Serendipitous indeed!

As I was never able to visit the Sackville Apartments or Bexhill, I relied heavily on Googling information and reading material for research. I can only hope that my research, even if not entirely correct, did justice to the Sackville and its residents, past and present.

Acknowledgements

The Blue Pendant was my first novel and possibly my best. Thanks are due to my mother Elizabeth (Betty) Jennings, for telling me the story of her mother, my grandmother, Anne (Nancy) Walker Blaine nee Neal, which gave me the original idea for this book. Secondly, thanks to Anne Grant of Long Ridge Writing Group for her teachings, encouragement, and faith in my storytelling that made me into a novelist.

My thanks to the beta readers of the original novel goes to, Sheila Macdonald, Audrey Starkes, Anne Raina, Myriam McCormick, Heather McKinnon, Angela Sutcliffe, Coralee Boileau and Kathi Nidd. All of these wonderful people deserve a whopping big round of applause for giving up their time to read the raw manuscript and offer their valuable feedback. Many other friends constantly encouraged me to keep writing, for which I am grateful. A special mention to Kathleen Bigras for her trust, confidence and financial assistance, and Cathy Burton for her never-ending emotional support. Without all these wonderful people, I could not have completed this novel.

Writing the book is only half the battle. Once the writing and critiquing is complete, it is time for the manuscript to be edited. Thanks goes to my friend and colleague, freelance writer and professional editor Brian McCullough, for giving up his time to read through the manuscript and make copious suggestions as to how I could improve the story. I am extremely grateful to Brian for his time and expertise. I do believe that had Brian not given me the thumbs up, this novel might never have been published.

My gratitude to professional editor Mark McGahey for the essential, second copy-edit and to my second editor Meghan Negrijn for yet another edit and proofread. And, I think this novel is the best it can be. My apologies to both American and British readers as the grammar and style is Canadian English which combines both American and British styles and I assure you the grammar and spelling are quite correct.

I had an idea for the cover. Thank you to animator and illustrator, Karoline Page (Anne Neal's great-great-granddaughter) for your artistic talent and ideas for the book cover. Thank you to the original designers, and product managers from Tellwell's publishing staff in Victoria, British Columbia for putting together the first edition *The Blue Pendant.*

As mentioned this is the second edition, with a new cover, a third edit and some minor changes to the interior. Last, but definitely not least my sincere thanks to everyone who worked on the new edition, including the Ladies Historical Writing Group who worked with me on the new cover. My gratitude goes to Bryan Cohen of Best Page Forward and to his team for the new descriptions and tons of advice and support, which made this new edition possible.

Resources and Research

The Sackville Hotel Trilogy spans half a century in a time of great change in the Western world. Although these books are mostly fictional, it was imperative that the historical facts be correct, which led to copious amounts of research. Information was gleaned from a plethora of online sites, which included Bexhill-on-Sea Museum, History of Bexhill, White Star Line (ocean liners of the early twentieth century), The Great War, WW II, the Cold War and military records, fashions and lifestyles of England and Canada in the various localities and time periods, and much more.

Much of the information about the day-to-day living came from books. Amongst the most helpful were the following: *The Perfect Summer – Dancing into Shadow in 1911* by Juliet Nicolson; *The Precipice, a Novel* by Elia W. Peattie, originally published in 1914; *The Great Silence 1918 – 1920 Living in the Shadow of the Great War* by Juliet Nicolson; *To End All Wars – A story of Loyalty and Rebellion: 1914 - 1918* by Adam Hochschild. If you have an interest in this time period, I highly recommend these excellent books, not just for research but also as interesting reads.

Numerous Google sites.

About the Author

Susan A. Jennings was born in Derby, England of a Canadian mother and English father. Drawn by her Canadian heritage, she settled in Ottawa, Canada where she now lives and writes, overlooking the Ottawa River. As an essential element of her writing, Susan interweaves British and Canadian cultures into her stories—a theme which is notably dominant in *The Sackville Hotel Trilogy*. Susan came to writing later in life; after raising five children as a single parent. There was little time for writing during those early parenting years. While writing her memoir, *Save Some For Me*, stories of a single mother, Susan was first bitten by the writing bug. Motivated by her love of writing short stories and cozy mysteries. Susan recently published a new women's fiction series, *The Lavender Cottage Series.* The romance is perhaps a distraction from the historical research and more the in depth writing of historical fiction. Susan returned to historical fiction in 2019 and published the Sohpie Series; *Prelude to Sophie's War* and Heart of Sophie's War a new series and a spin-off from *The Blue Pendant and Ruins in silk,* that takes place during the Great War. She is the founder of The Ottawa Story Spinners—authors of the eclectic story collection entitled *Black Lake Chronicles* Volumes 1 - 6.

You can connect with me on:

🌐 http://susanajennings.com

🐦 http://sajauthor

📘 http://facebook.com/authorsusanajennings

🔗 https://geni.us/CjRlF

Subscribe to my newsletter:

✉ http://eepurl.com/bgY6kb

Also by Susan A. Jennings

If you enjoyed **The Blue Pendant**, continue reading all of **The Sackville Hotel Trilogy**

Anna's Legacy - Book 2

Secrets and hidden agendas plague Anna but none are as dark as her own secrets. Might they be the deadliest?

Sarah's Choice - Book 3

Sarah, Anna's granddaughter has to make hard decisions in this final and exciting trilogy novel. Lives and livelihoods depend on Sarah's choices.

Her dream of fame through art or Anna's dream of a prestigious hotel?

Ruins in Silk - The prequel to The Blue Pendant and Prelude to Sophie's War

Sophie's young life - Her mother's death sets a path of tragedy; betrayal, misguided love and even murder. Devoted to her father Sophie faces one last unimaginable tragedy.

A special treat, available for .99c

Sophie Series - Novels of the Great War

Prelude to Sophie's War
Heart of Sophie's War
In the Wake of Sophie's War (coming 2022)

The Lavender Cottage Books - Love and suspense at Katie's B &B

When Love Ends Romance Begins
Christmas at Lavender Cottage
Believing Her Lies

More at Lavender Cottage (coming late 2021)

Nonfiction

Save Some For Me...and what about you?

Is a heartrending story of one woman's struggle to survive spousal abuse and, consequently, single parenthood.

Manufactured by Amazon.ca
Bolton, ON

24632727R00275